Liverpudlian by origin and once a Catholic, Keith Jacobsen read languages at St Catherine's College, Oxford. A former civil servant specialising in international health relations, he now divides his time between music and writing. A performer and teacher in piano, he has a special interest in the keyboard music of Bach. In addition to fiction and poetry, he writes on musical subjects.

Out of the Depths is his second novel. He sees the novel as a means of exploring aspects of the human psyche which lie dormant in everyday life but can erupt with devastating effect on the individual and society.

He lives in North London with his wife, Valerie, and has two grown-up daughters by his first marriage.

AUTHOR'S NOTE

Various Catholic priests and Christian Brothers in days long gone, dedicated to the spiritual and educational well-being of myself and my contemporaries, have contributed unwittingly to the body of memories and impressions on which this story draws. Those men were without exception kindly and well-meaning. Errors in the representation of what they tried to teach me are entirely down to faults in my understanding at the time and/or my memory since.

Central to the story is the intimidating ordeal of the Sacrament of Confession and its punitive doctrinal base. Less harsh alternative procedures are available today to Catholics who wish to be absolved from the burden of sin. But in other respects, such as the forbidding of 'artificial' methods of contraception and the rule of priestly celibacy, both relevant to this story, the harshness continues.

While Ridgeway Park Hospital is fictional, the conditions there as described through the eyes of a former patient were all too real. In the late 1960s and early 1970s a series of damning reports appeared on the state of several (now long since closed) large isolated psychiatric hospitals around the country. I have drawn on my general memories of those reports rather than on those relating to any particular institution.

Keith Jacobsen
May 2012

For Valerie

PROLOGUE

'Sure, now what does a good Catholic woman like that want to go and get herself murdered for?' asked Father O'Malley.

'I'm sure she didn't want to,' I replied. 'Who are you talking about anyway?'

He handed me a copy of the *Formby Times*, his plump red finger pointing to the article he had just been reading. I read it through, slowly. He drummed his fingers impatiently on the table.

Three days ago, we reported that the naked body of a woman had been discovered by an early morning jogger among the sand-dunes, three hundred yards from Formby woods. The police now confirm that she had been strangled the previous evening, some time between nine o'clock and midnight. They have named her as Mrs Frances Pickersgill, aged twenty-seven. Her husband, George, a local builders' merchant, identified the body. Mrs Pickersgill taught in a local primary school. In a statement from outside his five-bedroomed detached house on an exclusive Formby estate, a grief-stricken Mr Pickersgill told reporters that he still could not believe his wife was gone for ever. She had been such a vibrant person, always full of humour and vitality. The world was a colder, darker place for her loss. Detective Inspector Farrell told reporters that they had begun a murder investigation. They were still examining Mrs Pickersgill's clothes, which had been found in the woods, half a mile from the body. They stated categorically that she had not been sexually assaulted. They particularly wished to trace the driver of a grey Ford Anglia which had been seen in the vicinity on the night of the murder, with two occupants, a man and a woman. They were also very anxious to trace a Mr James Forsythe, a friend of the family who taught at Mrs Pickersgill's school. Mr Forsythe has been missing since the discovery of the body was first announced. His wife told us he had gone to stay with a relative in Wales in accordance with longstanding plans. She declined to disclose the name and address of the relative. The school's headmaster, John Cavendish, told us that as far as he was concerned Mr Forsythe's departure was a surprise and a mystery. He had had to recruit two supply teachers to cover Mr Forsythe's classes as well as those of Mrs Pickersgill. He told us he had expressed his deepest condolences to Mr Pickersgill. He was sure the close-knit local community would stand by him in his hour of need. Many of the pupils were still in a state of shock. Mrs Pickersgill had led an exemplary life, regularly attending her local Catholic church and devoting much of her spare time to charitable works. She would be sorely missed. The Pickersgills had no children.

'We don't usually get this paper, do we, Father?' I asked.

'No. I picked it up from Mrs Walsh when I was paying her a pastoral visit this morning. But I've asked Mrs Raferty to get the newsagent to add it to our delivery list. I want to follow the coverage.'

Father O'Malley was passionate about murders, though usually he only concerned himself with the fictional sort. The sad truth from his point of view was that local people did not go in for murder. Seaport, the home of our parish, was close enough to the city for smells of coal tar, molasses and chemical fertilisers to drift along from the riverside docks, warehouses and factories, when the countervailing winds from Wales and the Wirral Peninsula faltered. But the city's reputation for violent crime did not drift with them. And it certainly did not reach law-abiding, affluent Formby, a few miles further on up the coast, where no odour of industry or urban decay ever reached.

He was reading my thoughts. 'Would you not be realising what a fantastic opportunity this is, Father? A murder in Formby, of all places. The whole town will be in uproar for months. The *Formby Times* will cover it for week after week. Even the *Liverpool Echo* might pick it up. I mean, they have several murders a day in the city council estates and they don't even bother to report them. But this is different.'

I was not at all sure whether he had his facts right about the murder rate in Liverpool. He was from Dublin and was known to be prone to exaggeration on occasions. But I was aware that according to Seaport parish gossip all manner of violence and depravity was to be found in Liverpool. Bootle, which lay between us and the city centre, was reputed to be almost as bad. Not that either of us would ever have considered going near any of those neighbourhoods to find out for ourselves.

'And the wonderful thing,' he went on, 'is that she was a Catholic. Now who on earth would want to murder a Catholic? And not even a Catholic from Northern Ireland who might have got caught up in the troubles there and been followed over here by hired assassins.' His eyes shone as his imagination went into overdrive. 'Apparently she was from one of the old Lancashire Catholic families, the ones who own all

11

those country estates and can trace their roots back to the days of Elizabethan persecution. And a respectable married teacher in a reputable Catholic school at that. Now if you ask me, it was the husband. A *crime de passion*.' His strong Dublin accent faltered not one iota during his brief and rare excursion into the French language. 'And it won't be long before they find the body of the lover somewhere, this Mr Forsythe, despatched by the same hand. Maybe the husband'll do himself in afterwards, overwhelmed by grief and remorse. A triangle of love becomes a triangle of death.'

He rubbed his hands and went over to the sideboard to pour himself another whiskey in celebration of the speed and precision with which he had solved the case, and in anticipation of more deaths to come.

'But they surely won't find his body to have been despatched in the same way or in the same place?'

He frowned as he sat down, slightly deflated.

'I have to admit that that is a curious feature of the case. Naked among the dunes. Maybe there's a symbolic significance to it. Perhaps that was where they first made love. That was probably it. He led her there for the final consummation. Lust at the first and death at the last. Almost poetic, wouldn't you say? But then his body would have been found there as well, if it was a suicide pact. No, the love triangle is more convincing. I showed that article to the Holy Ghost yesterday but he showed no reaction at all. Too wrapped up in his mediaeval theology.'

"The Holy Ghost" was his highly irreverent term for Father Coffey, the most senior of the three priests still in post at our parish. A respected scholar of Church History, he was already in semi-retirement. He was due to move shortly to a remote parish in rural Derbyshire, where he would finish his ministry and where the number of remaining parishioners was so few that he was guaranteed all the peace and quiet he needed for his research. Father O'Malley had given him his nickname, which he shared only with me, in recognition of Father Coffey's habit of gliding silently about the church and the presbytery, so deep in thought that he barely noticed when he was greeted. I was not surprised to learn that the news of a murder in Formby was of no interest to him.

At first the crime correspondent of the *Formby Times* appeared to share Father O'Malley's belief in the love triangle theory, especially when the police issued a statement to the effect that they had traced Mr Forsythe and were holding both him and Mr Pickersgill for questioning. But the following day, they announced that they had been released without charge and no further arrests were imminent. The paper printed a highly critical leader the following day, denouncing the police for incompetence. Hoping to buy time or sympathy or both, or at least to stem the flow of critical comment, the police officers in charge of the case called in the reporters for a special briefing. The officers must have been dismayed to find that the additional detail they supplied stimulated an article in the next issue covering the whole of the front page. But the tone of the new article was at least less directly critical than that of its predecessors.

According to the article, the briefing had begun with an account of Mrs Pickersgill's journey to her place of death. Several eyewitnesses had seen a car on the road leading to the woods at the relevant time. All were agreed that the car contained a man and a woman, but they could not agree on which of them was driving. One was convinced the car was a grey Ford Anglia. The original purpose of the journey seemed clear enough, to the witnesses, the police and the reporters. The woods were a well-known place for lovers' trysts. Once there, the driver had pulled the car off the road onto a rough track of dirt and sand and driven on about a hundred yards. Tyre marks found near the clothes were compatible with the Ford Anglia theory, though they did not rule out similar models of car. It appeared that Mrs Pickersgill had got out of the car, stepped a few paces into the woods and taken off her clothes, confirmation, surely, that she and her companion had gone to the woods for sex and were setting about it in a businesslike way. There was no suggestion of coercion. Her clothes had been dropped onto the ground in an untidy pile. They showed no signs of having been torn and no buttons had been pulled off.

Everything appeared clear up to that point. But as yet the police had no explanation at all for what had apparently happened next. The woods were indeed an ideal place for covert sex. Why, then, had Mrs Pickersgill walked out of the woods with her companion to the dunes, where they were far more likely to be discovered? Could she have been killed in the woods and her body moved to the dunes, one reporter asked? The police were positive that she had been killed at the spot where her body had been found. It had been raining earlier that afternoon and the sand was still moist when the police first arrived on the scene. The prints of her naked feet were visible, leading out from the woods. And why was it that while she was naked her companion was apparently still clothed, at least to the extent of a pair of size eight shoes? (The shoeprints had been seized on as a possible early lead, but those of Mr Pickersgill and Mr Forsythe were size nine and none bore any traces of sand or the pinewood soil where her clothes had been found). They had not walked side by side, although the path was wide enough. His prints and hers were in the same track. It appeared that she had walked in front of him, because some of her prints were partially obliterated by his.

The only signs of a struggle were at the spot where she had been killed. It seemed that she was kneeling in the sand when she was attacked. According to the pathologist's report the bruises around her neck showed clearly that her killer had come up behind her to strangle her. There was no doubt that it was the man who had followed her from the woods. There were no other footprints nearby. Traces of skin and blood were found under her fingernails, evidence of her attempts to pull his hands away from her throat. She had not been raped or sexually assaulted in any way. Although her actions in undressing, walking out on the sand and kneeling down could not at that stage be explained, there was no indication that she expected the attack. She had made no attempt to run away and no screams had been heard, though several courting couples had come forward to admit they had been nearby in the woods at the time.

The police confirmed that they had finally eliminated both Mr Pickersgill and Mr Forsythe as possible suspects. Mr Pickersgill had a strong alibi. Mr Forsythe had admitted that he had been Mrs Pickersgill's lover. When he first heard of her death he had panicked and disappeared. But he had returned and gone to the police of his own accord to give them a statement. He had told them Mr Pickersgill had known about the affair for some time and accepted it. Mr Forsythe himself had no alibi for the night of the murder, but a thorough search of his house and close forensic analysis of his car and the clothes he had been wearing had failed to produce anything to put him at the scene of the crime.

The police frankly admitted that they were baffled. Without further evidence they did not want to speculate on the killer's identity or his motives. They were particularly puzzled as to why the killer had seemed to go out of his way to find an open spot for the crime and had made no attempt to conceal the body or the clothes. Public co-operation had so far been exemplary, but the police were desperate to talk to anybody else who might have seen or heard anything in the area at the time.

They had one further detail to disclose. Mr Pickersgill had told them he was sure his wife had been wearing a silver bracelet he had given to her for her birthday the week before. It had her initials on it. It was not on the body and had not been found with her clothes. They circulated a detailed description of it to all the reporters in the room.

At that point, a freelance crime reporter, drawn away from his usual hunting grounds in the inner city by the growing interest in the case, stood up and declared that he had the solution. The bracelet had been taken by the killer and he was still holding it. He had covered many murders in his time and he knew that psychopathic serial killers always took something away as a trophy. They also liked to provoke the police, which would explain why the crime had not been concealed in any way. If they looked in their records or enquired of other forces, they would find that there were other unsolved killings which followed a similar pattern. The officer in charge of the briefing had replied by saying he was sorry to disappoint him but that had already been tried. They were sure this was not part of a series already underway. But the officer had to admit that a serial killer has to begin somewhere and it was of course possible that this one could be the beginning of a pattern. They had alerted other forces to report any similar incidents. The briefing finished on that note.

So far, the article had reported the briefing in a reasonably factual way. Now it moved into feverish speculation mode. The police needed to show more imagination. Perhaps some form of pagan ceremony or witches' coven had been underway, involving a ritual which had gone horribly wrong. Those woods were notorious for strange goings-on in the dark. But they had to admit that that explanation had its shortcomings. It did not account for the move from the woods to the sand, or the presence of only two participants, or the fact that only one of the two was naked. Readers were invited to contribute their own ideas.

The coven idea caught the public imagination and was soon the preferred topic of conversation in the Formby pubs and clubs. Before long everybody seemed to know someone living in the ancient heart of the town who had had an ancestor who had been burned as a witch. The suggestion appeared more than once in the letters column. Eventually a prominent local historian took it upon himself to contribute an article in which he stated that no witches had ever been burned in Formby. Moreover, he knew of no evidence that witchcraft had ever been practised there.

The article had covered so much ground that it temporarily exhausted the energies of its authors. Then two weeks later the editor decided it was time for a dramatic gesture. In a leading article, he denounced the lack of progress and called on the local police chiefs to resign.

They ignored him. The paper, and presumably the police, found other priorities. The husband and the lover both moved away, no doubt to avoid the continuing local gossip and finger-pointing. Even Father O'Malley lost interest when none of his own increasingly implausible theories could be reconciled with the known facts. We cancelled our order from the newsagents and confined ourselves as before to the *Crosby Herald* and the *Liverpool Echo*.

It was August 1970 when the murder was first reported, very soon after my appointment as a parish priest in Seaport. It was the only local excitement I can recall in my first fifteen years there and it had not even been that local. Over the next fifteen years nothing memorable happened, either in our parish or in any of the immediately neighbouring ones. Father O'Malley pursued his love of murder vicariously through his favourite detective stories. I was barely aware of the passage of time, even less aware of what was happening in the city a few miles away. The riots in Toxteth came and went, and barely a ripple was felt in Seaport. They could have been on the other side of the moon for all that we or our parishioners knew or cared.

Even the arrival of my fortieth birthday came as only a slight shock. Father O'Malley never admitted to his age, though I well knew that he was sixteen years my senior. I like to think that physically he changed more than I did over that time. His waistline continued to expand and his face grew redder. In another ten years, I thought, he would retire and I would start to look like him. Perhaps I would even have started to tell stories like his. A few more years and I would have taken over his entire *persona*, perhaps even the accent I had always thought so inimitable.

One could do worse, I thought. I had never known such an irreverent priest. But our parishioners loved him. Mrs Raferty, our housekeeper, loved him though she scolded him endlessly. I loved him. In the company of Father Ambrose, my mentor and predecessor, I never felt holy enough, in that of Father

Coffey never clever enough. With Father O'Malley I could relax, and occasionally I could laugh, something a parish priest is not supposed to do, and salve my conscience by blaming it on his stories.

I was sure nothing would ever change the quiet drift of our lives. Then one evening everything changed, forever. It was the day Father O'Malley got back unexpectedly early from Dublin, and an envelope was left on our doorstep.

PART I

THE ANONYMOUS LETTERS

ONE

When I heard the knock on the door I expected Mrs Raferty to answer it. I had just finished dinner and was settling down to read the evening paper.

'Would you mind getting that, Father?' she called out from the kitchen. 'That was Father O'Malley on the phone just now to say he's on his way and I need to get his pie in the oven to warm.'

I opened the door. Nobody there. A prank caller. Children, probably. I was about to close it again when I saw the envelope on the doorstep. It was brown foolscap with scuffed edges. I picked it up. It bore only two words, "Father Jones", in large letters, scrawled with a red felt-tip pen. The rain was driving into my eyes straight across the Mersey estuary from the Welsh hills. The ink on the envelope was beginning to run. I peered through the darkness. There were no moving shadows, no sounds of receding footsteps.

I brought the envelope into the dining-room and left it in front of the fire to dry. Fido sniffed and licked it. Fido was the presbytery cat, female, black and white, and no bigger than a kitten, despite her eight years. We called her Fido because, unlike most cats of our acquaintance, she came when called, though in her own time, and followed us from room to room. That was as far as it went. She did not sit when commanded, or fetch pieces of wood or tennis-balls. The only dog-like attributes she had assumed were those suited to her innate sense of dignity. Her suspicious interest in the envelope suggested to me the presence of a dog or another cat at the time and place the contents were inserted. Congratulating myself on my powers of deduction, and wondering if Father O'Malley in the presence of the same evidence would have been able to match them, I turned the now dry object over in my hand. I could infer nothing further without opening it.

There were two plain sheets of paper, which looked as if they had been crumpled up and then smoothed out again. The contents had been inexpertly typed on a machine with uneven letters and a worn ribbon. I started to read but could make little headway at first because of the numerous idiosyncrasies of spelling, grammar and punctuation. The words seemed nothing more than childish ramblings. Until the story they told began to come into focus and I realised I was trembling.

But the more absorbed I became in the account the more I began to doubt its veracity. I was already shaking my head before I got to the end. No, I said to myself. It's not possible. Either this is pure invention or there has been a dreadful misunderstanding. It can't have been a priest. *No priest would ever do that.*

At that moment, Father O'Malley burst through the door, shaking his still open umbrella. Fido retreated under a chair just in time to escape a shower.

'Sure, it's raining blue murder out there, and that's the Lord's own truth.'

'Welcome back, Father,' shouted Mrs Raferty, still in the kitchen, 'and don't forget to leave your umbrella in the hall so it can dry out.'

Her warning had come too late as usual. Raindrops were already spattered around the room, including the back of my neck and the front page of my newspaper. His presence filled the room, his broad shoulders eagerly thrust forward. In his youth he had been a club level rugby player and his demeanour still suggested pent-up energy and purpose. But over the years what remained of the ambition of his early days had become slowly smothered under the influence of his favourite Irish whiskey and the comfortable routines of parish life.

'You're back early, Father,' I said, brushing the drops off my paper.

He had been to Dublin to visit his sick sister. We had served together as parish priests for the whole of the fifteen years since I had come to St Jerome's. But I still afforded him the courtesy of his title in recognition of his seniority and the fact that as a boy I had served at the altar while he said Mass. Usually he returned the courtesy of calling me "Father", only using my first name when he was cross with me.

Not that we argued much, and very rarely about parish duties. The more prestigious occasions were allocated to him without question. On weekdays we took it in turns to say morning and evening Mass. On Sundays I always said ten o'clock Mass, so that I had time to have coffee and attend to my correspondence before going to my mother's for lunch.

We heard Confession on Saturday evenings. We knew that there would not have been sufficient demand for both of us on any other evenings. Our parishioners were all aware that a State of Grace was required if they wished to receive Communion at Sunday Mass. St Jerome's was a quiet parish and few of them indulged in any Saturday night excesses, so there was at least a reasonable chance that a State of Grace from Saturday Confession would last until Sunday morning.

My predecessor, Father Ambrose, on the other hand, had only ever heard Confession on Wednesdays. It was an absolute rule with him. God is not only open at weekends, he would say to anyone who dared to question his rule. Father O'Malley had once tried to tease him, suggesting to him that he chose Wednesday so he would only have to absolve that handful of resolute souls who were confident they could maintain a State of Grace for several days. My mother was

25

always one of that select group. She would never have contemplated going to any other priest than Father Ambrose for Confession. Father O'Malley's remark was meant in good heart as always, but Father Ambrose was not the sort of priest you tried to tease more than once. He had frozen Father O'Malley with a stare and reminded him that it was a sacrilege to make frivolous remarks about any of the sacraments. I suspect it was a great relief to Father O'Malley when I replaced Father Ambrose. He knew I did not mind frivolous remarks.

'Sure, I am that,' he replied to my greeting. 'Caught the early morning ferry. Foul crossing. I think I'll take the plane next time.'

I did not believe him. He had never flown in his life. He sometimes said that if God had meant men to fly He would not have needed to make angels as well. He poured himself a glass of whiskey and sat down in front of the gas fire.

'Have you had your dinner already, Father?' he asked.

'Yes. Mrs Raferty's done a splendid steak and kidney pie. She'll get you yours as soon as she's warmed it up. So how was your sister?'

'Oh, fine. As soon I got there, there she was. Gone.'

'What, gone away? In her condition? Where?'

'No. Gone to the Lord, God bless her. I was just in time to help arrange the funeral. Sure, we had a great time, though. Our brother Jimmy came over from Cork. We were drinking a pint or few of Guinness. Then he drove us into Dublin centre for a bite to eat but nearly everywhere was closed. It's no wonder. It was three o'clock in the morning. There's me thinking it was about nine in the evening. The funeral was the next day at twelve. Thank God I wasn't taking the service. I'd have led them all in three verses of "Knees

Up Mother Brown", followed by the hokey-cokey round the coffin.'

'How old was your sister?'

'Just turned seventy. To tell you the truth, I hardly knew her, what with eight others between us. She was the eldest and I was the baby. Last time I went to see her was ten years ago, and she had no idea who I was. Said she was sure she only had eight younger brothers and sisters, not nine. But it was a great funeral, to be sure.

'Aunt Christine was there, despite having had the burglars in the previous week. Well, not the burglars exactly. The lad next door. She and Uncle John had gone away to Galway for a few days to stay with my Aunt Teresa, and they came back a day early because of an almighty row. God knows what about. Anyway, she'd told her next door neighbour how long they were going to be away, and her son must have overheard. When they got back, Uncle John went upstairs. He thought he heard something in the bedroom but he couldn't see anything. Something made him look under the bed and he saw a pair of shoes there. At first he thought they were his. Then he said to himself, "Lord bless us and save us, but who in their right minds is going to put their shoes away under the bed and stand them on end, and on the toes end at that?" He's something of a philosopher is Uncle John. He's a man who thinks deeply about things. So he sat there and thought for a good quarter of an hour. Then he says to himself, "well, maybe as there's some feet still in those shoes or how they would manage to be still standing up? And if there's feet in them, there's somebody attached to those feet and I wouldn't mind finding out who it is because I'm not so sure they're supposed to be here." So he bends down and grabs hold of the shoes and pulls with all his might. And sure enough there is somebody there. Young Bernard from next door. Just sixteen. Shaking like a leaf he was. He must have got in through the window and hid under the bed when he heard them come in. Probably thought he'd make too much noise if he tried to get out the same way. So they took him downstairs. He was in such a state they made him a cup of tea. Then they called the police. What a start to your life of crime, though. Caught *in flagrante* and given a cup of tea! The shame of it! The tea's the bit he'll never live down.'

He paused for breath at last. I smiled. It was quite normal for a simple question to elicit from him a story of considerable length and total irrelevance in response. It was no use trying to interrupt him once he had started.

He glanced sharply at me. 'So what's that you were reading when I came in?'

'A letter. A lot of nonsense, really.'

Of course it was nonsense. The words which had been going through my mind as he entered still resonated there. *No priest would ever do that.*

'Is it a sort of Confession, perhaps? Now, really, Father, what are things coming to these days? Since when has it been all right to send your Confession in by post instead of coming along in person? Would that be one of the reforms of the Vatican Council, now? No wonder it was twenty years after it ended before they could bring themselves to tell us about it.'

'No, not that sort of Confession. And it didn't come by post. It was left on the doorstep.'

'On the doorstep! Well, there's a thing. Still it could be worse. Aunt Christine told me one of her neighbours had something left on her doorstep only last month. Only that was a new-born child. What would we have done about that?'

'Now be serious for once, Father. Who's going to

leave a baby on a presbytery doorstep, to be looked after by a couple of old priests who only ever see a baby to baptise it and then give it back as soon as it starts squalling?'

'True enough. But less of the old please. Well what about this letter? Who is it addressed to? If it's to the parish priest, then that's me because I'm senior to you.'

'It's addressed to me. By name. Sorry about that.'

But why to me? Why go to the trouble of finding out my name and address and coming round to deliver it in person? Why tell me something I knew no priest would ever do? Why tell me something I could not possibly believe?

He looked crestfallen.

'Have you done the roster for next week?' he asked, after a sulky pause of several minutes.

'Yes. You're still happy to take Tom Kavanagh's Requiem, are you? I mean you haven't had too much of that sort of thing, have you? I didn't know you were going to a funeral when you left for Dublin.'

'I didn't know it myself. No, it's fine. I'll do it. As soon as I heard about Tom I went round to see Bernadette straight away. She especially asked me to take the service. No offence meant to you, I'm sure, but as I'm the one who sees her on pastoral visits and hears her in Confession it's understandable she should ask me. I've seen her grow up from a child of ten. I married the two of them. They were only eighteen. Same age as you. You had only just decided to enter the priesthood. They went to live with his mum and dad at first. Outside this parish. They moved back into the parish a few years later, when Tom got that promotion and they could afford that big new house. Much too big for her now. Tom was lapsed but we can give him a good Catholic send-off for her sake. Nothing I like more than a good Requiem Mass. Remember that flu

29

epidemic a few years ago? We had three or four every morning for a week. Saw one coffin on its way to the cemetery just as the next was arriving. Sheer bliss. One morning the first one was late, and there was a queue of coffins outside the church by midday. Mrs Davies was stuck there in hers for an hour. Nearly got her first and last parking ticket.'

I was relieved. This was one funeral service I did not want to take. Tom Kavanagh, accountant with Liver Assurance, forty, heart attack. Leaves a widow and one son. Bernadette Kavanagh. Thirty-nine.

Once, an infinity ago, she and I had both been eighteen.

'Shame, him dying so young though,' he resumed. 'She's still got young John, though. How old is he now? I heard he went to a college in Manchester but I'm not at all sure when. He might still be there. It's odd but I never met him. He was never there when I went round to see her and she never wanted to talk about him. She told me once that Tom had insisted he be brought up in the Anglican Church, so of course he never came to this church.'

'I never met John either.'

'Anyway, I'm sure he's old enough to look after his mum. Until she meets somebody else. She's still an attractive woman. Put a bit of weight on in the last few years, though. Not that I mind that. I like something you can get your teeth into. Not literally, of course. When it comes to a woman's figure, I like a real story, with a beginning, middle and end. Not like all these hard little epigrams you see everywhere these days. Oh, I'm sorry, Father. There's me going and forgetting again that you used to have a thing about Bernadette.'

He had not forgotten at all. Soon after my arrival in St Jerome's as parish priest he had shown me a list of parishioners he wanted to transfer to me for pastoral visiting. Bernadette's name was on the list. He told me he had been visiting the same parishioners in their homes for fifteen years and now wanted to see some fresh faces and hear some new life-stories. I had told him I was content to take over the ones on his list except that I wondered if for personal reasons he wouldn't mind keeping Bernadette on his. He had guessed right away from my embarrassed manner that a "thing", as he liked to call it, was involved.

'I knew there'd be something like this,' he had said. 'What can you expect when you were brought up in this parish and sowed your wild oats around here, and now you come back to set those hearts fluttering again?' It was not worth trying to explain that nobody was less likely than me to have sowed wild oats and set hearts fluttering. 'And maybe your own might still be prone to a slight flutter despite that collar you're wearing. So, Bernadette was the one, was she? Can't say as I blame you for having a thing about her. I think you're being very wise to be keeping out of her way now you're back here.'

No priest would ever do that.

'Sorry, Father?'

I realised I had missed the last words he had addressed to me.

'I said, now what would you be dreaming about? You were miles away all of a sudden.'

'Sorry. Wondering about that letter.'

'Hm...I wonder if it was something else you were wondering about. Something, or someone, I was just talking about, maybe?'

'Actually, no, Father. I wasn't thinking about her.'

That was not strictly true. There was a bedrock in my thoughts which was always devoted to her, more or less consciously. But over the years I had learned not to let him draw me into conversation about her.

31

'So what were you wondering about the letter?'

'Who would go to the trouble of leaving it on the doorstep and then run away?'

'Is there no address at the top?'

I picked up the sheets. 'No. No name at the end, either.'

'So why even bother to read it? You can't help them.'

'Whoever it is might come back. They might have left this to prepare me. I'll leave you to your dinner and say goodnight now. And, Father...'

'What?'

'Welcome back. We've missed you.'

'Ah, get away with you now.'

He waved me away with his hand and turned his attention to the plate Mrs Raferty had put before him.

I retired to my study, where I knelt every evening before a statue of the Sacred Heart of Jesus to say my daily Divine Office.

The words rolled off my tongue but my thoughts were elsewhere. If Father O'Malley had been able to see into my mind at that moment he would have grinned in triumph. Now he would have been right. I had put thoughts of the letter to one side. In their stead rose thoughts of Bernadette. Bernadette Reilly when I knew her. Large, green, almond-shaped Egyptian eyes. Long black Irish hair. Milk-white skin never ripened in the sun. A blue headscarf in church, head bowed at the altar rail. Soft, moist tongue protruding to accept Communion from my trembling hand. The altar boy holding the plate steady beneath her chin in case I drop the Host, or it slips from her mouth. 'The Body of Christ,' I murmur, as I hold the Host before her lips. Sacred words, at the most sacred moment of the Mass. 'Amen', she whispers, her response barely audible.

But that was years ago. Before we started to give Communion into the hand. Before she stopped taking Communion altogether. But why had she stopped? Maybe Father O'Malley knew but I had never dared to ask, in case the knowledge might be covered by the secrecy of the confessional.

The secrecy of the confessional, total and absolute in all circumstances. No priest would ever betray that secrecy.

I pulled the sheets out, spread them on the table and read through them again.

No, my first impression had been right. *No priest would ever do that.*

TWO

31 January 1985

dear father jones

    This is what they call an annonimouse letter. that's what tim calls it. tim's my friend and he knows everything. He said that's what it's called when you don't put your name at the end. is it all right so far because I've never writen a letter in my life before and I can't type very well yet either. tim told me I had to start with the date on the top but I had to ask him what the date was as I didn't even know the year.

    I'm going to tell you my story father jones. I was sixteen when it hapened. I was nothing speshal. a bit wild lousy at school not really good or bad. certainly not sweet sixteen. I did some wrong things so I went to connfession. things I couldn't tell her. I can't remember the priests name that's the trouble with me after all the drugs they gave me. I still forget things. I forgot everything for years but it's slowly beginning to come back now. I remember his questions he wanted to know every detail of how it happened. you lousy creep I remember thinking you're just getting off on this aren't you. I've told you what I did I've connfessed so now just say the mumbojumbo give me my pennance and let me get out of this stupid little box with its stupid little curtain between us so I can't see you can't see how you're getting off on what I'm telling you. that wasn't the worst though. the questions and all that. the worst was that he told her. but it's all supposed to be secret isn't it. the one thing no priest ever does is snitch on what he hears in connfession but he did.

she took me to his house like this great big manshon out in the country never been in such a large house before. big gardens long posh driveway and then this big stone porch with things like little statues at the top looking like eegles with the faces of devils. she left me there in this room told me she didn't want to see me ever again and she left. and the front door was locked I thought I was in prison on my own and nobody knew where I was so I would die there. I went upstairs and he was there in this dark room with no lights and I knew it was him because it was his voice though he was trying to talk funny so I wouldn't know it was him. he was going on at me about what I'd done telling me I was posessed by spirits but I wasn't having any of that crap. I could see where he was standing in the corner so I went for him. When I got up close I could see his face and I knew it was really him so I scratched his face as hard as I could but he got my arms behind my back Christ he was strong. I was kicking and screaming then he dragged me into a smaller room and locked me in and I was yelling and pounding the door for ages.

after a few hours I was dead beat and that was when he came back with the doctor and I laughed when I saw the priests face because he had scratches all down his cheeks that I had done. the doctor gave me a jab. I knew I had seen him before because he was our usual doctor and I was bloody relieved when I saw him I was sobbing trying to tell him what had happened but then I realised he wasn't listening he just gave me the jab and left the room. it calmed me down for a while but when it wore off I was worse than before so he gave me another jab and the priest kept saying I was posessed and he would need to call in a speshal priest. the second jab was much stronger because it put me to sleep.

the speshal priest came the next day. I was quiet by then and I just looked at him I saw he was very old with a beard. dead weerd he was quite a laugh really should have been on the stage. he had loads of old books with him and he wore fancy stuff like you wear in church and he made all sorts of funny gestures over me and sprinkled me with holey water. and tried to make me hold a prair book in one hand and a rosery in the other but I tore pages out of the prair book and I pulled the rosery beeds apart so they flew all over the floor. I was leading them on because they were saying I was posessed so I wanted to show them I was posessed all right. I mean if they wanted posessed I was going to give it to them right proper.

then two more doctors came I think it was a couple of days later but they were different ones so I didn't know them. and they examined me and made me unndress completely. and they asked me why I had atacked the priest when he had only been trying to comfort me and give me spirittual advice about my situation as they called it. I tried to tell them what the priest had done but they weren't listening they were writing things down in notebooks. I was dead cheeky with them because I asked them if they were drawing my tits and told them I thought they were only prettending to be doctors so they could get off on asking girls to unndress. but they just shook their heads and looked very serious and asked me if I had ever atacked anyone before and asked me if I had ever harmed myself. of course I said slit my wrists only last week. I was only kidding them but they wrote that down too. I told them I was only kidding and showed them my wrists but they kept on writing.

they took me away the next day I was very calm by then because they had given me loads more jabs so I was asleep most of the time. when I awoke I was in a tiny room with a narrow bed only a mattress no sheets or blankets. more men came to examine me. these ones had white coats they took away my own clothes and gave me a dirty grey gown. I asked them where I was and they told me it was a hospital where I would get better but I said I didn't understand what's wrong with me I asked but they never answered. it was all their doing. her and that priest. so you see why I need to find them don't you. now that I'm out of that place and now that I remember. I have to find them and make them pay for what they did to me.

THREE

'Father, if God knows all, why do we need to tell Him our sins?'

'Yes, George, quite right. He does know all. But the sacraments require us to interact with Him. If we just think about our sins, it is very likely that some, perhaps most, of our minds will be elsewhere. Life is full of distractions. That is only human nature. In speaking of our sins, we focus on them, and we focus our contrition on them.'

'I can understand that, Father. But why cannot we just talk to God, out loud? As in prayer. Confess our sins that way?'

It was the day after Father O'Malley's return. I was taking a class of instruction in the sacraments for would-be converts to the Catholic Faith. I had taken this same class every week for several weeks. Each time, the great majority of the questions concerned the Sacrament of Confession, the most difficult, intimate, and demanding of the sacraments. George, always my most persistent questioner, was a teacher at the local comprehensive school. He was engaged to a Catholic woman who did not want a mixed marriage. His willingness to convert was painfully sincere. He desperately wanted to understand everything about his new Faith, in the sort of logical terms he would have used in the classroom. I did not need to think too long about my answer. He had asked the same question the previous week and the week before that.

'Well, of course, you could. Say you were in the middle of the desert and dying of thirst. Or, a little closer to home, you have fallen down in the middle of the road and a bus is bearing down on you. You believe you are about to die. Then you would say an Act of Contrition. It only takes a few seconds. Less than a second if need be. I told you all a few weeks ago that in cases of emergency anybody can baptise a child who is dying. People who have no access to a priest can achieve Baptism of Desire. So it is with Confession. But in normal circumstances, it is the priest who acts as the instrument for God's Grace. When you hear the words of Absolution, and you know you are in the right state of mind, you know the sacrament is complete. Christ appointed His apostles and their successors, His anointed priests, to administer the sacraments on His behalf. That is what we try to do.'

'Father, when you go to Confession, do you actually see the priest?' This was not George, but a young woman, new to the class.

'No, not in this church, though that is no more than a convenient physical arrangement, to make it clear to you that the priest is not there in his own person. There is a screen between you and him. He cannot see you, and you cannot see him. There are two doors to each confessional box. He goes in one door. You go in the other. You will see a kneeler by the partition. In the partition is a grille, with a curtain drawn across it. The priest will be on the other side of it. He does not enter your space, and you do not enter his. When you are there, you must speak clearly and distinctly so he can hear you, but you should think only of the presence of God and speak as to Him. Yes, George?' I felt my heart sinking.

'But a priest is also a human being, and he must react in a human way to what he hears. What if someone comes in, for example, and confesses to being a serial killer who intends to go out and kill again, and the priest recognises his voice?'

'Your concern is very understandable. You are a professional man, George. You understand the duty to

39

respect confidences which are placed in you. But that duty is based on the rules of secular society. There are certain exceptions. A court might order you to disclose confidential information. In other circumstances your own conscience might allow you to do so, if the life or well being of a third party is at stake. But none of that applies here. There are no exceptions. The secrecy of the confessional is absolute.'

'Even if that means innocent people are going to die?'

'You have to ask yourself why the person concerned has come to Confession. Your example of the murderer, for instance. He will not receive Absolution if he is not truly sorry. If he is, God's Grace will prevent him from offending again. If, despite his contrition, he feels he is in danger of killing again, because of some psychological condition, the priest might well advise him to seek help. But he could not go to the authorities himself.'

'Father, does that mean that you, you personally, would go to prison rather than reveal what someone told you in Confession?'

'Yes, George, I would. Willingly. And so would any priest.'

I had given George this answer before. But the previous times I had known I was right.

But didn't I still know that? The letter had to be false. Not deliberate lies, of course. The letter had cost the writer too much pain and effort for that. But a sad tissue of paranoid delusions. Why, then, had a note of uncertainty crept into my voice when I had answered George?

The following morning, I rose early. It was my turn to say first Mass. Nobody stirred in the house except Fido, who urged me to ignore my holy duties to attend to her, by brushing against my ankles and emitting a plaintive squeaking noise. I stroked her and explained to her that Mrs Raferty would give her her breakfast with mine, after Mass. Then I relented and put out some dry food for her on the carpet. The pieces would be gone by the time Mrs Raferty was up so neither of us would be in trouble.

The house was much too large for two priests. The parish had once had four. There were five bedrooms, all painted in a uniform chocolate brown. Mrs Raferty now occupied one of them. Father O'Malley and I each had our own study downstairs. On the other side of the tiled hallway were the dining room and lounge. The lounge also served as a library. We had inherited a large number of books on religious subjects from our predecessors, among whom Father Ambrose and Father Coffey had been renowned for the breadth of their theological knowledge. I was ashamed at how little time I spent reading the books, though I had once spent several contented hours re-cataloguing them according to the Dewey decimal system, or what I had learned of it during my school holiday jobs at the local library.

The church was a low-roofed, brown-stoned building with narrow windows. A large, heavy oak double door at the back had long since been sealed. The only entrance for the congregation was a door at the side. There was no steeple or tower. The church beckoned gently to passers-by. It let in little natural light. It was a place of shadows where each could find light in his or her own way. It was not like the bright, modern churches where nothing can be hidden. At St Jerome's, the sinner could slip in unnoticed and pray undisturbed at the back, leaving others, such as my mother, sure of God's favour, to approach close to the Blessed Sacrament in the tabernacle over the high altar.

A passageway had been built onto the back of the

house, communicating directly with the church. At the end, a door on the right led to the room where the altar boys kept their cassocks and cottas, and where the candles and flower vases were stored. Another door directly ahead led into the sacristy. I unlocked the door from the house to the passageway. It was cold and dark. In the sacristy the acrid smell of candle-smoke and incense which had drifted in from the church during the Sunday services still hung in the air. The duty altar boy, who had had to rise even earlier than I to grope his way to church in the dark, had already been in to fill the wine and water cruets. I laid out the vestments. I put on my alb, chasuble and stole. I took out the chalice. I waited, praying. To my shame, I always felt a sense of theatre. I was dressing to play a part. I had my lines. They were well rehearsed. I had said them thousands of times. The clock pointed to half-past seven. The altar boy was waiting in the passage, rubbing his eyes. We moved out into the church and onto the altar. Twelve people. About the usual number for a winter weekday morning. The number had not changed in fifteen years.

On Sundays the church was always full for ten o'clock Mass. During Mass I faced the congregation. Those were the "new" rules, following the Vatican Council of the early 1960s. Most of our parishioners still referred to them as new with a tone of disapproval, and would probably do so for the rest of their lives. When I was an altar boy, it had been very different. We faced the altar. Now it was impossible for me to avoid the faces of my parishioners as I said Mass.

But, however large the Sunday congregation, there were only two faces I ever saw. My mother always sat in the front row. She beamed with pride. I told her it was wrong to feel pride because I was a priest. It was an office of humility which she should share. We were both there to worship God. She knew I was right but that did not stop her. The other face was Bernadette's. She always took a place near the back. Her eyes never met mine. Her head stayed bowed low over her missal. She remained there, motionless, even when others were coming forward for Communion.

The parish was in the Borough of Seaport. It was small in geographical terms, but a high proportion of the residents attended church regularly. Their Catholicism was rooted in the rural Ireland from which their forebears had emigrated in search of a new life. The area was neither poor nor rich. The houses were small, comfortable and meticulously neat and tidy. There was little debt and no ostentation. Many couples lived out their lives in the same house, though occasionally a person with ambition, such as my Aunt Mary, would move up the coast towards Southport, ascending the social and economic ladder in the process. Towards the water of the estuary, beyond the streets tightly packed with terraces and small semi-detached houses, lay a string of formal parks laid out in Victorian days by a local philanthropist who had made a fortune in shipping. The parks were strictly for walking and admiring flowers. They had assumed the respectable, slightly shabby character of the elderly ladies who liked to walk through them.

Evening leisure activity was confined to the few pubs, the Irish Centre, the YMCA and the Catholic Mothers' Union. In the pubs, animated conversation about the fortunes of Liverpool's two major football teams took precedence over heavy drinking. On the streets, Saturday nights after closing time were as quiet and safe as Sunday mornings. Beyond the parks and the beach lay the estuary and the Wirral coast. On clear days, the Welsh hills were visible in the far distance.

The air was constantly swept clean by moisture-laden winds.

Father O'Malley and I spent most of our lives within the walls of the house and the church and the passageway, only venturing out for our pastoral visits to parishioners. For these we each had an old bicycle. There was a rusting, red parish Mini, which we used for occasional business taking us further afield, such as diocese meetings at the Cathedral. But it was rarely necessary for us to go outside the parish, and we were grateful for that. We were content with Seaport. To the north, along the estuary coast, lay the affluent dormitory towns where the parish priests struggled to maintain attendances against the rising tide of worldly distractions. We did not envy them. To the south lay Bootle and the inner suburbs, by repute places of spiritual darkness and physical danger, to be avoided if at all possible. We envied even less the priests who worked there.

As I said Mass that morning, I found none of the usual sense of comfort and security in the prescribed routines and rituals. The letter haunted me, although I was still sure it was an invention from start to finish. I had read and reread it. I knew parts of it by heart. I told myself there was no reason for our lives to change, simply because of an anonymous letter which could not be true. We might never discover who wrote it and why. I would soon forget all about it. But I was still aware of a growing feeling of resentment. It was an unwelcome intrusion. I had seen nothing like it since coming to St Jerome's. Perhaps it had come from those benighted slums to the south. Quite apart from the content, the style and tone firmly indicated that it was not of local origin. But why then bring it all the way to Seaport of all places, and why deliver it in person?

After Mass, on the way back through the passageway, I smelt bacon and eggs. Mrs Raferty was up and about and Fido was having her second breakfast. When Father O'Malley rose she would have a third.

The next day was Saturday. Father O'Malley said morning Mass. I went into my study after breakfast. I resolved not to look at the letter again. I would leave it alone unless and until the author contacted me. I put it at the bottom of my drawer and caught up with my more routine correspondence. After lunch I visited an elderly bed-bound lady parishioner to hear her Confession. I then made three visits to the homes of parishioners. Such visits were called "pastoral", though they were usually no more than fireside chats over a cup of tea, with no talk of spiritual matters. I was anxious to adhere to my routines, to restore the equilibrium so harshly disturbed by the letter.

I returned to the presbytery at half-past three, my stomach swilling with over-strong tea. At four o'clock three prospective altar boys arrived on fragile, rusting bicycles. Father O'Malley had warned me of their arrival, asking me to take care of them as he had other important duties elsewhere in the parish. I knew from Mrs Raferty that he was going to Blundellsands, well outside our parish, to support his old rugby team in a local cup final. When I saw the boys, I commended him on his foresight in arranging to be elsewhere. They were aged about eleven, wearing shabby open jackets, dirty grey shirts which had perhaps once been white, and short trousers. All were missing buttons from all three items of clothing. Their noses streamed in the bitterly cold wind. They stared glumly at me, using their sleeves as handkerchiefs, as I sat them down in the sacristy and gave them an induction talk on their new duties. They made no responses and asked no questions.

With some relief, I handed them over to Francis, the head altar boy. Francis was eighteen and had been head altar boy since the age of twelve. He was plump, cheerful and patient. He served on the altar once every weekday, and at each of the four Sunday Masses. By means of relentless drilling he could turn even the least promising recruit into a useful altar boy in weeks. He taught all responses by rote, never deeming it worthwhile to explain their meaning. Francis was a living saint, though I knew there would be no point in advocating his cause to the Church hierarchy. His efforts, and those of Matthew, our eighty-five year old deaf organist who clambered unsteadily into the organ loft for eleven o' clock Mass every Sunday, never missing a week, or a note, or his place in the service, were really what kept our church going. It was work that would be taken for granted until the Second Coming, when Francis and Matthew could at last take their rightful places at the right hand of God. Until then they would have to be content with the knowledge that God, and a few insignificant mortals like myself and Father O'Malley, knew their real worth.

In the evening, I heard Confession and said Mass. After dinner I made notes for my sermon for the following morning. I sensed my usual Saturday evening mood of despondency creep up on me. The following day I would have to visit my mother for lunch. I did not have to, of course. But somehow it had become an immovable part of my routine. She knew what my duties were, and she knew I had organised them so as to be free at Sunday lunchtime. I could easily have invented an emergency which she would find reasonably credible, but not every week. I had long since decided that it would be less painful to numb myself into a pattern of weekly visits than to endure the dread which would build up each time if the visits were spaced out.

FOUR

Sunday lunch at my mother's was always timed for two o'clock. She needed time after Mass to clean the already spotless house and prepare a traditional meal of inedibly tough beef and watery vegetables. In winter the house was always cold. She had had gas fires installed some years before, deploring the fact that coal fires were no longer allowed and paraffin heaters were no longer considered safe. She was too nervous to switch on the gas fires herself. When I arrived I would switch them on for her, though she insisted on the lowest possible setting. I had to remember to take a warm pullover.

She still lived in the tiny terrace house where she and my father settled and where my sister, Angela, and I were brought up. She lived frugally and never complained about shortage of money. Her widow's pensions were sufficient for her purposes, plus the little she earned from sewing. She despised any form of luxury. She had no telephone, though I had often tried to point out to her that with her failing health it was a necessity. She had a radio, but no television. She never took a holiday. She never went on any of the parish outings for pensioners. I told her that she left too much on the collection plate. She was known throughout the parish as a good woman, a reputation which earned her respect but not affection.

For as long as I could remember her face had always been deeply lined and unsmiling. Her hair was a stiff, wiry white, the life long since leeched out of it by years of home peroxide applications. She had painful arthritis in her knee and elbow joints, but never complained. Each Sunday she had to allow a little more time for the walk to church. It had once taken her only ten minutes, but now she needed twenty. She still

48

attended Mass during the week, but only on alternate days. She refused to allow me to drive round to collect her, pointing out that her position as mother of a priest should not confer privileges which were unavailable to other parishioners.

I arrived at exactly half past one, as usual. The door was open, as it always was when she was at home, whatever the weather. She was sitting in the front room. The smells of relentlessly cooking lunch pervaded the entire house. She looked up from her prayer book as I sat down opposite her. I did not kiss her cheek. On another day I would have done, but physical contact was not allowed on Sundays.

'You were looking very handsome in church this morning.'

She said that every week now, though she had never called me handsome until I was safely ordained.

'Mother, you know you shouldn't be saying things like that, even if it were true. You should only see God, not his Minister. What the Minister looks like is not relevant.'

I said this every week. She expected it. My tone was never scolding.

'Still a handsome priest is a fine thing in the eyes of God, I'm sure. And why can't a mother be proud?'

'A beautiful soul is a much finer thing in the eyes of God. Father Ambrose was hardly handsome, but he made a finer priest than I ever could.'

'Yes, he's a true and holy priest, Father Ambrose. I still go to him for Confession, though it's a long way now, all the way to the nursing home. Two bus rides. I used to walk all the way from the main road. Now I ring up from the bus stop and they send a car to collect me.'

I sighed. 'I don't suppose there's any point in my offering to drive you there.'

'Certainly not. A little bit of hardship on the way to Confession helps to get me in the right frame of mind to confess my sins. I can't complain. His condition is far worse than mine. He's confined to a wheelchair now.'

'I know. I go to see him from time to time. Not as often as I should.'

'I was sad when he gave up this parish. Though I was pleased, too, because it gave you your chance to come here. I still don't like that Father O'Malley though, even though I know you do. There's too many round here who are too willing to share his irreverent attitude and he only encourages them.'

When my mother had first moved to Seaport from Little Penby, the village where she had been brought up, she had from the start found the local brand of Catholicism too relaxed. 'They go to Confession only to feel free to sin again until the next time,' I frequently heard her say. The arrival in the parish of Father Ambrose, whom she had known in Little Penby, was a great consolation to her. She knew he could be relied upon to raise standards of piety and observance. Between them they would bring the spirit of Little Penby to Seaport. Now that Father Ambrose had gone the spiritual wellbeing of the parish was in the fumbling, if well-intentioned, hands of Father O'Malley and myself. I knew the thought depressed her.

I did not want to talk to her about Father O'Malley. I waited for her to find another subject. I was relieved when she did. Until I heard what she had to say.

'Oh, I was meaning to tell you, Michael. I had a break-in here on Thursday. While I was at church. Somebody must have been watching and knew the house would be empty. There's just no morality around here any more. This used to be such a respectable area. To think, I might have caught them still here when I came home. I might have been murdered in my own house. But the funny thing is that nothing was taken. The back window was broken. That's how I knew. I searched everywhere. Nothing. They had had the sideboard drawer open. They hadn't shut it properly.'

'Probably looking for jewellery. They weren't to know you didn't have any.'

'Quite right. They chose the wrong house. No frivolous worldly things here.'

'Talking of burglaries...'

I told her the story Father O'Malley had told me about the break-in at his Aunt Christine's house, and how they had caught their neighbour in the bedroom and given him a cup of tea. She stared at me without the flicker of a smile. I had never been very good at telling stories. But then she would have reacted the same way if Father O'Malley had told it to her himself.

When I had finished, she grunted.

'You know, I sometimes think you can't believe a word that man says, though God forgive me for thinking such ill of him. Oh by the way, your Aunt Mary's back from her latest round of travels. She sent me a postcard. Maybe you were thinking of going up to see her. She's not as well as she used to be. All this travelling tires her out, and I'm not sure she should be driving at her age. But she insists she wants to get about and see places while she still can. Oh I think the lunch is ready. I'll just go and fix it. Then you can say Grace.'

'Penny for your thoughts, Father Jones?'

'Sorry, Mother.' We had started lunch and I had been silent for longer than she was usually prepared to allow. 'You mentioned Aunt Mary, and that started me thinking about Angela.'

She sighed and put down her knife and fork.

'You and your sister. There you go again. I wish to God you would try and forget about her. You know I don't like to bring back all those painful memories. So let's change the subject. You know Mrs Prendergast from up the road? She's going on retreat in a couple of weeks. To a place in Yorkshire. She says it's a beautiful, peaceful spot, up on the side of the dale. I've half a mind to go with her. Make my peace before I go.'

'Before you go where, Mother?'

'You know what I mean. I won't be around much longer. And I don't want that Father O'Malley taking my funeral service, thank you very much, however much he enjoys them. There's only one priest I want to do that, and that's my own son.'

'Mother, I'm not going to have this conversation. You know you've years ahead of you yet. But by all means go on retreat. It would do you good to get away. You never go on holiday or even a day trip.'

'I only said I had half a mind to go with her. And I wouldn't be going for my own enjoyment. Anyway, I think the other half of my mind has decided against it. I don't really enjoy her company. She's a gossip and a chatterbox. Can't imagine why she wants to go on retreat when she has to keep silent for days at a time. The experience will kill her. I think her husband must have talked her into it. Wanted a bit of peace and quiet for himself. No, I won't be going. That's definite. I only mentioned it because I thought it might interest you. I didn't expect you to pick up the idea so enthusiastically. Didn't think you'd be so keen to get me out of the way. I'll be out of the way for ever soon enough.'

Her change of subject had proved almost as much a

conversational disaster as my attempt to talk about Angela. It was time to move on rapidly. I chatted on about parish trivia. As always, I could tell that I was boring and irritating her. She wanted a visit from her parish priest to be a profound spiritual experience, as a visit from Father Ambrose would have been. I could not give her that because neither of us could forget that I had once been a boy with her in that house. I had struggled with my schoolwork and never won a single prize. I was not good at games. I had been too shy to make friends. In church, where I was dressed in the vestments of my office, where ceremony surrounded me and where altar boys waited upon me, she felt an unqualified sense of justification in her status as the mother of a priest. Now, at home, as I ate lunch with her and talked about mundane matters, she found it painful to be reminded that after all I was still only her son.

It was time to go. At last. I stood up.

'Oh, before I forget, Michael, Mrs Raferty left some net curtains with me, from the presbytery. They needed repairing. I've got them here. Could you take them back to her?' She handed me a carrier bag. 'Tell her to keep the bag. It's too big for me to go shopping with. I need so little these days.'

I always felt a sense of relief on leaving the house. With the relief came guilt. This was not how a man should feel when he has been to visit his mother. But the sense of being constantly observed and scrutinised always left me exhausted. She never relented for a moment. She knew I could never match her piety or that of Father Ambrose. But she still felt the need to ensure I was coming up to scratch, as far as I could within my limitations. The expression on her face as I left was always the same. Disappointed resignation.

FIVE

My father came from North Wales. By family tradition he was "chapel", a word which he pronounced as a spondee with the second syllable at a higher pitch than the first. He had no strong views on religion in any form. When he became engaged to my mother, he was content to convert to Catholicism and follow the necessary rituals in a half-hearted way. They moved to Seaport to be close to the school where he was a geography teacher.

I was eight and Angela was three when he died. My mother never spoke of him after his funeral, and as she had never "held with" cameras, regarding them as an encouragement to worldly vanity, there were no photographs of him in the house.

My last memory of him was a trip on the ferry across the Mersey to New Brighton. It was only a few weeks before his death. Angela was with us, in a pushchair. Mother was not there. She never joined us when we went out for the day, saying she had too much to do in the house. If she had been with us, he would never have done what he did. He would never have laughed. It was the only time I could remember either of my parents laughing.

It was a rare day of sunshine in the estuary. Although the usual numbing wind blew in from the Irish Sea, the mere absence of cloud had been enough to convince hundreds of pale Liverpudlians that it was time for a day out on New Brighton Beach. They would spend it making ramshackle sandcastles to impress children who remained stubbornly unimpressed, paddling in the oil-stained water with rolled-up trouser legs, shouting when their children brought pails of dirty estuary water to throw over them as they tried to sleep, smoking Woodbines, eating candy floss that dissolved instantly on the tongue with a taste of sugared disinfectant, drinking scalding, chocolate-brown tea in the seafront cafés, and eating a fish and chip supper from newspaper before catching the ferry home. The sun and wind would blister the skin of their faces and arms to the colour of the candy floss.

There was a woman on the outward ferry with two boys, each a little younger than I was. One was having a royal tantrum. His mother turned on him. She spat the words out, a separate breath for each, and each matched with a well-timed cuff about the head. 'I've brought you here to enjoy yourself, and you'll bloody well enjoy yourself or I'll belt the living daylights out of you.' Though the cuffs were light, I felt such sympathetic pain for the young boy that I started to cry. My father held me by the shoulder. He was shaking. I thought he was crying too. Then I realised he was laughing. The absurdity of the woman's words began to dawn on me and I too started to laugh. So did Angela. She was far too young to understand. But she was always ready to laugh.

There was nothing unusual about the last morning I saw my father. He was reading the morning paper at the breakfast table, as he always did. I walked to school on my own, as usual. It was just under a mile. After school, one of the neighbours was there to collect me. That had never happened before. The neighbour took me to her house for tea. I never asked why. After tea she told me my father had been taken ill and had gone to hospital. My mother had gone with him. Angela was with another neighbour. I stayed the night with the neighbour who had collected me from school. The next day, my mother called for me and told me I was to have the day off school. My father would not be coming home again. The Lord had called him to Him. We needed to pray for his soul.

We prayed endlessly together. I did not understand why. I was sure my father had been a good man. So why did he need so many of our prayers before he could enter Heaven? It was several days before the prayers ended and I started to cry. I thought I would never stop. My mother left me to cry, though her expression of hard resignation never changed. Angela was still too young to understand what had happened. When I had recovered a little, I told Angela that from now on I was going to be a father to her. She laughed.

SIX

Back at the prebystery, I handed Mrs Raferty the parcel containing the repaired net curtains. She took a packet of curtain wire out of a drawer in the hall and bustled into the front room to hang them.

'I'll give you a hand with those, Mrs Raferty,' I said, following her in.

'That would be grand, thank you, Father.'

I knew she did not require help with the curtains, but I felt the need to make myself useful. It was a mood which often came over me after a visit to my mother's. Mrs Raferty seemed to understand, and was always prepared to humour me on those occasions.

Mrs Raferty was sixty-five, silver-haired, slim, agile and strong. Her usual manner with us was one of good-humoured chiding. She and Father O'Malley constantly teased and scolded each other. With me, she was more reserved and gentle. In contrast to my mother, she was interested in knitting rather than in sewing. Their skills were complementary and they often did jobs for each other, using me as the carrier. In the evenings, when she was not in a mood for knitting, she liked to read airport blockbusters of adventure or romance, though she had never been near an airport in her life, never mind any of the exotic locations in the books. She bought the books second-hand at the monthly church hall jumble sales. Whenever I caught her on her own at a quiet time, reading, or polishing brass, I often sensed a mood of sadness in her eyes, and about her lips and her forehead, which wore a slight frown. This mood would only last a moment before the frown disappeared and she assumed her usual cheerful smile in response to my presence. At other times she cleaned and dusted with ferocious energy. Father O'Malley was convinced she had the gift of bilocality, sometimes attributed to certain saints. It was not unusual to hear her in the kitchen busily preparing a meal, while almost immediately afterwards finding her coming down the stairs with the feather duster in her hand, having completed a whirlwind tour of the bedrooms.

She had been the presbytery housekeeper for twenty-five years. Before that, she had lived locally, coming in each day for two hours to do the cleaning. A housekeeper had prepared the priests' meals, but did not live in. Mr Raferty had been a bus-driver. He had died of cancer when she was forty. They had lived in a comfortable and spacious council house. They had no children, and after his death she was under pressure to leave the house and move into a small flat in a tower block, situated on a notoriously dangerous estate. At the same time, one of the four parish priests retired and was not replaced. To save her from the tower block, she was offered the job of resident housekeeper, taking over the vacant bedroom. She assumed the additional duties of cook on the death of the non-resident cook a few years later. Her loyalty to the presbytery and its incumbents was absolute.

'How is your mother?' she asked, expertly threading the wire through the loop at the top of the curtains.

'Very well, I think, though she doesn't think so.'

'She's done a good job with the curtains, as usual. She's had a hard life, losing your father when she was still young and with you and your sister to bring up. Then she lost her. So sad, that. Still, she has you here, and your being a priest is such a consolation to her.'

'I try to be of some help to her, though much of the time I feel pretty useless. And she wasn't sad about Angela. Angela had exceeded her wildest hopes for her. And she knew she had a happy death.'

'I'm sorry, Father. I shouldn't talk about it. I know

you still miss her. And you're not ashamed to show it. I like that about you. Your mother is different. She was never one to show her feelings to the outside world.'

She sat for a few moments looking vacantly through the window, the curtains heaped on her lap like a discarded wedding-dress. Then she shook herself.

'Well, this isn't going to get the baby a new bonnet, is it? Will you hold the chair for me, Father?'

We had reached the dangerous stage of the operation. She climbed lightly onto the chair. I handed the first curtain to her. She stretched the wire until the eyes reached the hooks set into the window-frame. At that moment, Father O'Malley put his head round the door.

'You haven't been seeing my diary about the place, have you, Mrs Raferty? I'll swear the cat's got it, or you put it in last night's stew.'

'Don't be silly, Father. One of these days you'll lose your own head and you probably won't even notice. And neither will anyone else. I'll come and find it for you. Could you manage this one by yourself, Father?' She handed me the second curtain.

'I'll have a go, now I've seen how it's done,' I said.

They left the room. I moved the chair and climbed up gingerly. I fixed the first eye onto the hook with ease, as the wire was still loose. Then I stretched it towards the hook in the far corner. The taut wire slipped through my outstretched fingers and shot back, grazing the knuckle of my other hand. I swore. I hoped they had not heard me. I resumed my efforts, taking great care to keep tight hold of the wire. With a sigh of relief, I completed the task. I sat down, nursing my hand. She came back into the room, shaking her head and making tutting sounds.

'He'd left it on his desk, where it always is, only his

sermon for next week was on top of it. Oh, you managed to get it done, Father? Only I see you hurt your hand. I should have warned you. That wire can be lethal when it's stretched. Let me get something for that cut.'

She led me into the kitchen where she applied disinfectant and plaster. She gave me a long, searching look as she pressed it down.

'You're sure you're feeling all right now, Father?'

'Of course. There's really no need to fuss. It's only a graze.'

SEVEN

I have only one memory of meeting our grandmother, who still lived in the house in Little Penby where my mother and Aunt Mary had grown up. The village lay deep in the Lancashire hinterland, fiercely and devoutly Catholic, following a tradition of centuries. During the years of Elizabethan persecution, several householders had been executed for harbouring priests. A memorial to them stood on the village green. My mother's family had lived there for generations.

I was twelve, and Angela was seven. The invitation had been arranged some weeks before. Our grandmother had not seen us since we were very small and wanted to see how we were growing up. That was the reason our mother gave us for the visit. We were warned to be on our best behaviour.

We had several connecting bus journeys to make so we started out before dawn. Angela slept nearly all the way, her head against my shoulder. Our mother sat behind us, sewing, staring occasionally out of the window.

At first, the countryside was relentlessly flat and dreary. Gradually, it changed. I saw green curving hills, brown marshes, copses of wood, granite outcrops. The village crouched in a damp, sunless valley. There were about twenty houses, all built of grey stone blocks. An incongruously large church with an imposing bell-tower served Little Penby and several other nearby hamlets.

My grandmother's house had a single downstairs living-room, into which the front door led directly. When we arrived, she too was sewing. Angela and I had been dressed in our Sunday best, although it was a school holiday weekday. No visit would have been allowed on a Sunday, when my grandmother spent the entire day in prayer and Bible reading. We were paraded in front of her while she inspected us. Angela smiled at her, but the smile crumbled away when it was not returned.

'Look at me, the two of you,' she barked, sharply. 'Let's see what she's made of you. Good. Nice and clean.' We had been fiercely scrubbed before we had started out. 'Cleanliness is next to godliness. Michael.'

'Yes, Grandmother.'

'What school are you at now?'

'St Cuthbert's, Grandmother.'

'Jesuit Fathers?'

'Yes.'

'Good. Know your catechism?'

'Some of it, Grandmother. We haven't done it all yet.'

'What is the Holy Trinity?'

'God the Father, God the Son, and God the Holy Ghost, Grandmother.'

'So there are three Gods.'

'No, Grandmother. The Holy Trinity is three Persons in one God.'

The catch was familiar from school catechism sessions and my response was well-rehearsed. My grandmother stared at me. There was a gleam in her eye. She was not disappointed. On the contrary. She had known I would be too well-trained to fall into the obvious opening trap. But I knew she had further questions for me. Much harder ones. Ones which were not in the catechism. Ones to which there were no prepared answers. Ones which would reduce me to inarticulate mumblings, then to eventual silence. The gleam in her eye was in anticipation of the pleasure she was about to take in my humiliation in front of my mother and sister. I winced as she opened her mouth.

Her voice was softer and slower than before, savouring my helplessness.

'Three Persons in one God. Very good, Michael. So perhaps you can tell me, how...?'

It was Angela who chanced to come to my rescue, although she could have had no idea of how acute a predicament I was in.

'Can I have a drink, Grandmother? Have you got any lemonade? I'm very thirsty.'

A pair of frowning eyes swivelled upon her. I sensed Angela shrivel before them. 'No point asking you your catechism, I suppose, young lady.'

'We go through it on Sundays at home, Mother. But she has a head like a sieve, I'm afraid.'

My grandmother grunted. I wanted to hug Angela. Her intervention had taken the wind out of my grandmother's sails. She had lost the thread of her questions. She could not now recreate the moment when she had had me at her mercy. She turned to me again but I knew I was safe.

'Are you serving on the altar yet, Michael?'

'Not yet, Grandmother.'

'I've talked to Father Ambrose about it, Mother. He's promised to take him under his wing. He's asked to see Michael next week.'

'Good.'

She turned back to Angela, who had lowered her head, thoroughly deflated. All she had done was to ask for a drink and she had instead become the object of the ridicule which had been intended for me. If only I could have let her know at that moment how much I loved her, how much I wanted to take her away from that place and find somewhere where I could get her the biggest, fizziest lemonade she had ever had in her life. Not that there was anywhere within miles. At the least I could have gone to find her something to drink in the kitchen. But I knew that none of us dared to move anywhere inside her house until our grandmother gave permission.

'Where did you get that graze on your knee, child?'

'Fell over, Grandmother,' she murmured.

'Don't mutter, child. Speak up.'

I wanted to shout at her to stop bullying her. I bit my lip instead.

'She's always running around and falling over, Mother. Can't keep her attention on anything for more than five minutes. Sometimes I think there are wicked spirits inside her, though God knows ours is a house of prayer, where such spirits know they are not welcome.'

'Well, take her through to the kitchen, Margaret, and get her some of God's own water. Fancy her thinking I'd have lemonade here. You're spoiling them and giving them ideas. Michael can sit here and tell me about what he is doing at school.'

The hours dragged by. The lunch of dry, reheated lamb, boiled potatoes and cabbage was preceded by a Grace lasting a full five minutes. I could see that Angela was so hungry that she wanted to cry. When we were at last allowed to start, she ate everything on her plate, even the cabbage, though she did pull a face at me several times when she was sure the others were not looking.

We had to leave straight after lunch, or we would miss our bus connections. At the door, my grandmother called me back.

'Michael,' she said. 'There's no higher calling for a man than to be one of God's holy priests. Your mother and I are sure God is going to call you. Pray to God to make you worthy. Keep your heart and mind pure.'

'Yes, Grandmother. Thank you.'

There was a ghost of a smile on her face. I shivered.

EIGHT

'What do you think, Father? She must have got it wrong about the priest, of course. But even if she believes it all, why is she doing this now? Does she want us to stop her hurting the priest and the woman, assuming they really exist? And if so, why doesn't she come round, or telephone? We can't help her if we can't trace her. Should we tell the police? In case they know of anyone who's been getting threats? They might be able to do tests on the paper and the envelope.'

It was eight o' clock the same evening. We were in the presbytery library. My resolve to leave the letter alone had lasted no more than a day. On my return from my mother's I had taken it out again to read it. Then I made up my mind. I would show it to Father O'Malley after dinner. I was out of my depth. I needed help and advice. The letter contained serious allegations against an unnamed priest. I could not keep it to myself. Even though the allegations had to be unfounded, the author clearly believed them. The priest and the woman might be in danger. And what would happen if the allegations were publicly repeated? What if she went to the press with them? What if it came out that she had already made them privately to a parish priest? There would be many ready to believe her story. If a scandal were to break out, the repercussions would extend all the way to Diocese HQ and beyond. Perhaps to Westminster, maybe even to Rome. Some very senior representatives of the hierarchy would want to know why I had not sought advice immediately. I toyed with the idea of contacting the Archbishop's office. But what could I tell them, without any information about the identity of the priest or the woman, or their alleged victim? I decided that in the first instance I would consult Father O'Malley, as the senior priest of the parish.

I waited until he was sitting comfortably in his chair, with a glass of whiskey, a cigarillo and a volume of Sherlock Holmes stories. I could not afford to wait too long or he would become too absorbed in his story. I took out the sheets from the envelope and handed them to him.

'I think you might find that more interesting than what you're reading, Father.'

'I hope so, now you've been and gone and lost me my thread altogether. Would that be what you were reading when I got back from Dublin?'

'Yes. I need your advice on what to do with it.'

'It's not confidential to you then?'

'It doesn't say that I can't show it to anyone else. But before you read it, I want you to promise that if the author turns up you'll let me speak to her alone, and not let on you know about it. Just in case she only intended it for my eyes.'

'All right, I promise,' he said, wearily. 'I hope it's worth all the suspense and drama you're building around it.'

He read slowly, going back over several sentences and reading them aloud so he could catch the sense which had eluded him on first reading. When he had at last finished, he returned the sheets to me, looked me closely in the eye, then sat back in his chair and took a long sip of whiskey. He shook his head, slowly. I waited for him to speak. It was not like him to be at a loss for words. At last, I released my barrage of questions.

'Ah, yes,' he replied, as if relieved to have particular points to which he could respond. 'The police. They'd send it to forensics. Or is it ballistics? No, that's when someone's been shot. I've often wondered who this Mr

Forensics chap is. He must be very busy. He's in all the detective stories, the modern ones anyway. And the things they expect him to know. But I can't believe the police would be interested in this. Sure, assault and unlawful imprisonment are crimes. But there's absolutely nothing for them to go on. And if she wanted to involve the police she could go to them direct. Maybe she brought it to us precisely because she doesn't want to involve anybody like the police. Or rather she brought it to you. Now, that's the next question. How does she know your name?'

'The priests' names are on the church notice board outside.'

'I had noticed that, young Michael, in my thirty years here. But why choose yours rather than mine? I've been here twice as long as you have. I should be offended. And why this church? She must know you in some way. So, think who it might be. Anybody been to Confession recently who used similar language? Anybody you might have seen on a pastoral visit?'

'I have thought. Endlessly. I can't think of anyone.'

He frowned, deeply, as he had from the moment he started to read the letter. I was surprised to see how seriously he was taking it. It was not like him. I had expected him to be delighted. Not since the murder of Mrs Pickersgill, fifteen years before, had he had a real-life mystery to absorb his attentions. He shook his head at last.

'Sure, I think we might be approaching this in the wrong way. What about the priest she mentions? The one who betrayed the secrecy of the confessional. That doesn't happen every day, now. Surely that would be a more promising lead.'

'Every day? Never, surely. That's why I'm so sure

she's got hold of the wrong end of the stick. Some sort of paranoia about a priest, who is probably totally unaware of what she is thinking and saying about him. I can't see how we could possibly trace him from what we have here.'

He put down his whiskey and leaned forward.

'Well, I have something to tell you, young man. You say it never happens. But I happen to know that it does. Or that it has. A documented case. So what do you make of that?'

He sat back in his chair. I stared at him, open-mouthed.

'Surely not? Father, if this is another of your jokes...'

'Do I look or sound as if I am joking? Not at all. I'm deadly serious. And the thing is...' He paused, leaned forward, tapped me on the knee and whispered. 'It was around here.'

I whistled. 'So it really is true. And I had almost decided to take no action because I was so sure it could not possibly be. Where did it happen? Not in this parish, surely?'

'No, but nearby. I'm trying to remember the name. I was trying to recall it after I had finished reading. That's why I was so quiet. Gallagher. Christine Gallagher. Yes, that was it. The priest was Father James at St Monica's, the parish next to ours, in Crosby. I never knew him. All this was years ago. Before you came here. I can't remember much about it. She complained that Father James had told her aunt about something she had told him in Confession. She was an orphan. Her aunt was her guardian. Father James was kicked out of the priesthood. He may still be around somewhere. But it's much more likely he went a long way away, somewhere where nobody knew him. Where he could start a new life. Abroad, probably. I don't think we need worry about him. But the aunt may still be in Crosby.'

'To whom did Christine complain?'

'The Archbishop, I suppose. He would have appointed an independent priest to investigate and report back to him, then convened a panel to decide what measures to take. Usual procedure for allegations of serious misconduct.'

'So the independent priest may know their last-known whereabouts. Or someone in the Archbishop's office. It may be on the file compiled by the panel. All we need to do is find him and show this to him. Or go to the Archbishop's office direct.'

I was relieved, if startled, to hear him laugh out loud. He stood up and slapped me painfully on the back. He took out a tissue from a box on the desk, and sat down again, dabbing his eyes. He poured out two glasses of whiskey and handed me one of them.

'Here you go, Michael. A glass of my favourite, for getting me back into the ways of laughter. I feel like my old self again. Oh, Michael, you are such an innocent in the ways of the world. Let your Uncle Eamonn tell you a thing or two. First of all, the identity of the investigating priest would be known only to the Archbishop, his secretary and the complainant. Only the Archbishop and his secretary would know who the members of the panel were. And if you were to go up to the diocese office and ask for the papers on Father James, they would tell you there were no such papers and what's more there was no such person as Father James, past or present. Then in the middle of the night men in balaclavas would come and take you away. Well, that last bit is maybe a bit of an exaggeration. But what you have to remember is that as far as the Church is concerned this never happened. Of course they wouldn't be able to deny that a complaint had

69

been made, if the complainant were to pop up again and swear blind that she had made a complaint. And they couldn't deny that a certain priest left the priesthood at a certain time and place, as priests tend to do from time to time. But all the torments of Hell would never persuade a single member of the hierarchy from the Archbishop's secretary right up to the Pope in person to admit that there was the slightest connection between the two events. The official line is and will always be the same. No priest ever betrays the secrecy of the confessional.'

'All right, Father, you've talked me out of it. I don't like the thought of the men in balaclavas, thank you very much. I didn't become a priest to risk my life, though I know that many did in the past and some still do in some godforsaken parts of the world. But if Christine...what was her name?'

'Gallagher.'

'If she doesn't come forward, we could at least try to find Father James and the aunt and warn them that Christine has come back and is making threats against them. Without taking any view on the allegations one way or the other. Surely that wouldn't bring the wrath of the authorities down on us.'

'Less of the "us", please. You're the case officer here, remember. I'll deny I knew anything about it.'

'Of course if she does come forward, I can try to persuade her not to act on her feelings of hatred. Who's at St Monica's now?'

'Father Brennan. He's from Dublin, like me. I know him well. He took over from Father James. I tell you what, Father. I don't mind helping you out over this, so long as we only go as far as you say. Just find them and warn them, if we can. It could be fun. Make a bit of a change from the daily grind. So how about this. I go and see Father Brennan. He might be able to trace the address of the Gallaghers from parish records. And he might know where Father James went after he left there.'

'Good idea.'

I was relieved and heartened by his change of mood. I wanted to act on the letter in some way. I wanted some good to come of the disruption it had caused to my peace of mind. But the last thing I wanted was to cause our comfortable lives to unravel by drawing down upon us the unwelcome and unfamiliar attention of Diocese HQ. I needed his active support. Despite what he had said about denying any knowledge of the affair if I got into trouble, I knew I could rely on him.

'Perhaps Father Brennan could go and see the aunt, if she's still around,' I continued. 'Pretend it's a routine pastoral visit. Drop her niece into the conversation and see how she reacts. Ask if she has seen her recently.'

'And while I'm doing that I suggest you take this and show it to Father Ambrose. Best if you speak to him, not me. We were together here for quite a few years, but we never really got on. You were his protégé. He wouldn't allow me to take you under my wing. He knew what a bad example I would be. He's much more respected in the Church hierarchy than I am, and he's better connected. It's possible he knows a lot more about this case than I do, or most of us who were around at the time. He might even have been on the panel. The Archbishop often called upon him to help out in cases of potential scandal. He was so discreet. I could never get any details out of him. I couldn't even get him drunk so he would tell me. He was teetotal, as you know. If he had been on the panel, he wouldn't be allowed to tell you. But he might possibly be prepared to give you a lead on what happened to Father James, or where to find the

Gallaghers. Just pretend it popped out from somewhere in his memory. It's worth a try. Where is he these days?'

'In a nursing home near Southport. He moved there from his house when he became too ill to stay at home. The house belongs to his cousin, actually, the one in Australia. Father Ambrose has never owned anything in his own name. What a thing to happen to such a holy man. He still hears Confession in the nursing home. My mother goes to him. They've known each other from the time they lived in Little Penby. I haven't been to see him for ages. Feel quite guilty about it. This would be a good excuse.'

I looked through the crumpled pages again.

'She mentions another priest, the old one who did exorcisms. Ring any bells? If you'll pardon the expression.'

He gave me a long, hard look. 'I sometimes wonder if I'm a bad influence on you, Father. I don't remember any other priest being involved. Exorcists? Now, let me see. There was an old chap in a parish over in Manchester, used to do exorcisms. Could have been him. Bit crazy. He died years ago. I don't know whom we'd call on now if we needed anybody like that. Never been any need for it in this parish as far back as I can remember. It's a complicated business. You have to get permission from the Archbishop each time. I don't believe in all that mumbo-jumbo, anyway. But Father Ambrose might be able to help you on that. Now let's have another whiskey and try to put this poor girl's story out of our minds, at least until tomorrow.'

NINE

Father Ambrose. I thought about the time when I had first met him. I was shaking with terror.

When I arrived at the church I did not know where to go. I walked through the empty, echoing, shadowy building. I had never been there when it was not brightly lit and at least partly occupied. Now it was deserted, apart from a plump, smiling nun who was arranging flowers on the altar. I knew that when it was time for Mass, the priest and the altar boys all emerged from a door on the left. I had never been curious to know what lay behind the door. I had assumed that somehow they were always there, ready and waiting. It never occurred to me that their arrival had to be organised. There had to be rotas. There had to be places where the boys parked their bicycles and changed into cassocks and cottas, and where the senior altar boys allocated the duties of the service. Most mysterious of all would be the place where the priest prepared himself for Mass. The sacristy. I stumbled into the dark corridor beyond the door. Another door faced me, about twenty yards further on. It was partly open. On the other side of it, I could hear a man's voice. I could see he was kneeling, praying. I did not dare to interrupt. He finished and looked up. His eyes were intensely bright. His nose was hooked like that of a bird of prey. He smiled. I nearly fainted with relief. I was expected. As an intruder, I would have been thrown out of that hallowed zone, perhaps forbidden to come to the church ever again. He beckoned me in.

'Michael Jones? I'm Father Ambrose. I know your mother very well. Such a good, devout woman. Come on in. Don't be afraid. How old are you, my boy?'

'Twelve, Father.'

'And you want to be an altar boy.'

'My mother wants me to be one.'

'And don't you want it too, my boy? Don't you want the greatest privilege any boy can have? The privilege of being closer to the Blessed Sacrament than anybody else, apart from the priest himself?'

'Yes. Of course, Father.'

'Let me show you around. This is the sacristy. Where the priest prepares for Mass.' He pointed at the drawers where the robes were kept.

'Only the priest touches these. In this cupboard is kept the chalice and the Communion bread. Here, at the side, is where the cruets for the water and the wine are kept. What happens to them in Mass, my boy? The bread and the wine?'

'They are transformed into the Body and Blood of Christ.' The words came from the depths of my subconscious mind, into which hours of rote catechism learning at school had long since driven them.

'Good. Good. And what does that mean, "transformed"?'

'It means they become what God gave to His disciples at the Last Supper when He said "this is My Body and this is My Blood do this in memory of Me."'

The words came out in an unpunctuated tumble.

'Very good. But that is not exactly what I meant. I meant what actually happens to the substance of the bread and wine?'

I was floundering now. I had to find words of my own and I was not good at that.

'I don't think they change to look at. It's not transformed like you do in chemistry at school. It's transformed in a spiritual sense. God transforms them because He can do everything, and He does it in a way that we can still see them as they looked to us. Before.' I had ground to a halt.

He smiled again. 'Because if we saw them as they

really were we would be dazzled, we would be blinded, we would be terrified, wouldn't we? Because we cannot apprehend the spirit of God with our poor senses, except in the way He lets us. But never forget, boy, the spirit of God is everywhere though we cannot see it. Everywhere except where we choose to let evil take its place. But the spirit of God is stronger than evil. What is evil?'

'Evil is the absence of good.'

'Yes. Or rather, the absence of the spirit. But never think of it as just a vacuum. An empty space. When we let evil in, we let in a real force which, if we allowed it, would spread and contaminate the whole of Creation. We have to fight the spirit of evil with the spirit of goodness, and when we do so with a good and clean heart, then the spirit of goodness will prevail. Here's Sister Rose. She'll show you where you and the other altar boys prepare for Mass.'

Now I was forty and had been a parish priest for fifteen years. But the prospect of going to see Father Ambrose still made me nervous. I knew it would not be an easy conversation. With Father Ambrose there was no such thing. He always enjoyed setting me tests, trying to trip me up with theological and moral dilemmas. Despite his increasing physical weakness he was still the master and I was still the pupil. To calm my fears I tried to focus on the story my correspondent had told.

We now knew it was all true. If the bit about the priest were true, the rest had to be. We had a duty to warn them. We could not let vengeance take its course if it were in our power to do anything to prevent it. Vengeance is Mine, said the Lord. But what sort of people would we be warning? Father James had paid a certain price for his actions. He was no longer a priest.

But Christine had been abducted, abused and unlawfully imprisoned. The priests and the doctors and her aunt were all responsible. There was no indication from the letter, or from what Father O'Malley had told me, that they had answered for their deeds to the law of the land. But what concern was that of mine? God's law was higher. Whatever we as individuals might think of them, our duty as priests was to warn them of the danger they were in, and then to call them to repentance, to hear their Confession if no priest had done that already, to save their souls from everlasting punishment.

All that was clear enough. But what about Christine? She could be saved from sin if she could be deflected from her intended acts of revenge. But what about the sin of hatred in her heart? Could she be led to forgiveness, as Christ had enjoined us to forgive our enemies seventy times seven? If it had happened to me or to someone I loved, could I have found it in me to forgive? And if not, what right had I to tell her she had to forgive, when her youth and freedom and future had been taken from her? Repentance, Confession and forgiveness all round were all very well. Perhaps in the end they were the best we could do. But she would have every right to ask if they could give her back the life she had lost, a question to which I could give no satisfactory answer.

I took a right turn at the Formby Roundabout and drove along a narrow, twisting lane through large, ploughed fields, waterlogged after recent heavy rains. The nursing home lay at the end of a gravel driveway which had been laid through ancient woodland. The trees were gnarled and twisted with age. The house had once been a convent, and, before that, a private home belonging to the family who still owned most of the surrounding land. Now it was run by an Order of nursing nuns.

When I arrived, the sister on duty at the desk told me I would find him in the television lounge. He was sitting at the back, in his wheelchair, asleep. Several other residents were watching horse racing with varying degrees of apathy. I shook his shoulder gently. His eyes opened. They still burned as they had when I had first seen him.

'Ah, it's you, my boy. How are you?' He put out a bony hand. I took it. It was cold. 'I can still shake hands, just about.' His speech was slow and slurred.

'I'm well, Father. How are you is more to the point.'

'I'm as you see me. My mind and spirit are as strong as ever, but they are held captive in a body that is slowly shutting down. Soon I'll be totally helpless. But I will have my mind. I will still be able to pray. I can't say Mass any more, but I continue to hear Confession, in a little private room at the back. Your mother comes all the way out here to see me.'

'You know, if God had chosen to test me in this way, I am sure I could not bear it with the fortitude you display. You really are an example to us all.'

'Not at all. This is not a test. Pain, helplessness, even death hold no fears for me. God Himself became a helpless baby, to save us from our sins. That is what I will soon be. A baby again. Then I will be dead. It is a progression with a certain satisfying symmetry to it. You know, I never watched television in my life until I came here. Now I watch it every day. I often become too tired to read. Well, what is it, my boy? I can tell this isn't a social call.'

'I need your advice, Father.' I placed the envelope into his hands. 'This was left on our doorstep. Addressed to me in person. It's anonymous, but Father

77

O'Malley thinks he knows who it might be from. At least two people might be in danger. I think the person who wrote this will come to see me soon. Perhaps she left this to prepare me. Perhaps she could not bring herself to talk directly about the experiences she describes. I feel out of my depth. I want to know how to advise her. It's short. Could you read it now? Or shall I come back?'

'Open it for me. My fingers are no good now.'

I took the sheets out of the envelope. 'I must warn you. The language is rather coarse in places.'

'I'm sure I will have seen and heard worse in my time.'

I placed the papers in his hand. He glanced down the first page, then the second. He showed no reaction. Then he put his hand on my arm.

'It could be a blessing that this has come into our hands. Great evil has been done. But evil should not be met with evil. You may be the instrument chosen to prevent that. That is a great privilege, and a great responsibility. You said there was a possibility you know the case?'

I looked around the room. The other residents were now all asleep in their chairs. Although we were already speaking too quietly for anyone to overhear I lowered my voice to a whisper.

'I don't know it myself. There was a case at St Monica's. Years ago. A girl went to Confession and the priest told her aunt what she had confessed.'

'I remember it. There was discussion about it at a diocese meeting. The priest concerned was quite rightly expelled from the priesthood.'

'Should I warn him? If I can trace him?'

'He could be anywhere. Abroad, perhaps, with a new identity. Even if he were still among us, he is just a layman, indistinguishable from the rest of humanity.

I'm sure he is safe. What about the aunt?'

'Father O'Malley is going to St Monica's to see if she can be traced from the parish records. Father, what sort of priest would break the secrecy of the confessional?'

He smiled. 'You sound so shocked, my boy. You have much to learn about the hearts of men, even of fellow-priests. The principle is simple. Never reveal the secrets of the confessional. But reality is not always so simple. Let me put a hypothetical case to you. Somebody comes to you in the confessional. They tell you that they are holding in their hands a phial they have stolen from a laboratory where they work. It contains a deadly toxin. An air-borne virus. When the phial is opened the virus is released. In hours, thousands will be dead. This person tells you he is going straight into the city centre, where he will open the phial. You believe him. He leaves the confessional. What do you do?'

I hesitated. 'I should reply instantly that I would do nothing, other than advise him not to go through with it.'

'But you do not reply instantly. You are in two minds, am I right? Do not worry, my boy. That is as it should be. No priest with a strong sense of his own duty and a measure of compassion for the suffering of others could be other than in two minds. Let us say that the second of your two minds prevails. You decide to warn the authorities. What does that mean, in terms of the sort of priest you are?'

'That I am not a good priest.'

'Come on, my boy, you can do better than that. You must not seek to shelter behind a blanket excuse of imperfection. You were educated by the Jesuits, were you not? Come, let me hear you justify your position.'

'All right. The person you describe has come into

79

the confessional but has not come to the Sacrament of Confession. He has not confessed any actual sin. He has confessed to a sin of thought, but he has not sought Absolution. On the contrary, he has communicated his intention to convert his thought into action. He has abused the sacrament. He has abused the priest's office and his duty of secrecy, for whatever motive. Perhaps he is driven by an overwhelming urge to tell somebody what he is going to do. He thinks that only in the confessional can he be sure that his secret will be safe. But the duty of secrecy does not automatically apply to every word spoken in the confessional box. The spirit of the sacrament must be invoked and then sustained, both by the priest and the person who has come to confess.'

'Very good, my boy. The next time you come, I will ask you to justify the opposing viewpoint. I look forward to hearing you. It is a pleasure to talk with you in this way. But the fact that it is a pleasure warns us against continuing. We are being idle, when we have serious matters to discuss. Forgive me. The fault is mine. I miss the mental stimulation of theological debate. The case I put to you is perhaps a little extreme. Or rather, it is the sort of case anybody could understand, whether or not there is a religious dimension to their lives. But let us consider a case in a rather more spiritual context. This is not, I believe, a hypothetical one. I believe it is what we have here. I am trying to give you an insight into the mind of a priest who has done wrong, in the eyes of God, the Church and the wider community. You must try to understand him, at the same time as you condemn his actions. Imagine then that this priest is, in his own eyes, also in the presence of a phial containing a virus. The virus in the phial is real but invisible to the human eye. So is the virus of evil. He perceives that the person with him in the confessional is possessed by evil spirits. It is fashionable to laugh at such ideas these days. But then we read in Holy Scripture that Christ Himself cast out devils. Our priest does not believe that the devils will simply vanish when he gives Absolution. He believes that they will infect others, imperil their immortal souls. More must be done. But more cannot be done if the person simply disappears into the night.'

'So he follows her home. Tells her aunt.'

'Maybe he knew the girl already. Recognised her voice. We'll never know, of course. Unless you find him and he tells you the whole story.'

'Did nothing emerge about his motives at the meeting you mentioned?'

'Nothing at all. We were only told the nature of the complaint, in the broadest terms, the identity of the priest and the fact that he had been expelled from the priesthood. No, what we are indulging in here is speculation, though not, I believe, idle in nature. In the event that you do meet him you must prepare your mind to see into his heart.'

'But why should he think she was possessed by devils? The cases in Scripture may have been ones where these days a doctor would be called. A priest may help as well, if he senses the presence of spiritual evil. But people in that state of mind don't go to Confession. When you go to Confession, you are already half way to defeating evil. You are in a state of preparedness for Absolution and spiritual peace. Would somebody possessed by devils enter a church in a state of desire to confess their sins? Would not the very devils inside them hold them back at the door of the church?'

He smiled. 'Very good again, my boy. But beware of looking for evil in its too literal and obvious manifestations. And never underestimate it. Remember the phial. It is small. It looks harmless. The virus cannot be seen. It certainly does not boil over or jump out of its owner's pocket when he enters church. As for the devils which possess the soul, are we right to assume they have no power to hide in church, to escape the eye of God for a time, to retreat to allow the penitent to go through the motions of Confession and Absolution, only to return later with all their force, like a raging lion released from its cage? Perhaps this former priest was convinced an evil of great force and intensity was present, even in the apparently innocent form of a penitent young girl, kneeling before him in the confessional. When we speak of these things now, between ourselves, it is hard to believe, isn't it? But in earlier times his way of looking at the life of the soul and the dangers which can beset it was perfectly normal. Time has left him high and dry.'

'Is it possible that he perceived all this, when all she confessed was ...'

'What, my boy? Normal teenage behaviour? Or gross impurities of thought and deed, which in one so young would suggest a deep spiritual malaise? We cannot say. We do not know the sin she confessed. But we must not commit the mistake of confusing inner reality and outer form. Older people with a knowledge of the world and of themselves may choose evil. Evil may choose the young and innocent. Which is more dangerous? The person who chooses evil may later choose to renounce it. The person whom evil has chosen may not be able to do that. This young and innocent girl should have grown to maturity in the sight of God. Then if she were not chosen for a higher calling, she would have married, and submitted to her husband for the sake of procreation in accordance with

God's will. If her sin was indeed one of wantonness, what has such behaviour, especially in one so young, got to do with God's plan for womankind? Nothing, but it has a lot to do with the Devil's plan for the corruption of men.'

'But surely the Sacrament of Confession is a sufficient instrument against the will of the Devil, even if...'

'Even if you see it in the harsh, moralistic terms I have just stated? I can see you do not approve. You are absolutely right, of course. Confession is God's appointed means for the cleansing of sin from the soul. This girl, despite her sins, was granted sufficient Grace to avail herself of it. That should have been the end of it. You mustn't mind me, my boy. I'm only a crusty old bachelor who never knew anything of the world.'

'I'm an old bachelor, too.'

'Rubbish. You're a celibate young man, called to higher things than marriage or wantonness. You were in the world and you made the choice to respond to God's call. I had no choice to make. As young as twelve I already knew I had a vocation. I never had to renounce the world because I was never in the world. You are bound to see some things differently from the way I see them. I accept that. But what never changes is the nature of good and evil. Relativism is one of the great evils of today. "Society has changed so we must change too." I heard this all the time from the liberal wave, at conferences and diocese meetings. What dangerous nonsense it is.'

'I understand what you say. You said I was shocked at the betrayal of confessional secrets, and I am. But I am also shocked at what followed. The violence and the humiliation. The destruction of a young girl's life. I don't just want to protect the aunt. I want to help the woman. For some reason she approached me by name.'

'The consequences were indeed dreadful. Our priest could not have foreseen everything that was to happen, though that excuses nothing. The girl must have heard that you are a compassionate and approachable priest. I am sure she hopes you will deflect her from a course of violence and hatred. Why else should she write to you? But be very careful about how you approach her. She may still be ill in her mind. If you discover where she is, try to find out something about her before you talk to her. She may need a doctor more than she needs a priest. We do not have all the answers, you know, though there are people who think we do. When you have found out more, come to see me again. We will discuss how you should approach her, if you should approach her at all. I would be by your side in this, if I could, but God does not will it. I will help you as best as I can from inside this prison of a body, where for my sins I have been confined.'

'Thank you for all your wise words, Father. I will go now. I am afraid I have tired you. Give me your blessing.'

I knelt on the floor beside him. He made the sign of the cross on my forehead and whispered the Latin words.

TEN

Aunt Mary was two years younger than my mother. They had fallen out several years before and never spoken to each other since, though the occasional written communication still took place. Neither of them would tell me the cause of the quarrel.

Stifled by Little Penby and by the strict routines of religious observance followed by her mother and sister, Aunt Mary had left home at the age of twenty-one, finding a job as a trainee buyer for a prestigious department store in the centre of Liverpool. She rented a room in a large Victorian house in Aintree. Her mother, who had always intended both of her daughters to be nuns, accused her of renouncing the path of righteousness to wallow in the temptations of the world and the flesh, by which she meant Liverpool, which she had never visited in her life. She never spoke to Aunt Mary again. Aunt Mary had no regrets. She was relieved to be free of her mother's expectations. After a few years she married a local builder. Business conditions were poor. Within six months they had emigrated to Canada in search of improved financial prospects and wide open spaces in which to bring up the child she was already expecting.

She smiled when she opened the door. She had always had a ready smile, though in recent years it had seemed an increasing effort. She looked tired, and noticeably older than when I had last seen her, only two months before.

'Michael! What a lovely surprise.'

'Hello, Aunt Mary. Mother told me you were back from your latest trip.'

'Yes. No more gallivanting around for me now. I'm really starting to feel my age. I'll stay put from now on.'

'Mother said you weren't well.'

'I said something like that in my postcard to her. But I'm all right, really. There's nothing actually wrong with me. Just years. And a feeling that life has finally defeated me. But I don't want to get you down. I always feel better for your company. Come on through and sit down while I make us some tea.'

Her living room was furnished with mementoes of her time in Canada. There were paintings of the snow-capped Coastal Mountains, photographs of Stanley Park and the Vancouver waterfront, Native American woodcarvings and patterned rugs in deep reds and maroons. There were several photographs of her husband and daughter on the ski slopes at Whistler.

She returned with a silver teapot, and a plateful of buttered scones which she pushed towards me. She served the tea in delicate china cups.

'Well, all this talk about my health, but I'm not so sure you're all that well yourself, Michael,' she said, settling back into her chair. 'You're looking distinctly peaky. Are you eating properly now? Have another scone. They're home-made, as usual.'

'I'm fine, honestly. Mrs Raferty makes sure I eat properly, and she's the one in charge down there. Just in one of my down moods.'

'About Angela?'

'And a few parish things, not very important. Mainly about Angela. But I don't want to burden you with my feelings, when you have three of them to grieve for.'

She stirred her tea for a long time, staring out of the window.

'One thing you learn about grief,' she said at last, 'is that it never goes away. It enters your soul and becomes part of you. You accept it as a gift from God.

A sign that He wants you to reflect. And remember. That's why I keep the photographs there where I can always see them. That one there was taken the day before the car crash. They had been away skiing for the week, just the two of them. I didn't go with them. Skiing was not my scene. The camera was recovered intact from the wreckage. I was going to throw it away. Then I decided to have the film developed. So I could share their last times with them. She was only sixteen. Such a happy child.'

She pulled a tissue from a box on the table and dabbed her eyes. I walked over to her and put an arm around her shoulder. She looked up at me, struggling to smile.

'Thank you, Michael. I do look forward to your visits. You're always such a comfort. How is your mother these days?'

I returned to my chair and sipped the tea she had poured for me.

'Good, apart from the arthritis. She can still sew, though. Still doing jobs for the neighbours and accepting far too little for all her time and trouble. The arthritis hasn't got into her hands yet.'

'Yes, she was always gifted with her hands. Like your grandmother. She taught your mother to sew. Tried to teach me but I was all fingers and thumbs.'

I coughed. 'You know...you could ask her yourself. How she is, I mean. Instead of just sending her a postcard.'

She laughed. 'Playing the good priest, son and nephew, all at once, Michael? Trying to effect a reconciliation? That's so like you. You like peace, don't you? Conflict of any sort disturbs you. I know you mean well. But I'm afraid things have gone too far between us. Why do you think I sent her that card? It wasn't to open the way for us to talk to each other again. I was being totally selfish. I know you see her every week. I knew she would tell you about it and I hoped it would prompt you to come and pay me a visit, without me having to invite you directly. As you see, it worked. I use her to keep in contact with you, that's all. I still have some conscience left. I don't like to approach you directly, asking for your time and attention, when I know that your parishioners have prior claims on you and many of them need you far more than I do. There you are. Now you know how really shameless and manipulative I am. Your mother and I never really got on. She always thought I was too worldly. It's true. I saw no harm in enjoying material things. I was fortunate enough to marry a hardworking and successful man. I've changed now. I don't care about such things any more. But I can't be pious, either, like your mother. I just wish I could have done more good with my life.'

'You've done a lot of good, Aunt. You've always helped people in need. And you helped Angela find her way to God. More than I ever did. I wasn't there to help her.'

Although Aunt Mary had never embraced an openly pious way of life, she had always observed the minimum requirements of weekly attendance at Mass and occasional Confession. In Canada she had attended the church attached to the Priory of the Order of the Sisters of Saint Bernard, about an hour's drive from Vancouver. She had found it by chance while first exploring the area by car, and fallen in love with its combination of wild remoteness and tranquillity. After the accident she decided to change her life. She no longer took any pride or comfort in the possessions which she and her husband had accumulated. Instead she spent more and more time at the church and the priory, performing cleaning and flower-arranging duties, and visiting housebound parishioners in the widely scattered small villages and isolated farmhouses of the parish.

'Angela was the same age as Anne,' she said, looking again at the nearest photograph. 'What a shame they never met. They were very different but I think they would have been good friends. Angela received her vocation about the same time as Anne died. It was as if God had decided to take both of them to Him, each in a different way. But in the end He decided to take both their souls in the same way. Perhaps they met and became friends in Heaven. When I heard about Angela's vocation I suggested that she fly out to Canada to stay with me. I sent your mother the money for her fare. I had to admit I was surprised and none too pleased. I assumed it was just a passing teenage fad. I thought that if she could see the Order for herself and meet the Mother Superior, find out about their way of life, she might realise her mistake. I soon realised that I was the one who was mistaken. There was no doubt about it. She had changed. Her vocation was genuine. I thought so and so did the Mother Superior.

'After her death I couldn't stay there any longer. Too many tragic associations. So I came back here. Bought this house. Yes, I still do what you could call good works, for the local church and charities. But that's mainly for my benefit. I need to do things to keep me occupied, so they might as well be things that have a chance of helping others. And from time to time I need a change of scene so I go off on long car trips. I think I've been round the whole country at least twice since I returned. Though not any more, as I told you. You know, I sometimes think God was punishing me for leaving England in pursuit of a better life. But then I tell myself not to be so arrogant. Why should God bother to single me out for special punishment? Anyway, charity begins at home, so they say. Who does your mother go to for Confession these days? Not you?'

The sudden question and the unusually sharp tone in her voice startled me.

'No, not me. Father Ambrose. As always.'

'Yes. I remember him from Little Penby. Your mother's sort of priest, not mine.'

'Aunt, about Angela. Was it painful, her last illness?'

'You've asked me that many times before, Michael.'

'I know. I'm sorry.'

'I understand. You want to talk about her. You want to hear it from me again. I don't mind. She died peacefully. So they told me. And I believe it. I saw it in her face when she was laid out. She had collapsed suddenly, with no warning. She died only a few hours later. She never regained consciousness. The doctors said her heart was congenitally weak. The walls were paper-thin. There were no symptoms. Nobody could have known. The Mother Superior told me she was sure she would have accepted her death if she had known it was coming. She was happy because God had given her the time to be received into the Order. That was all she ever wanted. Just think of it. Our Angela, becoming Sister Veronica. Your mother was so delighted when she rang me with the news. You had gone to be a priest and now Angela had decided she wanted to become a nun. "My cup runneth over" she kept saying. I imagine she was telling everybody here the same thing. And Angela was such a scamp when she was little. I remember the first time I went back to England for a visit. It was the first time I had met her. Five years old and a real tomboy.'

'She was still a scamp when I last saw her. A great

big scamp. The change came over her afterwards.
When I wasn't there to see it.'

'St Bernadette was a scamp, too, by all accounts. A
real scatterbrain. God does not choose the way the
world does.'

'I still find it hard to come to terms with the fact that
I never saw her after she went to Canada.'

'It wasn't your fault. I didn't see her myself during
her novitiate. She wanted to focus all her spiritual
energies on her vocation. She set herself some harsh
penances, to put it to the test. One of them was not to
see or communicate with any family members, in case
they reminded her too much of the world. I think she
was afraid she might be pulled back. That's why you
only got the one letter. I had to write it down for her, if
you remember, because of her sprained wrist. She
loved the ice and snow in Canada, when she first got
out there, but she wasn't safe on it. Neither was I when
I arrived. I think that little accident was a warning to
her from God. A warning to settle down to a life of
contemplation. To stop running around like a two-year
old. It was probably the day her vocation was finally
sealed in her heart.'

'I do understand her wanting to keep to herself once
she had started her postulancy. I was the same. I could
only face the world when I was sure I did not want to
return to it.'

'And you've never regretted it?'

'Not once I realised it was what God wanted.'

Not once I realised that Bernadette had chosen another,
and God had chosen me. But why? Why had He
chosen me of all people, so poor in intellect and spirit?
What possible use was I to Him?

ELEVEN

At St Jerome's there were two confessional boxes on each side of the nave. When we heard Saturday evening Confession together, we used only one on each side. This was so that our parishioners could easily choose which confessor they wanted, with no danger of confusion.

There was a gentle rivalry between us as to who could attract the greater number. But there was no real contest. Father O'Malley was the clear favourite. I did not know if this was because he gave lighter penances, or because he told stories in the confessional. I suspected it was the latter. There was no doubt that his average time for each confession exceeded mine, despite his greater workload. He always teased me when I finished long before he did. 'For your sake, Father, I'm glad we don't get paid by piecework, like they used to down at the docks,' he once said to me after one particularly lean session for me.

The Saturday evening after my visit to my aunt, I entered the church at a quarter to six as usual. Before hearing Confession I always prayed before the high altar for ten minutes. Then I entered my side of the box, first sliding back the panel to reveal the letters which spelled out my name and to indicate that I was ready. That evening, there were already five waiting for Father O'Malley. There was nobody on my side of the church. It was not going to be a heavy session. I waited. My eyes were beginning to close.

'Bless me, Father, for I have sinned.'

My stomach lurched. I had not heard anybody enter. My breath caught in my throat. This was usually the point at which I made some reassuring sounds to calm the anxious person on the other side of the curtain. I could make no sound at all.

Why in God's name was she here? In all these years she had never once come to me for Confession. She always went to Father O'Malley. She had never come to see me for any purpose. We had never spoken since I had come to the parish.

'It is six weeks since my last confession.' The voice was soft and husky, with a slight nervous shake. It had deepened since I had last heard it. But there was no mistaking it. I knew it better than any voice in the world, even my mother's.

'Since then I have been late for Mass three times.' I knew that was not true. She had always been in her place at the start.

My mind raced. Father O'Malley was already at work on the other side of the nave. I had seen him go in. Had she really broken the habit of a lifetime just to tell me these trivial things? Or had she made a mistake? She was still recently bereaved and might be confused. But my name was clearly visible outside. I coughed, in such a way that she could not fail to realise I was not Father O'Malley.

'I had unkind thoughts towards a neighbour, who had spread false rumours about me. I wished her ill. That was on one occasion.'

'And do you wish her well now?' My voice was trembling.

'Yes.'

'Is that all?'

'No.' There was a silence of about half a minute. 'I am guilty of hatred. Over many years.'

'And the object of this hatred?'

'You.'

I heard her stand up. She had not said the Act of Contrition. I could not pronounce the words of Absolution. But then she had not come to confess. She had come to accuse. I heard the door on her side of the

93

box close gently. I waited. Nobody else came in. I could not leave until my allotted time was over.

The time dragged by. I tried to pray. I could focus on nothing but her last words. Finally I was able to leave the box. I looked round the church for her, wondering if she might have stayed to perform a penance she had set for herself. There was no sign of her.

In my bedroom later that evening, from the bottom of my private drawer of papers, I took out the letter she had sent me at the end of that week, twenty-two years before. The week which I knew would define my future. Bernadette or God. The letter telling me she had made a mistake. That she loved Tom after all. The letter telling me we could never see each other again.

She had not broken my heart. She had frozen it, for twenty-two years. After I had stupidly let myself believe she loved me. But if she never had loved me, how was it possible for her to hate me, and to keep her hate alive for all those years? And what reason had I ever given her to hate me?

I knew I had to go to see her, although it was the last thing I wanted to do. But first I had to think back. I had to try to remember what I had done or said that might have caused her to hate me. I had to go back to the beginning, to that day in the library.

TWELVE

'Excuse me.'

I had a holiday job in the local library over Easter, before my final school term. It had been a quiet afternoon on the counter up to that moment. Afternoons were usually quiet. A chance to tidy up the shelves and catch up on the fines notices for late return of borrowed books.

Mrs O'Hara had come in at three o'clock, as usual, to ask if there were any new murders. The question had startled me the first time she had asked, until I realised what she meant. We kept three separate sections among the fiction shelves for cheap paperbacks classed as romances, westerns and crime. It was the last category which fascinated Mrs O'Hara. The stock was replenished with new items every month but it would have taken a team of a dozen crime writers writing around the clock to keep up with her. I had shaken my head and told her the new supply would be in the following week. I promised to put some aside for her as soon as they arrived.

She had been followed half an hour later by Mrs Dodgson, another regular. Like Mrs O'Hara she was in her sixties, always respectably dressed. Her choice of fiction was more upmarket than that of Mrs O'Hara, usually consisting of serious novels with a social or historical background. This time there was an unusual gleam in her eye as she passed to me across the counter the slim volume she had borrowed, still holding on to it and covering the title and author with her hand.

'This book,' she whispered, glancing round to ensure nobody could overhear us, 'is...disgraceful! I thought it was the one based on that series on television, or I would never have taken it out.'

We had a special shelf under the counter for books

such as Henry Miller's *Tropic of Cancer* and *Tropic of Capricorn* and large medical dictionaries. Some customers, invariably men, who were aware of the existence of this section sometimes asked if they could browse through it. It took a certain nerve to make this request and those making it were usually given permission. The main purpose in keeping the books hidden from general view was to prevent their falling inadvertently into the hands of children. Mrs Dodgson's book had missed the librarian's initial scrutiny and ended up on the open shelves, to her obvious delight. It was clear she had read it from cover to cover. I glanced at the opening page and decided she had been right to declare it. I told her I would put it to one side and consult the librarian about putting it in the restricted section. She nodded, gravely. Although it was clear she thought she had done the right thing she seemed a little disappointed. It would have been unthinkable of her to ask to see the restricted books. Perhaps the scrutiny process would now be tightened up and the chances reduced of her finding another such unexpected treasure on the main shelves.

After that all was quiet. The evening after-work rush had not yet started. It was relaxing and congenial work and I enjoyed it. It passed the time and enabled me to earn a little money of my own. The last thing I expected that afternoon was a moment that would change me and my life forever.

When it came, it was in the form of those two little words, so innocent, so commonplace, spoken and heard every day in any street or shop or bus and meaning nothing in particular.

'Excuse me.'

The sudden lilting voice had startled me. I had not heard her approach. I looked up and saw almond eyes and long black hair. My heart stopped.

'Sorry, can I help you?'

'You really were miles away, then. I wonder if you can find this book for me. I've written out the title and the author. I need it for a school project. For next term.'

'I'll see. If you'd like to look around the shelves I'll come and find you when I've found out if we've got it.'

I dived into the catalogues. When I had the information I needed I searched for her. She was browsing in the French Literature section.

'Hello again. Do you do French?'

'Yes. A-levels coming up in June.'

'Me too. You're at Sacred Heart, aren't you?'

'Yes and you're at St Cuthbert's. I saw you speak in the last joint debate. You were very good. Bit serious. About the role of religion in modern society. I've seen you in church, too. Senior altar boy now. Bossing around all the nervous young ones. You do it very well, though. You're very good with that thing with the incense, at High Mass. What do you call it?'

'Thurible. The one doing it is the thurifer. I was very nervous in that debate.'

'Probably because of all the girls around. You wouldn't be used to that.'

She stared at me. I stared back, wondering what I was doing there, wondering how it had come about that she was standing there talking to me.

'Er, the book?'

'The book?'

'The one I asked you to find out about? For my project?'

'Oh, gosh, yes. That book. Reference only, I'm afraid. You can find it upstairs.'

'I suppose I'll just have to come in every day and make notes. My name's Bernadette Reilly, by the way.'

'Michael Jones.'

She startled me by laughing, giddily. Somebody at one of the nearby tables signalled her to be quiet. She blushed and put her hand over her mouth.

'Yes, I know who you are, silly,' she whispered. 'I saw you in the debate, remember. You were introduced. By Sister Serafina. Sister Semolina we call her.'

'Yes, of course. I remember.'

'Don't look so worried. We don't call her that to her face. Sister Semolina, I mean.'

'No. Of course not. I didn't imagine you would.'

'I'll go upstairs now.'

'What?'

'To find that book.'

'Oh yes. The book. I rang through to the reference librarian. He's expecting you. He should have it ready for you by now.'

When she had told me her name I had not said that I already knew who she was. But of course I knew. All the boys in the sixth form knew who she was. Nearly all of them claimed to have been out with her in the days before she had met her current, steady boyfriend, a classmate of mine, Tom Kavanagh.

The following evening, as I left the library, she was sitting on the low stone wall by the gate.

'Hello,' she said. 'I wanted to thank you. For helping me find that book.'

'Hello. Why didn't you come inside?'

'I've just got here. No time to change my books. I thought you could walk me home. I live...'

'I know where you live.'

She stood up and looked at me intently, her eyes widening.

'So, how could you possibly know that, Michael

98

Jones, when we only met yesterday, and I never told you then, because nice girls never tell strange men where they live? You haven't been following me, by any chance? You're not one of those weird stalkers, are you?'

There was a teasing edge to her voice and a gleam of laughter in her eye.

'Good Lord, no. I looked you up in the library records. The registration cards.'

'And what were you planning to do with that information?'

I felt my face redden.

'Nothing. I was just curious.'

I bit my lip. I was furious with myself for letting it slip out that I had looked up her address. I had done it on impulse the previous day, as soon as she had gone up to the reference library. It was so easy. The cards were kept under the counter. It had taken only a second, less than a second, for the details to be imprinted on my mind. To my relief she laughed.

'So as a result of your researches, just out of curiosity of course, you know it's only ten minutes away.'

'Yes. I suppose so. About ten minutes.'

'You don't mind, do you? I won't make you late home or anything?'

'A few minutes doesn't matter. I'd love to see you home.'

She walked very slowly, on the inside of the pavement. I kept to the edge of the kerb, a good foot away from her. As I matched my pace to hers she seemed to slow down further, so I had to go even more slowly myself. It was going to take a lot longer than ten minutes.

'You're going out with Tom Kavanagh, aren't you?' I said, after a minute. It was not something I wanted to talk about but I could think of nothing else.

'So you do know something about me.'

'Can't help overhearing gossip at school from time to time. With some of them, it's all they talk about. Who is going out with whom...'

'"with whom..."' She drew the words out, mimicking me. 'You're very good with your grammar, aren't you? You're right. Tom and I have been going out for over a year. He's...let's say he's steady and reliable. Not deep. Not like you. You think about things, don't you?'

'Not really. I'm just quiet. So people think I'm deep.'

'So that's how you get them interested in you. Very clever. Well, it works. I'm interested. We have gossip at school as well, you know. I did a bit of asking around this lunchtime. None of the girls say they've been out with you.'

'It's true. They haven't.'

'Why's that? I know quite a few I'm sure would be glad to go out with you. Why don't you ask them?'

'I never meet them. I don't go to parties or things like that.'

'Well, you've met me. That's a start, isn't it? Would you like to take me to the cinema on Saturday?'

She had moved closer to me. I stopped to look at her. She was smiling, but not in the teasing way she had used when I had told her I knew her address. I realised she was serious.

'Er, the cinema?'

'It's all right if you've had a better offer. I won't mind. Only I'd be curious to know who it is.'

'Better...?' It was my turn to laugh. 'No, of course not. Yes, of course. I'd love to take you. But isn't Tom taking you out?'

'He's away with his parents. In Wales.' We had

reached her house. 'Call for me here on Saturday. At seven.' A distinct tone of command in her voice.

'Fine. Er...see you then.'

She turned round when she reached the front door. The smile again. The sensation of my heart turning over.

When Saturday evening arrived and I was ready to go out, I was sure it was all still a dream. Until my mother's voice brought me down to earth. She was waiting for me at the foot of the stairs. She must have heard me getting ready and moved into the hall to intercept me.

'Where are you going, Michael?'

'Out, Mother.'

'Out where?'

'I just thought I'd go to the pictures.'

'So why have you put your best things on?'

'Might run into somebody we know. Don't want to disgrace you.'

It was an absurd thing to say. We knew nobody socially, and none of the neighbours or fellow parishioners for whom she took in sewing would have been seen dead near a cinema.

'Are you going on your own?'

'Yes.'

'I suppose I can't stop you, now you've got money of your own from that job. But the cinema's a godless place. Future priests shouldn't go to places like that.'

'I give you most of it for housekeeping. You know that. I only keep back a little pocket money. Anyway, I'm sure lots of priests go to the cinema.'

She stared at me, still barring my way to the front door. I was becoming anxious I might be late. At seven, she had said.

'Michael. Is there something you want to tell me?'

'No, Mother, nothing. I'm fine. Don't stay up. Goodnight.'

I eased past her. Once I was sure she was not watching from the front window I broke into a run.

'I enjoyed the film.'

'So did I.' The truth was that I could not remember a single word or image from it. 'I can't remember when I last went. I seem to remember my dad taking me to see some cartoons on a Saturday morning. Mother was furious.'

'And you haven't been since?'

'No. He died soon after that. Mother would never take me. I'm not sure she knows where it is.'

'You could have gone on your own. Or with friends.'

'I haven't really got any friends.'

'Don't you like people?'

'It's not that. There are other boys I get on with quite well. But they like to go out to places where I can't.'

'You mean, where your mother doesn't want you to go.'

'I suppose that's it.'

'And that's why you never meet any girls. Don't you want to hold my hand? Like you did inside?'

But it was she who had taken hold of my hand, in the smoky darkness.

'Yes. I'd like that.'

'Why are you walking so quickly?'

'My mother will be worried if I'm late home.'

'Did you tell her you were taking me out? I bet you didn't even tell her you were taking a girl out.'

'No. That would be a bit of a shock for her.'

'Wait a minute.'

She stopped, suddenly. I turned to face her. I could not tell if she was amused or angry.

'Come here. You've had a bit of a sheltered life, haven't you, Michael Jones? You don't know girls at all, do you?'

'I do. I've got a sister.'

'Not exactly what I meant. How old is she?'

'Thirteen. A tomboy.'

'Definitely not the same. Come here.'

She pulled me towards her. The taste of her lips, then her tongue.

'How was that?' she whispered. 'Not too awful for you? Your mother would be shocked at that, wouldn't she?'

'Very. I suppose...you do that with Tom?'

I wanted to bite off my tongue. The subject of Tom had come into our conversations twice and each time I was the one who had introduced it. It was as if I was determined to stick a knife into my heart just at the moment when it seemed so full that it was about to burst. She pulled away.

'What is the matter with you, Michael?' She hissed the words at me. 'Why do you always want to talk about Tom?' I had the impression she was about to burst into tears. 'I didn't ask you to take me out so we could talk about Tom. I just wanted to get to know you a bit. I wanted to see if I could bring you out of your shell. Reassure you that girls aren't terrifying creatures from another planet. And all you want to do is talk about my boyfriend. If I want to talk about him I'll let you know, thank you very much. I thought while you were with me you might find my company sufficiently interesting. I thought we could talk about you and me and nobody else.'

She pulled a tissue out of her handbag and dabbed her eyes. Then she brushed past me and ran quickly up the road. She stopped by a lamp post on the next street corner. When I caught up with her she had stopped crying and was struggling to smile.

'I'm sorry, Michael. Very sorry. I was upset. I'm all right now.'

'No, I'm sorry. It was stupid of me. I don't know why I said it.'

'No, it's all right, I understand. And the answer to your question is yes, sometimes. But somehow it doesn't feel the way it does with you. I don't know why. When we get to my house you can do it again. If you want to, that is.'

'I want.'

We walked on, hand in hand, so slowly that it seemed impossible we would ever arrive at her house. She was wearing a green cotton dress, with a white shawl over her shoulders. She had put on make-up and perfume. She looked ten years older than she did in her school uniform. Her dress swished and rustled as she walked. Her perfume hung about me like a pink cloud. Would my mother smell it on me? Her thigh brushed mine, as it had in the cinema.

THIRTEEN

'What's the matter with you today, Michael? You seem very preoccupied.'

I had gone to my mother's for Sunday lunch as usual. She sensed from the moment I arrived that something was wrong. As well as the anonymous letter, I now had Bernadette's visit to the confessional the previous evening to distract me. I could not of course talk to her about either of them.

'Just feeling a bit under the weather, that's all.'

'And if that's all, I'm the Pope. So can't you tell your own mother about it?'

'Not when it's a matter of confidential parishioners' affairs, no, I can't. One of our parishioners is having a severe personal crisis. I have to visit them tomorrow. It's preying on my mind. I'm not sure how well I'll handle it.'

All that was true. I had decided to visit Bernadette the next day.

'Well, you'd best be off then and pray for guidance. If your mother is no use to you in your hour of need, you'd be better off not wasting your time here.'

I sighed. 'I didn't mean to suggest you were no use to me. Of course I find strength in coming here.' Not as much as I need before coming here, I thought. 'It's just that I can't discuss the details with you. I'm bound to seem a bit distracted.'

'Well, before you go, there's something I have to tell you. I've decided after all to go on retreat with Mrs Prendergast. There is room for both of us in her car, though as you know I never did hold with women driving. But her husband can't take us because he's doing overtime this week. We're going on Tuesday.'

'But I thought you didn't like Mrs Prendergast.'

'I don't. But I only have to put up with her for the

journey. Once we get there the rules of silence apply, and I won't need to speak to her again until it's time to come back.'

'How long will you be away for?'

'I'm not sure. Maybe a week or two. I'm not sure of the address, either, but I'll let you know when I get there. I'd be grateful if you could call in every now and then to keep an eye on the house. After that break-in I need to be more careful. In the past, you could go away for weeks and leave the front door wide open and nobody would go in unless you had invited them.'

'Of course I will. I must say I'm surprised, after what you said last time. But I'm sure you'll find peace and joy there.'

'Peace and joy? No, Michael. Not at my time of life. I find it harder and harder to concentrate on my prayers these days. There I will be free of the distractions of my home, away from the world. I can prepare for the end. I know it won't be long now.'

I smiled. No home contained so few distractions.

'What are you smiling about? I talk about the end of my life and all you can do is smile.'

'I wasn't smiling, Mother. Not about that.'

I mumbled my usual assurances that she still had many years to live. She shook her head, slowly. I was not disposed to press her. Perhaps she was right. She suddenly seemed much older than she had on my previous few visits. Of course nothing could have happened to age her so quickly. The only explanation was that I was only now seeing her as she really was. I had been deceiving myself, in an effort to deny the advance of my own years.

When I left, I felt an even greater sense of relief than usual. For a few moments it masked my astonishment at her decision. She had not spent a night away from the house for many years. And why was she so vague about the address and the time she would be away?

But it was her business. I had other things on my mind. Like the letter. And Bernadette.

After our first date I was sure I would never see her again. I had been so awkward and insensitive. But to my intense surprise she had other ideas.

FOURTEEN

'Mike? What are you doing behind the counter?'

It was the Monday after I had taken Bernadette to the pictures. When she arrived at the library at three o' clock, I was just beginning my counter duties. She winked at me and went upstairs to the reference section. Tom came in an hour later.

'Hi, Tom. What it looks like. I'm working here. For the holidays.'

'What, stamping the books?'

'Yes, and other things. There's a rota. You do so many hours a week on the counter. Rest of the time, you're in cataloguing, or reference. What are you doing here? Need any help finding a book?'

'No. I was looking for my girlfriend. I've just been round to her house. Her old man told me she's been down here every afternoon this week, swotting up something for next term.'

'Yes, that's right.'

'Sorry?'

'I've seen her, I mean. She's upstairs in the reference section.'

'I didn't know you knew her.'

'What?' My heart jumped into my mouth. 'Oh no, I don't. But I've seen you with her. I know what she looks like from a distance. Long black hair. There's a girl who looks like that who's been in every day this week. So I'm assuming it's her.'

'Right. Yes, that sounds like her. I'll go and find her. Want to arrange something for Friday evening. I'm supposed to be swotting as well but I'm sick of it.'

He made no move to go. I looked up at him. His presence made me distinctly nervous. He was tall and broad-shouldered, with fair wavy hair and a ruddy outdoor complexion. He was good-looking. Of course he was. Otherwise Bernadette would never have chosen him as her boyfriend. Did he suspect I knew more about her than I had said? Even worse, did he know I had been out with her? Would he believe me if I told him it had been her idea and would never happen again? He would never see me as a serious rival of course. But he might feel obliged to teach me a lesson. Not in the library, but outside on the way home. Still he did not move, nor did he say anything. I had to find a new topic of conversation, quickly.

'So, er..., what A-Level grades do you need for university?'

'Two Bs and a C. That's the best offer I've had. From Leeds. I don't think I've got any chance. Might try the local poly. So I can live at home. I don't really fancy going away. What about you?'

'I'm not applying for university. I'd like to get a permanent job here. The chief librarian said he would have me. Mother has different ideas.'

He grinned. 'You know, you're the only one who refers to his mam as "mother". Everybody else, it's "mam" or "the old girl"'.

'If you met her, you'd understand. Neither of those quite fits.'

He grinned again. There was a mischievous twinkle in his eyes.

'Hey, want to come down the Brook tonight? Cartwell and Adams will be there. You know, the swotty ones who are going up to Oxford. They did A-levels last year and the entrance exam last term. They've left school for good now, the jammy buggers.'

'Er...yea, why not? What time?'

'About eight.'

'Okay.'

'See you there then. Oh, where did you say Bernadette was?'

109

'Reference section.'

He still did not move. He looked embarrassed. At last the penny dropped. He did not know where the reference section was. He had probably never been in the library. I had certainly never seen him there before.

'Sorry. It's up those stairs on the left. Straight ahead.'

He clattered noisily up the stairs. After no more than a minute I heard him coming down again. He ran straight out of the front door, without turning his head in my direction.

I allowed myself a faint glow of inner triumph. In every other situation I had seen him in, in the classroom, on the rugby field, in the playground, he was always brash and self-confident. But in the library he was out of his element and he knew it. He had invited me to the pub so that the next time we met it would be on ground where he felt at home.

But why did he want us to meet again at all? We had never been friends nor were likely to be. We had barely spoken. The circles in which he moved had always been closed to me and I had never wanted it otherwise. I did not flatter myself that I could now consider myself part of at least one of those circles, the one that met in the local pubs. Assuming I was right in thinking he knew nothing about Bernadette and me, there could only be one reason for the invitation. He wanted to amuse himself at my expense. He wanted to make me feel as uncomfortable as he thought I had made him feel in the library.

I wished I had refused, but I had not known how to do so. I could hardly say that I had never been to a pub before and did not know anything about them and would rather not know. I imagined the conversation which would have taken place if I had managed to refuse. Guess what, I asked that wimp Michael Jones to join us tonight but he chickened out. Yea, he's too much of a mother's boy to go out to a pub. Spends all his free time in the bloody church. It would be over the whole school by the end of the first day back. No, better to brave it out. If I was to be an object of amusement to Tom and his mates that evening, so be it.

Bernadette was waiting outside when I left the library. I had not seen her come down from the reference library. She must have left when I was putting books back on the shelves.

'Hello,' I said. 'I'm sure I saw Tom leave ages ago. You must have missed him.'

"No, he found me. He's gone home to revise. I wasn't waiting for him. I was waiting for you. Thought you might like to see me home again. If you don't mind.'

'Not at all.'

Tom would not be waiting outside. He would be nowhere around. He would have put as much distance as possible between himself and the library.

As we walked, I remembered her as she had been on Saturday, older, more sophisticated, so much more self-assured than I was. I had hardly recognised her when she had answered the door. It must of course have been the way she dressed and made up for any evening out. She would never have gone to any particular trouble for a date with me. As it was, her appearance had made me so nervous that I had hardly said anything for the first five minutes. She had not seemed to mind. Now she was dressed in a loose brown jumper and a black knee-length woollen skirt, a schoolgirl in the holidays trying to look as casual as possible. We were not on a date. I was just walking home with her.

'I wanted to thank you for taking me on Saturday. I

could have asked Tom to take me this week, if it's still on, but he doesn't want to see that film. Not his thing.'

I thought of Saturday evening, of everything about it except the film. I could not even remember the title. I thought of the perfume that formed a following mist around us, the unexpected firmness of her thigh against mine, the taste of her lips, burning and soothing at once, the moist, searching tongue. Each of these sensations was breathtakingly strange and exotic, as much now in remembrance as it had been at the moment it had seared itself into my brain.

But that was what boys with girlfriends did every Saturday evening. It was a natural part of their lives. Mine was divided between the four worlds of home, school, church and library. Until recently there had been only the first three. My mother had objected strongly when I told her I intended to take a job. At the time I could not understand why. It was surely a world as enclosed and sheltered as the others. Or it had been until Bernadette had given me a glimpse of another sort of world. Perhaps my mother had known that something like that would happen. But she need not have worried. It was not as if Bernadette would want me to take her out again. She had only asked me to see her home.

'You're being quiet and deep again, Michael.'

'Sorry. Just thinking.'

'About what?'

'About you. The way you looked so different on Saturday.'

'Different how? If you say older, I'll slap you.'

'How about mature and self-possessed?'

'I'll buy that. Do you like me like that?'

'Yes. But I was a bit scared at first.'

'Yes, I noticed. I didn't mean to intimidate you. I enjoy dressing up, trying to look older than I am. I wouldn't have slapped you if you had said I looked older. But I like what you did say. It was very sweet.'

We had reached her house. 'Are you coming in again tomorrow?' I asked.

'Yes. Every day this week.'

'It's my last week.'

'Better make the most of it then. Come here.'

Another long kiss. Different this time. A fresher, more natural taste. No lipstick. That was it. That had to be the reason.

Luckily I had not had to ask Tom where the Brook was. That would have been a total humiliation. I passed it every day on the way to work.

At eight o'clock I told my mother I was going out for a walk. She nodded and carried on with her sewing. I had put on my sports jacket and trousers, pushing my tie down into the pocket. It was not my school tie. I had bought the entire outfit with an advance the librarian had given me of my first week's wages. He was not being generous and I was not being vain. I could not wear school uniform to work in the library, but I had no other clothes. I hid the tie because if I had worn it my mother would have asked me why I was dressing up. Once outside, I took the tie out and tied it in a clumsy and loose knot, having no mirror to guide me.

At half past eight, I pushed my head sheepishly round the door. The smell of beer fumes and cigarette smoke hit me like a fist. Everybody was talking loudly and confidently. I wondered what they were all drinking. Men outnumbered women two to one. There was a jukebox in one of the bars, playing Elvis Presley. It would be another year before the Beatles took over. I wandered through the other bars. Nobody else was wearing a tie. I slipped it off as surreptitiously as I could. I heard a voice.

'Hey, Jonesy! Over here.'

Chris Cartwell, Brendan Adams and Tom were seated at a table in front of three pint glasses containing a brown foaming substance. There were two empty glasses near Tom.

Chris was tall and gangly, his arms and legs long and uncoordinated, his face always ready to break into a grin. A brilliant and hardworking mathematician, he disguised his academic propensities through the use of a comically exaggerated Liverpool accent, and thus avoided the reputation of being a "swot". Brendan was more outwardly serious and thoughtful, small and wiry, with horn-rimmed glasses. In his schoolwork he was every bit as clever as Chris, notably in physics and chemistry, and his carefully modulated tones, with no trace of a local accent, left him open to the dangers of social ridicule. But he attracted respect by means of an encyclopaedic knowledge of popular music and, above all, through a natural gift for mimicry, which when used at the expense of our teachers could reduce his classmates to tears of laughter. None of the teachers had been spared, though fortunately Brendan had so far always managed to exercise his skills out of their earshot.

'What'll you have, Mike?' offered Chris.

'Er...no, let me get them. I'm the last to arrive. What's yours?'

I desperately needed them to feed me some essential vocabulary.

'We've still got these,' said Chris, pointing to the half-empty glasses.

'You'll have finished those by the time I get served. What's it to be?'

'All right. Brown mixed. Pint.'

'All of you?'

'Mackeson for me,' said Brendan. 'Draught.'

'Brown mixed for me,' said Tom.

His speech was slightly slurred. The two empty glasses were clearly his. I wondered how long he had been there. I also wondered what a brown mixed was. Brown what? Mixed with what? Luckily the barman seemed to know. I got a brown mixed for myself. I brought the four glasses back in two trips, taking great care. Relieved that I had managed the operation without spilling any, I sat down.

'Cheers,' said Tom.

'Cheers,' we replied. I sipped and coughed most of it back on to the table.

'Quite strong, isn't it?' said Chris.

'Sorry. I'm not used to it.'

'First time Mother has let him out to the pub,' said Tom, with an emphatic sneer on the word "Mother." They laughed.

'Let me? No chance. She doesn't know I'm here. Thinks I'm out for a walk.'

'Better make sure he gets home sober,' said Brendan to the others. 'Or not so pissed that she notices. Mustn't let him get in the state you're in, Tom. Tom's been here since seven, you know.'

'You told me we were meeting at eight,' I said to Tom.

'I like to get warmed up first. How come none of us have met your mam?'

'Because she's a witch, and she's out on her broomstick in the evenings,' said Chris.

I sat back, letting the beer slowly fuddle my brains, waiting for the topic of conversation to change. That happened very quickly and alarmingly.

'What's this about you and Bernadette?'

I nearly choked again. Then I realised Brendan's

question was addressed to Tom rather than to me. My cheeks were burning. I tried to focus my eyes on my glass. If they noticed how flushed I was, I hoped they would attribute it to the effects of the unfamiliar beer.

'I'm going to chuck her, but I haven't decided when yet.'

'You're pissed, Tom. You don't mean a word of it. You two have been going out together for ages.'

'Yes. Because she's a nice girl. That's why I'm going to chuck her. She's too bloody nice. She's nice to everybody.'

'Saw her at the dance at the Old Boys last Sunday,' said Chris. 'You weren't there, were you? She had a really good time. Terrific dancer. She had that little red dress on. Nice and tight. I love the way she moves.'

He wiggled the upper half of his body, grotesquely. We all laughed, though I wanted to be sick.

'Seriously, Tom, what's the matter?' asked Brendan.

They had left me out of the conversation, assuming that the subject of girls had no interest for me. A week ago, they would have been right.

'Saw her out with someone. I was supposed to be away at the weekend but I changed my mind at the last minute. I didn't tell Bernadette. I stayed in Saturday evening. Wanted to think about things. Later on I went out for a walk. Saw her coming out of the cinema. I was on the other side of the street. She was talking to someone but there was a crowd around them so I couldn't see who it was. I could have followed her but I didn't want to find out. And I didn't want her to spot me and accuse me of spying on her.'

'Might have been with a girlfriend, or a group,' suggested Chris. I nodded as if to support the suggestion, but they had forgotten my presence.

'Don't think so. She didn't look as if she was having a girls' night out. Not the way she was dressed up. I wish I had followed her. I'd like to punch him.'

I took a large draft of my drink, which now tasted sour.

'Neither of us, we swear,' said Brendan, smiling. 'We were here. Got witnesses. So why don't you just ask her straight?'

'And have her accuse me of following her around? No thanks. I've still got some pride. That's why I didn't take her to the Old Boys on Sunday. I couldn't face seeing her. Anyway, I'm going to tell her. When we go out on Friday to the Irish Centre. If she wants to spread herself around like that, that's fine. It's nothing to do with me any more. I don't bloody care.'

'So, you don't care anymore,' said Chris. 'Is that why you're getting yourself pissed as a fart every night?'

'Sod off, Cartwell. How much I drink is my business.'

The atmosphere had suddenly become hostile. I excused myself and went to the toilet. I had nearly finished my pint. I did not dare to drink any more. I knew I had to leave before the next round. By the time I returned the tension seemed to have evaporated as quickly as it had arisen. Chris had just reached the end of a joke and they were all laughing loudly. I told them I had to go. Each of the three faces broke into a gleeful smile. Now they had a common target.

'Got to go back to...Mother?' They chorused the last word in perfectly timed harmony.

'Yes,' I replied. 'And you watch your mouths or I'll get her to put a spell on the lot of you.' I started to leave.

'Hey, Jonesy,' Chris called after me, still grinning. 'Why don't you ask Bernadette out, now Tom's letting her go? Should be your type. Right little raver. Smashing bottom.' I turned back, with a smile.

'Somehow I don't think Mother would approve, do you?' I mimicked their pronunciation. They laughed and waved. They did not take me seriously. Thank God. I threaded my way carefully through the crowded room and into the street.

'I'm home, Mother,' I called out as I put my key in the door. 'I'm going to bed. Feeling a bit tired.'

'All right, son. Don't forget to say your prayers. And don't disturb your sister. She went up half an hour ago. She'll be asleep by now.'

I ran up the stairs. I had lied. I was not tired. I was in agony. It was what Chris had said. About Bernadette dancing, in a tight red dress. I prayed that Angela would be asleep. I was in no state for one of her inane conversations, even less for one of her stories without an ending or one of her jokes with a forgotten punch line. The house only had two tiny bedrooms, so Angela and I had always had to share. Three years before, my mother had used her sewing skills to make a large curtain out of old dress material. She had fitted a pole across the room between our two narrow beds and hung the curtain from it, so we could have some privacy when we undressed for bed. This had done nothing to stop Angela's flow of bedtime stories and jokes. It only meant that she told them in a louder voice than before. This time, thank goodness, she was already fast asleep.

I knew the rules about impure thoughts, of course. We had been told about them often enough at school. It was accepted that they could arise unbidden, and that was no sin. But it was a sin to entertain them. Chris had put an image into my mind. All I had to do was put it out again. But it was far too late for that. The effect of the alcohol and my relief at escaping a beating from Tom had created a euphoric haze in my brain. I had no thought of sin. I thought only that I had to be quiet so as not to wake Angela. Then my thoughts were entirely of Bernadette's body, sometimes in a white confusion of vaguely imagined nakedness and sometimes encased in a red dress stained by a ring of sweat spreading outwards from the small of her back as she danced.

Afterwards I lay gasping. Had I made a noise? I was not sure. It did not matter. Angela snored on peacefully.

I could feel tears of shame stinging behind my eyelids. How could I have presumed to think about Bernadette like that? She had shown one aspect of herself to me, that of a serious mature woman who knew far more than I did about life, who was in charge of every situation in which she found herself, who could flirt and tease without losing her self-control. But there were other sides to her. Ones I would never see. Of course there were. She was a complete human being. She was at home in the world and open to what it offered. She readily gave and received love and friendship. She could enjoy life from moment to moment. She went to parties and danced. In company she would always be the centre of attention. She knew that to some of the boys at those parties she would appear only as Chris had described her. Afterwards they would find words to belittle her and parts of her body, particularly now that she was not available to anybody but Tom. As a woman of the world she knew what those boys were like. She would not expect anything different from them.

But she had not chosen to present that side of herself to me. She had trusted me to see her as she wanted me to see her. And I had betrayed her.

My eyes closed. I was suddenly very tired. Then I

remembered that what I had just done was a sin. I had to say an Act of Contrition. I would say it in the morning. But what if I died in the night? When I was first learning about sin from the priests at school and from my mother, I had been frequently warned of this possibility, as an inducement to say my nightly prayers. I was soon convinced that perfectly healthy young children were everywhere dying in the night for no apparent reason. If that happened to me now, the Devil would be entitled to take my soul. I mumbled the opening words of the prayer, but sleep claimed me before I could finish.

'Michael, I want to talk to you. Seriously.'
'Yes, Mother.'
It was the following evening. My heart was in my mouth. I knew the tone of voice and what to expect. She must have found out the secrets I had been keeping from her, my date with Bernadette, my visit to the pub. I always sensed her presence, even when I was out of the house. I was now sure she had seen me being kissed by Bernadette, seen me in the pub with Chris, Tom and Brendan, seen me in bed afterwards, seen my innermost imaginings about Bernadette's body.

'You seem to have changed, Michael, ever since you went to work at that library. Now I know I was wrong to relent and let you go there. When you go out into the world, you meet godless people. Most people are like that. They can lead you astray, unless you are sure of your path. You are sure of your path, aren't you, Michael?'
'I don't know, Mother. I don't know what path you're talking about.'
'Don't be obtuse, boy. I'm talking about the path to your holy calling. People out there see you and they think you are like other boys. They don't know you.

But I know you're not like other boys, and you know you're not. You should make it clear to them from the start.'

'How? Wear some sort of badge?'

'Don't you dare talk to me like that! Sometimes I think I don't even know you any more. There are days when I think you cannot possibly be the boy I devoted my whole life to bringing up in accordance with God's law. You could tell them you are going to seminary to be one of God's holy priests, that's what you could say.'

'But I don't know if I'm going to seminary. I haven't heard from them yet. How do we know they'll have me?'

'They'll have you because I pray every night to God that they will have you, and Father Ambrose and Father Taylor pray for it as well and their prayers are worth far more than mine. I hope and trust that you pray for it every day as well.'

'But who exactly is it I'm supposed to be making all this clear to?'

'I suppose you meet girls at the library? Girls who work there?'

'Oh, we're talking about girls. Yes, but they're all much older, and most are married.'

'There are other girls. Not older ones. Ones your age. They set traps for you. The way they talk and dress. The way they smile at you.'

'Mother, nothing has happened. There's nobody like that. I go out in the evenings sometimes because I need to be on my own. Think things through.'

'Think things through,' she echoed, slowly and deliberately. 'And what exactly would you be thinking through? Thinking about how to prepare your soul to be a priest? Or thinking about the girls you see, thinking about them in a way no decently brought up

boy should think about a girl? Don't deny it, Michael.
God knows it's a serious enough sin for any boy who's
been brought up to respect the human body as a vessel
of the Holy Spirit. But for a future priest there's no sin
more grievous than impurity of thought.'

She stood up and put her hand on my shoulder. I
shuddered and continued to look down.

'Just pray for strength, Michael. We're all weak
creatures before God. One day you will be a priest and
these impure thoughts will no longer trouble you. God
is testing you, that's all. He wants you to be a lot
stronger than you are being. So do I. I won't deny that
I'm disappointed, Michael. Bitterly disappointed.'

She got up and went to leave the room. She had had
no need to tell me about her disappointment. Her voice
was thick with it.

'Mother, I'm not seeing a girl,' I called out to her.
'That's the truth. I swear it.'

She turned back from the door.

'Never swear to me, Michael. Swear to God. He
alone knows the real truth.'

But it was the truth. I was not seeing a girl in the way
she meant. I was still seeing Bernadette home after
work, but that did not count. I was not her boyfriend.
Tom would never stop going out with her, whatever he
might say when drunk. When school started the
following week I would never see her again in any
circumstances, except perhaps from a distance, when
she came out of school with her friends, laughing,
sweeping her hair from across her face and tossing it
back. I would see, but I would take no notice.

FIFTEEN

I was returning along the passageway to the presbytery after saying evening Mass. I had devoted the day to routine parish matters. I had decided I was not yet ready to visit Bernadette. My long-frozen memories were returning but it was a slow and painful process. It was the first time I had really tried to confront the person I had once been, the person I thought I had left behind in the distant past.

Bernadette or God. That was the choice which had faced me at that age. Not my choice, of course, but the choice which would be made for me. But the more I looked back, the less I could understand why either of them could be even the slightest bit interested in so unimpressive a specimen of humanity as the eighteen-year-old Michael Jones. And if I was honest with myself, I could hardly pretend that I had become more impressive with the passage of time. All I had done was wrap myself in the cloak of priesthood, conferring on myself an automatic aura of authority and mystery while at the same time cutting myself off from any demands the real world might make of me. Inside I was still a coward and a runaway.

There was only one small window in the passageway, from which I could see the entrances to both the church and the presbytery. I glanced through it in the direction of the presbytery gate. The paper boy was just leaving after a delivery of the evening paper. Leaving rather quickly, I thought. Running in fact.

Paper boy? He came at five o' clock. It was now a quarter past seven. I ran through to the house and grabbed my coat and scarf. Mrs Raferty called out to my departing back that dinner was ready.

'Got to go out, Mrs R.,' I called back. 'Very urgent.

Don't worry about dinner.'

On the doorstep, I spotted the package. The same colour and size of envelope. My name in the same red ink. I resisted the urge to pick it up. When I reached the street, I looked right. A small figure in a blue duffel coat was just visible. The hood was up. The figure was half running and half walking. I crossed to the other side of the street, and walked as fast as I could. At the main road, the figure crossed at a pedestrian crossing, and waited at the bus stop. I was relieved. I was already out of breath. I checked to see if I had any money in my pocket. I did. Enough for a bus ride with a little to spare. I wrapped my coat and scarf around me to conceal my collar. Very slowly I crossed the road. I joined the back of the queue at the bus stop. Several people now stood between me and the duffel coat. It would have no reason to think it was being followed.

The bus came. The duffel coat went upstairs. I sat downstairs. I bought a ticket to the end of the route. I wondered where that was. I had not looked at the front of the bus. We were heading towards Bootle. On the right, we passed the massive container base which had finally ended traditional dock labour in the port and the local communities which had supported it. Huge cranes loomed in the dusk like sleeping monsters. The old disused docks lay beyond them, creeks of stagnant water where oil and debris gathered in the silent darkness.

The bus slowed at the junction with the old Dock Road. The duffel coat came clattering down the stairs and jumped out. The driver, anxious to get away from that desolate place, did not even stop. I managed to stumble out just before he began to accelerate. I shivered and gathered the lapels of my coat around me. There was a sharp, cutting wind. Heavy, black clouds scudded angrily across the greying sky. Globules of dirty stinging rain blew into my eyes. Papers whirled and cans rattled about my feet. I shivered again, this time with fear.

I had been there before, many years ago. My father had taken me on a trip on the overhead railway, known locally as the 'dockers' umbrella' and demolished a few years later. My mother had been furious when we had returned and told her where we had been. I had never been back since. I would not have recognised it. It was as if its living heart had been torn out. On either side of the road stood empty warehouses between large patches of waste ground. On some of the street corners, dimly-lit pubs still stood in defiant isolation, no sounds coming from within, the homes from which they had drawn their customers now just empty space, the occupants long since dispersed to the new towns of Kirkby or Skelmersdale. The street was deserted, except for a small scurrying figure in a duffel coat and a disguised priest in covert pursuit. My heart was pounding. If I had seen a bus coming in either direction I would have caught it. But there was nothing. Little whimpering sounds reached my ears through the wind and rain and I realised they were coming from me.

We at last reached a small development of flats and shops. I guessed that it had been built in the early sixties, using cheap, prefabricated units. It had probably assumed its air of shabby neglect the day after it had been built. Expertly executed graffiti denouncing the Thatcher government and supporting the aims of the now legendary Toxteth rioters adorned every wall. The shops were all fronted with metal shutters. It was impossible to tell what any of them sold. There was only one point of warmth and light, a small, smoky café, smelling of fried onions. The duffel coat was inside, still hooded. I looked around, pulled my coat and scarf tightly around me and entered.

'What can I get you, luv?' A tiny old lady in a grease-spattered overall flashed me a one-toothed smile from behind the counter.

'Tea, please,' I stammered.

I would have given anything for one of Father O'Malley's generous servings of whiskey. She produced a pint-size mug, and poured strong, black tea into it from a huge pot. She added milk and was about to pour into it an indeterminate quantity of sugar straight from the packet when I stopped her.

'No sugar, thanks.'

"Quite right, luv. Bad for you. There you go.'

There were only two tables. I went to the one where my quarry sat. By now, he had pulled back the hood. I sat opposite him. I noticed for the first time how dirty the duffel coat was. I guessed he was about nineteen. He was short, pale and thin, his face ravaged with acne, his hair an untidy tangle of ginger. I smiled at him. He smiled back. His teeth were yellow and several were missing. There was nothing on the table in front of him apart from a bottle of vinegar and a plastic dispenser of brown sauce.

'Sorry if I'm disturbing you. Do you mind if I sit here? Can I get you anything?'

'Yea, all right. Tea. Like yours. Only lots of sugar.'

I nodded to the lady. She had heard the order and brought it over. She gave me a long suspicious look as she placed the mug in front of him. She must have realised I had followed him in. In that place on a night like that the chances of two customers entering in quick succession must have been remote in the extreme. I had to be careful. If she thought that I was trying to pick him up, undeterred by the acne and the yellow teeth, she might call the police.

'I'll be honest with you,' I said, after we had sipped our tea in silence for a few moments. 'I'm not here by chance. I followed you from Seaport. You delivered a package at my door. I wanted to speak to you.'

The woman was listening, as I meant her to. She seemed reassured, and disappeared into the back.

'Can you tell me who it's from? Somebody asked you to deliver it, didn't they? Look, you're not in any trouble. I just want to know.'

'She paid me ten bob. Told me not to tell anybody.'

'What's your name?'

'Tim.'

'Mine's Michael. Where do you live, Tim?'

'Over there.'

He pointed through the grimy glass panel in the door across the street to a single-storey building. A small car stood outside. It was too dark to see its colour. It looked very like our parish car.

'What's that?'

'Hostel.'

'Does she live there too?'

'No. Not any more. Don't know where she lives.'

'What's her name?'

He put his finger to his lips and winked with a prolonged movement of his eyelid. I smiled, nodded and touched the side of my nose. He did the same.

'Secret?'

'That's right,' he whispered. 'She made me swear to it. Mind you, I don't think Dora's her real name, anyway. Oh, shit!'

He leaned back in his chair and covered his face with his hands.

'Never mind, Tim. If it's not her real name, it doesn't matter, does it?'

'No. Suppose not. She did make me swear, though.

127

On her prayer book and rosary. Don't go in for all that myself, though. She does jobs there now. Looking after people. She even drives that car. Gives me a ride in it sometimes. Let's me have a go at driving, though she hasn't even got her own license yet. I like her. She's really ace. I've got to go now.'

He rushed out quickly, leaving his cup only half-drained, before I could think of any way to retain his attention.

I finished my tea, left the café and crossed the road. There was a notice board outside the building. Community Care Centre. Enquiries to John Higgins. There was a telephone number. I looked round. There was a call box a few yards away. To my amazement it was in working order. I rang the number.

'Hello, presbytery.' It was a woman's voice. Strong city accent.

'Oh, I'm sorry. I must have the wrong number. I wanted John Higgins.'

'That's right. Father John Higgins. He's the parish priest here. St Joseph's. He'll be back in half an hour. Visiting a parishioner.'

'My name's Father Jones, from St Jerome's in Seaport. I need to speak to him urgently. But I'm not at home. I'm calling from a phone box. Can you give me the address?'

She told me. I found a scrap of paper and a biro in my pocket, and wrote it down.

I returned to the café. The old lady reappeared.

'Sorry to bother you again. Is there anywhere I could get a taxi from, around here?'

She laughed. 'Taxi? Not a cat in Hell's chance, Father. No taxi would come near here if you paid it a million pounds.'

I smiled. 'How did you know?'

'Obvious. Only a priest would dare come round

here, asking questions, not knowing their way. Even the police don't come down here after dark. You'd need the protection of the Almighty and you look as if you've got it. It's all right. Your secret's safe with me. Where're you trying to get to?'

I told her the address Father Higgins' housekeeper had given me. She gave me directions to the main road into the city.

'That'll take you about twenty minutes. Then you get any bus towards the city centre. Get off at the rotunda. Ask somebody there.'

I knew where she meant. The rotunda was a landmark junction on the route into the centre.

I was nearly sick with relief when I reached the busy main road.

SIXTEEN

After my Easter holiday job, I returned to school and tried to revise for my A-levels. I found it difficult to concentrate at the best of times. Now it was much harder because of what happened every day at four o' clock.

That was the time when I came out of the school gates with a group of classmates. We chatted on the street corner for a few minutes before dispersing in various directions towards our homes. Then I saw her, on the other side of the street, in her school uniform, talking to her friends. I imagined she looked in my direction. It must have been imagination. Why should she bother to look my way? She did not look away. I had to turn my eyes away first. Maybe she was looking at one of my classmates. They did not seem to notice her, or to realise that my face was burning. The same thing happened every afternoon at that time, for the whole of the first week back. She was always there at the same spot. She always looked at me, or I thought she did. I always looked away. In the evenings at home, I could not focus on my books because I was thinking about what had happened earlier. It was my fault that I could not work properly. There were no other distractions. I worked alone in our bedroom. Angela was forbidden to disturb me, doing her homework at the kitchen table.

The solution came to me at the beginning of the following week. I had an alternative way home, slightly longer, through a park at the back of the school. I told my classmates I wanted to feed the ducks. I had brought some stale bread from home for the purpose. They laughed and told me I was going crazy under the pressure of the coming exams. I told them they were probably right.

I took the park route home every evening that week. I saw no sign of her. My plan was working. I was not seeing her. Sooner or later I would stop thinking about her. My mother said nothing, but her frown was a little less tight and her lips a little less pursed. This meant that I was back in her favour, as much as I ever could be.

The following Monday I walked through the park as usual after school. I was approaching the pond. Then I saw her. She was sitting on a bench on the other side of the pond. She looked up. I could not avoid acknowledging her. I went round to her side of the pond, my heart thumping. I sat down beside her. She was dabbing her cheeks with a handkerchief. Her eyes were swollen.

'Bernadette, what's the matter? Are you all right?'

'I'm sorry, Michael.' She struggled to smile. 'I didn't want you to see me like this.'

'What is it? Is it Tom?'

I remembered his promise in the pub to tell her he no longer wanted to see her. Perhaps he had gone further, accusing her of seeing someone else. Perhaps he had even hit her.

'Tom? No, of course not, you idiot. It's you. You've been avoiding me. I saw you after school and you looked away. Not just once. You kept on doing it. The whole of the first week back. Then I found out you were coming home this way. I thought you liked me. I don't understand. What's happened?'

'I do like you. Very much. Of course I do. You must know that. I...never imagined it was me you were looking at. I thought you must be looking at someone else. I would never want to hurt you. Nothing's happened. It's just that you're Tom's girlfriend and I thought it would be best...'

'To cut me dead and make me feel as if I'm some

sort of insect.'

'No, of course not. I'm sorry.'

'You could have had the courage to explain it to my face. That you're scared of Tom.'

'I'm not...Well, maybe I am a bit. He is bigger than I am.'

She laughed, though tears were still trickling down her face.

'Michael, you really are a big baby. And so is Tom, if you only knew. He wouldn't do anything to you, or anybody else. I choose my friends. As it happens, he doesn't know you're one of them, but if he did he wouldn't object. What possible reason could he have? But it's not just Tom, is it?'

'What do you mean?'

'I heard rumours.'

'What rumours?'

'That you're going to be a priest. So you have to avoid girls.'

It was my turn to laugh. 'Who told you that?'

'I got it from my brother, James. Do you know him? He's at your school, two years below you. He said you went away to seminary for an interview. His teacher was holding you up as an example for them to follow. No chance of James doing that, though. He's much too fond of the girls and they of him. Still only sixteen but he knows much more about life than I do.'

'It is true that I went for an interview. Father Taylor arranged it, and the Order paid for my travel expenses. I could never have gone otherwise. It didn't go at all well. I can't imagine them accepting me.'

'So it is true that you want to be a priest. Or why would you have agreed to go for interview?'

'I wasn't asked. Father Taylor just told me I was going and when. He had arranged it with my mother, and contacted the head of the seminary himself. He knows him well, apparently. He looked so pleased with himself. He kept saying how the priesthood is short of vocations these days. He and my mother seem to have agreed it between them years ago that I would be groomed to be a priest. I got extra religious knowledge lessons right from the first year. I was told I had to do Latin for A level. But nobody ever asked me if it was what I wanted.'

'But you are an altar boy. You didn't mind that.'

'I wasn't too happy about it at first. But I enjoy it now. The priests are all right. Father Ambrose is a bit scary but Father O'Malley is a scream. I can't imagine how a priest could get to hear such stories. Unless he makes them up, which I think he does a lot of the time. But being an altar boy doesn't mean you're going to be a priest.'

'But it isn't a question of what you want, is it? It's whether God has called you.'

'I suppose so.'

'So has He?'

'Has He what?'

'Called you?'

'I don't think so. I'm not sure how it happens. I mean, you don't hear this booming voice out of the sky, "Michael Jones, you have been called."'

She laughed out loud. 'You don't think so. Michael, you must be the biggest noodle in the whole world. You do need someone to take you in hand, and I don't mean Father Taylor or your mother. If you have a vocation, you really know. There's no room for doubt. Didn't they tell you that?'

'Not in those words. They just seem to assume that I have been called and that I know about it.'

'So, calls from God apart, is it what you want? Really? If you haven't been called, are you hoping to be? Are you praying for it? Is that why you've been avoiding me? Michael, look at me.'

Her eyes were deep, wide pools, still swollen by her recent tears. The truth they drew out of me had been buried until that moment. I shook my head.

'No, Bernadette. It's not what I want.'

She smiled. 'Thank you for being so honest. To yourself as well as to me. I know that wasn't easy. Come here.'

She put her hand around my neck and drew my face towards hers. When she drew her mouth away again, it was my eyes that were brimming. We were silent for a minute, looking at the ducks, which that evening would have to do without the bread I had brought for them.

'Michael?' Her voice was so soft I barely heard it.

'What?'

'See me home.'

'Can't I meet your mother?'

It was a week later. We had a new routine. I saw her home every evening after school. We always met on the same bench in the park.

'I don't think you really want to.'

'I'll have to meet her sooner or later. If we keep seeing each other. Does she know you're seeing somebody?'

'No. I can't tell her yet. I mean, she might get the wrong idea.'

'The wrong idea? What sort of wrong idea?'

'I mean, she wouldn't understand about you and Tom. She might not realise we were just friends.'

'Michael, you're not ashamed of me, are you?'

'No, of course not. How could I possibly be ashamed of you?'

'That's how I feel when you won't acknowledge me to your mother. I don't understand that. I don't care if she doesn't like me or approve of me. I just want her to know I exist. So she'll realise you're growing up and meeting different sorts of people. If that's painful for her, too bloody bad. Sorry, I don't usually swear.'

'I'll tell her soon. I promise.'

She ran ahead of me, then turned back, a wide grin on her face.

'I've got something to tell you,' she called out. 'Liverpool University have offered me a place to do French. I need three Bs. Sister Semolina says I should get them.'

'That's wonderful. I'm very happy for you.' I ran up to her and kissed her. 'I wish I was as clever as you. I have to work like a dog just to pass exams. I'll be lucky to get three Es. They'd take me on at the library if I do get them. Then I could study for one of their diplomas.'

'Would you like to do that?'

'Yes. It's what I want. I'm sure of that now.'

You're sure? Really, really sure? Whoopee!'

The serious woman of the world had in an instant given way to the excited school-girl. She ran around me in circles while I stood still, my head dizzy as my eyes tried to follow her.

'Then go ahead and do it,' she shouted, still running. 'Whatever you do, I'll be proud of you. So long as it is what you want.'

She collapsed onto a bench, out of breath, giggling uncontrollably. I sat down beside her, grinning, unable to speak.

We were nearing her house. She turned towards me.

'I want you to come in this evening. To meet my parents. Just for a few minutes. Don't worry. They won't bite your head off. They're very sweet really. I adore them.'

'I'm sure they adore you.'

135

'I'm not so sure about that. Not when my mother shakes her head every time I dress up to go out. My dad always approves, though, whatever I do. I've got him round my little finger. That's what he says.'

Her mother was a plump, bright-eyed woman who in her youth must have looked very like Bernadette. Her father looked much older than her mother. He had worked on the docks, but been forced to retire early because of ill health. He did not move out of his chair, and he coughed a lot. Despite the cough, he smoked continuously. Capstan Full Strength. He offered me one. I shook my head, though part of me longed to accept it.

Her mother asked me about my plans for the future. Nervously, I told her I was thinking about becoming a librarian. To my surprise she seemed to find that a perfectly satisfactory response. Her father said nothing, but he smiled frequently at them both whenever his cough relented sufficiently to permit a smile. Her mother told me how proud they both were of her. Bernadette scolded her, pretending to be embarrassed, while rubbing her hands up and down her father's arms and brushing her hair against his cheek. They both seemed to treat him rather like a family dog, but he clearly did not mind.

I had dreaded the meeting, but to my surprise I began to feel comfortable after about half an hour. I did not want to leave and go home to my mother's silence and my revision books. At the door, I kissed Bernadette lightly on the cheek, in case her parents were watching. She came out onto the doorstep, half-closing the door behind her.

'That won't do at all, Michael,' she said. Her eyes were shining and her cheeks flushed red. I kissed her on the mouth. It was several minutes before she let me leave.

On the way home, I wanted to cry. Now I knew I was not worthy of her. My mother never smiled at me the way her parents smiled at her. My mother knew my inadequacies. Soon Bernadette would realise them too. She was still seeing Tom. Of course she was. Tom was not much cleverer than I was. But he was stronger and better looking. He was a sportsman. He was comfortable in the pub with his mates. He would do far better in life than I would.

Of course I had told myself many times that I was not her boyfriend and could never aspire to that state. I was only a friend. So why should I compare myself with Tom? We each had different roles in her life, though I often wondered what exactly mine was expected to be. Would they get engaged soon? Would she ask me to be best man at her wedding? Why was that thought so unbearable? Because it would be the final proof that she had not even begun to understand what I felt for her.

SEVENTEEN

An hour after I had left the hostel I stood outside St Joseph's Church. It was an imposing brick building, standing amid rows of terraces that had escaped the double devastation of wartime bombs and post-war development but were unlikely to escape much longer from the effects of creeping neglect. A light shower had fallen while I was on the bus. Only one of the street lamps was working, opposite the church. It threw a sallow shaft of light across the cobbles.

It took me several minutes to find the presbytery. A modest bungalow stood behind the church. There was a gate connecting the back garden of the bungalow to the land around the church. I went through it and round to the front of the bungalow. There was no sign to indicate it was the presbytery. I knocked. I took off my scarf to reveal my collar. A young man opened the door.

'Father Jones? My housekeeper told me you rang. I'm Father Higgins. Come in.' He was dressed in jeans and a loose sweater. He had just a trace of a South Yorkshire accent. There was humour and compassion in his eyes, despite the purple lines of fatigue beneath them.

'I'm sorry to call so late.'

'It's not late for me. I don't usually get to bed before three. And you're rather out of your way, with no transport, as far as I can see. Seaport, isn't it?'

'That's right, St Jerome's. Have you been in the diocese long? I'm surprised we haven't met.'

'A few years. You won't find me at those tedious diocese meetings. I think HQ regard me as a bit of a maverick. I suppose they'd be right about that. I have enough on my plate here. Things are a bit different from Seaport, I think. Though I'm pleased to say that there's some community spirit left around here. I can still leave the church unlocked for a few hours in the day. About six weeks ago, during the sermon, I read out a list of things which had been stolen from the church. It's a standard item now. Between the banns and the general parish news. I look round to see if anyone won't meet my eyes. After a couple of weeks some of the items started to trickle back. I think they realised they weren't much use. You can't really take candles and statues down to the local pub and flog them, can you?'

'We can't leave ours unlocked any time outside services and Confession. Not anymore.'

He took me into the kitchen. 'We can talk in here. I've taken over all the other rooms as offices, and there are papers everywhere. I sleep on a camp bed, when I can find it. Good job my housekeeper was in when you rang. I can never find the telephone. How about some coffee?'

'That would be great.'

He made it very strong and black and served it in two huge mugs. We sat around the small Formica-topped kitchen table.

'Now, how can I help you, Father?'

'I saw your name outside the hostel. But it didn't say you were a priest.'

'No. Some of our clients don't like priests. When I go there to see them I dress like one of them. Most of them don't even know.'

'You do this as well as all your parish duties?'

'Yes. I didn't intend it that way. A few years ago they started closing the large psychiatric hospitals. There was one only a mile from here. Ridgeway Park. They said they wanted to bring the patients back into the community. That's fine if you've got family or friends to go back to. Some still needed inpatient care.

They were moved to psychiatric units in general hospitals. Some were no longer ill, if they ever had been. There were some old ladies who had been in there since their teens. All they'd done was get pregnant out of wedlock. Their families certainly weren't going to have them back, if any of them were still alive. They just needed somewhere to sleep and eat, where they could feel at home. The younger ones needed to build up their daily living skills, maybe get work eventually. There are a few hostels that cater for them, but nothing like enough. So quite a few just fell through the net. Ended up on the streets. There was this woman called Dora, for instance.'

'Dora, you say?'

'That's right? Do you know her? Is that why you're here? Has she been in touch with you?'

'I haven't met her. But she could be the reason I'm here. What were you going to say about her?'

'She was the start of it all. She came to a drop-in centre we have further up the road here. She'd been in Ridgeway a few years earlier. Before she came here she'd been sleeping rough. I put her up in this house. In my bedroom. That's when my camp bed days started. I got used to it. Couldn't sleep in an ordinary bed now. My housekeeper had a few things to say about her staying here, I can tell you. I realised there was a need for somewhere more permanent for people like her. I knew she wasn't the only one, by a long chalk. So I started to raise funds. Found that place on the Dock Road. It's not even in my parish. It was empty. I got it dirt cheap. Some local worthy with more optimism than common sense had tried to start a community centre there, but had failed miserably and just abandoned it. I got some volunteers together and did the place up. Dora helped. She moved in there. Others came. They're not all ex-patients. Some came in straight off the streets.'

'Your optimism seems to have worked.'

He laughed. 'We had God with us. Or more likely, I had even less common sense than the chap who built it. I refused to give up. Even after the place had been set on fire twice.'

'How old is she? Dora, I mean.'

'She's in her late thirties, I would say. She's not sure herself.'

'Is she friendly with a young lad called Tim, who still lives in the hostel?'

'Yes. He follows her around like a faithful dog. He'd do anything for her. I'm sure Dora's not her real name. So how do you know about her, and about Tim?'

'She seems to know me. She never uses the name Christine?'

'No. To us, she's always been Dora. When she's there, she spends all her time helping the others now. I taught her to drive. She went on at me for ages to teach her. It was fun. She picked it up very quickly, though we had some scary moments. She hasn't taken her test yet. We've a little car down there. One of my parishioners gave it to us when he bought a new one. It's a big help when we want to follow people up after they leave the hostel. I used to do all that myself. Now she does a lot of it. It's strange. Any other car down there would be dismantled in minutes. It's a good job you didn't drive there tonight. But they leave ours alone. It's taken years to gain the trust of the locals. There's now a gang of youngsters who protect our premises and the car from the attention of gangs from outside. They even guard the telephone box in case it's needed if ours breaks down.'

'You've done incredibly well. I admire you.'

He waved his hand as if to brush aside my

comment.

'About Dora. I learned a bit about her history. She had been sectioned as a teenager. No idea why. Suicide risk, maybe. I never ask about our clients' pasts and she never showed any sign of wanting to talk about it. She was in Ridgeway for about eight years, as far as I can judge from what she told me. Her memory is still vague about those times. She said she had been before one of those review panels. They had told her she could be discharged, if she had somewhere suitable to go. But there was nowhere she could go. No family or friends outside that anybody could trace. Her records were incomplete. She had forgotten most of her past life. At that time she could not even remember where she had lived. Then she met a young man, another patient. From what she told me about him, I think he had schizrenia. He was there for about a year. They controlled his condition with drugs. One day they left, just before the place closed down. They lived together for a while. He refused to take his drugs and his condition worsened. They were living in a flat his parents had given him. Quite near here. She left. Or he threw her out. I don't know which. She doesn't know what happened to him. She slept rough for a while. She ended up at the drop-in centre. She didn't know it was connected with the church. Just as well. She really has a thing about priests.'

'Not surprising.'

'Sorry?'

'I mean...she seems to accept you, though.'

'I don't think she even knows. She's never been to Mass here, as far as I know, and I never wear my dog collar outside. This house doesn't look like a presbytery. There used to be a very grand presbytery next door to the church, totally out of place in this sort of neighbourhood. The land was sold to pay for repairs to the church roof. The parish priests had to move in here. I prefer it this way.'

'You were telling me how you found her.'

'Oh yes. Well, it was more a case of her finding us. One of our helpers found her sleeping on the doorstep of the drop-in centre, when she arrived in the morning to open it up. I visit there every day. The helper told me where she had found her. There's nowhere to sleep there, so I brought her here. She wouldn't tell me anything at first. Took weeks to gain her confidence. Then she started to talk about where she had been. It made my blood run cold. If they hadn't already closed the place down, I would have gone there and burned it down. Got the people out first, of course. Apart from some of the staff. You said she seemed to know you although you've never met her. How did that come about?'

'Tim has been delivering messages to me on her behalf. He leaves them on our doorstep. I spotted him leaving the latest one this evening and I followed him to the hostel. It's important that I find her and speak to her. I have no idea why she chose me. Our parish is not where she used to live.'

'How do you know where she lived?'

'We don't know where exactly. My fellow parish priest remembers an incident in which she was involved years ago, in the neighbouring parish.'

'Before she was committed?'

'That's right.'

'An incident involving a priest? Don't worry, Father. I'm not the nosy sort. I know they're obsessed with keeping these things secret at Diocese HQ. You probably know more than you should. I would rather not know. The last thing I want to do is draw attention to myself. They leave me alone and I leave them alone. My only interest in Dora is her present life, not her

143

past. Well, I'm sure there's no great mystery.
Presumably she's moved into your parish now. Got a
new boyfriend, perhaps. Obviously she was a Catholic,
before something happened to turn her against priests.
She's taken up the habit of going to Mass again. She
must take an instinctive comfort in it, despite the way
she feels about priests. She's seen you at Mass. She
may hate priests in general, but she feels drawn to you.
She thinks you may understand.'

'I know I would like to understand. From what she
has written I have good reason to believe her memory
is returning strongly now. There are certain people she
blames for what happened to her. She makes threats
against them.'

'So why would she tell you? Perhaps she wants you
to advise her, perhaps talk her out of her threats.'

'I would be happy to do that, if only she would
come to see me.'

'You don't want her to know you've traced her as
far as the hostel?'

'No. I don't want to scare her away. Or get Tim
into trouble with her.'

'I could try talking to her, without telling her I've
met you. Dora hasn't lived in the hostel for some time.
I don't know where she lives now. She still works
there as a volunteer. We're all volunteers, of course.
Nobody gets paid. So she comes and goes as she
pleases. But I can never be sure when she's going to be
there. I haven't seen her for a couple of days now. But
if I get the chance to talk to her, I'll certainly ring you.'

'She must have been at the hostel today, to give Tim
the envelope. What does she look like? In case I spot
her in church.'

'Small. Five-two or three, maybe. Looks fragile,
though she's really as tough as old boots. Greying hair.
Blue-grey eyes. Nothing special, really. You could

pass her anywhere and not notice her.'

'Thank you. How old are you, Father? If you don't mind my asking.'

'Thirty-five. Last time I counted.'

'I was twenty-five when I came to St Jerome's. I'm forty now. I'm sheltered there, like I'm in a cocoon. I have a congregation which never changes from week to week, just gets a little older. When I give the sermon, they listen to my every word, even though they know and understand it all already. During the week, we repay the compliment and go to see them. The outside world might not exist. You work with people who hate priests. I never even meet a non-Catholic, except for the would-be converts who come for instruction and desperately want to believe what I tell them. I never have to face an atheist, or anyone who can mount a sustained intellectual attack on the Church's doctrines. I have never taken my faith out into a world which is hostile or indifferent to it. I have never been the difference between life and death to anybody. You are five years younger than I am and you've done all this. You know what I really feel, here and now? Bloody ashamed. That's what.'

He sighed. 'Don't you think I feel ashamed, when I go down there and start yelling at people, because they're breaking things and there's no money to replace them, and because I'm so tired I just want to sit in the middle of the floor and cry? Oh, I'm no saint, Father, believe me. And I'm sure you do more good than you realise. You think your congregation doesn't change but it does. People up there are respectable, aren't they? They like to put a brave face on things. So when they sit there in church listening to you, they don't show what's inside. They don't show it when they've spent the week in despair at the loss of a loved one, or because they're ready to go mad with loneliness. No, on Sundays they dress up and put on their brave smiles and out they go. When they hear you they have the courage to face another week. Has this been bothering you, Father? Worrying about the value of the work you do?'

'Yes. I think it's been bothering me for a while, without me realising it.'

'And that's why you are so keen to help Dora. Because she represents something different. She has been to places you never dreamed existed. I'm not just talking about the hospital. I'm talking about where her heart and her soul have been. She's spoken to you through these letters she's sending you, and you want to find these places too. You want to lead her out of them.'

'You're a very perceptive man, Father. Yes. That's exactly how I feel.'

'Well I wish you luck. It took some courage to do what you've done tonight, leaving your safe harbour like that. I suspect that things will never be quite the same for you.'

'Look, when this is all over...I was wondering, well, if I could come and help out at the hostel? Disguised as a layman, of course.'

'I'm not saying we couldn't do with all the help we can get. But I'd be grateful if you didn't come. Not now. You'd just be doing it to salve your conscience. Wait until you want to do it for the right reasons. Come on, you look as tired as I feel. I'll ring for a taxi for you. Now, can you help me find that damned telephone?'

It was after midnight by the time I returned. Father O'Malley was waiting up for me. He leapt out of his chair as I staggered into the room.

'Thank God you're still up,' I gasped. 'I need some

money to pay off the taxi.'

'Michael, what in the name of all that's holy has happened to you? Come in here and have a brandy. You look like you've been through all the circles of Hell and out the other side.'

'Well, I have been to Bootle and beyond, if that's what you mean.'

I accepted the brandy from his outstretched hand and sat down.

'Bootle? On your own, and without the car and with no money? Have you gone completely crazy? There's only room for one madman around here and that's me. Only I'd never go and do anything like that. Mrs Raferty has been going out of her mind with worry. Wondering what she'll say to your mother if you disappeared. I've been facing the somewhat less terrifying prospect of finding something to tell the Archbishop. I'll go and pay the driver.'

He returned after a few minutes. While he was out I drained the glass and helped myself to another. When he returned, he picked up the second envelope from the table.

'It's another one, isn't it? Mrs Raferty said somebody delivered it and you dashed off after them. Fantastic! Just like me to miss all the excitement. You saw her and followed her. Did she recognise you? Did you hide in the shadows when she looked round? Did she dart into a waiting car? Did you hail a passing taxi and tell it to follow?'

'For God's sake, Father, this isn't Los Angeles. And when did you last see a passing taxi round here? It wasn't her I followed. It was her messenger. Her winged Mercury. With a bad case of acne. Young lad. Traced them to a hostel down the Dock Road. I talked to a priest who runs it. Father Higgins. He knows her. She calls herself Dora now, apparently. Ex-psychiatric

147

patient. Probably late thirties. She doesn't live at the hostel any more, but she does work there from time to time. He says he'll let me know when he next sees her.'

'Why not open this now? She may have left this to tell us she's changed her mind and she's gone away and we're not to worry anymore.'

'That, Father, would be a relief for which I would give a great deal. Though in that case I can't see why she should send Tim all the way down here to leave it on the doorstep. He charges a lot more than the Royal Mail for his services.'

I opened the envelope. A single sheet this time. I read it through and handed it to him. He looked down it.

'Bloody hell,' he whispered after a minute.

'You know, Father, when I saw the first letter I felt resentful. I was sure she was spinning us some story. Then when I thought she was telling the truth I still felt resentful. Why me, I thought? Why bring this here and disturb our comfortable smug lives? What can we possibly do to help?'

'And how do you feel now?'

'Sick. Angry. Partly with myself, for my earlier reactions. I don't want to persuade her not to confront them. Not any more. I want to help her. I want to be there when she confronts them. I want to see what sort of people they are. And if she does commit violence on them, verbal or any other sort, I'm not sure I'll be in any great hurry to stop her. There's one consolation, though. This place she describes has closed down.'

'Not much consolation for the people who were in there.'

'Let's think about the next steps, shall we? She says she's moved into this parish. Where would somebody go to live, near here? Somebody who doesn't have much money? Her work at the hostel is unpaid. She's probably living off benefits and that won't come to much. Do we have any accommodation for people who sleep rough, or come out of prison or anything?'

'None that I know of. Tomorrow, I'll get in touch with the local Council. Make a complete list of possible addresses. Then we'll split them between us and go and visit them. We'll be looking for someone called...what did you say she calls herself?'

'Dora.'

'Dora, or Christine. The name doesn't matter. She might change it again. Late thirties, you say. Arrived there recently. And we'll keep a lookout for new faces in church. Someone who might answer her description. Did he tell you what she looks like?'

'Yes. Not the sort of description the police would leap in the air over. Small, fragile-looking, blue-grey eyes, greying hair. Somebody you would pass by without noticing.'

'Oh that's great. That really pins her down. Go to bed now, Father. You look done in. Want me to say Mass for you in the morning?'

'No. I'll do it. I want to offer it up to Father Higgins and the people he looks after.'

'Goodnight then.'

'Goodnight, Father.'

I took the letter up to bed with me and read through it again.

EIGHTEEN

15 February 1985
(So Tim says!)

Dear father jones

I want to tell you about the place they sent me. It was a huge building with red bricks and tall narrow windows. it didn't look like a hospital or sound or smell like one. there were no prety nurses and no laughing or crying from the patients only howling. And the smells of piss and vomit everywhere. I had a few weeks on my own then they put me on a ward with loads of these old men who smoked all the time. There were nurses there in uniforms most of them men all burly and smirking. I had been in hospital once before and the nurses were really nice and they didn't hit me but these ones did. They weren't like nurses at all. The pills trolly came round twice a day and we were given handfuls at random. They never looked at the papers which said who was suposed to get what and if you shouted or broke anything they hit you just a slap usualy. I know I said the men were not like nurses but the women socalled nurses were worse than the men. They were even stronger and they knew better how to hurt because they didn't just slap. the pain of a slap is here and gone but they knew how to make the pain stay and get worse all the time until you went crazy. but that's funny because you were suposed to be crazy already because that was why you were there. They liked to pull my hair and pretend it was in fun. they would start all slowly laughing and pretending to

150

tease me and pull harder and harder. once I tried to hit them back so they took me to the bathroom and ran cold water in the bath and unndressed me and pushed me in and held me under the water. then they pulled me out and after that I learned to behave myself and become quiet so nobody would notice me. I began to forget and I couldn't remember why I was there in the first place. I just asumed I was bad and was being punnished but I wondered if it was the drugs because when I stopped taking them I started to remember some things. but they didn't know I had stopped because I hid them in my bed and threw them away and was sick for weeks but they never knew why. I still forget a lot of things but I remember what they did her and that priest and I think I know how to find her now that I'm living in your parish.

NINETEEN

'Mikey, have you got a girl-friend?'

'Keep your voice down, for God's sake! Mother will come up to see why we haven't gone to sleep.'

'Sorry. I said, have you got a girl-friend?'

'If I heard you the first time when you were shouting, then you don't need to repeat it in a whisper. No, I haven't.'

'But you are seeing somebody?'

'Why do you say that?'

'Because you go out on your own a lot, so you say, and when you're in the house you moon around all the time.'

'I do not moon around.'

'Do, so there. I should know. So who is she?'

'Well, if you must know, her name's Bernadette, and we're just friends. She has a boyfriend already.'

'Bernadette Reilly, is it? She's at our school. Wow, she's really something. Dead glam. She's a prefect. Bosses us around in the playground, sometimes. But she's nicer than most of them. Wait until I tell me mates.'

'You'll tell nobody. It'll get straight back to Mother, and then we'll all be in for it. And where did you learn to speak like that? "Dead glam...me mates." Don't let her catch you talking like that.'

'I can't go round at school talking like a fruit. They'd duff me up. Anyway, what's all the big deal? I've got a boyfriend.'

'You haven't.'

'Have, too, so there. I should know.'

'But you're only thirteen.'

'Yes. I'm a late starter.'

'A late..! God Almighty.'

'Don't let Mother catch you talking like that. She'll

make you wash your mouth out with soap.'

'What's his name?'

'I don't know. I'm still trying to find out. He waves to me from the bus. None of me mates know who he is, but they all fancy him. But it's me he waves to. They're all jealous as hell.'

'So you and your...boyfriend haven't exactly spoken yet.'

'Not as such. In words. But our eyes meet in unspoken passion.'

'Angie, I have never heard such utter bilge in all my life. If you did meet him, you'd probably hate each other.'

'Probably. Love and hate are different sides of the same coin.'

'Where did you get that from?'

'Book I was reading, yesterday. That romance you got me from the library.'

'Angie, didn't you take that back? You'll get me killed. It's two months overdue, and it's in my name. Just make sure Mother doesn't find it. I knew there'd be trouble, as soon as you started asking me to get those books out for you.'

'So have you kissed her yet?'

'Angie, this conversation is at an end. Goodnight.'

'You haven't then. Goodnight.'

'As it happens, I have.'

'You'll have to marry her then.'

'If you don't shut up, I'll throw a boot over.'

TWENTY

'Oh, I had a call last night from Father Brennan. No luck yet, I'm afraid. Nobody seems to know what happened to the Gallaghers. There's no address for them in the parish records. He says he'll keep his eyes and ears open, and let us know if anything comes to light.'

We were at breakfast, the morning after my nocturnal adventures and my meeting with Father Higgins.

'What about Father James?'

'He said he once had an address for him for forwarding mail. Over the water. He's looking for it. Of course he may not be there now. He hasn't had anything to send on to him for years. That's why he doesn't have the address to hand.'

'I might go and see him, if the address turns up. In case he's noticed anybody watching or following him. Though the thought of speaking to someone who did what he did does rather make me want to be sick.'

He looked hard at me. 'I know this is a worrying business, Father. But you're really not looking yourself at all. You're very pale. I'm wondering if there's something else troubling you. Is your mother not well?'

'She's fine, though she thinks she's dying. There's nothing new about that. She's gone away on retreat, with Mrs Prendergast. To prepare herself for the life beyond the grave, though I am sure she'll outlive both of us. But there is something else, to be honest.'

'Would it be Bernadette Kavanagh who's preying on your mind, now she's available again? I'm right, aren't I? So why don't you go ahead and marry her?'

'What! Father, there is the little problem of our vow of celibacy.'

'Vow, fiddlesticks. That's not a vow as far as parish priests are concerned, it's an administrative regulation.'

'All right, but it's still Church Law, whatever you call it. Priests can't marry.'

'Well they did for centuries and the world didn't end. Anyway, priests do marry, even Catholic ones.'

'Then they stop being priests.'

'Sure, there is that snag. You'd have to get a dispensation.'

'Dispensation? I'd have to sign a paper to say I was unworthy to be a priest. I don't think I am unworthy. Not as unworthy as that, anyway. So I'd be telling a lie.'

'Well, stretching the truth a bit, possibly. You know the Church could have been such a force for good in the world, if it hadn't got so hung up on sex. All because of an accident of history. If only Christ had lived a bit longer, it would have been all different.'

'What do you mean?'

'You do know Christ was an Irishman, don't you?'

I sighed. 'Why is it we never have a serious conversation about religious matters?'

'I am being serious. He stayed at home with his parents until he was thirty. Then he hung around with the boys a lot. *Quod erat demonstrandum.* An Irishman. Now if he had lived until he was forty, he would have got married in the end. Most of my friends from Dublin who didn't become priests or go to prison were married by then, but not before. It wasn't that Christ was against women. Not at all. He just never had the time. Neither did the apostles. How could they have married and settled down when they were running from place to place, preaching, then hiding, then getting themselves killed for their troubles? But because Christ didn't marry, and the apostles didn't as far as we know, the Church assumes marriage is a lower form of life, and sexual relations outside marriage a lower form of life still. But it's all a misunderstanding of history. Of course some of the saints we've had since haven't helped exactly. St Augustine, for example. He abandoned his mistress, claiming that women were such temptresses that they had forced him to sin. He was the one who said that sin in the Garden of Eden was about sex rather than apples. Then there was Thomas Aquinas. He said that women are more easily seduced by sexual pleasure because they have a higher water content than men.'

'I'll swear you're making all this up to make me feel better.'

'Well, you're smiling at last, so it's working. But no, I'm not making it up about Augustine and Aquinas. We both know I'm no scholar. But the Holy Ghost told me, and he is one. We're still reaping the harvest they sowed. Did you ever wonder why the Church is so keen to get you into its coils while you're still a child? It's because a child is sexually innocent. It's not that easy for a child to sin, as a rule. So you teach it the mechanics of guilt and Confession first, knowing the sin will come along later. The child says to itself, this is dead easy. I pull my sister's hair, ring a few doorbells and run away, go to Confession and then it's fine until the next time. Piece of cake. But what they don't know is that we've laid a trap for them. Like a net across the river to catch the salmon as they come jumping upstream. That net is puberty. They go crashing straight into it. Now we've got them. Because now it's not just the occasional venial sin we've got them for. It's everything they're thinking about every second of the day and dreaming about every second of the night. And the really clever thing is that just thinking about it is enough. You don't have to do anything in order to sin. A sin a second. Just think of that. A golden harvest of sin. And the poor little buggers never knew it was coming. They try going to Confession. And guess what? They haven't even left the church before they're sinning again. They might as well camp out permanently in the confessional box until they're ninety-five. What a wonderful trick! Signed up in childhood for a lifetime of guilt. But seriously, maybe it's time you did chuck it in. I've been in the business too long to change now. But you're still young. You could do other things. I've sometimes wondered whether your heart was in it.'

'My mind and my goodwill have always been in it. As for my heart, I seem to have lost that somewhere on the way. They told me at the seminary that God would be testing my vocation from time to time. Trouble is, I can't remember a time when He wasn't testing it. Once a priest, always a priest. That's what they kept telling us at the seminary.'

'Well, they would say that, wouldn't they, with all that time and effort and money invested in you.'

'Why did you become a priest, exactly, Father?'

'It was simple really. My parents sent off the other boys, one by one, to study in England. Law, accountancy, medicine, things like that. They wanted us all to be respectable. But when they got to me, there was no money left. The local bishop told them that there was a scholarship available for me to train as a priest, in County Donegal. So I went there. It was either that or go to sea.'

'Why only those two choices?'

'To escape the attentions of the young ladies, of course. I didn't want to end up like my parents, God bless them, going forth to multiply, and losing count after six.'

'I imagine you suffered a lot from those attentions, didn't you?'

'Sure, you're right there, Father. God inflicted grievous sufferings upon me in that regard. As you might have noticed, I have a certain gift for the blarney.'

'I had noticed.'

'And in those days, when I still played rugby, I was not bad looking, either. So there were quite a few of the Dublin lovelies who had a go at pinning me down. They never managed it, but that didn't stop them trying. Trouble was, I couldn't take them or myself seriously. So I thought, what better way of life for someone who can't take life seriously than to be a priest? So that was that. Not exactly an orthodox vocation, you might say. Anyway, we were talking of you, not me. And I think I know where you mislaid that heart of yours. You suffered the fate of tens of thousands of my countrymen. You lost your heart to a pretty Irish girl with a sweet smile, long black hair and ravishing....well, we won't go into the details. And a long time ago it was lost, I'll be thinking.'

'Yes, Father. A very long time ago.'

And more than my heart. Much more.

TWENTY-ONE

It was the last week of term. We walked to her house in silence, tired and relieved that the exams were over.

'My parents are out until late,' she said. 'Visiting my aunt over the water. James has gone with them. We're all by ourselves. Would you like to come in?'

I had not been in her house since the day I had met her parents. Then we had gone into a small parlour at the back. I expected her to take me into the same room. Instead she opened the first door on the left of the gloomy hallway. I followed her in. It was a spacious, high-ceilinged living-room. There was a small sofa in front of a bay window, and two small leather armchairs.

She walked slowly over to the sofa and turned to face me. I remained by the door, wondering where she wanted me to sit. She did not smile. She shifted from one foot to the other. I had never seen her so nervous and uncomfortable before. I was very surprised. Why should she feel nervous in her own house? The room was stiflingly hot. To my relief she took off her blazer. It was a signal that I could take off mine. I stood with it over my arm.

'I want to tell you something, Michael,' she said, still standing by the sofa, still neglecting to invite me to sit down. Her voice was flat and quiet. I felt as if a great weight were pulling my stomach downwards. This was it. The moment I had been expecting for weeks. She was going to tell me we could not see each other again. Perhaps she and Tom were engaged. I checked her left hand. Still no ring.

'I'm going to draw the curtains,' she said. 'The sunlight's too bright. Sit down.'

I walked over to one of the armchairs.

'Not there. Over here. We can sit on the sofa together and talk.'

To reach the curtains, she knelt on the sofa and leaned forward, her back towards me. The fabric of her blouse and skirt stretched against her straining body. I saw, heard and felt it at the same time, like a surge of electricity. I groaned, then prayed she had not heard me. I dropped my blazer into the armchair next to me, crept over to the sofa and sat down beside the place where she was kneeling, hoping that when she turned round she would not notice what had happened to me. I closed my eyes. I felt and heard her squirming round into a sitting position.

As I opened my eyes her face was immediately in front of mine. She loosened my tie and opened the top button of my shirt. 'That's better,' she murmured. I stared at her, scarcely able to breathe. She put her hand behind my head and drew it towards her shoulder. She moved her hand down to my lap. She had noticed. Her fingers worked. She undid the buttons of my trousers and slipped her fingers inside.

'Bernadette, don't, please.'

'Poor Michael.'

I was whimpering.

'So helpless.' Her voice croaked. 'You want me so much, don't you? I knew you always wanted me. From the moment you looked up when I first spoke to you. But you couldn't do anything about it, could you? It's all right now. I'm not teasing you this time. I love you. That's what I was going to tell you. I want to show you. Come on. I know what we have to do.'

I was on the point of crying. She was sinking backwards on the sofa into a lying-down position. I followed her, and at the same time she drew me down onto her. Two pairs of hands fumbled frantically at her clothing but whose was doing what it was impossible to tell. Before my eyes I was aware of a blur of grey, lifting skirt, white thigh and blue knickers loosening about her knees. Then my face was level with hers, my mouth on hers. Savagely, uncontrollably, I began to tear her apart. I expected her to scream. But I heard only rapid, shallow gasps. She held me far too tightly for me to withdraw. So there was only one way to end her agony quickly, but first I would have to increase it by thrusting deeper and faster. Still she was quiet. In the end I was the one who screamed.

I buried my face in her hair and cried. Her hands clung to my neck, damp with sweat. Slowly, we drew back from each other and tidied our clothing. I glanced up at her. There was a pink blush on her neck and cheeks. Her eyes and hands were suddenly shy. She turned away. Outside, the sound of a ball being kicked against a fence. Children shouting. The world carrying on blindly as if nothing had changed.

'I'm...sorry if I hurt you,' I stammered, at last.

'And what makes you think you can hurt me, big boy? Well, just a little, at first.'

She forced herself to look at me. She leaned forward and kissed me gently.

'I'm the one who should be sorry, Michael. I'm really wicked, aren't I? Taking advantage of you like that. You must think I'm a whore. But I'm not. That was my first time. Only, I did know a bit about it, about...what to do. I saw James. A week or two ago. He had left his bedroom door open. He had one of those girlie magazines. Suppose he must have got it from the other boys in his class. He had no idea I was watching. Good job Mum or Dad didn't catch him.'

'Bernadette. Was there something else you wanted to say? When we first came in, I had the impression you wanted to tell me something.'

She nodded slowly.

'Yes. There was. I wanted to say that I'd finished with Tom. Last week. It wasn't fair to him. I don't

161

love him. It's you I love. You know that now, don't you? Tom and I never did...what we just did. You're the first, Michael. Honestly. Do you love me?'

'Of course I do. Will you marry me?'

She drew back and stared at me, her eyes wide with mock surprise.

'If you'd asked me before, I wouldn't have believed you meant it. But now, when you've already had your wicked way with me...well, I suppose you must mean it.'

'I do. Please don't tease. I thought you weren't going to tease me again.'

'I didn't say I never would. Just that I wasn't teasing you then. And I won't now. I'm sorry. But when? After university? It's a long time to wait.'

'No, now. I'll get a job. At the library, like I said.'

'I was going to live at home anyway, if I got my place at Liverpool. We could both live here. Get a place of our own later on. Mum and Dad wouldn't mind. Even if they did they always let me do what I want in the end.'

She shivered. I put my arms around her.

'What's the matter?'

'Nothing. I'm very happy. Really. It's just that...it seems only yesterday I was still a child, being spoilt by my parents, teasing James, knowing nothing about the world, not caring that I didn't know anything because I thought my childhood would go on forever. And now it's over. So soon. I'd just started to play at being a woman. Making up, dressing up, flirting, dreaming about boys, then having a real boyfriend. They knew I was just playing. They still saw me as a child. That made me feel safe. I always knew there was somewhere I could go back to, a place in their hearts as their child, if I got hurt or scared. I could lick my wounds and they would look after me and tell me

162

everything would be all right. Just as they always have. Then after a while I could venture out again, knowing they would always be there for me. For me as their child. But it can never be like that again. Now suddenly I'm a woman. And here we are, talking about marriage. It all feels so different. A bit frightening, I suppose. When it's not a game anymore. It'll be such a shock for them. They'll still love me and support me. But they'll never be able to see me as a child again. And I'll never be able to go back to them as a child. All that's finished.'

'Will they think we're too young?'

'My mother was my age when she married my father. I might have to remind her about that. He won't say anything. He'll be happy for me. She will as well. It might take her a bit longer to come round, that's all. She'll be so glad it's you. She really likes you. But are you really sure? I mean sure you don't want to become a priest?'

'Of course I'm sure. I want to marry you.'

'It's all happened so quickly. I need to think about how to break it to them. They'll need time to come to terms with it. Give me a week. Please? I'll tell you then. If it's yes, we'll marry right away if you want. I suppose I should snap you up while I have the chance. Or word will get around how good you are. And I don't mean good as in holy.'

'How would they know?'

'How do you think? They'll tell from that smirk on your face. I suppose you'll be wearing it forever now.'

'I'm sorry, I didn't realise. I'll have to get rid of it before Mother sees me.'

'How will your mother take this? She was the one who had set her heart on your being a priest, wasn't she? I haven't even met her yet and already I know she's going to hate me.'

'She'll just have to put up with it. It's my life, not hers. She won't hate you. Nobody could hate you. All right. One week. I can wait that long for an answer.'

She stood up and walked over to the window.

'Michael, do we have to go to Confession? I suppose we should. But we can say we are going to marry. Then it's anticipation. What we just did, I mean. Not a mortal sin. It can't be a mortal sin, can it? Not if we're going to marry.'

'No, it can't be.'

'I kept Tom hanging on for too long. I should have told him before about my feelings for you. And told you, of course. We could have discussed it properly, instead of just falling into...what happened just now. I can say I'm sorry about how and when it happened. You have to be sorry about something, don't you? Or you don't get Absolution. But I'm not going to say I'm sorry we did it. Nobody can make me say that. Not in a million years. Because I'm not sorry, and I never will be.'

She turned to face me. I had never seen her with such an intensely serious expression before.

'You're not sorry, Michael, are you? Tell me you're not sorry and never will be. Tell me.'

'No. Never.'

'Just never? Is that all?'

'Never in a trillion years.'

'That's better.'

It was a mortal sin, though. I was sure of that. It was the one sin I had thought impossible. It was not because I was too virtuous. I had already committed the sin many times in my mind. But that was a sin of thought. There were far too many practical obstacles to what was called actual sin. She had to want the same sin, and to want to do it with me of all people. The whole idea was absurd and ridiculous. Even if it were not, the operation had to be discussed, planned and carried through jointly, stage by stage, each stage a carefully choreographed act of collaboration. At every point, even as late as the gradual removal of clothes, there was a chance for either of us to say no, this is a sin, we must go no further. With so many obstacles there could be no danger. This was the safe sin, the out-of-the-question sin. And yet in an instant, miraculously, all the barriers of impossibility had simply melted away.

But if it was such a great sin, why were the signs of it not upon us? I remembered what her face looked like, when it had finally come back into focus. Like the face of one receiving the Beatific Vision. How was it possible for the face of sin and the face of blessedness to look the same? Was this how the Devil was able to dress up sin, so that we did not even recognise it afterwards?

I was nearing home. The singing sensation in my stomach had given way to a knot of misery and dread. I had to tell my mother I could never be a priest.

'Mother, I'm home.'

As I entered the living-room she jumped out of her chair. She was clutching a piece of paper in her hand.

'You're very late, son.' Her voice quivered with excitement. 'Where in God's name have you been? I've got a letter to show you. Here it is. It's wonderful. Father Taylor brought it round himself, but he had to leave half an hour ago. He couldn't wait for you any longer. Look. It's from the seminary. They've accepted you. All my prayers have been answered. You can start in September. You'll be a priest. We must get on our knees and give thanks to God. Michael, what's the matter? Are you ill?'

165

I slumped into a chair. 'Mother, I'm sorry but I can't be a priest. I'm not worthy. I have no vocation. I know that now.'

She sucked in her breath. Her face contorted, horribly. She raised her hand as if to strike me. I waited. She held her breath. She brought her hand down, slowly. For a minute her breath was rapid and shallow. Gradually it became deeper as she regained control. A look of intense fatigue came over her face as if the effort had exhausted her.

'That's all right, Michael.'

Her voice was gentle, soothing. I had never heard her speak like that before. It was the opposite of what I had expected. I was prepared for rage, even violence. I was ready for a tirade of abuse so harsh that it would signal the inevitable end of our relationship. I was prepared to accept full responsibility for her unhappiness, even despair. I would take the blame for my total and final failure as her son. I had told myself that I would accept whatever she chose to say and do so without argument or resistance. I had tensed every limb in my body in readiness for her reaction. But what I had not prepared myself for was her kindness. I felt the resistance in my bones and muscles, across my chest and at the back of my throat ebb away. In its place came an uncontrollable shaking throughout my whole body. I could not have spoken to save my life.

'I understand. You're nervous. You've got your doubts. That's natural. Remember how worried you were when you went to see Father Ambrose about being an altar boy? And that worked out so well, didn't it? Well, don't let's talk about it now. Let's wait a while. I'll leave the letter here on the mantlepiece. You can read it when you're ready. They don't need to hear from you until the end of July. In the meantime you can talk to Father Ambrose and Father Taylor about it. I won't interfere now. It's not my decision. Nothing to do with me. I'm just a silly old woman. It's in God's hands. I'm going upstairs to lie down now. I'm tired, with all the excitement. I've left your dinner in the oven. Good night, Michael. God bless.'

TWENTY-TWO

Bernadette's house was double-fronted with bay windows and an oak-panelled front door with a frosted glass pane. It was part of an estate built about twenty years before, when demand for new exclusive, executive-style housing well outside the city was at its peak. At least four bedrooms, perhaps five. There was a double garage. Tom had done well for himself. She had made the right choice. I could never have matched him as a provider. But there had only been the three of them. Why had they needed so much space? I noticed there was a new For Sale sign outside the front gate.

I rang the bell twice. I was about to leave, assuming she was not in, when from inside I heard a door open and close again. Hesitant footsteps approached. The door swung back slowly. She was still wearing black, a loose pullover over a long skirt. She wore dark-brown slippers. Her hair was tied up. She looked up at me with no sign of surprise, pleasure or annoyance. She turned away. I stepped onto the doormat and followed her inside. Neither of us had said a word. I followed her through the hall into the front room. Her body moved sluggishly. The weight of her grief had crushed her spirits, I thought. I wondered if Father O'Malley was right to assume she would recover quickly if at all.

'Sit down, Father.'

She had sat down in a huge, black leather armchair, part of a three-piece suite which dominated the room. The walls were wide sweeps of white, textured wallpaper broken only by small china ornaments. There was a glass coffee table on which lay several back copies of Woman's Own. A piece of discarded knitting lay on the other armchair. There were more china ornaments on a maple mantlepiece over a large imitation coal fire. There were no books or records. It was a room for the formal reception of visitors who were not expected to stay long. I sat opposite her on the sofa.

'Are you on your own?' I asked. 'I wondered if John might have stayed with you for a while. After the funeral, I mean. I assume he came home for that.'

'Home?' She frowned. 'Oh yes. He was here. But he had to get back.'

'To college, I suppose.'

'What? Yes, college. Of course.'

She looked away, around the room, towards the window, the door, the mantlepiece. Anywhere but in my direction. Her hands fluttered nervously. Her voice sounded empty, as if the words had no meaning for her and she was only repeating them to fill the silence that hung in the air.

'I wanted to say how sorry I was about Tom.'

'Thank you. But that's not why you're here, is it?'

'I think you know why I'm here. You came to me for Confession. I came because you left the confessional before I could give you Absolution.'

'So you did recognise my voice. I wondered if you would. But that's not the real reason, is it? It's because of what I said. I'm sorry about that. It was unforgivable. Saying personal things to you in the middle of Confession. That's sacrilege, isn't it? I suppose I should confess that as well.'

'You just did. And nothing is unforgivable. You know that.'

'I wish I believed it. I intended to go to Father O'Malley as usual. Then I saw you go in first. There was nobody else on your side of the church. I went in on an impulse. I started to confess in the normal way. I didn't intend to say what I did. It just came out. When I realised what I had done, I couldn't stay any longer.'

She sighed, shrugged her shoulders and looked up at me with a tight smile, formal and polite, utterly unlike the one I had once known. I wondered when she had learned it. When, during all those years since we had last spoken to each other, had she drawn down the curtain between her inner self and the outside world?

'Cup of tea, Father?' she asked, in a tone of brisk, forced cheerfulness.

'Yes, please.'

While she was in the kitchen, I stood up and walked around the room. I was relieved to be on my own for a few minutes. Among the china ornaments on the mantlepiece was a wedding photograph in a silver frame. I picked it up. They smiled radiantly at me. Two eighteen-year olds in love. I was replacing the photograph when she brought in the tea.

'Good photograph isn't it? Very convincing. It would fool anybody.'

I sat down again and drew a deep breath.

'Bernadette, I came here because you told me you hated me. I don't understand. I want to know why. If it was something I did or said before you...before you sent me that letter, something that caused you to send it, then I want to say I'm sorry. But I can't think what it could be. I misunderstood your feelings, obviously. If that's it, then I apologise. But I was very young. We both were. But whatever it was I did, how could you possibly carry on hating me all these years?'

'Sugar?'

The same brisk tone, the same wall between us.

'No, thank you. Just a little milk.'

She handed me my tea. She sipped her own for a few minutes. I was about to get up to go when she spoke. She did not look at me. She was half-turned towards the window. She spoke as if to herself.

'Tom was a good husband. Better than you or

anybody else will ever know. He worked hard. We could afford nice things, as you can see. His only weakness was drink. He went to the pub every evening. Never got really drunk. Not until the last year or two. He started smoking heavily then as well. I tried to stop him, because it was smoking killed my father. I'm sure of that.'

'I'm sorry about that, too. I liked your father. Your mother died too, I heard.'

'Yes. She was heart-broken. About dad, I mean. She had a stroke. Six months later. Anyway, there we are on our wedding-day. Two young love birds. Only it wasn't quite like that.'

'I'm sorry, I don't understand. In your letter you said you had made a mistake. About us. That you really loved Tom. You just said he was a good husband. He provided a good life for you and John. Now you say you've hated me all these years. And that thing you just said about the photograph. Not being what it seems. Are you saying you were unhappy with him all these years? Perhaps it was because you were both so young, you didn't really know each other.'

To my surprise, she laughed, harshly. The sound was unfamiliar, dissonant.

'We didn't. Not before we were married anyway. But very soon after. Things changed then pretty quickly.'

'But didn't John bring you closer together?'

She laughed again, a note of hysteria in her voice. I wondered if she were about to have a breakdown, if her repressed grief were finally about to break forth. She shook her head.

'I'm sorry, Father. Please forgive me. It's all been a terrible strain. Tom going so suddenly and me having to arrange the funeral and sort out his affairs. I still can't get used to him not being here.'

'It's all right. I understand.'

'Oh I very much doubt that. No, John didn't bring us closer together. And I didn't want any more. So I went on the pill. There's another sin for you, Father. I never confessed that. What was the point? I wasn't going to come off it, and I wasn't sorry.'

'So you stopped taking Communion.'

'Oh, you noticed. Tell me something. Can you imagine what it is like to go to Church every week, desperate to feel the warmth and consolation everybody is feeling, sick with envy as you watch them all going up to the altar rail to receive the Body of Christ? But you can't go up with them because there is an icy hand around your heart and a hollow voice in your ear that's telling you all the time that you don't belong there, that you're an unrepentant sinner, that God's love is available to everybody else but not to you. Can you imagine how that feels, Father? No, of course you can't.'

'I can imagine it must be terrible. But of course God's love is available to everybody, you know that. And as far as birth control is concerned, you could have talked it over, if not with me then another priest. There are methods approved by the Church.'

'I know. The rhythm method. But that wouldn't have worked for us. Believe me.'

'Couldn't you have tried? How could you have gone on paying such a price for something you could have sorted out between you?'

'Because I had no choice. There was more at stake than you realise. More than I can talk about.'

'Not even to me?'

'Especially not to you.'

'Because of your feelings about me. But surely you don't hate me because your marriage wasn't what you had hoped for? I'm not saying I would have been a better husband. I'm sure I wouldn't have been. But you did choose him, Bernadette. I asked you to marry me, and you chose him instead. That was your right. But how can you blame me if it went wrong?'

She put her head in her hands.

'God, Michael, you really don't understand, do you? You have no idea how what you did to me changed me, made me hate myself, made me unable to love anybody. If you don't understand now, you never will.'

'Bernadette, help me to understand. If the only reason you turned me down was because you realised you didn't love me, then why marry Tom? Why not wait until you met someone you could love?'

'I've just told you, Michael. I couldn't love anybody by then. I was desperate. I needed security. Tom could give me that. I did love you once, Michael. There was a time I was able to love. I didn't turn you down. There was nothing to turn down. Your proposal meant nothing. You were going to be a priest. You never meant it when you said you wanted to marry me.'

I felt a tide of nausea rising in my throat. How was it possible that her memory of events could be so different from mine? How could she have taken away from those events such a wrong interpretation of my feelings and motives, and held onto them with growing bitterness through all the subsequent years? Or was it only her recent grief that was altering distant events in her mind?

'That's not true, Bernadette. How can you say that I was always going to be a priest? I was waiting for you. If you had said yes, I would never have become a priest. I would have married you. There was nothing else in the world I wanted, nobody else I wanted to be with. How can you possibly have thought I had already decided on something else?'

173

She leaned back in her chair, staring at the ceiling.

'Michael, I'm not saying you're lying. But you have forgotten the most important thing. Your life was not your own to give. Not then. Not now. It belonged to somebody else. Somebody who in church stands triumphantly between us.'

'Bernadette, I don't know what you might have heard about me or who might have told it to you. But I swear to you...'

'No, Michael. Don't swear. Please. I want you to go now. I'm sorry for what I said to you. Let's just leave it at that. We'll never see or think about each other again. I'm leaving. Selling up. I'm going to Birmingham to be with James. He's going through his second divorce. He didn't turn out to be a very good Catholic either.'

I stood up. 'I'm sorry. I shouldn't have come. It was a mistake. Thank you for the tea.'

'Can I ask you to do one thing for me, before you go?'

'Of course.'

'Could you give me Absolution now? For everything I said to you in the confessional, and for the way I abused the Sacrament? Or shall I go back to Father O'Malley?'

'Look, about the pill. I'll give you Absolution for that too. It's all part of the past now. I know it's been on your conscience and for me that's enough. And quite frankly, though I'd rather you didn't quote me on this, there are some Church rules that don't seem to me to have much to do with living a good Christian life. You have always done that.'

She made a sound half way between a sob and a retch.

'Oh, Michael, if you only knew. Please give me Absolution for the sins you know about. The ones I've

174

told you I am sorry for. No more.'

'All right. But talk to somebody else about the rest. Not just the pill. Everything. Including all the things you didn't feel able to tell me about. Maybe you think you will never be able to. But time changes many things.'

'But not everything. Some things are there all the time, with you every day, whatever you do, wherever you go. Do I need to go over the words again?'

'No. Just kneel down.'

She knelt in front of me. I made the sign of the cross over her bowed head as I pronounced the words. She remained kneeling as I walked towards the door.

'What about my penance, Father?' She did not look up.

I turned round. 'Your penance? After what you've told me, who am I to impose a further penance?'

I went straight back to the presbytery. I walked through the passageway to the sacristy and on into the deserted church. I knelt in front of the high altar. I looked up at the tabernacle. I prayed aloud.

'Dear Lord, forgive me for what I am about to say to You. I thought You had given me a clear sign, through her. Now I know that You only planted confusion in both our minds. I was willing to make the sacrifices I thought You were demanding of me. If You wanted my life, it was Yours for the asking. It will still be Yours, if that is what You want. But why did You demand the sacrifice of her life as well? And his? If I had known what I know now, that I was offering up all our lives, not just mine, I would have refused You. I thought we understood each other. Now I know I understand nothing. And I understand You least of all.'

TWENTY-THREE

'In the name of the Father, and of the Son, and of the Holy Spirit. The Grace of our Lord Jesus Christ and the love of God and the fellowship of the Holy Spirit be with you all. As we prepare to celebrate the mystery of Christ's love, let us acknowledge our failures and ask the Lord for pardon and strength.'

It was the following Sunday. I was saying the opening words of the Mass, or rather stumbling over them. My voice was usually fluent and strong. Something was wrong with me. Perhaps I was coming down with something. The congregation had responded in the prescribed form. They were waiting for me. What was next? I looked for my place. Mustn't panic. There it was.

'May Almighty God have mercy on us, forgive us our sins, and bring us to life everlasting.'

No, the problem was not with me. It was out there in the congregation. For the first time since I had come to the parish, neither of them was there. My mother was on retreat. Bernadette had gone. We would never see or think about each other again, she had said. But since my visit, I had thought about nothing but her and the words she had spoken to me, words of which I could make no sense.

I looked again at the spaces where they should have been. My mother at the front, Bernadette at the back. What was it she had said? *Someone who stands triumphantly between us.*

I had somehow reached the stage at which I was to deliver the sermon. I entered the pulpit. Everybody sat down. I took out my notes and laid them in front of me. I looked out on the sea of strange faces. Why were they strange? The same people came every week. They were strange because I had never seen them before. I had seen only Bernadette and my mother. *Triumphantly between us.* I had thought her words were an irreverent reference to God, excusable because of her grief and bitterness. But what if she had meant someone in the congregation? But she had never met my mother. She did not even know her by sight.

I looked at my notes. They contained only jottings, to prompt my memory. Usually I knew well enough what I intended to say. This time the jottings meant nothing. They were random scribbles. I folded the papers up, and pushed them to the side. They slid on to the floor by my feet. I had a few parish announcements to make. I mumbled through them. At the end of the announcements would come the sermon I had prepared earlier in the week. The sermon which had now vanished for ever from my mind. The announcements were over. I looked up.

'Dearly beloved Brothers and Sisters in Christ. For once, the shoe is on the other foot. I have a confession to make to you. The sermon I had prepared for today has gone right out of my mind. My notes are no help to me. Some recent events have put other thoughts to the front of my mind, where they tumble about in confusion. Let me share my confusion with you. That, I am afraid, is the best I can do this morning.'

Many were now shuffling uneasily in their seats. They expected certainties, not confusion.

'I have been thinking recently about what we expect of our priests. We want them to appear worthy vessels for spiritual truths. So we dress them up. We call them Father. Ironic, that, isn't it? That's the one thing we are not allowed to be.' Someone tittered nervously.

'We expect them to look and sound the part. It is not difficult to define a bad priest. He is one who oversleeps and is late for Mass, who puts on the wrong

177

vestments, stumbles on the altar, drops the chalice, falls asleep in the confessional, delivers a sermon like this one. A good priest on the other hand gets all the rituals right, delivers a brilliantly organised sermon and spends the week visiting the parishioners who came to see him perform on Sunday, telling them what they already heard then.

'The other day, I met a priest from another parish. I want to tell you about him, in case you are becoming concerned about what a bad priest I am, based on my performance today. You see, he is really bad, in a different league from me. You are so lucky you have me, not him. I have my faults but I would never let you down the way he would. I have not seen him say Mass but I have an idea he is even worse at it than I am being today. He doesn't spend much time on pastoral visits. He devotes a lot of time to providing shelter for a group of people most of whom have never been near a church. What truly dreadful people they must be, living on the streets the way they do. Most of those people do not know or care if he is a priest. What a terrible influence they must be on him!

'I am in no such danger, you will be reassured to know. I have been trying to remember the last time I spoke to anyone I did not know to be a Catholic, or an intended one. Let me see. I met a bus conductor the other day, and it is possible he was not a Catholic. But don't worry, I only bought a ticket from him. And there was a young boy in a café, and the lady who served us tea. I spoke to both of them. She might have been one, though. She knew I was a priest, even though I had hidden my collar. But clearly I mustn't make a habit of this. I owe it to you all not to put myself in spiritual danger, with the risk that I might drag you down with me. In future I will check people out before going near them, in case they are not one of us. I will certainly not do what Christ did, and what Father Higgins does, go out among the sick, and the possessed, and the lame and the lepers, and not even ask them if they are Catholics. What a terrible example Christ set us. Luckily, we have learnt a lot since His day. Thanks be to God.'

I had seen her every day that week as usual, hadn't I? I always saw her home from school. It was the last week of term. Or did I? Try to remember, for Christ's sake! It was so long ago, over twenty years. No, I hadn't seen her. That week was different. It was on the Monday evening we had made love and I had proposed to her. After that she had kept out of my way. I understood why. She did not want to be distracted while she thought about my proposal. She needed to think about how she would turn me down. Would she do it by letter or word of mouth? Letter would be best. But what would she say in the letter? Long or short? Better keep it short. She would need to speak to people first. To her parents, and to Tom. She had no time to see me. So she sent me the letter and I never saw her again. Not until I first said Mass at St Jerome's, seven years afterwards.

I shuffled down the spiral steps leading from the pulpit. I heard the sounds of puzzled muttering. I gabbled through the rest of the Mass and hurried out to the sacristy. I had remembered something. I had thought nothing about it at the time. But if that was how it happened...I needed to know, for her sake as well as mine.

I told Father O' Malley I needed the car urgently to visit a sick parishioner. He shook his head.

'I wouldn't be in such a tearing hurry, Father. They'll still be ill when you get there, or they'll be dead. Just remember to say the right prayers depending

179

on whichever it is.'

He settled down to enjoy the cup of coffee Mrs Raferty had just brought him. Fido was on his lap.

I was outside her house again in twenty minutes. The For Sale sign had been replaced by one which read Sale Agreed. I rang the bell repeatedly. No reply. No sounds from within the house. The neighbours told me she had left the day before. She had a heavy suitcase. One of them had given her a lift to Lime Street Station. She had not left a forwarding address.

TWENTY-FOUR

My admission to the seminary was not as final as my mother appeared to think. They had only assessed me as potentially suited. My application needed to be endorsed by Father Ambrose and supported by the Archbishop.

I had a long series of private interviews with Father Ambrose. He talked and I listened. He spoke of the rich inner life of his soul. He had been lucky. He had always known he had a vocation from the time he had been able to understand the concept. He knew my path had been more uncertain. I had had more conflicts to overcome. He had watched me from the time I had come to him to be an altar boy. He had done more than that. He had watched over me and prayed for me. He had sensed an inner struggle in me. I had been torn between the worlds of the flesh and the soul, he said.

I wondered how he could have known. I had never confided in him about my personal life and feelings. I had always gone to him for Confession. But no word had yet passed my lips in the confessional box about the sins of mind and body which I had committed since meeting Bernadette.

Now it was different with me, he told me. God had calmed the turbulent waters in my breast. My heart was clear, my eyes focussed, my purpose settled. He was sure in his own heart God had called me and he knew I was sure.

He was right to sense that the struggle was over. My eyes had indeed been turned away from the world. What he could not see was that it was neither God nor myself who had wrought the change. A few simple words in one short letter had been enough, each of them a finger of ice pressing into my heart, holding it, freezing it. *I am sorry, Michael. I made a mistake*

*about my feelings. I do love Tom. I know that now. I
cannot marry you.* He had mistaken the death of my
heart and soul for a new inner calm of the spirit.

He wrote his report. My visit to the Archbishop's
palace and my five minute interview with him were a
formality. He was a small, kindly man, with the
distracted manner of someone who is always looking
for some important piece of paper he has just lost. I
had seen him at St Jerome's from time to time, for
special ceremonies such as Confirmation. Here in his
own office he seemed much more insignificant, as if he
had wandered into the building by mistake and could
not find his way out. He gave me tea and biscuits and
told me that I had a lot of hard work ahead of me. But I
had been luckier than most to have had Father Ambrose
as my mentor. Father Ambrose had prepared me well
and had assured him he would always be ready to
advise and assist me. He shook my hand and that was
that. It seemed that in that diocese the endorsement of
Father Ambrose was all that was needed to seal any
admission to seminary.

My mother did not come to see me off. She told me
she was not feeling well. Angela insisted on
accompanying me as far as Lime Street Station. When
we heard the honk of the taxi's horn outside in the
street, my mother rose and clasped me awkwardly in
her arms. It was an uncomfortable moment for both of
us. As far as I could remember she had never
embraced me before. Then she fixed her eyes on me.
There were tears in them, though I had never seen her
cry. She spoke in a trembling voice.

'Work hard, my son, and pray for God's help to be a
good and holy priest. It will be a long and difficult
road. But we will be praying for you. Father Ambrose
will say Mass for you next Sunday. He will tell the

congregation that you have gone to be a priest, and he will ask for their prayers. Write to me every week. And write to Father Ambrose as well. You will be free from temptations there. Free from the pernicious influences of this godless world. One day you will come back and face that world, but you will have the strength of God's armour about you. You will be an Apostle of Christ. Your grandmother would have been so proud of you. It was not God's will that she should live to see this day. But He spared her long enough to know that you had listened to His voice, and had put aside the temptations of other, siren voices. She died a happy death in that knowledge.'

The taxi honked again.

'Goodbye, Mother.'

I could find nothing else to say. I could have told her I was grateful for her help and encouragement. I could have told her I loved her and would miss her. But at that moment I did not have enough strength to lie. I felt sick. My legs were like jelly.

'Come on, Angie.'

I carried my bags to the taxi. The driver opened the boot and helped me to put the bags inside.

'Lime Street, isn't it, mate?' he asked, cheerfully.

'That's right. Two o' clock train to London.'

'Ah, London, eh? The great metrolopiss. Never been there meself. Me kid brother went down there for the cup final once. Couldn't understand a word anybody said. All foreign, he said. Asked this Japanese bloke the way to Wembley and he just smiled and took a photograph of him. Staying long, are you?'

'No. I'm not staying in London. I'm going on to college. In Surrey.'

'Yea, Surrey,' said Angela. 'Dead posh down there. He's going to be...'

'Shut up, Angie. Just get in, will you?'

I found a seat on the train, stowed my bags and went back on to the platform to say goodbye to Angela. She was crying.

'Mikey?'

'What is it, Angie?'

'You're a great big mutt, you know. You always were. And you've been mooning around for so long you've forgotten I'm here. But I have to say this. I'll miss you.'

'I'll miss you too, cheeky-face. And I'm sorry I've been preoccupied. I never forgot you were there. Of course I didn't. How could I forget my daft kid sister?'

'Mikey, I've been thinking. I want to be like you. Go away and become all dead holy. I know I can't be a priest. But I'm thinking of becoming a nun.'

'Don't be silly, Angie. You're much too young to be even thinking of anything like that. Anyway, what about your boyfriend? The one on the bus.'

'Gone off him. Last time I saw him, he didn't even look my way. Men are so fickle.'

'That's no reason to go away and be a nun. Just because somebody you've never even spoken to doesn't look your way for once.'

'I know it sounds silly.'

'Anyway, you'll meet lots more boys, and you'll forget all about becoming a nun.'

'Maybe. But you've got to admit. They do look nice, all dressed up in black and white like that. Like those mixed chocolate bars.'

The whistle was blowing. I hugged her.

'Take care, Angie. I'll write special letters for you. Every week. Don't let Mother see them.'

'She said I mustn't write to you. In case I distract you.'

'That's all right. But that doesn't stop me writing to you. And I know you'll be thinking of me. Don't cry, Angie. I'm not going away forever. It's not like prison. I'll be home for a break at Christmas. That's no time at all.'

She sobbed, turned away and ran off.

Father Ambrose had told me that I would soon find profound spiritual joy in my vocation, so long as I worked and prayed hard. I worked and prayed and waited. The joy did not come. I reminded myself that I was not training to be a priest to satisfy my own emotional needs.

The years passed. My visits home were tense and difficult times. My mother questioned me constantly about my progress, searching for evidence of any backsliding or loss of motivation. Angela had changed. She was not the sister I had known. She was silent and morose. Whenever I asked her what the matter was she said nothing and ran off upstairs to be alone. Sometimes I went up after her to see if she would confide in me in private. She still refused to talk. Mother ignored her and shook her head when I asked her what might be troubling her. She would only tell me that her school reports were very poor and the nuns were concerned about her behaviour in class. I suppose she's just going through a difficult phase, I suggested. Her response was as I expected. So like you to make excuses for her.

After my first three years I was away from home for much longer periods, attending courses and seminars at theology colleges during the summer. I had not seen my mother or Angela for over six months when I received a letter from my mother which made me gasp with surprise and disbelief. Angela had come through her difficult time, my mother wrote. She was now happy and serene. What was more, she was sure that she too had been called.

My first reaction was that Angela was having a joke at her expense, one I knew our mother would not appreciate when she realised it was a joke. She was still only sixteen, after all, far too young to decide she had a vocation. My mother had anticipated that reaction. She assured me Angela was completely serious. My mother had talked things over with Aunt Mary in Canada, who had offered to introduce Angela to the Order of the Sisters of Saint Bernard. Father Ambrose had let her use the presbytery telephone for the long and expensive phone calls. Angela had already left to stay with Aunt Mary, who had sent her her plane ticket. The validity of the ticket was limited and she could not delay her departure for me to return to see her off.

At the time the letter was posted, I was on a three-week pilgrimage to Lourdes. When I got back, Angela had already been in Canada for two weeks. Aunt Mary wrote to me soon afterwards. Angela could not write herself. The two of them had been for a walk along a forest trail near Whistler. Although it was spring there was still a lot of ice and snow around. Angela was running on ahead when she slipped and fell. She had fallen heavily on her wrist and sprained it. That was typical, I said to myself. How could she settle down to a contemplative life if she continued to run around like a mad thing? Those were my first thoughts.

Then I read the rest of my aunt's letter. Angela was attending a residential college run by the nuns for girls aged sixteen to eighteen. Some, though by no means all, of the students were potential postulants. In their spare time they would do work in the priory and the gardens and get to know something of the life led by the nuns. The Mother Superior took a close interest in the college and made it her business to get to know all the students. Once Angela was eighteen she would, if she was still sure of her vocation and if the Mother Superior agreed, begin a nine-month postulancy. If after that she was accepted, she could begin her novitiate. Aunt Mary told me of the transformation in her. She was in no doubt Angela was in a state of profound inner peace and joy. The Mother Superior had already noticed her and was convinced her vocation was real.

My heart ached to see her again. But there was no way in which I could afford to pay for a flight. My aunt had already spent so much on Angela's behalf and I could not bring myself to ask her to send me the money. I wrote back to my aunt to explain why I could not visit, and to ask her to get Angela to write to me as soon as she felt in a position to do so.

It was some months before the letter arrived. I noticed that the envelope was in my aunt's hand. So was the letter itself. She began by explaining that Angela had been waiting for her hand to heal but it was still painful for her to write. What followed would be Angela's words which Aunt Mary would write down for her. Angela had wonderful news. The Mother Superior had agreed that she could start her postulancy earlier than usual, as soon as she had reached her seventeenth birthday. That was only weeks away. She hoped I would understand if she told me that this would be her last letter to me as Angela. She begged me not to write to her. Not until she had been received. Not until she was no longer Angela Jones. Then I could write to her. Then I could visit her. By that time I would surely be a priest, God willing. How happy we would be when we met again, brother and sister, priest and nun.

I completed my studies, including a year at a seminary in Rome. To my mother's delight, the Archbishop agreed that my ordination could take place in my home parish church, where I had served for years as an altar boy under the kind but strict tutelage of Father Ambrose.

I then served as an assistant priest in several parishes around the country, alternating between rural and inner city areas. I deputised for other priests, often at very short notice. I felt restless. I sensed that I was learning a trade rather than following a calling. I was intensely lonely. I had no chance to settle anywhere and make friends. I did not want to keep in touch with my mother, though I wrote to her from time to time. I was afraid she would sense the lack of spiritual commitment in me. She would be disappointed and resentful, even angry. I would wait until I was finally blessed with the inner joy of my calling before I went to see her.

Then the news came at last, in a further letter from my aunt. From now on I had to forget about a sister called Angela. She had completed her novitiate. Her vocation had been confirmed and she had been received. She was now Sister Veronica, Bride of Christ.

I continued to move around the country, still profoundly unsettled both in my way of life and my emotional state. Part of me longed to see Angela. Her absence had left a void in my heart which I was now sure my vocation would never fill. But another part of me held back. It was the Angela I had grown up with, the one I had known up until the time I had gone away, that I missed so terribly. That Angela had gone forever. She had already gone by the time I returned for my holiday visits, to be replaced by the sulky teenager who would not even talk to me.

Now yet another Angela had taken the place of the sister I had known and loved. Sister Veronica. Her vows to Christ would only serve to magnify the distance which had started to grow between us, if I were honest with myself, from the moment I had boarded that train at Lime Street.

Of course her letter had not suggested any personal distance between us. She had written of our happiness when we would meet again, as brother and sister, priest and nun. But had she? It was Aunt Mary who had actually written the letter, because of Angela's accident. Were they really Angela's words? And if they were, did they represent her true thoughts and feelings? The style of the letter was one I would never have associated with the Angela I had known. Had my aunt written what she thought Angela intended to say, without understanding what was really in her heart and mind? Or was the accident itself an invention, to disguise the fact that she did not want to write to me at all, did not actually want to see me again? In which case, my aunt's letter was also an invention, designed to protect me from the pain of Angela's rejection until such time as she thought I could cope with the truth. She had sent me a letter purportedly coming from my sister, but had not offered to help me out with the costs of visiting her. I was sure she was acting from the kindest of motives. But I told myself I would have preferred to know the truth, however painful.

But why should Angela have chosen to distance herself from me? With the benefit of hindsight and a little more maturity on my part since my departure for seminary, I imagined I was beginning to understand. She had been only thirteen then, on the threshold of adolescence. At that age she could not possibly understand why I had gone away. She would be alone in the house with a mother who had never understood or appreciated her, and who would react to the troubles of her adolescence with even greater distance and disapproval. Maybe, despite all my inadequacies, she had looked up to me as a sort of substitute father. A desperately poor substitute, admittedly, but at least someone who would listen to her and not judge her. I imagined how hard those years must have been for her, years when I was no longer there for her, when I was selfishly absorbed in my own concerns.

Quite simply, in her eyes, I had abandoned her when she needed me most. She was entitled to resent me, even to hate me. I was relieved and delighted on her behalf that she had come through and found happiness in a way that had so far eluded me. If she were true to her vows, as I was sure she would be, she would have forgiven me. A Bride of Christ does not bear grudges. But I was deluding myself if I thought she would welcome me as if nothing had happened between us.

Whatever the real truth about her attitude to me, I knew I had to visit her as soon as I could. Even if she had forgiven me, I wanted to tell her that I now understood and was deeply sorry for having hurt her in any way. I had finally managed to save a little money. What I needed next was to obtain some leave of absence and that was proving difficult. The best I could hope for was a two-week period beginning the following summer, some six months hence. I would just need to be patient.

The next letter from my aunt, only a few weeks before my leave was due, was on black-edged paper. It took three weeks to reach me, forwarded from parish to parish. It contained the news that God had called Angela to Him a second time. The funeral had already taken place, in accordance with the rules of the Order.

They could not wait for me to be located and flown over. Now, when it was too late, my aunt finally sent me the money for my plane ticket.

I was given permission to bring forward and extend my leave. I spent three weeks in Canada, in my aunt's house. We mourned together. Sister Veronica had been buried in the priory churchyard. I visited her grave every day for a week, saying to her in death those words of regret I had not been given the time to say to her in life. The priory was indeed a place of deep tranquillity. I understood why my aunt and sister had both fallen in love with it. I sensed the presence of the Order on the other side of the churchyard wall, that company of nuns where she had spent her final, blessed years. Sometimes I heard their singing. I sensed no sadness among them, only acceptance.

The Mother Superior told me she had been profoundly happy in her short time as a nun. As for her death, she had not foreseen what was to happen and had had no consciousness of it. She had gone straight from an earthly to a heavenly paradise. I knew she deserved it. But I still felt a powerful resentment against God for taking her from me.

After the end of the three weeks I flew home to England, to the news that Father Ambrose had asked for me to return to St Jerome's to replace him in my first posting as a full parish priest. He was taking over a small parish in Formby. The Archbishop had agreed, so I was hardly in a position to object. When I arrived, I went straight round from the church to see my mother. I sensed mixed feelings in her. She was pleased that I was to be her new parish priest, not, I suspected, because she expected great things from me but because she could keep an eye on me. But her feelings of pleasure were more than outweighed by her

191

disappointment at the departure of Father Ambrose. Her only consolation was that he was still near enough for her to go to him for Confession. He had raised no objection to the arrangement, only expressing concern that the longer journeys would not tire her too much.

The first task I set myself when I took up my position was to conduct a memorial service for Angela. I thought it would help my mother to get over her grief. She had declined Aunt Mary's offer to pay the costs of her fare to Canada, saying that she could not start globe-trotting at her time of life. I understood that decision. But I was surprised when she opposed my plans for a service, saying that she had already grieved enough in her heart and that to grieve further would be to oppose God's will. I told her I intended to go ahead. She refused to attend. Only Father O'Malley, Father Ambrose, Father Coffey, Mrs Raferty, Sister Rose, who kept the altar clean and supplied with fresh flowers, and our organist Matthew were there. Mrs Raferty cried. So did I, after they had all left me alone in my study.

I had two fellow-priests at the time. Father O'Malley was forty-one and had already been there for fifteen years. Father Coffey was the senior priest, fifty-five, his reputation as a scholar of Church History already secure. He had known Father Ambrose since childhood, though the two men were amicable rather than close. They had been brought up together in the same orphanage. He had already started to wind down his parish duties to complete an important piece of research and to prepare Father O'Malley and myself for the time we would be on our own. He was absent for long periods and no longer heard confessions or made pastoral visits. He left two years after my arrival to take over a small rural parish in Derbyshire.

On his departure our establishment was reduced to

two priests, so we replaced Father Coffey with a dog called Tiddles. Tiddles was a dachshund, who liked nothing better than sleeping in front of the fire, who never came when called, and who hated going out for walks. When Tiddles died ten years later, we replaced him with Fido.

'Nice to have a real dog, at last,' said Father O'Malley, when we became acquainted with our new cat's behaviour patterns.

PART II

THE SEARCH FOR DORA

TWENTY-FIVE

After an hour of persistent telephoning Father O'Malley had drawn up a list of addresses where Dora might have taken shelter. There were only six. We split them between us.

Mine were all within walking distance. I set out briskly, after morning Mass. It was a bright, sharp, cold March morning. I walked through the parks along the sea front. Sheltered from the wind, I soon became warm. I took my coat off and put it over my arm. Tiny crocuses and frail early daffodils pushed their way nervously through the enriched soil of the flowerbeds, sniffing the salt sea breezes. They knew they had no right to grow there, so close to the estuary. Without the protection of a high brick wall on the seaward side, and the results of years of patient cultivation of the ground, there would have been nothing there but coarse grass in sand.

I was like them, I thought. With a wall blocking out my past and my feelings, I could flower as a priest, on the outside at least. But my wall had blown down. Dora, Bernadette and Father Higgins had done it between them.

Pull yourself together, Michael, I told myself. Stop being self-indulgent. You've got a real job to do. For once.

I reached the first address. It was a derelict hall. All the windows were smashed in. The words *Seamen's Mission* were still legible in flaking blue paint on a creaking notice board outside. I see the Council's information is right bang up to date, as usual, I said to myself.

I moved on to the second address. It was a bright,

modern single-storey building on the edge of a new housing estate. I could hear sounds of laughter and shouting as I approached the front door. I found the administrator's office to the left. The administrator was a well-built lady in her forties with a loud, horsy laugh. She was shuffling piles of paper around her desk, while conducting simultaneous conversations over the telephone and with a young girl in the room who seemed to be her assistant. When I peered in through the door she put down her papers and waved me inside and into a chair. She put the phone down and flashed me a smile which exuded energy and efficiency.

'Hello there, Father. It is Father isn't it? You are from the Catholic Church? I don't go myself and I can't tell who's who these days. We had a Church of England Minister here a few weeks ago and he wanted to be called Fred. It didn't seem right somehow. I much prefer Father.'

'Yes, Father is fine by me. I'm from St Jerome's. Father Jones.'

She turned the information over in her head for a moment, then darted towards me to shake hands, vigorously and painfully.

'Sandra, get Father Jones a cup of coffee. And one for me too.'

Sandra glared sullenly at both of us and disappeared.

'Well, what can we do for you, Father? Is this what I believe they call a pastoral visit? You'd certainly be welcome to come and talk to our residents here any time, though some of them can be a bit disconcerting at first. My name's Jean, by the way. Jean Mottershead.'

'Well, Jean, of course I'd be happy to talk to anybody here any time. But I'm actually looking for a particular person.'

'Name?'

'That's the problem. I'm not sure. Dora or Christine. We believe her real name is Christine, but she now goes by the name of Dora. She's been trying to contact me. I mean, she has been contacting me, by letter. The issues she raises are of course confidential and very sensitive. But it is very important I trace her and speak to her personally. I have been to a hostel where she used to live but she's left and nobody knows where she is now. All the information we have is that she is now somewhere in this parish.'

The coffee had arrived. I sipped it, gratefully.

'Hostel, you say. What sort of hostel?'

'For ex-psychiatric inpatients.'

'Condition?' Her directness was both reassuring and intimidating.

'She has suffered from amnesia, but that appears to have been the result of shock and the drugs she received. I will go so far as to tell you that she believes she was unlawfully detained. I can't go into the reasons.'

'No head injuries?'

'No. Not as far as I'm aware.'

'Description?'

'Short, slight build, blue-grey eyes. Not much to go on, I'm afraid.'

'Photograph?'

'Nothing. Sorry.'

'Age?'

'About thirty-five.'

'I don't think I can help you, Father. We are a specialist unit here. All our clients have suffered serious head injuries. We try to provide some form of community care. We're a halfway house between hospital and the outside world. We have several women, but none fits what you have told me. They are mostly much younger, for a start. It is the young who are particularly prone to accidents which give rise to head injuries. I'll show you round, if you like. You can meet some of them. One other thing. Where was she detained?'

'Ridgeway Park.'

She looked up with a sharp movement of her head that took me by surprise.

'The place that was closed down a few years ago?'

'That's right.'

'Then maybe I can help you. We have someone who was there. He's about the same age. He may remember her.'

I followed her out of the office. At the end of a corridor was a large, open space like a gym, but furnished with several soft cushions and beanbags on which clients reclined.

'Problems with head injuries can vary enormously,' she told me in a ringing voice, without breaking her stride. 'Some of our clients have severe behavioural difficulties. They are profoundly anti-social. Others have problems with mobility and balance. It depends on what part of the brain has been damaged. Oh, this is Jim. The one I was telling you about. Jim, this is Father Jones.'

Jim was lying on one of the beanbags. He was very thin. His limbs seemed uncoordinated. He pointed at my collar.

'Priest,' he said. 'I know about priest. Used to go to church.' His speech was slurred.

'Did you, Jim?' I asked. 'Which church?'

'Don't know. Catholic Church.'

'St Jerome's? Just up the road? That's where I'm from.'

'Don't know. Can't go now. Can't sit still.'

He offered me a shaking hand. I took it. He could not grip properly.

'Jim,' said Jean. 'Father Jones is looking for someone who was in Ridgeway Park. A woman, about your age. Name of Dora, or Christine.'

He frowned. 'Dora. I knew a Dora. Not Christine, though. Nobody of that name. I was in there because of what I done. They sent me to Hell.'

I bent down. 'Sorry, Jim,' I whispered. 'I didn't catch that. Where did they send you?'

'Where you go when you do wrong. To Hell. You know. That's what I thought. But it can't have been. They closed it down. So I came here. Nice here. Like it here. So it wasn't Hell. Must have been that other place. Purgatory. That's it.'

'Why Hell, Jim? What made you say that?'

'Lost souls, Father. Empty, staring eyes. Shuffling feet. Screaming voices. Nobody listening. If that's not Hell, what is?'

'Jim, I'm sorry to revive bad memories. But I have to ask you. Tell me what you remember about Dora.'

'She helped out in our ward. At first I thought she was one of the staff. But she couldn't have been because the staff didn't care about us. She did. So I asked her if she came from outside. You know...'

'A volunteer, you mean?'

'Yes. But she said she was a patient, like me. She said she was going to go home soon. When they found out where her home was. She couldn't remember. I don't think they ever did find out. So she had nowhere to go.'

'Was she your age, Jim? Smallish, blue-grey eyes?'

'My age. Yes. Can't remember what she looked like.'

'Jim, have you seen her since you left there? Try to remember. It could be very important.'

'Never saw her again.' His head slumped forward. His eyes closed.

201

'Thank you, Jim. You've been a great help. It was nice to meet you.'

He did not respond.

'What happened to him?' I asked as we retraced our steps to her office.

'Familiar story. He had a motorbike, when he was nineteen. Saved up for it for years. Saturday jobs. Paper rounds. First time he was out on it. Not wearing a crash helmet. His behaviour changed. He became violent. Attacked several people, including his own doctor. The courts committed him to a secure psychiatric unit.'

'Ridgeway Park.'

'That's right. He was referred here when it closed down, because his family come from round here. We're not secure in this building but he's no longer subject to the detention order. His moods are well under control. He has problems of co-ordination, as you can see. But I think he could easily live at home now.'

'Will he be all right? I'm afraid I've brought back some distressing memories.'

'He'll be fine. I would have stopped you if I thought you were harming him. I sometimes try to get him to talk about those times myself because I believe it does him good. He still has nightmares about them but less and less these days.'

'I suppose his parents have died.'

'Oh no. They live two streets away. They disowned him. After the attack on the doctor. They know where he is but they never even come to visit.'

'I don't suppose you could give me their name and address?'

She looked at me very severely.

'I'm afraid not. That information is strictly confidential. I feel I have told you too much already.'

The third address was the basement to a large house in one of the most respectable streets in the parish. Another mistake by the Council, I thought. I rang the bell. I still had my coat over my arm. A small, bearded man in jeans and open neck brown check shirt and wearing spectacles opened the door. His mouth opened. He looked nervously up the street, then grabbed me by the arm and pulled me inside.

'Get in here, quick, Father, before she sees you,' he whispered. Then he turned his head towards the dark interior and called out loudly.

'Which one of you bloody idiots called for the bloody priest? I told you he was over the worst. We don't need the bloody last rites for him. She could be here any second. If she sees him there'll be blue murder. It'll be hard enough as it is to convince her he's not dying. Quick, Father, in here.'

He pushed me through a door to the right of a hallway. There were several shabby armchairs and a settee, taking up between them most of the floor space. A small black and white television stood in one corner, showing flickering images of a cookery programme. A wire coat hanger served as an aerial. Three teenage boys watched it listlessly.

'Wait in here, Father. Oh Christ, she's here.'

The street-door slammed. A strident woman's voice cut through the shadows in the hallway.

'What's that bloody priest doing here? You told me he'd be all right. I'm telling you, Brendan Adams, if my boy's dying I'll murder him. Then I'll murder you. I never knew he was into all that stuff. You just said it was an overdose, and the hospital was sending him here to rehabilitate, whatever that means. So if he's rehabilitating, what's the priest doing here? I want to see him rehabilitating. Now. This instant. Now, where is he? The priest, I mean. If I find him, I'll murder him too.'

One of the boys watching television suddenly came to life.

'Here you are, Father. Through here. Get the collar off and get this on.'

He pushed me into a tiny, filthy kitchen. I obeyed. A primitive instinct for survival had taken over. I removed my collar, and put on the grey overall he handed me. It was much too large for me. I buttoned it at the top to cover my black shirt.

'Catch this.'

He handed me a large, rusty spanner. I stared at him in bewilderment.

'The boiler, over there!' he hissed. He was losing patience. 'Pretend to be fixing it, you dummy. Don't worry. You won't hurt yourself. It hasn't done anything but rattle for weeks.'

Wondering when I would wake up, I turned to the boiler and started to bang on the rusty exterior with the spanner.

'Not like that!' whispered my saviour. 'You'll bring it off the wall. You've got to be gentle with it. Try to look scientific about it.'

'Right, thank you. I'll try.'

I gently prodded some screws with the edge of the spanner, and assumed the air of a puzzled diagnostician. Voices from the corridor filtered through my fuddled senses.

'Of course he'll be all right, Mrs Foster. The hospital said so. You can come through and see him. We never sent for a priest. You must have seen the funeral director going to the upstairs flat. Mrs Jenkins passed away yesterday.'

'Do I look like I'm eleven pence halfpenny short of a shilling? Do you think I don't know a priest from a funeral director? And if he was going upstairs, what was it I saw coming through this door and through that door there? A Scotch mist?'

While continuing to tap with my spanner, I looked furtively round. My rescuer had gone through into the room and was making signals toward the bearded man in the corridor.

'He's through here, Mr Adams. The boiler chap. Says it'll need new parts. Going to be expensive. Isn't that right, mate?'

I realised that the last few words were addressed to me.

'Er yes, absolutely, this is a really difficult one. New parts, definitely.'

A large black shape loomed in the doorway to the hall.

'Don't sound like a boiler chap to me. Never heard a boiler chap use long words like that. Sounds more like a bloody priest to me.'

I wiped my hand against the side of the boiler. Dirt and grease came off it. I transferred some of it to my face. I turned round and came into the room, facing my accuser.

'There you are, Mrs Foster,' said Brendan. 'The boiler chap. I'd forgotten he was due here as well. I never saw him come in. Fred here let him in.'

'At exactly the same time as the funeral director arrived for upstairs?'

'Looks like it. Life is full of coincidences, isn't it? What's the problem, exactly?' He was speaking to me. There was a wicked gleam in his eye.

'Problem? Er, difficult to say. Looks like something wrong with the...the flue.'

'The flue?'

'Yes. Should have a spare back at the office, I mean the shop. I'll go and get one now.'

'Where's your van?' barked the black shape, still filling the doorway.

'Van? Oh, my colleague... my mate, he's got it. Urgent job over in Bootle. We're within walking distance from here, so I didn't need it.'

'Mrs Foster, we should go through and see Bill,' said Brendan. 'That is why you came.'

'Right. Yes.'

She eased herself back reluctantly, allowing a few shafts of sunlight from the still open main door to squeeze past her into the room. Then she was gone. Brendan had escorted her down the hall. I slumped into Fred's chair, while he listened at the door. Then I heard her raised voice again.

'What the hell have you been doing, son? I told you about messing with those drugs. Your dad'll beat the living daylights out of you when he hears. Come on. Get your things. You're coming home with me, now.'

'Mrs Foster, I don't think that's a good idea. He's been sent here for rehabilitation.'

'You and your bloody rehabilitation. Well, get on with it. How long will it take? All right, you've got ten minutes.'

'Mrs Foster, it could take weeks or months. Bill has a serious addiction problem. He needs care and treatment. The doctor will come in to see him regularly. He'll use other drugs to wean him off the dangerous ones.'

'Weeks! Months! Bloody hell. You said it was just an overdose.'

'That was the critical point, yes. Mrs Foster, he could have died. If you take him away now, without proper aftercare, he could still die.'

The voices became quiet. I could no longer hear what they were saying. Fred signalled for me to return to the kitchen. I heard her shuffle towards the front door. She was crying now.

'Thank you, Brendan. God bless you. Look after him. I'll come and see him next week. Sorry I was a bit...You see, that boy's my world, and the thought...'

'It's all right, Mrs Foster. We'll do our best for him. Goodbye now.'

The door closed. He came into the room, sighing, his face in his hands. I stood up. 'Hello, Brendan.'

His eyes widened. 'Jonesy? Is it really you?'

'Yes, it's definitely me. Despite appearances.'

He grinned. 'Christ, you do look a sight.'

'Thank you for saving my life. And thank you, Fred. Very quick thinking. She wasn't really convinced, though, was she?'

'No, I don't think so. But we bought ourselves some time. I think you'd better get cleaned up, Father. Out here.'

He showed me into a grimy bathroom. I washed in the cold water from the only tap which worked. I returned to the room with the television. Fred had sunk back into his chair and into the torpor in which I had first seen him, and in which his two companions had remained throughout. He ignored us. It was hard to believe that he had so recently galvanised himself into action on my behalf. Brendan and I found some cushions in the corner near the window and sat down. He handed me my collar, which Fred had evidently hidden during the crisis and then returned to him.

'Bill will be all right for a while. The doctor gave him something to calm him down. I don't think he even recognised his mother. Just as well.'

'I think you have the patience of a saint, Brendan.'

'I wish I had. I just have to remind myself sometimes that when people get angry, it's because they're scared and they're blaming themselves. Anyway, how are you? I heard you had gone to be a priest. I wasn't surprised. No idea you were in this parish. I don't go to church any more, I'm afraid. What brings you here? We've never had a pastoral visit before.'

'This isn't actually a pastoral visit. I'm looking for someone who might have moved into cheap accommodation in this area. A woman in her thirties. Goes by the name of Dora. Real name might be Christine. Ex-psychiatric patient.'

'We have some of those from time to time, but all our clients are men at the moment. What did they tell you about us at the Council?'

'Nothing. Yours is just one of the addresses they gave us for places where someone coming into the area with no money might stay.'

'Well, you've seen what we do, only it's not usually as dramatic as that. We're part of a joint local and health authority programme. For registered addicts. Mostly heroin. Fred and the others here are on methadone. The doctor comes in every day from the clinic. I'm not sure what we're going to do when we close down here.'

'Close down?'

'Yes. This is my place. People in the ground floor flat complained. Said there was too much noise. Usually there's no noise at all here. The truth is they don't like the look of them, coming and going. The Council have promised to find us somewhere more suitable.'

'How did you get into this, Brendan? You were always so ambitious.'

'I was. Went into management consultancy after university. Pat and I bought this house. We got married when we were both twenty-two. We had one son, Peter. We were well off. Sent him to a private school. He was a good lad. Nice and steady. Until

208

someone introduced him to heroin. He died two years ago. Sixteen. One of his friends was hooked too. George. He moved in with us. He pulled through, eventually. Pat and I got divorced. Our marriage had broken up under the strain. She moved back to London, where she came from. I had given up my job to look after Peter, and then George. Couldn't afford to keep this house, so I sold it and rented back the basement. George moved out, but others came along. I applied for funding. That's how it started. So how's priesting?'

'I'm not sure. I've been a priest for fifteen years and I still haven't found out what I'm really supposed to be doing. I go through the motions well enough, most of the time. But we can't have done much of a job if we didn't even know you were here. The funny thing is that I'm sure I know this address.'

'I'm sure you do. The couple on the ground floor. They own the house and want us out. They're your parishioners. Go to church every Sunday without fail. Then they come home and write letters of complaint about us. They say they're not against what I'm doing. They just want me to go and do it somewhere else.'

'I remember them now. Mr and Mrs Munro. I think I might just be paying them a pastoral visit soon. How long have you got before you have to move?'

'Oh, I'm not moving until there's somewhere to go. I didn't ask to come here and I haven't anything like enough space. They seem to think I came here just to annoy them. Will you stay for a cup of tea, Father? We've a kettle somewhere and it sometimes works.'

'Call me Michael, please. We were at school together. No, thanks, I'd better get on. You know, I've been visiting around this parish for fifteen years. I feel as if I'm just getting to know the place for the first time. Oh, by the way, you heard that Tom Kavanagh died? Heart attack.'

'No, I didn't. Poor Bernadette. I always knew those two would get married. Though he was always talking about chucking her. Truth was, he couldn't live without her.'

I looked up at him, feeling my face redden. His expression was open and honest. There was no hidden meaning in his words, no unspoken question. He hadn't known. Neither had Tom. Nor anybody else. I stood up and we shook hands. 'Well, goodbye, Brendan. Been good to see you. I'll call again if I may. Maybe get to know your clients a bit more.'

'You'd be welcome any time. They're all good lads, really. And you've seen what Fred can do when he's fired up. Which is not very often.'

'Oh, and if you get a woman here in her thirties, short, slim build, blue-grey eyes, greying hair, it could be the one I'm looking for. Could you give me a ring? Don't tell her anything. I'll just come down and see her. Have a chat.'

'What's she done? Stolen the chalice?'

'No. I'd say she was more sinned against than sinning.'

'Bloody hell. What's that from?'

'*King Lear*, wasn't it?'

'Yes, something like that. I was never very good at English Lit.'

At the door, he called after me.

'Oh, Michael. About the boiler.'

'Yes?'

'Don't give up the day job.'

I walked down the street, mumbling a prayer.

And then the cock crew. I remember the story so well. I preach about it every Easter. How Peter denied You thrice. But I didn't deny You, Lord. Only my priesthood. And it wasn't for me. It was to spare her feelings. Oh, come on. Who am I kidding? No, Lord. You're right. I did deny You, and not to spare her. I have never faced hostility before, just for being a priest. I failed Your test miserably. This is not the stuff of which martyrs are made, Thomas More is supposed to have said of himself. He was wrong. But this is the stuff of which cowards are made, and that is Your own truth. Forgive me, Lord.

On my return, Father O'Malley was still out. I had just sat down to recover from my escape from Mrs Foster when the phone rang.

'Father Jones? Father Higgins here.'

'Hello there. Any news?'

'No, I'm afraid I still haven't seen her and nobody else has either. Listen, I had a thought. I'm sorry I was a bit sharp with you the other night. Got on my moral high horse a bit. I wondered if you would like to come and spend a morning down at the hostel and get to meet some of our clients. There's always a chance she might turn up. If she does, I'll take her to one side and talk to her while you keep an eye on the rest of the show.'

'Yes, I'd be delighted.'

'Tomorrow morning suit you?'

'Fine.'

'Remember, don't bring the car. Come the way you did last time. It's reasonably safe during the day. And come as plain Mr Jones. Don't put the glad rags on. Remember to call me John.'

Father O'Malley returned an hour later.

'Any luck?' I asked.

'Not a sausage,' he sighed, slumping into his armchair. 'One of the addresses didn't exist, though the Council assured me that they are funding it. I wonder where that money is going. Another was a day centre for old dears. Run by a terrifying middle-age lady called Hazel something. Think of it. All the saints in heaven and...'

'I know, it's a bloody nut they call her after.'

'Very good, Michael. I'll soon be able to hand over everything to you, even the jokes. I had four cups of tea before they let me go. And only then after I'd promised to come and talk to them next week. I told them you would go instead. You're better than I am at that sort of thing.'

'You never did!'

'All right, I didn't. But I thought about it. I'll go myself. The other place was a youth centre. For sixteen to nineteen year olds. Only three lads there, kicking a football about this concrete yard. I think they were the staff. What about you?'

'One was closed, one was a hostel for drug addicts, run by an old school pal of mine. I ended up pretending to fix their boiler. Don't ask. Do you know what a flue is?'

'Haven't a clue.'

'No, neither have I. No trace of Dora. I thought I had struck lucky with the third place. Chap there had been in the same hospital and he remembered her. Or it could have been her. Same name.'

'Christine?'

'No, Dora. He seemed to recognise the description. But he hasn't seen her since they closed the place down. I'm going to go back to those places from time to time. I feel so ashamed we never knew they were there. There's also some of our parishioners who should feel ashamed. How little we know about them, all those faces staring piously towards the altar. One has been complaining to the Council to get the drug addicts out of the basement because their presence upsets her. Oh, Father Higgins rang. He hasn't seen Dora, either. He's showing me round his hostel tomorrow.'

'Would you be sitting down for a moment, Father? I wanted to have a few serious words with you.'

I could tell from the change in the tone of his voice that I was in trouble. I sat down opposite him.

'I did a few pastoral visits as well this morning. Just what exactly have you been doing to upset the parishioners? Nobody wants to talk about anything but your sermon last Sunday. Mrs Johnson is going to complain to the Archbishop, so she says. Mr Johnson said it was the best sermon he had ever heard. They were still rowing about it when I left.'

'Well, that's half for and half against. Not too bad.'

'You're missing the point, Michael, if I can respectfully explain something which may not have occurred to you. The sermon is the point in the Mass when people sit back and relax. Have a little nap, maybe. I pride myself on how many of them I can send to sleep within one minute. I got to five last week. They're not supposed to be even listening, never mind remembering it days later and arguing about it. Next thing is, they'll be listening to mine. Waiting for me to say something interesting they can argue about. And for the first time in all these years, they'll realise what a load of inconsequential drivel I've been spouting. And some might even realise that it's the same drivel I spout every week. All I do is change the order of some of the sentences. It's too late for me to start to become a preacher. But that's the sort of pressure you're putting me under now.'

'I'm sorry, Father. I really didn't intend to put anybody out. It's just that I had made my notes as usual, and I couldn't make any sense of them. I couldn't remember what I had intended to say. So I just made something up, on the spot. I've no idea what I actually said.'

'Well, Mrs Johnson said it was pure subversion and sedition. Said you wanted us to go out and be nice to non-Catholics. Or that's what she thought you said. Now that is going a bit far, Michael. I've never had any objection to Christian unity now. So long as people see the error of their ways and come to join our flock.'

'I'll try not to do it again. Perhaps you could lend me your standard sermon for next time, and I'll just read it out. I'll change the order of sentences, of course.'

The phone rang again later that evening.

'Michael? It's Brendan here. No news about the woman, I'm afraid. I just wanted to ring and thank you for intervening with Mrs Munro. She came down this afternoon to apologise for complaining about me. Said she'd written to the Council to cancel her complaint. She even asked if she could do anything to help. I've got her out the back now, making tea for them. You must have given her a right bollocking.'

'I wish I could say that I had. But the truth is that I still haven't seen her. I had put her on the list for a visit later this week.'

'Sounds like a true miracle then.'

'I don't think so. I gave a sort of improvised sermon last Sunday, for which I think I am shortly to be defrocked. Perhaps she took it to heart.'

'Well, that's as may be. But I know her, and I say it's a miracle. Thanks anyway. Keep in touch.'

I put the phone down, with a smile. I wondered if I would next hear from the lady at the head injuries centre, asking me how I had managed to locate Jim's parents and persuade them to come round and see him.

Then I shook my head. God had wrought enough miracles in the Parish of St Jerome's for one day.

TWENTY-SIX

I arrived at the hostel at ten o' clock. Tim answered the door. He gave no indication that he recognised me. I stepped into a large unfurnished room. It was draughty and damp, with peeling plaster and wallpaper. There were about fifteen people in the room. Most were watching a group of youngsters attempting to redecorate one corner with wallpaper. The wall was too damp to hold the paper, and it peeled down as soon as it was in place. They laughed and got in each other's way. A large tortoiseshell cat fed noisily at a green bowl in the corner. I walked over and stroked the back of her neck. She ignored me and continued to feed.

'Hello, there.'

John came briskly through the door. Loud greetings met him from several parts of the room. He came up and shook hands with me.

'Is anybody getting you a cup of tea? Tim. Cup of tea for our visitor.'

He turned to me. 'That could take some time. Tim is easily distracted. We can get some from Vera in the next room if it hasn't emerged soon. She has tea on the go all the time. I see you've met Lucinda. Hostel cat. All the helpers and most of the clients bring food in for her. She lives in cat heaven. Life for her is one long dinner. Let's have a look round. We can start in the office. What's your first name, by the way?'

'Michael.'

'Pleased to meet you, Michael, in less desperate circumstances than when we last met.'

The office was not a separate room but a desk and telephone near the door. Papers lay scattered over the desk. Behind it was a row of hooks for keys, with a label beneath each one. He pointed to an empty hook.

'That's for the car key. As you see, it's not there.

And neither is the car. Dora was the last person to have it. There's a spare front door key missing as well. So, as you can imagine, I'm rather anxious to find her myself. I'll have a few sharp words to say to her. Anyway, this is the office. Rather better organised than the presb...sorry, the bungalow. We have a unified filing system covering both premises. If it's not here, it's at the bungalow. If it's not there, it's here. If it's in neither place, God knows where it is. Simple, isn't it?'

I turned over some of the papers. There were brown foolscap envelopes with scuffed edges. Red felt-tip pens. An old Olivetti typewriter. Crumpled sheets of plain paper. I looked at him.

'It was here,' I said. 'She typed the letters here. At this desk. With Lucinda for company.'

'Probably did it when she was on night duty. Only time there's any peace here, and not often then. Shall we look round?'

'Yes, of course.'

'One of our helpers is leading a decorating task force. That's it, over there. I never interfere, unless someone is in actual physical danger. You know, wobbling on top of the ladder. They learn to do things for themselves. If they get frustrated, they shout and scream and throw things. Sometimes I throw them back.'

We walked through a door to a smaller, quieter room. The walls had been haphazardly painted in various shades of green. An elderly, smiling lady in a huge grey cardigan and brown ankle-length skirt was pouring out tea from an urn. Several other ladies were standing nearby, waiting to take their cups back to their armchairs, from which padding leaked and springs protruded.

'This is Vera,' said John, indicating the tea-lady. 'Any chance of one for Michael here? He's come to visit. And for me.'

'Yea, no problem, luv. Sit down.'

The chairs remained understandably empty. The ladies who had been served with tea preferred to stand near them and lean on them.

'It's all right, Vera. We'll stand here and chat. Vera, tell Michael about what happened to you.'

'To me? Well, I was in that big place, before they closed it down. I wasn't really crazy or anything like that. Just had this thing about counting everything. Didn't dare open a can of baked beans. Drove my old man mad. He never got his tea, but I could tell him exactly how many spoons we had. I don't mean drove him mad in the sense that he needed to go there as well. No point taking both of us, was there? Just imagine. Him on the ward, having a quiet fag, and me running in to him, saying, "Hey, George, I've just been down to the kitchens and they've got five hundred and thirty-two spoons. I'm just going back there now to count the forks." They'd have discharged him, just to give him a chance to get his sanity back.'

'Vera, did you know Dora there?' I asked.

'Oh yea, nice kid. She should never have been in there. Couldn't find anything wrong with her, apart from her memory, and I'm sure that was the pills they gave her. She couldn't remember how she came to be there. But they couldn't find her family, so they couldn't send her home. More tea, luv?'

She was busy with her next customer. I turned to where John had been standing. He had disappeared. Perhaps there was an emergency with the ladder next door. I took my tea to a corner of the room where a couple of small wooden chairs looked safe enough to sit on. I put my tea on the floor, and tested one of the chairs with my hand. I sat down, carefully. The ladies chatted quietly among themselves. They seemed to have forgotten my presence. Then I noticed that Tim had slipped into the chair beside me. He was holding two polystyrene cups, each containing a steaming liquid.

'Got your tea, at last, Father. Sorry about the delay. Went over the road for them. Vera doesn't make it strong enough for me. Then I remembered that was where I had met you. The café over the road.'

'That's right, Tim. Clever of you. You're Dora's friend, aren't you? The one who delivers messages for her. You haven't any more for me, have you?'

'No. Sorry. I haven't seen her since the day she gave me the last one. We all miss her. Place isn't the same without her. I miss the car as well.'

'Tim, you know when you came to deliver the messages...did she show you where to leave them, or did she just tell you the address?'

'Showed me. We were driving around in the car. She stopped outside your pad. Sorry, your church. She asked if I could get there by myself on the bus. I said, course I could. Then she told me she would give me some dosh if I left a letter there for her. Told me she couldn't trust it to the post. Only I mustn't be seen or heard. So I had to leave it on the doorstep, knock and then get the hell out of there. She gave me the first letter a few days later.'

'How did you come to live here, Tim? Don't you have any family?'

'Just me dad. He was always on the booze. Me mam died years ago. When I was sixteen, he threw me out. I had earned some money in a local garage, and he stole it for drink. I was swearing at him and calling him names. He tried to belt me but I got away. I was always too quick for him. I lived on the streets. Went down to the stations in the Centre. Lime Street, Central, Exchange. Begged off the people coming into work and going home again. Even turned tricks sometimes.'

'You mean, people paid you for sex?'

'That's right. I didn't like doing that. Then one night this guy picked me up and paid me, but he said he wasn't interested in sex. He wanted to help me. Said I could get a job if I could find somewhere to kip down. A proper address, like. He told me about this place. He'd lived here himself. He brought me down here. I didn't like it at first. But John and Dora looked after me. Got me signed up for these classes, doing metalwork, car maintenance and the like. I want to be a car mechanic. I do the repairs to the car when it goes wrong.'

'Tim, does Dora have anywhere special to go, apart from here? When the two of you were driving around, did she stop anywhere and talk about memories she might have of the place?'

'There was a house somewhere. She stopped near it. Looked at it for a few minutes. It wasn't anything special. Ordinary street. Ordinary house. A woman came out. Quite old. Dora stared at her. But she never got out of the car. When the woman had gone, we just drove off. She never said anything about it.'

'Could you find that street again?'

'Not sure. Like I said. There was nothing there to remember. It wasn't very far from your church. Couldn't say how far, though. We'd been driving round and round in circles. Like she was looking for it.'

At that moment, John came rushing back into the room.

'Sorry, Michael. Got called to the phone. I see Tim's been looking after you.'

He sat down in the chair which Tim had vacated as quickly as he had left the café on the evening we had first met. I suspected that his life with his father had taught him the value of a quick and inconspicuous exit. I had a sudden thought.

'John, I wonder if I could borrow Tim for the afternoon. Take him for a drive. He might see something to remind him where he went with Dora. That might help lead us to her.'

'Sure. If you can find him. He can be a bit slippery at times. Vera, did you see where Tim went?'

'I think he went next door to help out with the decorating.'

John and I followed her directions. Tim was pretending to hold the ladder, but was actually shaking it so that wallpaper paste was slopping onto the floor. A young boy on top of the ladder protested noisily. I thought I might be doing John a favour if I took Tim away for a while.

'Tim,' I called out. 'Like to come down to Seaport? We've got a car just like the one here. I'd like to take you for a drive. Then if it goes wrong, you can fix it.'

He gave the ladder a final push which almost toppled it and ran over.

'Will you give us ten bob as well, like she does?'

'Sure. Let's go.'

We took the bus back to Seaport, where I picked up the parish mini. I drove along the main road to the border of St Monica's parish.

'Tell me more about the street where you went with Dora, Tim. Where you stopped. What were the houses like? Were they joined together, or set apart from each other?'

'You mean terraced? Why don't you say so?'

'Sorry. Yes, Tim. I meant terraced.'

'Yes, they were. Very small front gardens. And back to back, with the back jigger in between.'

221

'Jigger?'

'You're not very good with words, are you, Father? Space between the backs of the houses where you can play footy.'

'Yes, I know what you mean. I grew up in a house like that.'

'So did I. Off Scotty Road. They knocked it down.'

We had just passed St Monica's.

'Did you come this way with her? Did you pass that church?'

'No. Don't remember coming here.'

'Never mind. We'll try the streets between here and the beach.'

There were several streets of the sort he had described in the immediate vicinity of the church. Further away, however, in the Blundellsands sector of the parish, the houses suddenly became much more spacious and exclusive. Some had been turned into private schools or nursing homes. There would be no point going there. We drove up and down the terraced streets. Tim shook his head each time. We turned back into the road which led past St Monica's. Suddenly, he twisted round in his seat.

'It's there behind us, Father! The car from the hostel.'

I looked in the mirror. There was a double-decker bus immediately behind me. Behind the bus was a large red Ford hovering as if trying to overtake it.

'Are you sure, Tim? I can't see anything.'

'Course I'm sure. I'd know that car anywhere. Turn off here and see what it does.'

I indicated right and moved into position. The bus and the Ford moved past on the inside. I could see no other minis. I turned into the side road. It was a dead end. After three hundred yards, it ran into the sands. I pulled to a halt. The parks were on my left. The beach lay ahead. A small dredger moved sluggishly towards the open sea. The Welsh hills lined the horizon. There was nothing behind me.

We waited for five minutes. No other cars came near. A few elderly men shuffled onto the sand, some walking large dogs.

I drove him back to the hostel, remembering to give him his fifty pence. After he had scrambled out, he turned back and told me to open the bonnet. I did so. He fiddled around inside for a few minutes, then shut it. He put his now oil-smeared face through my window and grinned.

'The tuning was a bit off. It'll be better now.'

I gave him a pound. Driving home, I could notice no difference in the engine sound or performance. He has a great career as a mechanic ahead of him, I thought.

TWENTY-SEVEN

'So she seems to have disappeared?'

'Yes, Father.'

I had gone back to the nursing home to see Father Ambrose. I had told him everything I had discovered about Dora.

'She left another letter, saying she had moved into my parish and knew how to find her. Her aunt, I presume that is. That was last week. We've searched hostels in the area but there's no sign of her. There's no trace of the former priest, either.'

'Do not be too concerned, my boy. You have done what you can. She will come to see you if God wills it. If not, there is nothing more you can do. Just keep your eyes and ears open. I haven't seen your mother here for a while.'

His speech was noticeably more slurred than on my previous visit.

'No. She's on retreat.'

'On retreat still? She told me she was going, of course. You haven't heard from her?'

'Not yet. She said she might go for a few weeks.'

'When time is spent in prayer and contemplation it can no longer be counted in human terms. A day, a week, a month is nothing there. It is a truly blessed place. I know it well. I am sure she is happy there. Do not be anxious for her. Do not disturb her or press her to return. Let her be. She will return when she is ready. I need to sleep now. Come to see me again soon, my boy.'

'I will, Father. Goodbye.'

TWENTY-EIGHT

'Nice car out the front, Father,' said Mrs Raferty. 'I don't recognise that priest getting out. Are you expecting anyone?'

'No, I'm not. Is Father O'Malley in?'

'No. Went out half an hour ago.'

A small, dapper figure was walking briskly up the path. I saw a flash of purple.

'Priest? That's no ordinary priest, Mrs Raferty. It's the bloody Monsignor!'

'Father Jones, I sometimes think your language is getting as bad as Father O'Malley's.'

'Put the kettle on, Mrs Raferty. And get out the best china cups.'

She disappeared into the kitchen. The doorbell rang. I checked in the hall mirror that my collar was not crooked, brushed the dust off my jacket with the clothes brush we always kept by the door and opened it.

'Father Jones, isn't it? Monsignor Winstanley. From the secretariat. At the palace. Archbishop's office.'

A limp, damp hand was extended in my direction. I touched it. It slipped back into his ample sleeve.

'Well, what a nice surprise, Monsignor. Won't you come in?'

'Er...actually, I wondered if...Father O'Malley is out, I take it?'

'Yes. Was he the one you wanted to see? If we had known...'

'No. Actually. It was you I wanted to see. I wonder...I've been indoors all day, and then in the car. You have good sea air here, don't you? And some nice parks down the front. Could we walk a little? There's no rain forecast, though I appreciate it's not very warm.'

'Here, Monsignor, it is never very warm. Fortunately, it is never really cold either.'

He frowned, as if searching his mind for a theological parallel to be drawn from the observation. He gave up, with a shake of his head.

'I'll get my coat.'

I shouted to Mrs Raferty to cancel the tea, and returned to the door. He had disappeared. I found him at the end of the pathway, shuffling from one foot to the other.

'I'll leave the car here if that's all right.'

I looked at the black Mercedes with leather upholstery.

'It is rather grand, isn't it?' he said apologetically, following my eyes and my thoughts. 'We use it for Arch's visits to the more salubrious parts of the diocese. Today, he's gone somewhere where something a little less ostentatious is appropriate.'

I wondered what the local youths would make of the car in the unlikely event that it made an appearance outside Father Higgins' hostel. Or rather, how long they would take to strip it down and sell the parts.

We walked down to the parks briskly and in silence. He had a wide, greasy smile which never left his face. His hands fluttered by his side. We reached the first of the parks. The breeze stiffened appreciably. We had the park to ourselves. His pace slowed. I slowed mine to match his.

'Father Jones, we hear nothing but good reports from this parish. Church attendances and revenues from collections are well up to scratch. You do well to maintain the level of interest and support.'

'No credit to me, Monsignor. People around here are creatures of habit. They hate change. Many still grumble about the Vatican Council changes, even after all these years. It was Father Ambrose and Father

226

O'Malley who earned the parish its reputation, and Father O'Malley who maintains it inasmuch as it needs it. I try to do my small bit to help out.'

'You are too modest, Father. You are well thought of in high places. Father O'Malley has indeed done well, and he is very popular. A little eccentric for some tastes. He and Father Ambrose did not always see eye to eye, so I hear. But he will go no further. He will finish out his time here, and retire in a few years. But you are still very young, Father. You could go far. You could do very well indeed for yourself. You are intelligent, energetic and conscientious.'

'Thank you. But it is not for myself I would want to do well.'

'Well said. I stand rightly rebuked. I deal with establishment matters in the diocese. From where I sit, I could be in any large organisation. A big company, a bank, or a government department, perhaps. Everybody is jostling for positions. Ambition and backbiting are everywhere. It really is most disillusioning. I forget what business we are in sometimes. But you have not forgotten. That is good. You should not forget. But you should also not limit your horizons to this pleasant but rather uneventful locality. The Church faces great challenges. To its teaching. To its authority. Its role in the world is being constantly questioned. These days, there is great social unrest, especially in the inner cities. Why, only a few years ago we had those riots in Toxteth. Funny, I'm not sure where that is. I'm a Londoner, you see.'

'I think you'll find that it's less than a mile from your office.'

'As close as that? Oh dear, the enemy really is at the gates.'

'I'm sorry, Monsignor. I'm not trying to sneer. I don't have your excuse of coming from down south. I was born and bred here, and I've never been to Toxteth either.'

'Well, whatever. The point is that we need people who can respond to those challenges. Bring the Church and the modern world together. So let us say that your potential has been spotted.'

'Was that what you came down to see me about today, Monsignor?'

We had completed one circuit of the park and had commenced another. He looked around to ensure we were still alone.

'Not entirely that. Mostly that. But not entirely. As I say we have noted your potential. But it would be a shame if anything happened to prevent that potential being realised.'

I stopped walking and looked at him. Slowly, his smile faded. It reminded me of a deflating balloon.

'What sort of...thing?'

There was a bench nearby. He sat down and waved for me to join him. He looked round, then spoke so quietly that I had to strain to hear him.

'It has been brought to our notice that you are looking into a certain case, a case of great sensitivity. Fortunately it was disposed of satisfactorily many years ago. Quite a few eminent priests of the diocese at that time worked very hard to dispose of it. I wasn't here myself then. I was a parish priest in Cricklewood. You would still have been at seminary. But I have had access to all the relevant papers at Diocese HQ. Privileged access. I have read and studied and inwardly digested them. The Archbishop of the day was greatly disturbed by the case. I am sure everybody was who knew about it. But it was promptly and thoroughly investigated in accordance with established procedures. Appropriate action was taken in the authorised manner.'

He looked around furtively, as he had already done several times while he was speaking.

'Now, the point is this,' he continued. 'The current Archbishop does not know about the case. But if he were to find out about it, and if he were to hear that it is being looked at again, by a junior parish priest acting on his own initiative, I could not foresee the consequences. Needless to say, he has heard nothing yet. I have some influence on the matters which pass across his desk and reach his ears while he is in the palace. But I have no influence on what might be whispered to him while he is out on a visit. Nor can I always prevent pieces of paper being pressed into his hand, at which he might glance before I can relieve him of them and seek proper advice on them. The arsenal might explode at any moment and the shock-waves would be felt out here, and much further.'

He rubbed his hands together. Then he detached his left hand and rubbed the back of his neck with it. Then he transferred the knuckles of the same hand to his mouth, as if he were about to say something momentously indiscreet but had managed just in time to restrain himself.

I coughed. He was waiting for me to respond. There was clearly no point in denying all knowledge of the matter. He was too well briefed. But how could he possibly know? It was inconceivable that Father O'Malley would have contacted the Archbishop's office on his own initiative. He hated any sort of attention from on high. And, even assuming he could have done any such thing behind my back, our investigation, incompetent and bordering on failure as it was, was the only excitement which had come his way in years. Why would he want to do anything which would bring it to a premature stop, and at the same time tarnish our reputation with our seniors?

What about Father Brennan? I knew him slightly. I would never have thought him capable of any sort of deviousness. In any case, Father O'Malley had known him for many years and obviously trusted him implicitly.

He waited patiently while I gathered my thoughts. I decided that it would be best to focus his attention on the plight of my correspondent and avoid the issue of the priest's actions for as long as possible.

'Your sources are, I am afraid, misleading you, Monsignor. I am not trying to open up anything already dealt with by due process. I would not be so presumptuous. I have received an anonymous communication from a deeply troubled soul, a woman who complains of ill treatment at the hands of a female carer, probably her aunt. As a result of this treatment, according to her own account, she spent years locked up in an asylum. The treatment there was not exactly humane and enlightened. She speaks of revenge. My enquiries are aimed only at finding where she might be, so that I can talk to her.'

'That is a compassionate reaction, Father Jones. It does you credit. There are of course some priests who would not react at all to such an anonymous communication. They would say that it is up to the person concerned to come forward, perhaps in the confessional. There may be something to be said for such passivity. The woman has chosen to remain anonymous, and there is a case for saying that that should be respected.'

'I have no intention of speaking to her without it being clear that that is her wish. But if she could be identified, someone who knows her could, without betraying her secret, perhaps establish whether anybody is in real danger. The danger of course is not just to the aunt, but to the soul of the woman, if she proceeds to a violent crime.'

'Forgive me. I do not wish to split doctrinal hairs. I am more of an administrator than a theologian. I hope I am not getting out of my depth if I say that the role of a priest is not to prevent sin where the prospective sinner does not seek to have it prevented. You have perhaps rather over-reacted to this communication. You see, once you start to dig around in the flowerbed you may find you are not just pulling up weeds but your favourite summer flowers as well.

'Let us not beat about the bush, Father. You and I know we are talking about the same case here. And we know that behind the events you mention lies a case of betrayal on the part of a certain priest. Terrible betrayal.'

His voice rose steadily in volume. He had forgotten his fear of being overheard. Fortunately an ever-stiffening sea breeze ensured that we still had the park to ourselves.

'It is impossible, absolutely impossible, to exaggerate the seriousness of the matter. The secrets of the confessional are holy, sacrosanct, beyond all earthly laws. The trust placed in the priest who hears Confession comes direct from God. In full recognition of its dreadful, appalling gravity the case was properly investigated and disposed of by all the appropriate resources of Holy Mother Church. This was twenty years ago, Father. Twenty years dead and buried. Do you really think you can resolve your correspondent's problem without disturbing the grave in which that hideous corpse lies? And if not, and I am sure that on reflection you will agree with me that you cannot, have you given thought, even a moment's passing thought, to the consequences to the Church in which you hold the office of an anointed priest, in succession to the Apostles of Christ?'

By the time he had finished this speech he was shouting. He pulled a handkerchief out of his sleeve and wiped his brow with it.

'I do not know if I can resolve anything,' I said, as quietly and calmly as I could.

'But you are following your conscience.'

'I always try to follow my conscience.'

'That, Father Jones, can be a very dangerous thing.'

He sighed. To my relief, he seemed to have nothing more to say.

'I am grateful to you for your advice, Monsignor. Will you come back and have tea?'

'No thank you. I must get back to the palace.'

He stood up and began to walk briskly away in the wrong direction. I caught up with him and tugged at his sleeve.

'This way, Monsignor.'

We stopped outside the presbytery. He stood by the door of the car. He had recovered his composure. The greasy smile was back. I knew he had more to say. My heart sank.

'Are you sure you won't come in for a cup of tea, Monsignor?'

'No, thank you. One last thing. I would be grateful if you would keep this conversation to yourself. Regard this as an...informal warning. There will be no record of it on your file. Nobody at HQ knows about this visit. Arch thinks I am visiting an elderly relative who lives over the water. I will not even report that I have spoken with you. Of course, should there need to be further communication about this matter between us, it could not be on so friendly a basis or in such pleasant and relaxed surroundings. I would need to ask you to come to the palace. We would need to be much more...formal. That would be a pity. I have enjoyed our chat. Goodbye.'

He disappeared into the huge interior of the car. I walked back up the path to the house. Once inside, I went up to my bedroom, picked up a pillow and threw it against the wall.

Father O'Malley was back in time to take afternoon tea with me in the library. He settled himself into his favourite armchair. Fido jumped into his lap.

'We had a visitor today, Father.'

'Oh, and who might that be? Whoever it was hasn't exactly put you in a good mood.'

'Monsignor Winstanley. From the Archbishop's office. He has got wind of our little investigation and wants us to stop. Doesn't want the Archbishop getting upset. Thinks he will be if the Gallagher case resurfaces. I said I was only bothered about finding the woman.'

'He thinks we should not even try?'

'That's right. Says it is not the job of a priest to prevent sin if the sinner does not want it prevented.'

'Just clean up afterwards?'

'Something like that.'

'And what happens if we don't stop?'

'You'll be all right. But I'll be taken away and put in charge of supplies of staples and rubber stamps at Diocese HQ. Under the direct and constant supervision of Monsignor Winstanley.'

'Perhaps we should call a halt then. For your sake. If you're not going to do as I suggest and marry Bernadette, you should think about your career. In any case, I don't know where we go from here. And all this rushing around is making me feel very tired.'

'Yes. I think I'll forget all about it. Unless she comes forward.'

'Yes.' He paused. 'So, er, you don't want to do

anything more, then? Just leave it?'

'Yes.'

'That means you won't be wanting this, then?'

He took a piece of paper from his pocket.

'What's that?'

He smiled, roguishly. 'No, you wouldn't be interested. Not now.'

'Father! What is it?'

'Only something that came in the post this morning. From Father Brennan. Father James' last known address, that's all. I'll just be throwing it away now.'

'Don't you dare, Father! Give that here.'

I jumped up. With surprising speed he stood up, the sudden movement depositing a startled Fido on the floor. I chased him twice round the room before I caught him and prised the paper out of his hand. He collapsed in the chair, out of breath and laughing.

'So you might be visiting outside the parish tomorrow, Father?' he gasped at last. 'Would I be right about that?'

'You might.'

'Fine. I'll say evening Mass in your place if you're not back in time.'

He looked at his watch.

'Time for Confession soon. Talking of Confession, did I ever tell you about Mrs Jenkins? It was before your time.'

'You wouldn't be about to betray any secrets, would you?'

'No, that's the point. I couldn't if I wanted to. By the time I met her, she was in her seventies. She was deaf and half-blind. But in her past she had, by all accounts, been quite a beauty, and had a reputation for wild behaviour, well into her middle years. She came to Mass, but she had neglected Confession for decades. Then at last she summoned up the courage to go. With some difficulty she found the box, went in and confessed her sins. It was my box. Unfortunately she had not noticed that I had not yet arrived. She was too early. I entered the box as she was just finishing. Just in time, I managed to shout at her through the screen to say an Act of Contrition. Then I yelled Absolution at her. Jesus, Mary and Joseph! I mean, just think about it. Trust me to miss the best catalogue of sins ever pronounced in our church since it was built. I'll never forgive myself. I'd always wanted to know what she'd been up to. There was my chance, a chance nobody else would get, and I blew it. So there's me giving Absolution for sins I had never heard. She could have confessed to murdering the Pope for all I knew. And what penance was I supposed to give her? She got fifteen Our Fathers. She was probably expecting ten novenas and a pilgrimage to Lourdes on her knees.'

Twenty minutes later, I heard the confessional door open. Someone knelt down. I could hear rapid breathing.

'Take your time,' I said, gently. 'Begin when you are ready.'

Silence. Stage fright and temporary memory loss are not unknown among people who come to Confession, particularly those who have not been for some time.

'If you have forgotten the form of words, I will remind you. Say after me, "bless me, Father, for I have sinned."' Silence.

'Would you prefer to use only your own words? If so, please do so. God does not mind what form your confession takes.'

Silence. I desperately wanted to pull the curtain back, but I knew that was strictly forbidden. I leant forward and whispered through the grille.

'Is that you? Is that you, Christine? Or Dora? It doesn't matter. I don't care what name you use. You've been leaving me those letters, haven't you? Please let me help you. You know that nothing you say to me here can go any further. I know you believed that once, and you were betrayed. I will never do that. Never. Please. Just tell me where I can find you.'

I heard the door to the confessional shut. Immediately afterwards, it opened again. Another parishioner had entered. I could not leave.

TWENTY-NINE

Early the following afternoon I was "over the water." It was the local expression for anywhere requiring a trip across the Mersey, whether by ferry, or train or through one of the two road tunnels. I had taken the ferry to Birkenhead, and then a series of local buses. I was in a remote village on the Wirral Peninsula. I found the address at last, a small cottage set back from the road. The building looked crestfallen, though the flower garden in the front and the vegetable garden to the side were meticulously tended.

I slipped my coat off before ringing the doorbell. I wanted my white collar to be instantly visible. From the outset he must not mistake my calling or the likely purpose of my visit.

The man who answered the door was about sixty, tall and straight-backed with a shock of wavy, white hair. He was wearing a huge, shapeless, badly torn pullover and grey, baggy trousers. Pullover and trousers were stained with soil. He was rubbing his hands with a towel. He dropped the towel on the floor and smiled broadly. To my surprise I took his proffered hand without hesitation. He gestured for me to enter. There was no hallway downstairs, only one low-roofed room, from which a wooden staircase led upstairs. Newspapers covered the floor, on which stood numerous plant-pots.

'I run a small plant nursery here,' he said. 'It's a very peaceful calling. Can I get you anything?'

The voice was firm and resonant. What an excellent preacher he must have been, I thought.

'Thank you. A glass of water would do fine.'

He fetched two, handed me one and sipped from the other. We sat down. I watched him. I had expected the cruel stare of defiant fanaticism, or else the weary inward-looking gaze of the defeated. I saw neither. His was the expression of a man at peace with himself and the world. Could it be that he knew or guessed nothing of the terrible harm which had followed his misdeeds? What right had he to a clear conscience? I intended to undeceive him. I would not deny him peace of mind in the end, but he would need to work much harder for it. But perhaps I was completely wrong. Perhaps this was not the former Father James. He might have moved on. But where better than here could a defrocked priest come to hide from the world?

'Well, Father, what can I do for you? Not a pastoral visit, I presume. You're not from our local church. You look as if you've had a long and tiring journey. I haven't seen you before, and I know most of the priests on the peninsula.'

So he still went to church. Had he confessed everything? Was his conscience free because of that? Why was Confession so often thought to be the answer to everything, when the victims of sin continued to suffer grief and pain?

'I'm Father Jones, from St Jerome's, in Seaport. You are Mr James? Father James as was?'

He smiled. 'I think you know I am.'

'I know that business is all finished with, strictly speaking.'

'You mean the business as a result of which I became plain Mr James.'

'Yes. But something new has turned up. I'm trying to tie up one or two loose ends.'

'Something, or somebody?'

'We think Christine Gallagher is back, living in our parish.'

'I didn't know she ever went away. She has contacted you? For what purpose?'

'Do you know what became of her? After the

incident in which you were involved?'

'No. I never met her. You said she is one of your parishioners.'

'No, I said she had come back and was living in our parish. My understanding is that you did meet Christine, after you had heard her confess, with terrible consequences for her. You abused her, under the pretext of purifying her soul. After her encounter with you, she was committed to an asylum. She spent years there. Lost her memory. She's out now and her memory is returning. She says she wants to make you and her aunt pay for what you did to her.'

He whistled. 'How dreadful. Truly dreadful. I knew nothing about her being committed. He gave me the impression she was living in the parish. St Monica's. Not yours.'

'Who are you talking about?'

'Christine, of course.'

'No. You said, "he gave me the impression..." Who is he?'

'I'm sorry, Father. I was thinking aloud. Is Christine with you at St Jerome's? Do you want to arrange for me to meet her? Is that why you have come here?'

'Her letter doesn't give her address, just the information that she is in our parish. I came to warn you. And her aunt, if I can find her. Have you noticed anybody following you? Have you heard of anybody enquiring after you?'

'Who would trace me here? I know you did, but you have the resources of the Holy Church behind you. Well, as you have come a long way, let me tell you what really happened. I wasn't lying just now. I never met her. I don't suppose you saw the report of the investigating priest? Normally only the Archbishop and the disciplinary panel ever get to see those.'

'No, I haven't seen it. I'm here in a personal capacity, because Christine has approached me. All I know is that you heard her confession and told her aunt. Christine complained. You were suspended, then thrown out of the priesthood. According to Christine's letter there was much more. Before she complained about the betrayal of her confession secrets, she was abused and maltreated. By you.'

'Do you have the letter with you?'

'No. It's in a safe place, back at the presbytery.'

'I thought you said she was committed and lost her memory.'

'That's right.'

'Then how was she in a position to complain?'

'I...I don't know. Perhaps somebody made the complaint on her behalf. Another family member, perhaps.'

'You said she wanted to make me pay. Does she know that action has already been taken against me?'

'I don't know. We don't have all the facts. But I doubt if she would regard what has happened to you as sufficient punishment. If you had been subjected to the laws of the land for what you did I might have been visiting you in prison rather than in this pleasant retreat.'

'Yes, I understand what you are saying. Tell me something, Father. Have you ever substituted for another priest at Confession? At another church, perhaps?'

'Yes, of course. We all have.'

'So have I. And has anybody ever substituted for you?'

'Of course.'

'That night, when I was supposed to have heard Christine's confession, my mother was taken ill. I asked another priest to take my place. It was all done in rather a rush. I expect my name was on the door as usual.'

'You're saying someone else heard her confession? And then told her aunt? After all these years, what is the point of lying again? You've been punished, and you live with the consequences of that every day. I admire the way you've come to terms with your new life here. I accept you didn't know about the long-term consequences of your actions. I was prepared to hold you in some contempt when I came here. Against all my instincts you have won my respect. Doesn't that mean anything, when you have lost the respect of so many? Why throw it away?'

He laughed. 'Look into my eyes, Father Jones. You are a good man, I can see that. You can recognise the truth. Look at me and tell me again that I am lying to you.'

I stared into his clear blue eyes. They smiled back at me. I shook my head and sighed.

'No, I can see you are not lying. But then in God's name, why didn't you speak up for yourself? Your mother could have verified your story. Is she still alive? Can she remember?'

'Eight-five last birthday. Sprightly as a lamb and memory as sharp as a razor. Much better than mine.'

'Then it's not too late. She can still verify it. Why are you here and why is another priest still out there, accepting the title of Father when he doesn't deserve it? Saying Mass and hearing confessions when he has no right? It was your duty to speak up then and it is your duty now. Why didn't you tell the investigating priest who your locum was?'

'The investigating priest? Ah yes. The Archbishop appointed a senior priest of impeccable character to assess whether the charges against me were sufficiently credible for him to appoint a disciplinary panel. Yes, I could have told the investigating priest. But what was the point of telling him what he already knew?'

'But how...? Oh my God.' I covered my face with my hands. 'I am so sorry, Father. I have done you a terrible injustice. The investigating priest. What was his name? Please.'

'I promised you the truth, Father. I have told you the truth. Forgive me if that does not extend to meeting one act of betrayal with another. I have forgiven him for what he did to me. Whether others can or should forgive him for what he did to them is not for me to say. God sees into his soul and He will punish him as He pleases.'

I smiled. 'That is the reply I expected from you, Father. Forgive me for asking. But could I ask you to consider again from a different perspective? Christine was abused by this priest. He is an evil and dangerous man. He must not be allowed to continue his wrongdoing. Neither of us can allow it to be on our consciences if another such incident were to occur.'

'I expected that reply, too. I am pleased we have met, Father Jones. I feel we know and understand each other. What a pity we never had the chance to work together as parish priests. I appreciate your motives for coming here, and I understand why you want to find this priest. Let me reassure you. I have not just buried myself here. I have, as you say, lost the respect of some, but I have gained the respect of others. I act as a sort of spiritual counsellor. People come to me when they cannot talk to anybody else, not even to their priest. Not all priests are as approachable as you are. And a priest always has the trappings of his office, which divide him from others. I find I can be more use to people without them. I am content here. I feel I am doing what God intended for me. Some of the people who come to me know that I was once a priest, but nobody knows the reason for my dismissal. They assume I left voluntarily, if they think about it at all. As for the priest who betrayed me, I have been kept informed. Somebody has been here before you. Suffice it to say that the situation is under control. I cannot tell you any more, but I must ask you to accept my word. There is no more danger.'

'He has died, then?'

'You can put that construction on my words, if you wish. I would prefer to leave the matter as I have expressed it.'

'You have put my mind at rest in one respect at least, Father.'

It was his turn to smile. 'You have forgotten I am not entitled to the form of address you persist in using with me.'

'Oh, I think you are.'

I reported the results of my visit to Father James to Father O'Malley that evening, after Mass. We were sitting in the library. I thought he looked tired and strained. There would be no amusing stories that evening.

'So, it looks as if we've come to the end of the road,' he said. 'Dora has disappeared. We know the priest appointed to investigate her complaint was the one who had been the cause of it in the first place. Now that, I must say, is an ingenious arrangement. It appeals to my sense of order and economy. Only Holy Mother Church could come up with that one. Think of all the time and trouble it saves. Father James refuses to name him but tells us that he is no longer considered a danger. Probably retired from the priesthood. Nothing more we can do.'

'No. Nothing more.'

'Well, I'll be off now, Father. I'm meeting Father

Brennan down at the YMCA for a drink. I'll bring him up to date, and thank him for his efforts on our behalf. Fancy coming along?'

'No, thanks, if you don't mind. I'll say my Office and get an early night.'

'I'll be off then. Goodnight, Father.'

'Goodnight.'

Half an hour later, I realised I had dozed off in my chair. I tried to remember the voice which had been pounding in my head while I had been asleep. It was my own. It was telling me something. What was it? Oh, yes. That was it. *More than one.* More than one what?

There was more than one priest involved. Neither of us had given any thought to the other one. The old one, who had come to carry out the exorcism. He had a beard. He wore vestments, and carried holy water. He made her hold a prayer book in one hand and a rosary in the other. She had pulled the rosary apart.

Exorcism? An exorcism had prescribed forms. It required the prior permission of the Archbishop. That would take time. There would need to be supporting documents. A case would have to be made. But what had Dora written? *The special priest came the next day.* The next day? How could that have been possible? Had she been mistaken? I did not think so. This had been no exorcism. It had been a ritual humiliation, dressed up as a ceremony.

I looked up the catalogue I had once prepared of the books in the library. There was only one on exorcism. I took it off the shelves. It was a slender leaflet. The information it contained was equally slender. There was the briefest possible description of the procedure. *The essence of the exorcism is a solemn command to the evil spirits to depart.* There had certainly been no solemn command here. I turned to the back page. There was a short bibliography. Perhaps other books would be more forthcoming. What about that one? *Exorcism – a Historical Survey of Practice in Nineteenth Century Britain.* The author was a Father P Coffey.

Father Coffey? Of course. The Holy Ghost, as Father O'Malley called him, though never in his presence. He had been at St Jerome's for two years after my arrival. He was a well-known Church historian. He had spent nearly all his free time writing and reading in this very room. His book was not in the catalogue. I looked out his last-known address. He had been the parish priest in a small Derbyshire village. But he had to be seventy now if a day. He had surely retired. But they might have a forwarding address.

I rang the number. He was there. He sounded pleased to hear my voice. I explained that I wanted to consult him urgently on matters which he may have covered in his book. Could I come to see him the following day? He would be delighted to see me. I left a message for Father O'Malley, to tell him I would be out all the next day.

THIRTY

I parked outside the tiny slate-roofed cottage which served as the presbytery to St Mary's Church, Daleford. The rain had stopped at last. The final ten miles of the journey had been a hair-raising experience. The single-track road wound its way down the side of the valley through a dozen hairpin bends. The rain lashed horizontally against the windscreen. The road disappeared repeatedly from my line of vision as rainwater streamed across it.

Father Coffey was waiting for me at the door. We shook hands. His grip was still firm. He ushered me inside. The floors of his hall and living room were covered with books and papers. I picked my way through them to one of the two armchairs. He brought in a tray with a pot of coffee and two cups. He wore the same horn-rimmed spectacles he had always worn. He had on his favourite shapeless grey pullover and slacks. Since I had seen him last, he had faded rather than aged. He had always been small and thin, his face hollow, and his forehead deeply lined, the result of a lifetime of poring over old books and documents.

'I remember you don't take sugar, Father.'

The same voice. Dry, precise, slightly clipped.

'You're looking somewhat burdened,' he continued. 'Are parish duties weighing heavily on you? You should come here when I leave. I have only six parishioners left now, all older than I am. The only problem is that I won't be replaced. The church is due to be deconsecrated. That's why I'm still officially a parish priest, at the age of seventy. They'll deconsecrate me along with the church as soon as they've sorted out the formalities. Then my remaining parishioners, if there are any, will have twenty miles to go to the nearest church, along country roads with no

Sunday buses. Still, it suits me here. I have plenty of time for my writing and my research.'

'It's not my parish duties that are burdening me, Father. Life goes on much as it always has there. But a few weeks ago, I received this. An anonymous letter. I wonder if I could ask you to read it, particularly the bit about the exorcism. Don't mind the style or the language.'

I handed him the letter. He replaced his spectacles with a pair which to me looked identical to the ones he had just been wearing. He read it through, twice, slowly. He shook his head.

'That was no exorcism. I should know.'

'Yes, you should. That's why I brought it to you.'

He handed it back to me, reluctantly, as if he wanted to examine it much more closely.

'When was this? Do you know?'

'I would say, about twenty years ago. I have been trying to contact the woman, but with no success as yet. I have found out where she was living until recently. I have spoken to a priest who knows her. Father O'Malley thinks he remembers the case because there was an investigation into the actions of the priest mentioned in the letter. It was before my time.'

'But if Father O'Malley remembers it, I should remember it too. Did Father O'Malley mention a name?'

'Yes. Christine. Christine Gallagher.'

'Curious. I don't remember that name. But I do remember a case where a priest betrayed the secrets of the confessional. St Monica's. Father James.'

'That's right.'

'Good. I'm pleased to see my memory is still partly functioning. But it's not like me to forget any name. So why do I remember the priest's name and not hers? Yes, that was it. There was a meeting of all the parish priests in the diocese, chaired by the Archbishop in person. Three line whip. No excuses. Father James was conspicuous by his absence. We were told why. He had been expelled. We were told that he had betrayed a confessional secret. No more than that. We were solemnly enjoined to keep his betrayal a secret. He was telling us about it so we would know how to deal with any rumours. So we could truthfully deny it if word got about that he had been touching up the altar boys, for instance. But on no account were we to breathe to a soul the real reason for his expulsion. If anybody suggested it to us, we were to deny it. It would be an authorised denial, not a lie, not a sin, to protect the Church. There was of course another reason why we were being told the truth. He was warning us, telling us that in such cases there would be no warnings, no second chances. I suspect he was acting on orders from the Archbishop of Westminster. The Pope's envoy might even have been consulted. But we never knew the name of the complainant. The investigation itself would have been very hush-hush. Are you sure Father O'Malley mentioned that name?'

'Positive.'

'He didn't say he was involved in the investigation? Or on the disciplinary panel?'

'No, I'm sure he wasn't. He would have said.'

'Twenty years ago. Then the disease may well have finally run its course. Pray God it has. I am only astonished that it persisted for so long.'

'Disease?'

'Yes. I think that is not too strong a word. A disease. A canker. A corrupting force. In every religion, there are pockets of fanaticism. It has been that way through the ages. Sometimes their leaders break away and form religions of their own. Most of these splinter groups die away from lack of interest or support. Some are more insidious. They do not break away. They work from within. They feed off the main growth. Let me show you something, Father. It may take me some time to find it.'

He disappeared into a back room through a connecting door. I could see that it housed even more books and papers than the rest of the house. There was no room there for any furniture at all. He came back after ten minutes. He carried a small box-file.

'I'm afraid all the sheets have come loose. It's quite old. That's why I keep it in here. Well, that's one reason. The other...I'll explain later. No need to read it all. There's a lot of tedious, half-baked stuff about evil and devils and the like. Let me find the bit which is relevant. Yes, here we are. You can read Gothic script, can you? The style is archaic, even for the time it was written.'

With great care, he placed in front of me two yellow, dog-eared sheets. He leaned back in his chair, while I started to read.

In first Order after the Angels cometh Man. In second Order cometh Woman. Such is the Divine Will of the Creator, according to the Book of Genesis. Man was created first. Woman was created as Companion for Man. For those Men whom God hath not called to higher Things, and who, in the Words of Saint Paul, do not have the Gift of Continence, God hath ordained the Sacrament of Holy Matrimony. In Matrimony the Woman shall submit to the Will of the Man for the Procreation of Mankind.

In the Act of Procreation within Matrimony, it hath pleased God to allow Man Gratification of the Flesh. No such Gratification hath been allowed Woman by God, because only the

249

Gratification of the Man is needful for the Fulfilment of the Act. Indeed, Gratification for any Man or Woman is a Sin, unless it be Part, and that the smallest needful Part, of such lawful Act of Procreation. God hath placed in Man the Capacity for Gratification, to be used only in accordance with His Holy Law. He hath placed no such Capacity in Woman.

However, the Devil hath the Power to enter and corrupt the Soul of any Man or Woman. The display of Wanton Desire on the Part of any Woman is clear Evidence of the Presence of the Devil within her, because the Source of such Desire can only be the Devil. As Women grow to Maturity in the Sight of God, their Souls become strong and resistant to Temptation. Young Women, mature in Body but not yet in Mind or Soul, are in great Danger of Possession by evil Powers. The greatest Vigilance is required of those who have care of such young Women.

Where, in spite of such Vigilance, Possession is found to have taken place, how can it be countered? As Christ appointed his Apostles to continue His Work of preaching and administering His Holy Sacraments, so to this Day and until the End of Time He anointeth His Priests to continue their Work. Christ and His Apostles cast out Devils, as is revealed to us in Holy Scripture. It must follow then that only a truly anointed Priest can cast out Devils, in the Name of Christ. He must first compel the Woman to confess her State of Possession. The Priest must pray over her. Some Castigation of the Flesh of the Person possessed may be needful. Such Flesh is no longer the Vessel of the Holy Spirit. No Reverence is due to it until the Devils have departed and the Holy Spirit is once again present. Some Devils are weak and cowardly. They depart instantly in the Presence of Divine Power. Others are strong. They resist. The Soul of the Person possessed becometh a true Battleground of Good and Evil. If the Person possessed be kept away from the Temptations of the World, if Prayer and Exhortation continue, the Evil will, in the Completion of the Time appointed by the Will and Grace of God Almighty, be that Days, or Months, or Years, or the entire Duration of the possessed Person's earthly Life, be at last vanquished.

I handed the fragile sheets back to him, as carefully as he had given them to me. He replaced them in the box-file, and carried it back to the room from which he had fetched it. He returned to his chair.

'You might expect to find that sort of thing in a mediaeval library. Indeed, I have, on numerous occasions.' He sounded as if he were delivering a lecture. 'But what you have just read, Father, was written and printed as recently as 1840. The author was one Father Sebastian Johns. On the foundation of the crude arguments you have just read, he carried out so-called exorcisms. They were more like acts of sadism, carried out for the perverted pleasure they gave him. He even went so far as to found an Order. The Order of the Followers of Sebastian Johns, he modestly called it. They dressed like friars, and went round the towns and villages practising their obscene rituals. But of course he never had permission to found an Order. When he heard about it, the Pope ordered the Order to disband and all Father Johns' writings to be destroyed.

251

Yes, Father, I am afraid I have inadvertently led you into the sin of disobedience, though as you were in an ignorance which was not wilful the sin is entirely mine. As a scholar, I do not believe any book should ever be destroyed. We should be prepared to let mistaken beliefs see the light of day so that truth and reason can prevail against them. If I found a book written by Lucifer himself I would not destroy it.

'We can easily see Father Johns' work for the evil nonsense it is. Nobody would take him seriously on the basis of his writings alone. But the man himself was charismatic. So were some of his followers. Anyway, when I found that pamphlet, I knew it should be destroyed. But I could not bear to do it. It is probably the last remaining copy. You won't give me away, will you?'

'Certainly not. I agree with you.'

'After reading it, I began to research Father Johns and his so-called Order. It is a murky story. Father Johns' writings were not so extreme as to be deemed heretical, but his practices were condemned by the Pope as contrary to Church Law. He was eventually excommunicated. He died soon after that.'

He poured some more coffee into our cups.

'That should have been the end of it. But it was not. There is evidence that the Order went underground. Its members no longer dressed like friars. On the surface, they were ordinary parish priests, who took great care to appear orthodox. They carried out their so-called exorcisms in secret. They preferred remote villages, where superstition was rife and where no priest would ever be challenged, whatever he said or did. The trail goes rather cold after that. Then, in the 1920s, a priest called Father Lamb published an article in one of the proscribed journals, supporting Father Johns' beliefs and practices. I have, again to my shame, seen a copy of that article, though I do not have one here. Father Lamb was reprimanded and threatened with expulsion from the priesthood. He recanted. Officially, that is. But it is possible that in his heart he did not recant. He was withdrawn from his parish duties and put in charge of a boys' orphanage, on the condition that he changed his name and kept his past secret. I got all this from a ninety-year old retired Monsignor who had been in charge of making the arrangements. It cost me six brandies to get him drunk enough to tell me the story. He didn't know the orphanage or Father Lamb's new name, though. That was a pity. I had wanted to interview him if he was still alive, though I knew that was unlikely. That, I always assumed, was the end of it. What you have told me is profoundly disturbing. It seems that as recently as twenty years ago, Father Johns still had his followers, or at least one.'

'Or two. There were two priests involved.'

'It is possible that Father Lamb himself was the older priest. If so, it seems he had a protégé. Let us hope and pray the protégé has ceased his evil ways and has not passed the disease on again.'

'Amen to that.' I stood up to go. 'Well, thank you, Father. You've been most informative and helpful. If anything further comes to light from your research, let me know.'

'Of course. Though these days my interests lie in other fields than possession and exorcism. You may find out more yourself, if the writer of your letter comes to light.'

'In which case I will keep you informed.'

I walked to the door, accidentally knocking over a pile of papers in the process. I apologised and stooped to clear them up.

'It's all right,' he said. 'Leave them. They don't matter. I keep all the important stuff round the back.'

'Oh, just a couple of final questions, if I may,' I said. I was standing on the doorstep by then.

'Of course.'

'Where did Father Lamb come from?'

"Sorry, didn't I mention it? Sebastian Johns was Irish. So was Father Lamb. My drunken source had been a senior figure in the Dublin Diocese, close to the Archbishop. The remote villages in Ireland were ideal hunting grounds for Johns and Lamb. Hotbeds of superstition.'

'And the pamphlet. Where exactly did you find it?'

'That was a very happy chance. A scholar's dream. I could have searched all the libraries in Christendom and not found it. But there it was. In our little library at St Jerome's. In one of the drawers for loose papers. God knows who put it there. Oh, give my regards to Father O'Malley, will you?'

'Of course I will.'

On the way back, as I drove recklessly along the winding lanes, my mood steadily darkened. I talked to myself. I felt tears on my cheek.

'I loved you, Father O'Malley. You and your teasing and your irreverence and your stories. I didn't care if they were true or not. You made it bearable all these wasted years. So was it a façade I loved? Did you assume it to hide the evil in you? Has the façade now become the man? Is that what Father James meant when he said you were no longer a danger? Is that enough for me to ignore the past and continue as we are? And how could Father James be so sure? What does he really know about you? What did I ever know about you?'

THIRTY-ONE

I arrived back at St Jerome's just after half past six. Father O'Malley was saying evening Mass. It was Mrs Raferty's evening off. She would have gone to bingo, as usual. I went into the library and poured myself a brandy. I sat sipping it in front of the gas fire. Fido sat on the rug, purring with contented warmth. At last I heard him come in through the passageway.

'You're back, Father,' he called out.

'Yes. I'm in here.'

He pushed open the door.

'Well, come on. Tell me. Where have you been? Did you find out anything more?'

'I went to see Father Coffey. He sends his regards.'

'You went to see the Holy Ghost? All the way down there? So why did you go and do that and not tell me where you were going or why?'

'Why, Father? Would you have tried to talk me out of it? Is there any reason why you wouldn't have wanted me to go and see him?'

'You're sounding very strange, Michael. Is anything the matter? Would you be coming down with something, now?'

'No, thank you, I'm fine.'

'So what put the idea in your head?'

'Why, what's the matter? Are you worried about what he might have told me? About a certain pamphlet, perhaps? Written by a certain Father Johns, which he found here in one of the drawers. Which you brought here from Ireland. Which should have been destroyed decades ago. Perhaps you never noticed it was missing. But then, I expect you know it off by heart.'

'What in the name of all the saints in Heaven are you talking about, man? Why would I bring anything

255

into the library, when I never so much as take anything down off the shelves to read from one year's end to the next?'

'I don't know. You tell me. Maybe it was important to you once and it isn't any more. Is it true what I was thinking on the way back? That you started years ago to put on an act, and now the act really is you? Yes. It must be true. I can sense no evil in you now. Did you confess it all? Put it all behind you?'

'Michael, if you don't start making some sense soon, I'm going to call the doctor. You've been under too much strain lately. That's plain for all to see.'

'Do you remember when I showed you the first letter? You told me it might be the Gallagher case.'

'That's right.'

'How did you know?'

'I didn't know. It was the only such case I had heard about. It's not exactly an everyday occurrence.'

'No, I mean, how did you know the name of the complainant? These cases are confidential, aren't they? The name would only be known to the priest against whom the complaint had been made, the Archbishop who received the report, and, of course...the investigating priest.'

'Yes. That's right, I suppose. I...can't remember how I got to hear the name.'

'Father, before we get any further into a bog of lies and deceit, is there anything you want to tell me?'

'No, Michael. I'm afraid there isn't.'

'You wanted us to find the aunt, didn't you? To prevent any further harm being done. You wanted me to find Christine, too. So she could be helped. I'll give you credit for that. When you got those addresses from the Council you hoped I would be the one to find her. I know you couldn't have foreseen all the consequences. You were genuinely sorry about what had happened to her. But how could you...how could anybody be complicit in such cruelty? I just can't understand it. The only excuse I can find for you is that you were under his influence. That old priest from Ireland. A follower of Father Johns. I suppose you met him in Dublin. He must have cast a sort of spell on you. He's dead now, isn't he? So the spell is broken. Now you would like the chance to make amends. You even put me on to Father James in case that would lead us to them. That was risky for you, of course. But then if he named you, it was his word against yours. And why should he name you now? He didn't at the time when he could have saved himself from being thrown out. You were safe. The case was closed. Still, I bet you were relieved when I told you he hadn't named anybody.'

'Michael, what in God's name are you talking about?'

'Just...'

I felt the anger breaking through my voice. I stopped and controlled it.

'Just tell me how you knew the name.'

'I am telling you, for God's sake. I can't remember. I just knew it. It was just in my head.'

'Just in your head. I see. There's nothing else you want to tell me?'

'No.'

'Then I'm going to bed. It's been a long day. Goodnight.'

'Fine. Well, goodnight then. I think you need a good night's sleep. I'm going out for a walk. Try to clear my head a bit. Try to remember.'

'Father?'

'Yes?'

'When you get back from your walk...if you want to speak to me, however late it is, come and see me, if you want to. I won't mind if you wake me up.'

'Right. Fine. I'll be off then.'

He shook his head, put on his hat and coat and slipped out.

Upstairs in my bedroom, I began to draft a letter to the Archbishop, requesting a transfer. The words came easily. I thought I had been too long at St Jerome's. It was about time I went to serve in a parish where the social conditions were more challenging. I was in a rut. The false words flowed. I did not mention the real reason, that I no longer wished to share a parish with Father O'Malley.

The telephone was ringing. I could hear Mrs Raferty's voice as she picked it up. I looked at my watch. Christ, it was a quarter past eight! I was supposed to be saying Mass. I put on my dressing gown and rushed downstairs. Mrs Raftery laid the receiver gently down on the hall table.

'Oh, good morning, Father. Father O'Malley is saying Mass for you this morning. We agreed we mustn't disturb you because you were very tired last night. There's a call for you here. A lady. I can't quite catch the name. But she did ask specifically for you. I'll get your breakfast on for you.'

'Thank you, Mrs R.' I picked up the receiver.

'Hello?'

I heard a woman's voice on the other end of the line. It was very faint.

'I'm sorry, who is that? It must be a bad line.'

'Father Jones?'

'Yes, this is he.'

'This is Christine Gallagher. I wonder if you could come to see me?'

'Yes, of course.'

258

I tried to sound calm, but I knew my voice was shaking.

'Give me the address. Yes, I've got that. I'll be there as soon as I can.'

I put the phone down, and ran upstairs to get dressed. In five minutes I came down again.

'Sorry, Mrs R., I've got to go out. Fido can have my breakfast.'

I heard her sighing in the kitchen as I grabbed the car keys from the hook by the front door.

PART III

REVELATIONS

THIRTY-TWO

To my surprise, the address she had given me was a few miles away, well inside St Monica's parish. It was a large, detached, double-fronted house, faced with a discoloured crumbling stucco which might once have been white. The house wore an air of genteel decay. There was a long, narrow front garden, in which alpine flowers had been tidily cultivated in a sequence of terraced rockeries. On the other side of the road in front of the house was a broad, levelled patch of sand in which coarse grasses struggled for a secure foothold. Beyond it lay a concrete dyke designed to hold at bay the erosion of the coastline by sea and wind. Further away still, the grey waves of the estuary swelled angrily.

I checked the address several times before approaching the front door. I was puzzled. In her second letter she had told us she had come to live in our parish. She could easily be mistaken as to its boundaries. But it did not seem the sort of place I expected her to be, wherever it was located. Did she have a friend or relative who owned this house? What did this person know of her history?

I rang the bell. The door was opened almost immediately.

'Hello, I'm Father Jones. I'm here to see Christine Gallagher.'

'I am she. Please come in.'

She fitted the description. She was the right height. She had greying hair, tied up in a bun. She was about the right age, as far as I could tell from my first impression. I had not noticed her eyes yet. There was definitely something fragile about the petite figure who closed the front door behind us. Why then had I hesitated to assume she was Christine when she had first opened the door?

She moved slowly and gracefully, leading me into a spacious sea-facing lounge with a wide bay window. An open grand piano stood in one corner. There were two sideboards adorned with silverware, and a Welsh dresser with intricately designed china plates. In another corner stood a mahogany writing desk.

'Good sea views, the estate agents would say,' she said, with a nod towards the window. 'Pity the sea is so far away you can never see it. Sit down, Father.'

She seemed at home, as if she had lived there for years. She sat down with her back to the window. I sat down opposite her.

For a moment her eyes tried to focus on mine, then looked quickly away. I had a fleeting impression that they were hazel. But they could have been blue-grey. She was sitting in the shadow so it was hard to tell. Her face was a regular oval, her complexion pale. Her lips were full and slightly parted, pale pink, no lipstick. There was no hardness of hatred or violent intent in her features. I sensed only resignation beneath a surface of tremulous anxiety. Had the act of writing the letters done enough to draw the angry feelings out of her? Her eyes flickered back to mine and away again. I realised she had caught me staring at her. I lowered my eyes. She had long, delicate fingers, which fluttered nervously in her lap. She wore a long, green, faded dress with a grey cardigan with over-long sleeves.

She spoke again. Her voice was low-pitched and slightly husky, her words formed with careful precision and delivered with no trace of a city accent. I was puzzled. Neither Tim nor Father Higgins had mentioned that she "talked posh" as Tim would have put it. Yet her lack of a local accent would have stood out like a sore thumb at the hostel.

'Somebody who knows me told me you were trying

to find me. She goes to St Monica's. Father Brennan was paying her a pastoral visit. She must have mentioned she knew someone who still lived in the parish, who used to go to church a very long time ago but doesn't now. When she told him my name it seemed to ring a bell with him. He asked her if she would let me know you wanted to see me. I suppose it's about all that business years ago. You're from St Jerome's, aren't you?'

My mind was whirling painfully. How could such a deliberately schooled manner of speech possibly belong to the author of the letters? Yet there seemed nothing forced or unnatural about the way she spoke. No, it was the style of the letters which had to be false, along with the deliberate errors of grammar, spelling and punctuation, a style assumed to preserve an anonymity which, for reasons best known to herself, she had now decided to shed.

'That's right.'

'Looking into it all again? There's no point, really. It was all sorted out.'

'I wanted to find you, Christine, because I was afraid for you and for others. What I've seen and heard here has reassured me already. We can leave it here. I don't want to cause you any further pain. We can forget everything now.'

She shook her head slowly.

'No, I want to tell you. You have a kind, honest face. It's about time I told somebody. I even kept the full truth from him. From my brother. He never knew what really happened. Nobody knew.'

She paused and looked down again into her lap. She rubbed her hands together. She took several deep breaths.

'Perhaps you should start at the beginning.'

'Yes. I'll try. God, I'm so nervous. And I've been

preparing for this for days. Simon and I were orphans. Our parents were killed in a car crash, so we were brought up by my aunt. She was very strict, very distant. She never maltreated us, but she never showed any feelings. She was very good about observances. Went to church every day, Confession every week. Over the years, she seemed to grow more and more bitter and angry. She resented us. She had never married. Never wanted children. Until we were thrust upon her. We never received any guidance from her about...growing up. Simon joined the army. He was about five years older than I was. When he left I was on my own with her.

'I spent a lot of time in my own company. I followed my aunt in her observances, but I found myself able to take more joy in them than she ever could. I became ludicrously pious, an object of scorn at school. I ignored the classmates who ridiculed me. I knew I had access to higher truths than they ever would. I decided I would become a nun. I didn't tell my aunt about my decision. I would wait a few years to ensure my vocation was true.

'When the blow came, right out of the blue, it was devastating. Now I realise that what I took for spiritual delight and yearning for the presence of God was nothing more than my body preparing itself for a far more physical sort of fulfilment than the one for which I thought was destined. I fell in love. My feelings were perfectly normal for a normal teenage girl. But I wasn't normal. I thought I would be above anything...like that, if I ever thought about it at all.

'It was ridiculous, really. I was only fifteen, scrawny-looking with crooked teeth. The first time I had any money of my own, I had them straightened, the only act of vanity in my whole life. The object of my love was my English teacher, twenty years my senior. I followed him around. He probably didn't even notice. When I was on my own, I fantasised that he was making love to me. I had no idea what that would involve, in a physical sense. But, more or less by accident, I discovered how to arouse myself. At school they told us we should pray to make our bodies vessels of the Holy Spirit. The other girls had laughed but I hadn't. I had taken it seriously. I prayed until my head reeled. At last I thought my prayers had been answered. I was sure that my body belonged to God. Then I found to my horror that it belonged to my teacher. Or it would have done if he had been in the least bit interested. He would have laughed himself silly if he had even suspected.

'I had other fantasies, such as killing his wife as proof of my love, then killing myself if he rejected me. But I knew I could never have declared my love in any way. It was as solitary and one-sided a love affair as the world has ever seen. Just me, alone in my bedroom, a mass of aching longing in my stomach, crying each time I managed to bring myself a moment of release, because it was only at those times that I knew how really alone I was.

'I knew what the nuns had told us repeatedly, as soon as we reached what they called the dangerous age. I was abusing my body. I was committing a sin. As well as the anguish of my feelings of passion, I suffered torments of guilt. As the former became more and more intense, so the latter became ever more excruciating. In the end I could bear it no longer. I had to find some sort of release from my guilt. It took me ages to pluck up the courage. Finally I managed it. I went to Confession. Not as part of my usual routine. I went specially to confess this sin.'

'To Father James?'

"Yes. I hadn't been to him before, but his name was

on the door. He was quite new to the parish. I had never met him.'

'Was that important to you? The fact that you had never met him?'

'Yes, very important. You see, it was a ...new sort of sin for me. I didn't want to go to my usual priest, Father Sullivan. He was quite old by then, close to retirement. I would have been too embarrassed. He would have recognised my voice. He always did. I went to him every week, you see, confessing the usual stuff. Being late for Mass, which I never was, misbehaving at school, which I never did. He knew me because I helped out in the church with the other volunteers, cleaning and changing the flowers. He would often come and chat to us, distracting us from our work. I think he was a bit lonely, that's all. He dreaded retirement, the end of all the social contact you get as a priest. He was making the most of it while he still could. Sometimes, at the end of Confession, he would chat to me, through the grille. It was obvious he knew who he was speaking to. He knew me by name and he knew me as an innocent. There was no way I could tell him what was happening to me now. I was afraid he would be disgusted with me, stop talking to me, not let me carry out my duties in the church. That would have broken my heart.

'I wish to God I had gone to him. Whatever he thought of me he would never have treated me the way Father James did. It was awful, far worse than I expected. He wanted to know exactly what I had done, in every detail. That surprised and horrified me. I hadn't read the sort of books or magazines you get these days. My aunt would never have let them in the house. I didn't have the words to tell him about it. But still he insisted. He didn't shout or anything. He whispered, but louder and louder so that it was like a

hiss. I nearly ran away. But then I would still be in a
state of sin. Eventually, he gave me Absolution, and
my penance. Told me I had to say it in the church
before I went home. Obviously he didn't trust me. I
said my penance as quickly as I could and rushed
home.

'My crush on my teacher was not cured. I still
sometimes committed the sin which I had confessed.
But I could not go back to confess it again, not to
anybody. I couldn't face the risk of all that shame once
more. Anyway, there was no point. I had expected the
feelings to stop. But they were stronger than ever. If I
could not help myself, what was the point of saying I
was sorry and promising not to do it again?

'Just about that time, my aunt's attitude to me
started to change. She looked at me in disgust. She
kept asking me if I was entertaining impure thoughts.
She made me kneel down and say long prayers with her
every evening. It was as if she knew exactly what I had
confessed. Then, one night, she caught me. She must
have been just outside my room. I always tried to be
quiet but I suppose she heard me make a little noise.
She came rushing in and jerked the covers off me. I
pulled my hand away but my nightdress was up around
my waist. I didn't have time to pull it down. She
didn't say or do anything. She just threw the covers
back over me and walked off.

'After that she ignored me as much as she could and
I tried to avoid her. The evening prayers stopped. I
never went to Confession again. Finally I stopped
going to Mass. I couldn't face going near the church.
It broke my heart but I couldn't pretend any more. I
felt that God had rejected me.

'Then something very strange happened. I suppose
it was about three weeks after the time she had caught
me. She told me she was taking me to see a cousin of

hers I had never met. She said this cousin was very nice and had a piano I could play on. I love music. I had piano lessons at school and played the piano there, but my aunt didn't have one. I needed no persuading to jump into the car with her. I was so relieved that she was speaking to me again, and was actually doing something to please me. I wondered why I had never met this cousin before. I had always thought we had no other living relatives.

'We seemed to drive around for ages. I had no idea where we were. At last we arrived at this large house, standing on its own in the countryside. I thought my aunt's cousin must be an eccentric recluse. My aunt did not knock or ring the bell. The front door was open. I thought that was strange. When we were inside she bolted the door behind us. I panicked and tried to pull the bolt back. She grabbed me by the arm and pulled me up the stairs. She seemed to know exactly where she was going, as if she had been there before.

'There was a huge hallway with a grandfather clock. I remember it didn't work. The time was wrong. Funny, the silly little details you remember, isn't it? The stairs led to a gallery. There were several rooms off it. The door of one of them was open. She pushed me inside. It was dark. There were heavy curtains. They had been pulled across. I heard the door close behind me and a key turning in the lock. I heard her footsteps retreat. I was terrified. I could not move or make a sound.

'Then I realised I was not alone in the room. There was a figure in the shadows at the far end. Then a light was switched on. There was a lamp in the corner. The light was shining on me. It hurt my eyes. The figure was still invisible. Then he spoke. He asked me why I was afraid of the light. Was I afraid of the light of truth? Was I afraid to let the light of God shine into my

270

sinful soul?'

'Did you recognise the voice? Was it the priest who had heard your confession?'

'I suppose it must have been. In the confessional he just whispered, as I told you. I had heard him at Mass, of course, but here it sounded different. But voices are different in church, aren't they? All those echoes.'

'Did he have any accent, that you noticed? An Irish accent, perhaps?'

'Irish? But Father James wasn't Irish. Are you saying...? Oh my God, that's why you're here. You're saying it wasn't him. It was somebody else. Somebody you're still looking for.'

'Forgive me, Christine. I can't really say any more about it at the moment.'

She had gone very pale. She shook her head, slowly.

'My God, it's my fault. What happened to him. It never occurred to me it might have been...I'm sorry, you asked me a question. The answer is no, I didn't notice any sort of accent.'

'Please go on.'

'He told me I must let the light into me so I could be cleansed and the devils frightened out of me by its power. He...told me to undress. I was petrified. My hands wouldn't move. Eventually I managed to get my blouse and skirt off, and my shoes and socks. He told me to remove everything. I did. I looked down. There was a puddle on the floor and an acrid smell. I had urinated, without even being aware of it. He told me my body was meant to be a vessel of holiness, but devils had possessed it. He told me to show him where they had entered. I didn't know what to do. I pointed to my mouth. He told me that was wrong. I was shaking and crying. He kept shouting, "point, point!" Eventually, I pointed to my...to...down there.'

She stopped. She put her face in her hands and started to sob. I found myself kneeling in front of her. Through the loose woollen material of her cardigan I felt her arms tremble. I caught my breath. I could not remember reaching out my hands to touch her. I could not even remember rising out of my chair. If I had been conscious of what I was doing I would have held back. A priest never touches another person, except for a formal handshake, or the slight brushing of the finger involved in some of the sacraments or forms of blessing. He learns from the outset never to go too close to a distressed person, particularly a woman or child. I knew I should have stayed in my chair and relied on my well-rehearsed forms of verbal comfort to try to ease her pain. What, in God's name, had led me to forget myself like that? Slowly, I drew my hand away, my heart thumping painfully.

'It's all right,' I said, still kneeling. I was only inches from her, still far too close. But I did not want to alarm her by jumping back.

'It's over now,' I continued. 'It was many years ago. You've come through it all, though God only knows how. You've been strong all these years. You have every right to cry now.'

'I'm so sorry. I was sure I could do this. I was sure I could stay in control. I was wrong, wasn't I?'

'Stay there,' I said. 'I'm going to make you a cup of tea.'

I stood up and left the room. I found the kitchen and put the kettle on. I was relieved to be on my own for a few minutes, and to have a task to occupy me. I was sweating and my hands were shaking. I fumbled with the teacups and came close to breaking one of them. Slowly I regained my composure and tried to think. I was sure she was telling the truth, although there were some inconsistencies between her written and verbal accounts. In her letter, she had described being left downstairs in the house and finding her own way upstairs. Now she had told me her aunt had dragged her up the stairs. But that was a minor detail. Her memory could still be playing tricks on her.

She had not yet mentioned the hospital or the hostel. I would not press her. Why put her through further distress when I already knew the rest of her story? I would not even ask her why she had left her letters anonymously and why she had now decided to tell me face to face. Once I was satisfied she had recovered sufficiently, I would go straight home and burn her letters. I was now sure she would take no further action and that there would be no more such incidents. I knew who the guilty priest was, and I knew there was no longer any evil in him. I would let it rest. I would move on to another parish and forget the whole episode.

From the lounge came the strains of a haunting melody. I shivered. How could this be possible? Where and when had she had the chance to learn to play with such a sure and refined touch? It would have taken many years of continuous practice and concentration. Certainly not in that hospital or anywhere she had been since. She may have learned to play as a child, but surely not to that level. And much of what she had learned she would have forgotten since.

Unless...

'My God, Michael, you stupid..!'

THIRTY-THREE

I spoke the words out loud. She would not have heard them. She was still playing. My hands were shaking again. I took a minute to collect myself. I must not drop the tea tray. When at last I felt calm enough, I took it in. She had returned to the sofa. She was as composed as she had been on my arrival.

'Music has great healing powers for me,' she said.

'So I see.' I poured the tea. 'You play really well. Where did you learn?'

'At school, as I said. When I went to university I found a private teacher and played a lot of chamber music there. My brother bought me the piano. This was his house. He died of cancer a few years ago.'

'That piece you were playing. It was beautiful. What was it?'

'Chopin's Waltz in A minor, opus 34 number 2.'

'Gosh, what a mouthful! I don't know much about music. I'd like to get a recording of it, but I'll never remember all that.'

'I'll write it down for you. I recommend the first recording by Lipatti. He recorded the waltzes twice towards the end of his life. The second time was a live performance. His last. He was desperately ill by then, and only thirty-three. He didn't have the strength to play all of them. He died soon afterwards. I can't bear to listen to that recording.'

She went over to the writing desk, and wrote on a piece of paper. She folded it and brought it to me.

'Thank you. Christine, we really don't need to talk about this business anymore.'

'No, it's fine. I don't mind now. It has done me a lot of good. You see, I never told Simon about the episode in the house. I only told him that I had been to Confession, and the priest had told my aunt about it.

Simon didn't know what I had confessed. I told him only that my aunt had rejected me because of it. He was apoplectic with rage. Wrote off to the Archbishop on the spot. He then went to the Herald and told them. Said he was determined to expose Father James and see that he never worked as a priest again. I didn't want my name in the papers but it was too late. Simon gave it to them, along with that of Father James. I was furious with him. I never gave the press any interviews. They left me alone after a few weeks.'

'When he received your brother's letter of complaint, the Archbishop sent a priest to investigate. Did you meet that priest?'

'No. When Simon told me what he had done, I told him I wanted to take no part in any inquiry. Simon must have met the priest and told him he couldn't see me. When Simon saw how distressed I was he was sorry he had ever complained or told the press. But it was too late by then. I forgave him. He was always impulsive, but he acted from the best of intentions.'

'Have you any idea who the investigating priest might have been? Did Simon ever mention a name?'

She smiled and looked up at me.

'This is unofficial, isn't it? I did wonder. I don't want to be rude, but you don't look or sound like an official investigator. If it were official, you would know the answer to your question. You would have access to the files. It's all right, you don't have to tell me anything. If you can clear his name, please do. It'll be on my conscience for the rest of my life, the harm I did him.'

'You didn't harm him. You had every reason to believe it was he. He could have cleared his own name, but he chose not to. He chose a different way of life. He found his true vocation. You mustn't worry about him.'

'Thank you for telling me that. It is a great comfort to me. He is a saint, isn't he? To act like that, with no bitterness or concern for his own good name.'

'Yes. In my book he is.'

'You have seen him?'

'Yes.'

'Is he happy?'

'Yes. One of the most contented men I have ever met.'

'Thank God. No, Simon never mentioned a name. I'm sorry. I can't help you.'

'You said you went to university. When was that?'

'When I was eighteen.'

'What do you do now?'

'I teach music part-time in schools, and I give private lessons here. It was the mother of one of my pupils who told Father Brennan about me. We were chatting once and she told me she went to church. I told her I used to go when I was a child. That was all. The next time she brought her daughter here for a lesson she gave me the message from Father Brennan that you wanted to see me. You seem surprised. Don't I look like a teacher?'

'Yes, you do. Sorry, I mean that in a nice way. What surprises me is that you recovered so quickly.'

'It wasn't that quick. Or that easy. And I have never recovered fully.'

'Can you tell me what else happened in the house? How long were you there?'

'I was there about a week, I suppose. I lost all sense of time. I was telling you about that time he made me undress. He told me to get dressed again and sit on this chair in the middle of the room. I heard him come up behind me. He said a lot of prayers over me. He told me to keep my eyes closed. There were other noises in the room, but they seemed to be coming from where I had first sensed his presence, not where he was standing now. I wondered afterwards if there had been two people there all the time, though only one spoke.

'Then he told me to open my eyes. I noticed for the first time that in front of me there was a connecting door to the next room. He told me to go through. I heard the door being locked behind me. It was a bedroom. The windows were nailed shut. The glass was too thick to break. Not that I had any thought of escape. It was very small, sparsely furnished. A narrow bed. The sheets and covers were clean. There were two doors, apart from the one by which I had entered. One led through to a tiny bathroom and toilet. The other must have led to the gallery. It was locked as well. There was a Bible on the bedside table. He told me to read from it.

'My meals were left outside the gallery door. I didn't see who brought them. There would be a knock on the door when they were placed there, and I heard the key turn. When I opened the door, there was nobody there. Once I was back inside, the door was locked again. When the next meal came, I left the used dishes outside when I picked up the new ones. Once they left some spare clothes outside. They were mine. My aunt must have brought them.

'I kept as quiet and as still as I could. I read from the Bible until I was too tired to read any more. I slept. I prayed. I don't know how long this went on for. It must have been several days. It seemed like an eternity. I wondered if I was going to be kept there on my own forever. Then one night I was woken up by the sound of the key turning in the lock of the connecting door. The door opened. I heard his voice telling me to come through. I crept back into that room, shaking, whimpering, wondering what was going to happen. It was dark as before. I couldn't see him.

Then he spoke again. I jumped. His voice came from right behind me, telling me not to turn round.

'He put his hands on my shoulder. He said more prayers over me, mostly in Latin. One of them sounded like the words of Absolution. Then he told me that by the Grace of God the devils had departed from me, though I would need to be continuously vigilant against their return. He told me I had a weak soul. I needed to pray constantly to God and ask Him for strength. He told me to go back into the bedroom and wait. My aunt would come to fetch me home the next morning.'

'So you never saw him?'

'Never. I returned home. My aunt said nothing. She didn't ask about what had happened. We never spoke to each other. For weeks I was severely depressed. I couldn't attend school. I tried to kill myself. I cut my wrists with a kitchen knife. Then I went upstairs to my bedroom to wait. My aunt was out shopping but she came home earlier than I expected. She found me just in time. There was a trail of blood from the kitchen to my room so she must have realised right away what I had done. She just stared at me, then went to ring for an ambulance. I was taken to hospital.'

'How long were you there for?'

'Only a week. A psychiatrist came to see me once, for half an hour. I couldn't answer any of his questions. He seemed to think it was all my fault. He asked me why I was seeking attention like that, when I had a good, comfortable home and a kind, loving aunt to take care of me. I was discharged. You can still see the marks on my wrist, or I imagine you can, so I wear long sleeves.

'When Simon heard about it he came home and stayed with us. I often heard him arguing with my aunt. Asking her what she had done to cause me to cut my wrists. She wouldn't talk to him. He tried to get me to talk about it, though he was always gentle with me. I couldn't say anything to him. I tried, but always ended up crying. He decided I had to move away from there as soon as possible. He left the army and got a job. He had qualified as an engineer. He bought a small flat and moved both of us into it. That was when I finally told him about the confession and Father James, as I thought it had been.

'Simon took me to see this private psychiatrist up in Rodney Street. I had months of therapy with him. I thought I was cured. I went back to school. I had lost a lot of time. I wanted to catch up. I resumed my studies, frantically. To my surprise I got a place at university. I did quite well there. I was very quiet and studious. I didn't make friends. I got a good degree. Simon was very proud of me. He came to the degree ceremony. My aunt didn't. I went to London. I got a clerical job in the civil service.

'After a year, I had another breakdown. I came back here, to be with Simon again. He had bought this house. He married. I lived here with him and his wife. There was plenty of room for the three of us. They didn't have any children. This was my room. The music room. Simon died and my sister-in-law moved to New Zealand, where she had come from. The house is hers now, but she always refused to sell it or take any rent from me. I had the house to myself. I recovered, month by month, year by year.

'But every few years the depression has returned, each attack a little less severe than the last. I am almost content now. I never married, of course. I was too absorbed in my own efforts to cope with the world, to cope with my...sense of disgust with myself. Tell me something, Father...'

She looked up at me, a tense smile flickering across her face.

'I know he...that priest, was wrong to betray me. But was he wrong in the way he reacted to what I confessed? Was I really evil and corrupt? If I had gone to you in Confession, what would you have done with me?'

I smiled. 'Well, if you had told me about your feelings about your teacher's wife, I might have given you a few Hail Mary's to say.'

To my surprise she laughed.

'They were only fantasies, never intentions. I could never hurt anybody. I knew that as soon as those thoughts crossed my mind. If I had met her I would probably have thought she was wonderful. But...' she looked away again, 'about the other thing, I meant.'

'You just said you could never hurt anybody. Don't quote me on this, but for me sinning is about hurting. People or animals. Deliberately or negligently. But what you did...I have a confession to make to you. I know all about those feelings. I will never forget. I was a little older than you were. I was madly in love as well, with someone I thought would be forever out of reach. Just like you. Then, for a moment, I thought she might not be. Out of reach, I mean. But she was. Or so I concluded.'

She smiled again. 'You sound as if you were a typically confused adolescent. Funny, I never thought about priests being adolescents first and lusting after girls.'

'Well, this one was, and did.'

'So why did you become a priest? You could have chosen somebody else, if your first love really was unattainable.'

'No. I had decided. It was her or the priesthood. When she turned me down...'

'What a sad story. It's strange, Father. Since I opened the door to you just now I've been finding it

280

hard to think of you as a priest, at least the sort of priest I've had the misfortune to have contact with. I'm finding it even harder now. We seem to have a lot in common. But, going back to my question, you see, we were told that impure thoughts hurt God, caused Him pain.'

'I was told that, too. But somehow I think God has better things to do than be hurt by our thoughts. But, as I said, please don't quote me. I am supposed to be a priest, after all.'

'I'm sorry. I didn't mean to embarrass you. I know you have a job to do. I can tell you still have some more questions. Please go on.'

'You never go to church now?'

'Never. Except for the occasional wedding or funeral.'

'So you've never been to St Jerome's?'

'No. I know roughly where it is, that's all.'

'You don't know a Father Higgins, by any chance? Runs a hostel off the Dock Road.'

'No. I don't think I've ever been up there. I've heard it's not safe.'

'Is your aunt still alive?'

'I don't know. She moved away at the time Simon and I moved into the flat together. She broke off all contact. I don't know what would happen if I saw her again. I couldn't trust myself. I tell myself I don't hate her any more, but if I actually saw her again...'

'I understand.'

'I don't hate him, either. The one you're looking for. Not anymore. I did, of course. For many years. But it was destroying me, consuming me, stopping me finding any sort of life for myself. I still think about him. I think about how awful it must be to live in that sort of darkness. If you find him, I'd like to know. But I don't want to see him or talk to him. Will you get into trouble for what you're doing?'

'I already have. That won't stop me.'

'Is there anything else?'

'No. Thank you for everything, including the music and the tea.'

'You made it.' She smiled again. 'It has been good for me, honestly.'

'Could you do me a favour?'

'Of course.'

'Play me some more Chopin, while I see myself out.'

THIRTY-FOUR

When I returned, Father O'Malley had already gone out on his visits. A letter had come for me in the first post. I recognised the handwriting on the envelope. It was from my aunt. I took it upstairs to my bedroom and read through it. I sighed. The news it contained saddened me. I would miss her.

I expected Father O'Malley to be back by lunchtime but he did not appear. Mrs Raferty served me my lunch on my own, giving me extra portions as I had missed breakfast. I left most of it. She shook her head when she came in to collect the plates. I told her I was not feeling very well. I went upstairs to lie down. It was Father O'Malley's turn to say the six o'clock evening Mass, though I was duty bound to offer to say it for him as he had deputised for me in the morning. When he had not reappeared by half past five, I went along to the sacristy and prepared myself.

I said Mass in a daze, barely conscious of what I was doing or saying. Afterwards, I went straight upstairs to my room. The draft of my letter to the Archbishop was still on my writing desk. I tore it up.

I took out the note Christine had given me about the Chopin waltz. Then I took out the envelope in which the first letter had been enclosed. I laid the two pieces of paper side by side. I nodded. There could be no question about it.

I opened my drawer of personal papers. I wondered what it was I was looking for. There was a folder my mother had given me when I had come back to St Jerome's as parish priest. She had told me she did not have room for it. But I knew the real reason. Angela would be in that folder somewhere and she did not want mementoes of her in the house. At the time I had put it away without opening it, knowing the contents would revive painful memories. I opened it now. The ink on the yellowing sheets had faded. There were old school reports on both myself and Angela, none of them very complimentary. 'Grammar is a continuing weakness'. That was my report. 'Spelling is a continuing weakness'. That was hers.

I hadn't realised. Mother had always hidden away her reports. She had never told me about them until much later, when I was on leave from seminary. She had told me then that her reports were poor and the nuns were concerned about her behaviour. But I had never known what her particular weaknesses were. I could not even remember seeing anything in her hand. Mother had forbidden her to write to me while I was away.

I took out the letter Aunt Mary had written to me from Canada on her behalf. Only one letter. Even that was not in her hand. But there was an explanation for that. She had hurt her wrist. Naturally. Typical Angie. But why not more letters, when she was better? There was an explanation for that too. She did not want to be distracted from her vocation. She still harboured some resentment against me for leaving her. There were always explanations. Why, then, was I still asking questions?

What happened to you, Angie? The Angie who dared to ask our grandmother for lemonade. Who brought laughter into my life after our father died, when it seemed I would never laugh again. I needed your laughter and your courage, all the time I was away learning to be a priest. And afterwards. If you had only been there. Living nearby, married, with lots of cheeky, spoilt, laughing children to make fun of me and tease Father O'Malley and listen to his stories. Things would have been so different. I would have been so different.

But you went away. You left me. Because I had gone away and left you. Even if you hadn't died, you had already left me. The Angela who wrote to me through my aunt, if it was indeed she who was behind the letter, was not the same as you. Those words were not those of the sister I had known. When was it that I lost you? Was it already too late by the time I got on that train? Why didn't I try harder to keep you? Why did I ever go away? Is there anything of you left here for me to remember you by?

At the bottom of the drawer, I found one of her old exercise books. I glanced through it. It contained short stories, most of them shorter than a page, all of them breaking off in mid-sentence as she abandoned them for a new idea which had struck her. She had often told me she wanted to be a writer. But she never showed me anything she had written. She preferred to tell me her stories at night when we were in bed, making them up as she went along, usually unable to find a conclusion. There was a date at the front of the exercise book. She was ten.

I started to read the last one, knowing it would, like all the others, finish in mid-air. As I read the first two lines I smiled. It was a fairy tale, as I expected. But the inspiration was an event which had been only too real, our visit to our grandmother two years before, when she had asked for the lemonade. The grim memory had embedded itself deeply into her subconscious mind where her fertile imagination had worked on it and transformed it.

Once upon a time there was a litle boy and a litle girl who went to see their grand mother who lived in a cotage deep in the forrest the grand mother was a wiked wich and she made them say lots of prairs and gave them cold bread and potatos to eat after making them stand still for hours then she made them sleep on the bare floor. In the morning she gave them cold porige to eat which made them sick and she made them clean it up then she made them chop up wood for the fire but she did not put any of the wood on the fire because she was too meen and they were so cold that they hudled together to keep warm. Now deep in the forrest lived some good fairys and they came to the window of the cotage and looked in at the boy and the girl who were trying to sleep but were too cold and were keeping each other warm because they were cold and were crying because they were hungry and the fairys went and wispered in the ear of the wiked wich grand mother who was asleep because she was all right because she was waring a speshal warm wiches cloke and she had had lots and lots to eat because she had eaten the boys diner and the girls diner to and they said to her you are a wiked old woman because you are making the boy and girl cry and you go about as if you are good and holey but you are not so in the morning you must go to the priest and connfess and tell him you are sorry and he will tell you to make it up to the boy and the girl and give them lots and lots of sweets and lemmonade...

There was no more. Inspiration had dried up. Typical. I looked back over the last few lines. I had seen something but it had gone again. What was it?

I started to move the papers around the top of the desk, idly, wondering when I would hear the sound of Father O'Malley's return. I placed the envelope and the exercise book side by side, the book open at the page I had just been reading. I stared for a minute.

Then I froze. I had stopped breathing.

I gripped the edge of the table. The room began to swim. The chair in which I was sitting gave way.

THIRTY-FIVE

I already had my coat on when Father O'Malley returned. Mrs Raferty stepped out of the kitchen, stared at both of us for a few moments, then decided to leave us on our own. He looked closely at me.

'I've remembered. Christ, if I haven't been walking the streets battering my brains out and praying to all the saints in Heaven. Then it suddenly came back to me.'

'I know, Father. I made a terrible mistake. Forgive me, please, for God's sake. How in the name of Heaven could I have thought it was you? You knew the name because it was in the local paper.'

'That's it. That's what I remembered. How did you find out?'

'Christine. She rang me this morning while you were saying Mass. I've been to see her.'

'We were wrong all along, weren't we? Those letters. Christine didn't write them. Fine bloody detectives we turned out to be.'

'No. It wasn't Christine who wrote them. It was...somebody else.'

'Somebody else. That's right. And from the look in your eyes you know who it was.'

'Yes.'

'Michael, why have you got your coat on?' His voice shook.

'I have to go out.'

'To see those responsible for what happened.'

'Yes.'

'Take me with you.'

'No. I have to go on my own. It's my past. I have to go and face it. And not run away. Not this time.'

'Michael, listen to me.' He spoke urgently. 'You look as if you have murder about your heart. Remember, the Bible is right some of the time.

"Vengeance is Mine, said the Lord." That's the bit they got right. The rest, particularly all that stuff about being perfect, can go to Hell as far as I'm concerned. Christ, Michael, you're scaring me.'

'It's all right, Eamonn. I'm not going to commit any violence. It won't be necessary.'

He took me by the arm.

'Michael, I'm thinking that after tonight things are never going to be the same. I'm right, aren't I? Christ, why has it taken fifteen years before you call me by my bloody name? I know I'm a silly old fool who enjoys a joke more than attending to his spiritual duties. But we've been happy enough here, haven't we? At least I have. I know this isn't exactly the spiritual and intellectual centre of the universe, but it's not been so bad, has it? I'm not one for saying things like this, but I have grown a bit fond of you, and...what I'm trying to say is that if you don't stay on here, after what happens tonight, you may still need me. And here is where I'll be. And don't you forget that. And you just be bloody careful tonight and stay in one piece and don't do anything stupid. Do you hear? This is your elders and betters speaking. Well, your elders anyway. Well, what the hell are you waiting for? Get on with it.'

He threw his arms around me. Then, just as suddenly, he pushed me away and ran upstairs.

THIRTY-SIX

I parked outside my mother's house. I turned my key in the door as quietly as possible. I stepped in and closed the door behind me. Silence. Not even the familiar ticking of the mantlepiece clock. It had wound down. She had told me the sideboard drawer had been disturbed in the break-in. I looked through it. On top was a scrapbook about me. I had never seen it. She had never shown it to me, or told me she was keeping it. She had cut out and inserted a report in the local paper about my ordination at St Jerome's. Then another, a few years later, about my arrival to take over from Father Ambrose as parish priest. A blurred picture taken by their own photographer because she would not have had one to give them.

I padded upstairs, into the bedroom we had shared. The twin beds were still there, made up in case she had unexpected visitors, though nobody had visited for years. I looked at the one Angela had occupied, where she had kept me up night after night, telling me ghost stories and fairy tales that never had an ending. There was a crumpled blanket on it.

I sat down on the bed, where I had sat beside her all those years ago. I waited. I had to let the memories return. I had to let my acts of betrayal and my broken promises step forth and accuse me.

It was during the summer holidays, a year after we had been to see our grandmother, and a week after she had fallen over and fractured her arm while playing football in the street with the two young sons of our next door neighbour. They were two years older than she. They did not mind her joining in their games, though they made no allowances for her being younger and a girl.

Mother minded a great deal. She had forbidden her

to play with them. She had also refused to buy us a football so I could play with her, in what I hoped would be a less dangerous fashion. I was reading in the front room. Mother was sewing. When Angela's screams flooded the room from the pavement outside, I ran out, convinced she was dying. The two boys had rushed in to tell their mother, who had promptly telephoned for an ambulance. I managed to get Angela into a sitting position so I could cradle her head in my arms and try to persuade her to stop screaming. When Mother came out, some minutes later, by which time Angela was only sobbing, I told her the ambulance was coming. She was shaking with anger. She spoke to Angela, pulling out the words from the back of her throat as if they had lodged there and were preventing her from breathing.

'When you get better, young lady, I'm going to give you the thrashing of your life for disobeying me.' She turned away and stamped into the house just as the ambulance was arriving.

I stayed by Angela's side in her hospital bed that evening. Her arm was in a sling. The fracture was not serious and was expected to heal in a few days. They had decided to keep her in overnight for observation, in case there were any after-effects of shock. Mother did not come to visit. It was Wednesday, her evening for Confession with Father Ambrose. Angela was already her former self. She was the centre of attention. She chatted to the nurses and the patients in the neighbouring beds. I went to fetch her the next day.

'Can I go back again, soon?' she asked me, as I helped her on to the bus. 'It's much nicer in there than at home. Everybody smiled at me.'

'If you think you're going to break your arm every week just so you can go back there, you'd better think again. Next time, Mother will break your other arm and both your legs, and keep you at home as a punishment.'

'Yes. And she'll tell me not to come running to her if I break my leg again.'

She collapsed into peals of laughter, so that everybody on the bus turned to stare at us. After a few moments, I joined her. By the time we got home we were exhausted with laughing, having completely forgotten about the punishment Mother had promised her.

Mother had not forgotten. But she decided to change the punishment. She confined Angela to our room for two hours each afternoon, during which time I was forbidden to enter. Not only was I not allowed in the room, I was told to stay out of the house.

I did not have a watch. To ensure I did not inadvertently disobey her by coming home early I would stay out much longer than the prescribed two hours, walking round the local streets and parks, and sometimes along the shore. When I returned the two of them would be sitting silently in the front room, Mother sewing and Angela reading. Or pretending to. I could tell she had been crying. But I could not say anything to her. Part of her punishment was that she was forbidden to speak until after the evening meal was finished, and I was not allowed to say anything to her until then.

One day I got it wrong, although I thought I had been for a particularly long walk that afternoon. I came home too early. Or her confinement had gone on beyond the prescribed two hours. There was no sign of either of them downstairs. I should of course have gone straight out again. But what if Angela had fallen ill and Mother needed my help?

I crept up the stairs. The door to our room was slightly ajar. I heard Mother's voice. She was reading from her prayer-book. Through the gap I could see that she was sitting on the bed. Angela was kneeling on the bare floor in front of her. Her arm was still in the sling, so she could not hold her own prayer-book. Instead she repeated, in a whisper, her mother's words, a few at a time. I tiptoed downstairs again and quietly let myself out by the front door. When I returned after half an hour, they were downstairs.

After a week, Mother told me the confinements were over and Angela and I could see and talk to each other as usual. But she was forbidden to go outside on her own or talk to any of the neighbours' children. On the first day of her freedom she refused all my offers to take her out for a walk. Whenever I spoke to her she muttered something inaudible in reply.

Each night during the previous week, when she was still wearing the sling, Mother had undressed her at bedtime and put her pyjamas on her. Now her arm was free and she could dress and undress herself. That night, I returned to our room from the bathroom where I had been cleaning my teeth, expecting her to be in bed already. She had not yet put on her pyjama trousers. I saw that her knees were red-raw. I returned to the bathroom to fetch a damp sponge. She winced as I dabbed her knees as gently as I could.

'She made me kneel the whole time,' she whispered. 'While we prayed. The whole time.'

I put my arm round her shoulder. 'It's all right,' I murmured. 'The pain will go now. And I'll stay with you all the time. I'll make sure she never hurts you again.'

I had betrayed her. I had promised her I would never leave her. I had promised her I would make sure Mother would never hurt her again. I had broken both promises. And to make it easier for me to live with my betrayal I had buried the memory of it.

I crept downstairs again. I knew the house was empty. Why was I acting like an intruder afraid to make a noise? I did not want to disturb the ghosts that floated around me, the memories that were at last stirring in the dark corners and only now venturing towards the light. Mother had always said it was a house of prayer. But in a real house of prayer the memories of words and deeds do not slink away into the shadows.

I looked for the spare key my mother always kept in a cupboard in the kitchen. The third cup from the right on the top row. The cups she never used. Nobody could know the key was there unless they had grown up in the house. It was missing. Several empty food-cans stood on a ledge. A tin opener lay next to them.

I closed the front door noiselessly and returned to the car.

THIRTY-SEVEN

It was half past eight when I arrived at the nursing home. Dinner would be over.

'Good evening, Father,' said the sister on the desk. 'Father Ambrose is in his usual place in the lounge. I think you'll find he's asleep, though. These days it's impossible to wake him up until he does so of his own accord. It's as if he's in a coma.'

'How's his speech, when he is awake?'

'Very slurred now. If you're used to it, as we are, you can still understand him.'

I smiled, thanked her and went through to the lounge. The back of his head was motionless. I pulled up a chair and sat beside him. I put my hand on his arm and shook it gently. I looked round. There were three other residents in armchairs, all asleep. He did not stir. His eyes were closed. I put my hand on his and pinched it. No reaction. The nerve connections had gone. His body was close to the final stages of shutting down. The duty sister had been right. I would save my words until I knew he could hear them.

I went back to the desk and smiled cheerfully at her.

'He was awake when I went in but he's dropped off again now. We had a little chat. He asked me to pick up a book from his cousin's house. He told me the title of the book and where it is kept. But I don't have the house key, and as I said he's fallen asleep again. I don't want to disturb him, even if I could. Could I possibly ask you to get it for me?'

'That won't be necessary, Father. He used to ask us to fetch things from the house from time to time. Told us the key is kept under the mat outside the front door. There's a housekeeper who goes in to clean, and she picks it up and leaves it there when she goes. She doesn't take it with her in case he wants to send for anything while she's not there. Didn't he mention that? Shows how forgetful he's getting now.'

'No, he didn't mention that. Well, that's fine then. But there's still one problem. I've gone and forgotten the address though I have been there before. It's a bit out of the way, isn't it? Have you got it?'

'Yes, here it is.'

She took out a card from a box-file beneath the desk and wrote out the address on a loose scrap of paper. Then she produced a local map and showed me the best route to take.

'Should take you no more than twenty minutes by car, Father.'

'Great. Thanks a lot. I'll bring the book here tomorrow morning. It's a bit late now. Good night.'

I parked the car by a dilapidated five-bar gate. I walked slowly up the gravel pathway. The house loomed out of the shadows. There was the porch. I looked for the gargoyles. There they were. Eagles with devils' faces she had called them. I picked up the key from under the mat and unlocked the door. My footsteps echoed. A silent grandfather clock in one corner. A thin strip of feeble light under one door. I opened it. My eyes adjusted to the combined light from a gas-fire and a reading-lamp.

I could see a wisp of thin, stiff hair above the back of a chair in front of the fire. On the table next to the chair was a large brass poker. Thin, gnarled fingers stroked it. Piles of books and papers littered the other side of the table.

'Who's there? Who's there?'

Her voice, thin, wavering, terrified. Her hand tried to tighten on the poker but could not grip it.

'You won't need the poker, Mother.'

'Oh, is that you, son? I wondered if you would get

296

here first. Couldn't use this anyway. My hands are too far gone now.'

'So why are you hiding here, Mother? Fancy you telling a lie, telling me you were on retreat. I would hide that poker if I were you. It could be used against you.'

'You wouldn't hurt me, would you? Michael, I'm your mother. You can't hurt me.'

'No, I won't hurt you. But there's somebody who might. Is that why you're here? Because you're afraid of her? Ironic, that, isn't it? She grew up in terror of you, and with good reason as it turned out. Go on, tell me why you're afraid of her. Tell me what you and he did to her. I've read her version. I want to hear it from you. I'm a priest, so you keep telling me. So make your Confession.'

'Won't you come round and face me?'

'No. I don't want to see you. Father Ambrose told you about the letter I showed him and offered to hide you here.'

'Yes. How did you find out?'

'It doesn't matter. She broke into the house while you were out. She was looking for information about me. She discovered I was a local parish priest. You had a folder of stuff about me, articles in the local press in that drawer that was left open. She also took the spare key. You never noticed that had gone, did you? She's been living there, while you've been here. Sleeping in her old bed. Waiting for you to go back. She found out where I was and wrote to me. I haven't seen her. She hates priests. Understandable, that, isn't it? So she didn't want to contact me directly. She knew a priest had betrayed her, and I had gone to be a priest. As far as she was concerned I was one of the enemy. Now she wonders if I have become like him. She wants me to know because I'm her brother. But because I'm a priest she doesn't want to talk to me. So she left me that anonymous letter.'

'But why now? After all these years? Why is she coming after me now?'

'Her memory was affected by the drugs they gave her. It may have only returned recently. Since they discharged her, she's been slowly recovering, remembering her past, deciding how to confront it. Is that what you're doing here, Mother? Confronting your past? Let me help you. That's why I'm here.'

'What do you want to know?'

'Why you sent her away.'

'We sent her away because she was possessed by evil. We told you she had gone to Canada and died out there. We did that to protect you.'

'Protect me or protect yourself? You were wondering what I would have done if I knew what you had done to her.'

'You always had a weakness about her. Even after you had gone away to seminary I couldn't be sure you were safe from the world. If you had known you might not have understood. You might have given up your vocation.'

'Too right I would. And I would have taken her away from that dreadful place. And I would have seen that that evil priest answered for his misdeeds to the laws of the Church and the land.'

'So you would have defied God's will. That means we were right to do what we did.'

I stepped closer to her chair. I sensed her shudder.

'How long have you been here, Mother, alone with your thoughts?' I spoke gently, almost in a whisper. 'And not a chink of light has yet penetrated your soul. Well I'm going to see that it does. Because I'm not afraid of you any more. So tell me, why was it so important that I become a priest? Why were you so more certain than I was that it was God's will? Why did you need to construct such a monstrous fabric of lies to ensure I didn't come back before I was ordained?'

'Your grandmother wanted both of us to become nuns. Mary was always much too worldly. Mother pinned all her hopes on me. But I wanted it too, more than anything in the world. I went away to the convent and began my postulancy. You know what the word means, don't you? A postulant is someone who seeks admission to a religious order. There is always the possibility they might be refused. That happened to me. I nearly died of grief. I felt God had spurned me. The Mother Superior told me she was not satisfied that I had a true vocation. She was very kind about it. She told me that some women have a different sort of vocation. It might be their calling to bear children who would be called.'

'No, Mother, that's not good enough. You might hope that your children might be called. You might even pray for it. But what right had you to expect it? Just because you had been refused didn't give you that right. There's something else, isn't there?'

'Yes. I hoped I would never have to show you this.'

Slowly and awkwardly she raised a shaking hand. There was a crumpled piece of paper in it.

'Leave it on the table. What is it?'

'There was evil in the family, Michael. There was a danger it might have passed into you and Angela. There had to be...atonement.'

'Atonement? What in God's name are you talking about? The only evil in the family is in you, Mother. As your actions show.'

'My actions?' Her voice was suddenly harsh and shrill. 'When all I ever did was try to keep your hearts and souls pure? Don't you dare talk about my actions.

299

What about his?'

'Whose?'

'Your father's. Your father who now suffers the deserved torments of Hell and will do so for eternity.'

'My father? In Hell? Oh no. Hell is where you and that priest belong. My father was a good man and I know he is in Heaven. The day he died was the worst day of my life. The sun set in our house on that day and never rose again.'

'You never knew, Michael. You are still such an innocent. So I will forgive you your words. But ignorance can no longer be an excuse. You have to know. He was seen, Michael, seen committing obscene unnatural acts. Acts forbidden in Holy Scripture. Somebody saw him and sent him a letter demanding money. He couldn't pay of course. Even if he had, he would have been exposed in the end. It would have ruined all of us.'

'You knew about this?'

'Never while he was alive. Do you think I would have stayed with him or left the two of you in his presence for a second if I had known? He didn't have a heart attack. He took an overdose of sleeping pills. The first I knew about his...nature was when I read the note he left. This one. I kept it to this day. I never showed it to anybody. I suppose he had hoped marriage to me would cure him. A good Catholic marriage blessed by the Holy Church. But he was still rotten to the core of his soul. The law in those days was right. Then they made it legal. In private between consenting adults.' She spat. 'But sin is never private. God is always present. Adults can consent but God never consents. What is forbidden in Scripture is forbidden forever. And at the Last Trumpet all our sins will be revealed.'

'Yes, Mother. They will. Including yours and

mine. So it was all hushed up. He had a heart attack.'

'Thank goodness we had a good Catholic doctor in Doctor Grant. He was the only one who knew. He understood he had to conceal the truth for the sake of the Church as well as for the family. He signed the death certificate, stating he had died of a heart attack. I was going to burn the note. Then I thought that one day I might need it. I might have to explain to you. That day has now come.'

'So that was what all those prayers were about, after his death. You weren't praying for his soul. You were promising God that we would make up for his sins.'

'Only you, Michael, not her. You were weak in many ways but only you had it in your soul to do what was needed.'

'You mean only I was weak enough to be manipulated by you.'

'Don't blaspheme, Michael. I am talking of His holy will. After your father's death I prayed for weeks. I was in despair. Then one day I knew my prayers were answered. I sensed it in my soul. It was a moment of the purest joy. You would make up for your father's sins. God would call you. I swore to Him that I would do everything in my power to help you overcome your weaknesses. And you had many weaknesses, Michael. There were other voices than mine or God's, voices calling you to a life of wantonness. For a time you were listening to them, until I saved you from them. I never told you about what I did for you. I never asked for your thanks. I did what I had to do and waited. Then, one evening, you came down from your room. Do you remember? You had been up there all day, on your own. You told me you had decided. You would go to the seminary after all. You were sorry about the way you had spoken to me the week before, when you had said you were unworthy and could not go. Then I knew God had brought His will to fruition through me. But I knew I had to keep silent, in case you wouldn't understand. I had to let you think He had given you His sign directly. My thanks would come in the life hereafter. And one day, when you joined me in that life, you would know what I had done for you. I'm telling you now because you are putting your own soul in danger, by questioning His will.'

'I know it was you. I've known for some time. I thought she had made a free choice and that God had given me a sign. But it was you all along. You were not only prepared to destroy the lives of your own children but those of anybody who stood in your way.'

'I was only a weak and foolish old woman. I could do nothing on my own. But His hand led me. He gave me the power. He guided my mind and my heart. He took me to the place where I could confront the evil which threatened you. And by His Grace I vanquished it.'

'Did you really need the power of God and a host of His angels to vanquish one terrified eighteen-year old girl trying to make sense of her feelings and mine? You didn't even know her. But you brushed her aside. That was all it took to ruin her life and that of the man she married.'

'Ruin? How could I ruin a life devoted to leading astray those who were dedicated to God? She had already ruined her own life by letting herself become the instrument of the Devil. She was a whore, Michael. And you were putty in her hands.'

'How dare you say that about her! She was no whore. What she and I did together was the first time for both of us. And she stayed faithful to her husband, even though she didn't love him. So you were God's instrument, were you? And I suppose He was guiding you when you destroyed Angela.'

'I knew I could hope for nothing from Angela except that she might grow up as free from sin as possible for one of her nature and make a good Catholic marriage. She might not be capable of leading a holy life, but she might avoid the worst excesses of evil. That was the extent of my prayers for her. But her weakness was far greater than yours. It allowed the evil to enter her.'

'Evil? The natural feelings of a healthy, lively young girl? Was that all she confessed? A few so-called impure thoughts?'

'Thoughts? You are a fool, Michael. She was sixteen. Sixteen and already experienced in the ways of the world. The ways of the flesh, I mean. Sixteen, Michael, and the wicked girl was pregnant. And she hadn't even told me, her own mother. She had told him, in Confession. The devils had taken possession of her. She did not have the strength to resist them.'

'Is that what he told you? Instead of telling you it would never have happened if you had loved and accepted her and given her the guidance she needed? Why in the name of God was I so blind and stupid as to go away and leave her in your hands?'

'I tried to bring her up by God's law, as you had been. But she was wild, out of control. I couldn't fight the devils who had taken hold of her. Not on my own. Only a holy priest could do that. What could you have done? You were still only a weak and foolish boy, always ready to excuse her, always unable to see the bad in her. And you had to go away. God had called you.'

'No, Mother. He hadn't. I never had a vocation.'

'May God forgive you, Michael. You're angry because you don't yet understand. That's why you're blaspheming. There can be no mistaking the call of God, and no questioning it afterwards.'

'No, but we can mistake our ambitions and weaknesses, and attribute them to God's will. That's what you did when you promised me to Him. And what I did when I didn't have the strength to stand up to you. And don't you dare talk to me of blasphemy. What he did, in betraying her secrets, was a terrible blasphemy. And so was what you did, in allowing it to happen.'

'I absolved him from his duty of secrecy because her soul was in danger. He knew I had to know what she had confessed. He said he would try to purify her before she was sent away. But it might go wrong. He said that sometimes the devils cannot be driven out, even with exorcism. Then God and the Devil fight over a person's soul. It can take years. So it was with her. The exorcism didn't work. He told me what happened. She attacked him. She attacked the person of a holy priest. She was truly possessed. The Devil has still not given her up. Or she would not have written all that dreadful stuff about wanting to hurt us.'

'You took it upon yourself to absolve him from a duty from which nobody but she had the right to absolve him. As you both knew very well. Then you stood by while he brought her here and abused her. Finally, you had her certified and locked away, forever as you hoped.'

'That wasn't part of the plan, Michael. The original idea was to send her to Ireland, to work in one of those convent laundries. Have her baby there. Then they would have taken it away for adoption. But all that changed when she attacked him. They would never have accepted her, not someone who had viciously attacked a priest who was trying to give her spiritual guidance. They would have seen she was still possessed. So I asked Dr Grant to go to see her. He said she was a danger to herself and to others. She would need to go to hospital for a while, to receive the treatment she needed. He called in two colleagues who agreed with him. They signed the papers. I signed too. We followed all the proper procedures.'

'Was it a proper procedure to commit her under a false name? What name and address did you give when you signed the papers? Did Doctor Grant give you details of a former patient living on her own, someone who had died and whose house had been demolished in the slum clearances? That would have done the trick, wouldn't it? It doesn't matter. Anything would have done, so long as the trail didn't lead back to you. So long as nobody suspected what had really happened. That would have been unthinkable, wouldn't it? Imagine the whispering and shaking of heads as you passed in the street. People staring at you in church. Shifting away from you as you took your place. The pitying looks would have been the worst. The ones that said, there's the poor woman whose daughter went funny in the head so they sent her away. And then the gossip machine would start in earnest. Maybe she wasn't locked up because she was crazy. Maybe she had disgraced her mother, by getting herself...well, you know what I mean but I can't say the words. But you won't tell anybody else, will you? And so the word would go round and by the same evening the whole parish would know.

'Imagine the conversations. You'll never guess what I've heard. You know that woman whose son went to be a priest, the one who was bragging about it until we were all sick of it? Well, I know for God's own truth that her daughter got herself knocked up and had to be sent away in disgrace. Fancy that, the poor woman. Serves her right, though. Shouldn't have pretended to be all holier than thou. God took her down a peg or two for that. Oh no, Mother. That wouldn't have done at all. Anything to stop that. So you took away her freedom, her past and her future, all so you could hold your hypocritical head up in church.'

'No, Michael, it wasn't for me. It was for her. She had to be taken to safety while the battle for her soul went on. Now those idiots have let her go. I thought she would only be released when God had reclaimed her. She's out there and still in the Devil's hands. And she wants to do even greater evil.'

'Did you ever see her? After she had been taken away?'

'God's will was clear. We had to leave her alone while He fought with the Devil over her. I didn't know where she was. I didn't want to know. I told Dr Grant I didn't want to know, because as far as I was concerned what had happened to her was a curse and a judgement from God, because of your father.'

'What about the baby?'

'Dr Grant told me he had heard she miscarried. It was the only piece of information he ever gave me about her. The only information I would ever have wanted to hear. I was glad. Glad there would be no child to inherit her evil.'

'She miscarried because of the way she was treated in that dreadful place.'

'She miscarried because the child was a product of sin and evil possession. I never wanted to see her again. You do understand, don't you, son? You're a priest, so you must understand why we had to do what we did.' Her voice was cracking. 'For the sake of Almighty God, tell me you understand.'

'I'll tell you what I understand, Mother. My father's only fault was that he was not honest with himself. But in those days, few men like him dared to be. As for Angela, you never saw the goodness in her, your own daughter. She was worth a hundred of me.

Understand you? Never. And I can never forgive you, either. As a priest, I know I should. But as your son, and her brother, I cannot. No, Mother, it's not good enough. You haven't made a proper Confession. You haven't yet faced up to your sins, and you feel only fear and hate, not remorse. When you do face up to them, and you decide you want Absolution, find another priest. Not me, and certainly not your accomplice. Or pray directly to God for forgiveness. Tell Him you were led astray by one who assumed a holy form but whose evil nature surpasses yours. I don't want him to find forgiveness. But I do want you to. I want you to see in your heart the wrong you have done. And when she comes here, get on your knees and beg her to forgive you. She'll come eventually. You can't hide forever. She will find you. If I can, she can. She's very resourceful. Or go to her, if you have the courage. Go back home.'

'I can hardly move now. I couldn't get back. Not without help. And I don't want you to help me. I don't want to go back. I've decided to die here.'

'Does somebody come in here to look after you?'

'Yes. His housekeeper. She prepares some food for me. He told her I'm staying in the house while he's ill, to sort out his papers, decide what to destroy and what to leave for the Church archives. She doesn't know how sick he is. I sleep over there on the sofa. When I can sleep.'

'I'll leave the key under the mat outside. When she comes, she'll find it. Or if she doesn't, she'll find a way in. You can be sure of that. Goodbye, Mother.'

'Wait, Michael. Don't go. Don't leave me here like this. Michael, wait. You have to find her and stop her coming here. You have to explain to her. I couldn't see her. It would be too dreadful. Michael, for God's sake. Michael!'

She screamed as I left the room, strode through the hall and slammed the front door.

THIRTY-EIGHT

I was approaching Crosby. A mile from home. I knew I had driven much too fast. There was something wrong with the car, but I could not work out what it was. The engine sounded strange. Tim had noticed something was wrong but he hadn't fixed it properly. No, it wasn't that. The lights weren't all working. But I couldn't see which ones were out of order. Or was it the gears? Or the steering? Better get home as quickly as possible. Mustn't break down tonight. I can take it to the garage in the morning. I turned off the main road. One more turning and I would be home. I skidded to a halt and banged the steering wheel.

You bloody fool! The problem isn't with the car at all. It's outside. You sensed there was a problem every time you looked in the mirror on the way back. It was what you didn't see! The grey mini which was outside the hostel when you first went there, which she took with her when she went back to the house, which followed you and Tim, which Tim noticed but you missed. Which was there behind you tonight, never immediately behind, always two or three cars in-between, following you all the way to the nursing home, then all the way to...

Christ, what had I done? I would have gone back the next day, of course. When my anger had subsided. Promised Mother I would try to find her and stop her going there on her own. Found the housekeeper and told her not to leave my mother alone, not to let any visitors in, to contact me right away if anybody came looking for her. Now it was too late!

I drove like a maniac. When I reached the gate I jammed the brakes on just in time, jumped out of the car and ran up the driveway. Jesus Christ! The door was open, creaking on its hinges. She had gone in. I

309

might just be in time. Please God I had returned in time. They would be talking. I listened for the voices. They would be raised, angry voices. But that did not matter. Because voices meant life. Voices meant that nothing dreadful had been done. Not yet. I was in time to prevent it. If only I could hear something.

Nothing. No voices. Only silence. Deep, deepening silence.

Five minutes later I stumbled out, retching. When I reached the car I looked around. Still nothing to see or hear. Only the wheezing of air in my lungs. Nobody around. No sign of the other car.

Of course! I knew where she had gone. She had unfinished business. My mother and her priest accomplice. First one, now the other. The job was only half done. I wrenched the car into gear. The tyres screamed as I hit the road.

THIRTY-NINE

As I drew up towards the front of the nursing home I saw the approaching ambulance just in time to stop myself from colliding with it. It swerved and carried on, picking up speed as it approached the gate. The siren blared.

I swore, very loudly. She had been following me. Now I was following her, on the path of destruction she had been planning for weeks, and I was destined always to be one step behind. And it was all my fault. If only I had waited for her at home so we could have gone to face her tormentors together. If only I hadn't left my mother alone in that house. If only, if only. Well, whatever had happened here, it was too late to prevent it now. But I had to know the worst.

I dashed into the hallway. The same nurse was on duty at the desk. She looked up. She had been crying. She was dabbing the corner of her eye with a handkerchief.

'Father Jones, you're back already. That's amazing. I rang the presbytery and left a message with Father O'Malley and he said you were still out. I can't believe you got back there and then here again so quickly.'

'What's happened, Sister?'

'It was like I told Father O'Malley. Sister Teresa had gone in to check on him, only a few minutes after you had left. It was his breathing. She could tell right away that he was nearly choking. We sent straight off for the ambulance. You must have seen it leaving. Oh, Father, why did it have to happen so soon?' She was crying again. 'It's not as if we weren't expecting it. Doctor Michael had told us it could happen any day. But we kept hoping and praying he'd be with us a bit longer. Doctor Michael came at the same time as the ambulance. He's gone with them. He told us we should pray for him but we shouldn't expect him back here. He'll need intensive care now until the end. That could come any moment. I know it's God will, but it seems so cruel. Such a good and holy man.'

I stared at her.

'Sister, I'm sorry, I can see how distressed you are. So am I, of course. Such a sudden shock. It must have been awful for you all here. But I need to be clear. Father O'Malley doesn't seem to have got your message right. You're saying it was a sudden deterioration which could have happened any time?'

'That's right, Father.'

'Nothing else? I mean, he didn't have any visitors? After I left, I mean?'

'No, Father. Nobody. He was where you left him. Oh...' She put her hand over her mouth. 'I'm sorry, Father. I didn't mean to imply your visit was anything to do with it. I'm sure there was no connection. He always looked forward to your visits. And your mother's. He was always better for them. Until now.'

'Have there been any other visitors since I left, not for Father Ambrose I mean, for anybody?'

'No, Father. Nobody at all. It's been as quiet as a grave. Oh, I'm sorry...' She started to cry again. 'I just can't seem to find the right words. It's the shock. Since you left nobody has been through that door until the ambulance men arrived. Then it was like all hell let loose. Oh, I'm sorry! There I go again. I never meant to mention that dreadful word. They dashed in to get him ready and help him with his breathing, and then Doctor Michael came. They just got him out and then you arrived.'

'Does anybody have visitors through the back door at all?'

'Oh no, it's always locked. Unless there are deliveries and there have been none of those today.'

312

I sighed, allowing myself a glimmer of relief.

'Do you mind if I go in to where he was sitting, Sister? I know it doesn't make much sense but I just want to...remember him as I last saw him there earlier tonight.'

'Of course, Father. I understand completely. Go on in. I'll get the kitchen to make you a cup of tea. You look as if you could do with it.'

'What? No, no thank you. I'll be fine. I'll only be a minute.'

I glanced tentatively round the door, then tiptoed in. It was empty. The staff had obviously decanted the other residents to bed so as not to upset them as soon as they had realised Father Ambrose was in a critical condition. No doubt it was a well-rehearsed routine. I looked in and around the chair in which he had been sitting. I did not know what I was looking for. Something an unseen visitor might have left, a visitor whose hands had quietly closed around his wasting neck muscles, unnoticed by the others as they dozed in their chairs? But that would have left bruises. Sister Teresa would have spotted them long before the doctor or the ambulance men and would have raised the alarm about an intruder.

I was about to leave when I thought about the windows. There were two large sash-windows, covered with thick, velvet curtains. I eased back the curtains and checked the fastenings. To my inexpert eye nothing had been disturbed. I looked around the room again, my mind playing out the drama which had taken place there a few minutes before my arrival. Less than an hour before, another scene of horror had taken place in the house where my mother had stayed. But this was different. This one had been triggered by the inexorable progress of a hideous disease and not by any outside intervention. I was sure of that now. I went back to the desk.

'Thank you, Sister. I'll have to be off now. Which hospital did they take him to?'

'St Jude's, just outside Southport.'

'I'll ring them later. Thank you. I'm sorry you've had such a terrible time here this evening. But maybe it's for the best in the long run. God has decided to be merciful. His sufferings will soon be over and he'll be with his Maker at last.'

'I'm sure he will, Father. If anybody has earned a place in Heaven, it's him.'

She managed a tearful smile.

Not if my prayers are answered, I thought, as I walked slowly out of the front door. Go to sleep now, Father Ambrose. Slip from sleep into death. Don't wake up and make an Act of Contrition. Slip into death, and go to Hell for all eternity.

I drove back carefully, conscious that I was shivering although I had put the heater on to its maximum setting. I parked some distance from my mother's house, and let myself in as quietly as before. Nobody had seen me. The street was deserted. There were no lights on in the house, upstairs or down. I checked quickly through the rooms, knowing I would find them unchanged from my visit earlier that evening. I slipped out again, returned to the car and drove on to the presbytery, trying desperately to hold the steering-wheel steady, somehow forcing my shaking foot on the accelerator to keep within the speed limit.

FORTY

Father O'Malley had been waiting up for me. The door opened as I stumbled towards it and I nearly fell into his arms.

'Eamonn,' I gasped. 'You've got to help me. She's dead. I saw her there. It was horrible. We have to go back. Can't just leave her there. Better call the police. Oh no, that's just what we mustn't do...'

'Christ, Michael, you're rambling. Get yourself inside, get your breath back and some whiskey inside you and tell me what happened, for God's sake. But one thing at a time and start at the beginning.'

He would not let me speak again until I was seated in the armchair by the fire and had taken some sips from the glass he had handed me. My hand was shaking so much that most of it went on the floor.

'Now, tell me, Michael. First of all, are you all right? You're not hurt?'

'No, no, I'm fine. Just shock, I suppose.'

'Then who's dead? What happened?'

'My mother's dead. It's my fault, Eamonn. I left her. I went to the house...'

'Her house?'

"No. She was staying in Father Ambrose's house. His cousin's house, I mean. Hiding there. I tried to have it out with her. Tried to make her see what she had done. Then I left her there, on her own. Stupid of me. But I was so angry, I couldn't think. She was very ill, could hardly move. She'd been following me and I hadn't realised until too late. She must have gone in after me and...I'm sorry, Eamonn, you don't know who I'm talking about.'

'Oh yes I do. I guessed as much. When I saw you earlier tonight, before you went out, I knew this had to be a family affair. God, I'm sorry, Michael, I should have made you take me with you. How did your mother die?'

'When I went back there was blood on the floor and I could see the side of her head, by the temple. She had a poker with her, when I was there earlier. Some crazy idea of protecting herself with it. She could barely lift it. It was lying beside her. Blood on it...'

I leaned over the side of the chair and retched, dryly. He stood up and put his arm round my shoulder until I had recovered. He poured me another drink and returned to his chair.

'She never got to Father Ambrose,' I stammered. 'He's safe now in hospital.'

'Safer than you think, Michael. The nursing home rang again a few minutes before you got back. They had just heard from the hospital. He's dead. Never recovered consciousness.'

'Thank God.'

'I'm surprised you say that, Michael. I don't thank Him. God have mercy on me for the thought but if anybody deserved killing, and knowing why he was being killed, it was him.'

'I'm glad he never had a chance to confess, I mean.'

'You can't be sure he never repented, while he still could. Anyway, that's between him and God. So, it was that holy bastard all along. Talk about whited sepulchures.'

'I went to see him first, but he was asleep. I tried to wake him but it was impossible. Then I got them to tell me where the house was. I said he had woken up briefly and had asked me to fetch something. I found her there. She was terrified. I told her to ask her for forgiveness when she came. That happened sooner than I expected. She had followed me. Probably been following me for weeks. I had come nearly all the way back here before I realised. I went back. Found her there.'

'No sign of...?'

'No. They told me at the home that the housekeeper left the key under the mat. That was how I had let myself in. She must have been watching me, out of sight. I checked back at my mother's house. That's where she had been staying. No sign of her there, either.'

'What about her car?'

'Nowhere to be seen.'

'Any sign of the front door key when you left?'

'I never looked.'

'When you were there, both times, did you touch anything? Think carefully.'

I thought for a few moments.

'No. The first time I stood behind her chair. I wouldn't let her see me. The second time I didn't need to go near the body. I could see it all from by the door.'

'You never touched the poker, either time?'

'No. I wish to God I had. I wish I had taken it off her. I even warned her it could be used against her. What are we going to do?'

'For the moment, nothing. We're not going back there. And we're certainly not going to contact the police. Not yet.'

'They'll find her, Eamonn. Her fingerprints will be on the key, and the door handle and the poker.'

'Not necessarily. Maybe she wore gloves.'

'Christ, Eamonn, don't be such a bloody fool! Of course she didn't wear gloves. This isn't one of your detective stories you're so fond of reading. She didn't intend this. She went round to confront her, as I did. I never knew what anger was until tonight. But imagine hers, Eamonn. She had a thousand times more cause to be angry than I had. It must have boiled up to the point where she did not know what she was doing. The poker was just there. She probably didn't realise until afterwards what she'd done. If they catch her...I don't think I could bear it, Eamonn. After all she's been through. Wait a minute. I've got an idea. We'll go back there. I'll need your help. We'll wipe the poker clean. Then I'll put my prints on it. Then I'll go to the police and confess.'

'And she'll read about it somewhere and just let you go right ahead and do it? Forget it, Michael. The police won't believe you, anyway. You're such a pathetic liar. You'll need to show them her letters to convince them you had a motive, and the letters will put them on to her. But if we just leave things be, they'll never make a connection between her and the crime. All they'll have is a set of unknown fingerprints. If she hasn't been in trouble with the law before, and keeps out of their way in the future, they'll stay unknown. No more daft ideas like that, thank you. I'll decide what we do. Let me think. Who was looking after your mother?'

'There was nobody else living in the house. There's a housekeeper who comes in every day. She used to prepare some food for her.'

'Okay. So for the moment we do nothing. The housekeeper goes round tomorrow. Bit of a shock for the old girl but nothing we can do about that. She'll find her and call the police. Now, does she know her visitor was your mother?'

'No, I don't think so.'

'Let's assume not. The whole point of Father Ambrose hiding her there was that nobody would know where she was, not even you. Her anonymity was crucial to that. Tomorrow you will start getting worried about your mother. Get in touch with Mrs Prendergast. She should be back from retreat now,

318

because she has a husband who doesn't know how to boil an egg and she'll be afraid he'll have wasted away in her absence. She'll tell you your mother never went on retreat with her and she has no idea where she is. Then you go to the police and report her missing. Will your mother have any identifying papers on her?'

'She doesn't have any. Only her pension book.'

'That'll still be at her house. She wouldn't have been planning on popping out to collect her pension while she was supposed to be in hiding. The housekeeper will tell the police that Father Ambrose knew who she was but of course it's too late to ask him anything now.'

'If they go to the nursing home they may find out I had asked about the directions to the house.'

'They've no reason to go asking questions there.'

'Say they did. And say they fingerprint me and match the results to prints on the key or the door handle.'

'You went there on an errand for Father Ambrose. You had no idea your mother was in the house. You went in and out. You never saw her.'

'They'll suspect I'm covering for somebody.'

'Even if they do that's as far as they'll get. That trail leads nowhere. And as I said, I doubt if they'll even think to start down that road. The most likely course of events is this. They find this mysterious body. Obvious signs of foul play but not forced entry. They'll conclude it was intruders, burglars maybe, who had been watching the house and seen the housekeeper leave the key under the mat. Only you and I know who killed her and she will have disappeared without trace. Even if she reappears as Dora there'll be no connection to your mother. We must let her disappear. We both know how good she is at that. You mustn't make any attempt to contact her, or to let her know you know she's alive. I know that will hurt, but you have to let her go. If she got in touch with you or came here, of course, that would be different. But something tells me that won't happen. You have to reconcile yourself to that.'

'Okay, so the police conclude it was intruders. But why should they kill an old lady who was barely able to move?'

'They couldn't find anything in the house. They threatened your mother, wanted to know where the valuables were hidden. She wouldn't tell them. One of them lost control. Picked up the poker. When you've reported her missing they'll soon put two and two together. They'll tell you they think they've found your mother and she's dead. You'll say you think she was staying there to keep an eye on the place for Father Ambrose, because of his illness. She was getting forgetful and didn't let you know. You thought she was going on retreat but she must have changed her mind. No trail leading to you or to anybody connected with you.'

'But what about the letters?'

'Good thinking, Michael. We'll burn them, and the envelopes. Right away. Go right on upstairs and get them.'

When I came down again I went into the kitchen. It was unfamiliar territory, Mrs Raferty's jealously guarded domain. Taking care not to make a noise which might wake her I opened the cupboards and searched through them until I found a large iron saucepan. My mother had had one just like it, handed down through generations. I took it into the library. The gas fire was still burning. I put the pan in the grate, tore the papers into shreds and put them in the pan, all except the first sheet of the first letter. I glanced down it for the last time, lit it at the fire, dropped it into the pan and watched the fire spread. At the last moment before the fire expired, while I was sure he was not looking, I threw in the piece of crumpled paper I had picked up from the table next to my mother's body.

I had lied to him. I had touched something, the note from my father which might have led the police to suspect my mother's visitor had not been a stranger to her. As the paper burned, I ran through the scene again in my mind. My mother lying there, motionless. I, tiptoeing to the table, picking up the note with two fingers, taking care not to touch the table itself or anything else, watching my steps to ensure I did not leave a footprint in her blood, hoping and praying that my nerve would last until I could get outside and into the car.

He examined my handiwork.

'All done? Good. Tomorrow, we can bury the ashes in different parts of the garden,' he said, in a conspiratorial whisper. 'You can explain to Mrs Raferty about the pan. I leave that to your powers of invention. You should be off to bed now, Michael.'

'I couldn't sleep. Not now. Let's have another drink. I need to talk.'

He fetched the drinks and handed one to me.

'Did you ever suspect it might be her, Eamonn? During our investigations, I mean? I only found out myself by chance. I was looking at some old papers of hers from when she was only ten, and saw some similarities in the handwriting on the envelope. But what really clinched it was the spelling. Nobody else in the world spells "confession" the way she does. And she must have seen the correct spelling a thousand times on the church notice board.'

'Michael, every time you talked to me about your

sister, there was a certain look in your eyes. And tonight, that same look was there, only it was lit by a fire I had never seen in you before. I have to confess that the possibility had occurred to me. I prayed again and again that it would not be the case. I desperately wanted it to be the Gallagher girl. Or somebody else. Anybody else. Not her. But the more I thought about it, the more I believed it couldn't be Gallagher. It just didn't fit. The circumstances were so different. And what reason would she have had to send you a personal letter when she didn't know you from Adam? Michael, when you talked to your mother tonight, did you hear her Confession? Did she seek Absolution?'

'No. She didn't accept she had done any wrong. What they had done was for the good of Angela's immortal soul, she said. All her life my mother had allowed people to poison her mind. Her own mother, Father Ambrose. She allowed herself to be turned against her own children. As far as I know she never sought forgiveness, from God or Angela. But I can't be sure what happened in those few minutes after I left, before she met her death. If I had known it was going to be so soon...'

'Don't blame yourself, Michael. She had plenty of time. More than most sinners. Alone there in that house, with only her thoughts for company. All the time in the world to face up to what she had done. If she chose not to, that's her business. There's something else I must ask you about, if you're up to it.'

I nodded. 'Go ahead.'

'How come you suspected me? What was all that stuff about a pamphlet and a priest called John something?'

'As I told you, I went to see Father Coffey. I was curious about the so-called exorcism. He's something of an authority on them. When he read the first letter, he confirmed it was not a true exorcism. Then he saw a connection with the perverted beliefs and practices of a certain nineteenth century priest called Sebastian Johns. He was excommunicated and his writings ordered to be destroyed. Except they weren't all destroyed. He had produced a pamphlet. Father Coffey had found a copy of it here. Dreadful stuff. A torturer's charter. Instead of destroying it, he took it away with him, like the true scholar he is. Then he told me Father Johns had been Irish. He had followers.'

'Also Irish?'

'Yes.'

'And they operated in Ireland?'

'Yes.'

'So let's look at the case against me, Michael, in the cold light of day, well, early morning. You had a pamphlet that could have blown over from Llandudno and in through the open window for all we know, and the fact that there were once a couple of priests in Ireland who liked to go around torturing and humiliating young girls. And on the basis of that you constructed a case against me. I was from Dublin so I had to be part of some Irish mafia of priestly perverts.'

'Well I suppose if you put it like that it does seem as if I rather jumped to a hasty conclusion. I did ask you to forgive me.'

'And I have forgiven you. Because I rather think I would have come to the same conclusion.'

'But I had other grounds as well. I can say this now I know you've forgiven me. There was the name. You knew the name of Gallagher when you shouldn't have, unless you had been the investigating priest.'

'Sure, Michael. And a very convincing piece of evidence that turned out to be, when everybody who read the Herald at the time knew the name. So you went to see Christine. Did she name Father Ambrose as the investigating priest?'

'No, she never knew. Her brother handled the whole complaint on her behalf. He's since died. What happened to her was very similar to what happened to Angela, except that there was no immediate breakdown. She was taken to the house and made to undress and make humiliating confessions. She didn't react the way Angela did. She didn't get hysterical. She played along with them. So they told her she was cured. She broke down months later. Tried to kill herself. She told me her brother had made the complaint to the Archbishop on her behalf, and had also told the press.'

'Which let me off the hook.'

'I didn't know it was Father Ambrose until I got back here and discovered it was Angela who had written the letters. It had to be him. We all went to him for Confession. Mother insisted on that. And I found Mother hiding in his cousin's house, a house that exactly matches the description in Angela's first letter. She admitted that Father Ambrose had told her about the letter and suggested she hide there.'

'And you think he was a follower of this Father Johns?'

'Not directly. It was too long ago. But Father Johns had followers, as I said. I believe he was a disciple of one of them. Probably got the pamphlet from him. One of the followers might have been the other priest Angela describes in her letter, the older one who pretended to be an exorcist. Christine also thought there might have been someone else there when she was being abused.'

We sipped our drinks.

'There's something else I want to do, when the dust has settled,' I said, after a long pause.

'What's that? Pilgrimage to Lourdes on your knees,

324

in sackcloth and ashes, flogging yourself, all for suspecting me? It's all right. You don't have to do that. A bottle of the best Irish whiskey will do.'

'You've got it. But I meant, clear Father James' name. Christine begged me to do that.'

'That'll take years.'

'I'm not going anywhere.'

'The Archbishop will have your guts for garters. And you can expect daily visits from Monsignor Winstanley.'

'I'll tell the Monsignor it's all your idea. All the Archbishop can do is throw me out of the priesthood. And I'm leaving anyway. You were right to say my heart was never in it. There are witnesses who could help. His mother is still alive and she can testify he didn't hear any confessions that night.'

'What about Christine?'

'She told me she couldn't be sure whose voice she heard in the confessional. And she never saw his face clearly.'

'Angela didn't mention Father Ambrose by name in her letter.'

'Even if she had, we've just destroyed the letter. But remember, they don't have to find Father Ambrose guilty. Only conclude that Father James was innocent.'

'All right. I'm with you. We'll start lobbying as soon as the dust is settled from this other business. They'll probably throw me out as well. We'll make a right pair won't we? Two crazy defrocked priests haunting the parish. You're looking just about dead, Michael. Better get to bed.'

'I will. Good night, Eamonn. Thank you for everything. We'll do it all exactly the way you say. I'm in your hands.'

FORTY-ONE

'Come on in, Michael. It was good to hear from you. I am sorry about your mother. What a ghastly thing to happen. And her all alone like that.'

Father Higgins looked even more tired and dishevelled than usual, and his sitting-room even more cluttered. He moved several piles of paper from an armchair so I could sit down. He looked round, seemed to decide that the effort of finding a space for himself to sit would not be worthwhile and hovered over me. He looked uncomfortable. I coughed and began slowly.

'Father, this isn't just a social call, as you might have gathered. I'm looking for...connections.'

'I think I understand. I'll help if I can. But I think it would be best if you put your cards on the table first.'

'All right. Can I ask you a question before I do? Has Dora shown up again? Have you heard anything from her since we last spoke about her?'

'Not a sausage. Except that the car has been returned. That was a pleasant surprise. It was left outside the hostel during the night.'

'When?'

'A couple of nights ago.'

'No messages left on it or inside it?'

'Nothing. The key was in the ignition. Tim looked it over. It was in good nick. Had done a hell of a mileage since it disappeared, though.'

'All right, Father. I'll do as you ask. Put my cards on the table.'

'Call me John, please. I have an idea that as this conversation develops I'm going to become more and more uncomfortable with the fact that I'm supposed to be some sort of priest.'

'I know that feeling, John. Dora's real name is Angela.'

326

'You thought it might have been Christine.'

'I was wrong about that. I was mixing Dora up with somebody else altogether. Then I found out the truth. Dora...Angela was...is...my sister.'

'Yes, I know,' he whispered.

This time he made a determined effort to find a space at the table where he could sit. He started to shuffle through some papers. At first I thought he was trying to calm his nerves by finding something to do with his hands. Then I noticed he was holding up an envelope in his hand.

'Come and look at these, Michael.'

I went over to the table. From the envelope he had pulled out three faded black and white photographs. Three men with white collars. Three priests. All the faces were known to me. He spread them out.

'I got these from library archives, records at the Crosby Herald, the museum, anywhere with old parish photographs. They are the best I could find. The three priests who were there at the time. We spent hours poring over them. It was no use. She couldn't remember which one it was. Not by name, not by appearance. They're none of them very good likenesses, as you can see. All we knew was that it had to be one of them. One of these three. Yes, Michael, she had told me what had happened. All the details, as they came gradually back to her. After months of wrestling with herself, she decided to confide in me. That was how long it took for her to trust me. I was sworn to secrecy, which is why I couldn't tell you when you came here. I was helping her. She had found her mother. She would deal with her in her own way in her own time, she said. Now she wanted to find the priest. I was helping her, even though I knew what it might lead to. She never threatened violence, but often I could see it in her eyes. What the hell was I supposed to tell her, Michael? Forgive and forget? After what they had done to her? No, I threw aside the teaching of Christ and I helped her to get her revenge. What sort of priest does that make me? Now it has come to murder. Murder of a mother by a daughter. I prayed it wouldn't but inside I was sure it would. And it had to be your mother as well. Meeting you, liking you, wanting us to be friends, has made it all so much more painful. Oh, God. My fault. Michael, I am really so sorry.'

He covered his face with his hands.

'No, John. You couldn't have stopped that. I could, but I didn't.'

'She never told me about you. I can't even remember if she said she had a brother. Must have been strange for her, when she found out her brother was a priest. When you came here, saying she had been leaving you messages, I wondered what was going on. I couldn't ask her because she had disappeared by then. I just held my breath, waiting to hear or read about something she had done, wondering if she would be caught, deciding I would give up the priesthood so I could testify on her behalf, even if it made me an accessory. Then I read about your mother. It had to be her. It was too much of a coincidence. She looking for her mother, you coming here after having had messages from her, your mother being killed. Okay, tell me. I have to know. Which of them was it?'

'Father Ambrose. That one.'

'Did he confess before he died?'

'No. I found my mother hiding in his house. Angela followed me there.'

He picked up the photograph and stared at it.

'The papers only mentioned a remote house in the country. I never met him. Knew him by reputation. Was his death...?'

'Natural causes. He had had motor neurone disease

for some time. God had punished him in His own way.'

'Your mother...What do they think happened?'

'Intruders, looking for money or jewels. One of them hit her when he couldn't find any and she wouldn't tell him where they were hidden.'

'Plausible, I suppose. They're not looking for anybody else?'

'No.'

'And I take it from your visit that Angela has not been in touch with you.'

'No. She's disappeared again. This time for good, I'm sure of it.'

'So am I. So it's over.'

'Yes. There is one thing I want to do, though, before I can feel that it is over. I didn't go to Father Ambrose's funeral. You can understand why. All those eulogies, everybody saying what a holy man he was. But I do intend to visit his grave. I have a few words to say to him. Personal. On Angela's behalf.'

'Yes, so do I. Your sister was part of my life as well. I suppose I loved her, in a way. My way. When I imagine what she might have been, what she could have done, if her life had not been torn apart like that when she was so young...Michael, let's go together. To his grave. Would you mind?'

'Of course not. You've earned the right to be with me.'

'When are you going to go?'

'Not for a week or so. I'm taking a short holiday first. Leaving tomorrow. I'll ring you when I get back.'

'Good. You look as if you need it. Where are you going?'

'Canada. Vancouver.'

FORTY-TWO

For the second time in my life, I looked down on the peaks and glaciers of the Coastal Mountains as they slid behind the plane on its descent to Vancouver Airport.

I took my aunt's letter out of my pocket and re-read it.

My dear Michael

Now that I am getting old I have decided I cannot stay in England any longer. The thought of dying here, away from my family, is just too much for me. I want to be with them now. With Bill, and Anne, and of course your sister. Though my own sister is nothing to me now, the thought of being away from you causes me a great deal of pain. I am returning to Vancouver. I want you to visit me as often as you can. I am enclosing an open plane ticket for your first visit. I do not know where I will be living. Come as soon as you are free. If I have not yet sent you an address, write to me care of the priory. I have been in touch with the Mother Superior. She is looking forward to the renewal of our friendship. I hope to find peace there. Please forgive me for not saying goodbye in person. By the time you get this I will be already on my way. I cannot bear airport farewells.

Your loving Aunt Mary.

She was waiting for me in the arrivals lounge. As soon as she saw me she ran up to me as if to hug me. Then she thought better of it and held back. I nodded but could not force myself to smile. I barely recognised her. In the short time since I had last seen her grief and age had ravaged her.

We drove through the centre of Vancouver, and on through Stanley Park and over Lions Gate Bridge to North Vancouver. There we took the left turn towards Horseshoe Bay, then north along the coastal route in the direction of Squamish and Whistler. Heavy mists rolled across the waters of the Strait of Georgia. The grandeur of the panoramas that unfolded with each bend of the road meant as little to me now as they had on my first visit. Now, as then, I was in mourning, for a sister who had died to me a second time.

After about half an hour we took a right turning along a narrow road, leading sharply uphill over a pass. I saw the church and priory below, on a plateau by a rushing stream. We had not spoken a word during the entire drive.

She parked the car outside the cemetery where I had spent so many hours on my first visit. We walked slowly through the gates, towards the grave we each knew so well.

'The Mother Superior gave me your letter,' she said, at last. 'I did as you asked me. I burned it right away. I'm staying inside the priory as a guest. I haven't found anywhere permanent to live yet. I join in the routine of their lives. I try to make myself useful. Help out in the kitchens and the gardens. Did the funeral go all right? I'm sorry I couldn't be there. It would have been hypocritical of me to go.'

'I wasn't there either. Father O'Malley took it. I was officially sick. Everybody understood. Nobody expects a priest to take the funeral of his own mother when she has been battered to death.'

'And the police think it was a casual intruder?'

'More likely a planned robbery that turned violent when nothing of value was found. Either way the case

331

is closed.'

We had reached the grave.

'I still come here every day to pray. She was a beautiful child, so quiet and self-possessed. Your mother hated me for her. Said that Anne was the child she should have had. She had prayed for such a child. Instead she had Angela. But Angela was blessed, too, in her own special way. Why couldn't she see that?'

'Anne wasn't in the car with her father, was she?'

"No. He was on his own.'

'Where was Anne?'

'Staying with some school friends. Your mother told me Angela had fallen very ill, and had had to be sent away. We discussed it, by phone, by letter. We worked it all out. Anne was sure by then that she had a vocation. I explained the situation to her. She agreed to help. The Mother Superior had never met Anne. Anne had been educated at a boarding-school in Edmonton. She did go to one of the Order's preparatory colleges, but in Rome, not here. I thought it would be good for her to travel a bit. Before she...' She paused and dabbed her eyes with a tissue. 'I introduced her to the Mother Superior as my niece, Angela Jones. It didn't matter to either of them what her name had been while she was in the world. Once her vocation was confirmed she would have a new one. Anne started her postulancy. I wrote a letter to you from Angela.'

'Pretending she had hurt her wrist.'

'Yes.'

'That was very true to life. If Angela had come here she would have broken something within a week. All this open space to run around in. The style and language of the letter wasn't exactly her, either. But I assumed at first you were acting as her ghost writer, taking her thoughts and finding a suitable style for

332

them. Then I thought you might have invented the accident and the letter, to disguise the fact that Angela did not want anything more to do with me. I would have understood that. I had left her alone with Mother at a time in her life when she was intensely vulnerable. Only I had no idea just how vulnerable.'

'When did you realise that Angela wasn't here?'

'She sent me an anonymous letter, telling me what had happened. I think she was going to identify herself to me later on, when she was sure I would be on her side, when she knew I was not the sort of priest who had betrayed her. But then the...it happened. It was too late. She won't make contact now.'

'But you recognised her from the letter, even though it was anonymous?'

'Not at first. It was typed, but she had written the address on the envelope. Later on, I happened to be looking at one of her old exercise books, from when she was a child. I saw how bad her spelling was. It obviously never improved. The typed letter had the same mistakes, unique to her. Then I compared the writing on the envelope and in the exercise book. They were similar enough to confirm my suspicions.'

'Anne had a serious congenital weakness of the heart. She was a premature baby. They did various tests on her and discovered the condition. They told us she would be lucky to survive more than a few years. Every year of her life was a special blessing to Bill and me. I knew she was likely to die before me. She did not know about her condition. The Mother Superior did. That was why she agreed to let her start her postulancy early. She wanted to give her every chance of taking her final vows before she died. When Anne died, Angela could die too. I was sure she already had. You could mourn for your sister, knowing nothing of the terrible things that had happened to her. I could mourn for my daughter and my niece.

'Shall we walk around the gardens? Spring comes earlier to Vancouver than to nearly anywhere else in Canada. I love this time of year.'

She took my arm as we began to stroll.

'When your mother told me Angela was seriously ill, she said she had been showing signs of mental instability for the past two or three years. Now it had suddenly got much worse. Angela was prone to violent outbursts. She was a danger to others and a serious suicide risk. The doctors had said she would have to go away for treatment, possibly for some years. I believed her. I had no reason not to. I had not seen Angela for a good few years. Your mother was desperately concerned about you. She seemed more worried about you than about her in fact. She thought that if you found out what had happened, you would give up your studies and come back. Nothing meant more to her than for you to complete your preparations and become a priest. We decided on our plan. For your sake, so she said. At the time, I was persuaded it was the right thing to do. Of course you would have to be told the truth in the end. The time would come when you would insist on visiting your sister. But by then you would be a priest or well on the way to becoming one. If Angela had come home by then, you could give her spiritual guidance. You would understand why we had done what we had done.'

'My mother suggested that? That she would have had Angela home again? She was lying to you. She would never have acknowledged her. Angela really was dead as far as she was concerned.'

'I realised later that she was lying to me. When Anne died, we had no choice but to continue with the deception and pretend it was Angela who had died. To your mother it was a solution sent from Heaven. Now you need never know what had happened to Angela, unless she returned and you found out. I didn't see it that way. Your mother hadn't lost a daughter in the way I had. Not a daughter who was blessed to her. To me, it seemed that I was being punished for my part in the deception. Though even then I had no idea of what had really happened.

'As time went by I grew more and more uneasy. There was no news of Angela. I expected your mother to send me reports of her progress, or tell me if she had got worse. I wrote to your mother, telling her I wanted to see Angela for myself. I didn't care what condition she was in. She didn't reply. I knew something was badly wrong. I took the next flight to England. I went round to see your mother. I demanded to know where Angela was. She told me I had no right to know. We had blazing rows. At last, she admitted she did not even know where she was. To her, she was dead. She had never even existed.

'I kept on going round to see her. I demanded to know what had really happened. Eventually I forced it out of her, bit by bit. She told me what she told you, the way you described it in your letter. I was horrified, sickened to the depths of my soul. At first I could hardly bring myself to speak to her. Then I told her she had committed a terrible sin. I said she was a cruel and unnatural woman, and a hypocrite, doing all this evil under a cloak of religious fervour. She threw me out of the house.

'I had never really understood her. She was so different from me. But I had always looked up to her. Thought she was a holy woman. It was such a shock to realise that holiness can be a cloak to hide anger and hatred. Our mother was much more severe with her than with me. She ignored me. Let me go my own way. Thought I was a hopeless case. I knew your mother hated and feared her, but she never showed it. I thought she overcame it in the end. I thought Father Ambrose had shown her the way to come to terms with it. Instead he only fanned the flames of her anger and resentment. Turned it into a form of sick obsession. He hid his real nature from the world as well. I never liked him but I would never have suspected him of doing what he did.

'From the moment I knew what had happened, I never spoke to your mother again. I came back here and sold up. Then I returned to England and went in search of Angela. All I wanted was to be with her. Even if she had no idea who I was. Even if they had to lock me up with her. I went first to Doctor Grant's surgery. He had died by then. His successor could find no records in the surgery about her committal to an asylum. The health authority had no record either. They gave me a list of the large psychiatric hospitals in the region. I visited them all. Then I went round the rest of the country. Many had already closed down.'

'Why didn't you tell me, Aunt? I would have come with you. We could never have found her. But you wouldn't have had to shoulder the burden on your own.'

'I know. God knows I wanted to tell you. But I was so afraid I would find out she was dead. You had mourned for her once. It would have been terrible for you to have to mourn again, this time knowing how she had lived and died. And you are no fool, Michael. Not like me. You would have wanted to know how she had got that way. You are her brother. You two were inseparable when you were young. You knew her better than anybody. You would have guessed that she had been maltreated. You would have asked questions, until you discovered what it had taken me years to discover. I hoped you would never have to know. Of course, if I had found Angela alive, that would have been different. I would have told you the whole truth then. But if she were dead you could continue to believe she had died a happy, painless death here. Where had she been confined?'

'Quite close. Ridgeway Park.'

'I remember. I went there. It was closed down. I tried to get a list of former patients and where they had gone. It was hopeless. It was as if they had disappeared into a black hole.'

'She was using a different name, anyway. The original records at the hospital would have had the name Doctor Grant had given them for her, whatever that was. Certainly not her real one. She called herself Dora.'

'So I could never have found her. About your mother's death...There's no chance, I suppose, that the police could be right? That Angela might have had nothing to do with it? That she might see that God has punished your mother and Father Ambrose for their sins, and make herself known to us?'

'No, Aunt. No chance at all.'

'No, of course not. The way you explained it in your letter. It had to be like that. I let her down, Michael. Terribly. I should never have come out here in the first place. I should have stayed to keep an eye on the two of you. When I went back eventually it was far too late. I tried to make up for it by looking for her but it was no use.'

'I let her down, too. Leaving her alone there while I went away to seminary. Just at the time of her life when she needed me most.'

'Is this God's way of punishing us, Michael? Letting us know she's still alive somewhere, but telling us we'll never be able to see her, talk to her, make our excuses to her, ask for her forgiveness? We have to

337

live with that, don't we?'

    'Yes, Aunt. We have to live with it.'

FORTY-THREE

'Can I get you another cup, Father? That one's gone stone cold.'

'No. Thank you. I'm sorry, Mrs Raferty, I'm still feeling the after-effects of the flight. Nine hours on a plane is a long time. And when you land it's not the time of day your body thinks it is.'

'I wouldn't know, Father. I've never flown in my life. How was your aunt? How did she take it? The news of your mother's death, I mean?'

'She was shocked about the way it happened, of course. But they had been estranged for a long time. Her sister's death wasn't a loss to her. It's very odd, Mrs Raferty, isn't it? Many people spoke of my mother in terms of admiration. Everybody said what a good woman she was. But nobody really seemed to like her. I mean, you did knitting for her and she did sewing for you, but the two of you weren't really friends, were you? I acted as your courier for the jobs you did for each other. You never went round there for chats by the fireside. Neither did anybody else. I was her only regular visitor, and that...'

'Out of duty? That was plain for anybody to see. Your mood and the expression on your face come Sunday lunchtime. I think I will get you that fresh tea, and have one myself. Sometimes people need to talk.'

She returned in five minutes with two cups of fresh tea, and sat down opposite me. 'I met your mother a few times when you were still a boy, serving on the altar here. Sometimes she would come round after Mass to talk to one of the priests about something or other. I would sit her in here, get her a cup of tea, we'd have a little chat while she was waiting. She was very proud of you being on the altar. She often said that when she saw you up there she had this vision that one day you would be the priest and some other boy would be serving for you. She was sure the vision came from God. After you had gone away to seminary I felt a bit sorry for her. Thought how she must be missing you. I had heard she was good at sewing, which I'm not. So I thought I would take her a few things to keep her occupied, and keep an eye on her that way.

'I met your sister at your house. What a bundle of mischief she was! Made me feel years younger. After a while I realised that I was going round there for Angela's company rather than anything else. I understand why you loved her so much. I could tell your mother didn't approve of her. Once I told her she had to make allowances for a lively teenager. It wasn't the right thing to say. I knew that as soon as I'd said it.'

'My mother didn't believe in making allowances.'

She took a long sip of tea and looked up at me.

'I still went to visit her after your sister had left, though I knew she would never open up to me about what had really happened.'

'What...What do you mean, Mrs Raferty?'

She put down her tea and made a dismissive gesture with her hand.

'I knew it wasn't true. What she had been telling everybody. I knew your sister hadn't gone to be a nun. It just didn't add up. Your mother was round here one evening. Here in this very room. It was a few weeks before Father Ambrose told me Angela had gone away to Canada. I was outside, cleaning the mirrors in the hall. The door was closed. I couldn't tell which priest it was she was speaking to. His voice was too low. I wasn't eavesdropping, but I couldn't help hearing her when she raised her voice. She was saying something about there being a curse in the family. That's a strange thing to say, isn't it, when your son has gone to be a priest and your daughter has told you she has a vocation as well?

'The next day I was doing the flowers in the church, because Sister Rose had been taken ill all of a sudden. Your mother was there on her own. Saying her rosary. I smiled at her but she didn't notice I was there. Her eyes were burning. She was biting her lips. Then she got up and started to do the Stations of the Cross. She looked like a soul in Purgatory. I was so worried about her I went round to her house the next day. As a pretext I took some things that needed sewing, but I wasn't bothered about them. I knew she was in. I could hear her voice. I think she was reading from her Bible. She didn't come to the door.

'Then three weeks later, Father Ambrose told me the news. I went round to your mother again, with the same package of sewing. This time she opened the door. She was different now. Very proud. Almost defiant. I told her I had heard the news from Father Ambrose. I wanted to be among the first to congratulate her. She told me God had been good to her and had answered her prayers for both her children. I asked her when Angela had left, because if I had known I would have taken something round for her as a parting gift. Three weeks ago, she said. Three weeks! Just at the time I had heard her at the church, talking to one of the priests about a curse, and just at the time I had seen her praying as if she were calling for death to take her and release her from her pains. I knew she was lying. I don't know if she realised. I think she did. The way she was looking at me. I was almost scared, and it takes a lot to scare me, Father. It was as if she were warning me not to ask any questions. Angela had no more time for gifts, she told me. She was past such things now. She no longer craved worldly goods. Maybe not, I replied, but at least I could have wished her well and said goodbye. I could tell she didn't want to talk to me anymore, so I left.'

'Why are you telling me this?' I stammered.

'Because I believe you know at least some of the truth now. Probably more than I do. You know your sister isn't buried out there in Canada. You know she never went there, don't you?'

'Yes.'

'I can read you like a book, Father. All these years I've watched you, watched your grief for her as it became part of your life and your soul, part of what made you such a good and understanding priest, watched how you consoled yourself with the thought of her blessed, final days. Then I saw you change, suddenly, horribly. It wasn't your mother's death. This was just before that happened. That same evening, before you went out. I saw things in you I had never seen before. Anger instead of grief, despair instead of consolation.

'I don't know where Angela spent her life after she left here. I don't even know if she's still alive. What you might know about all that is none of my business. But as far as the reasons for her being sent away, I have a pretty good idea. In my young days, if you brought disgrace on your family, you were sent away and as a rule you did not come back. Some girls were put away in those dreadful asylums. Morally feeble, they called them. As if it were a sort of illness, when all that had happened was that nature had taken its course because nobody had told them of the dangers. I knew Angela had always had an eye for the boys. But if she had been careless, and been sent away to have her baby, why did your mother come here to discuss her condition with one of the priests? That was the bit I couldn't understand. And why had she talked about a curse?

342

'Then I began to understand. For your mother it could never have been just a social disgrace. It was a betrayal of everything she stood for, everything to which she had devoted her life and in the name of which she had sent you to be a priest. It was hardly surprising that she should seek spiritual guidance at such a time. But what was the guidance the priest had given her? Why wasn't it a Christian message, one of love and forgiveness for Angela? There was no need to send her away. I would gladly have taken her under my wing myself. Found somewhere quiet for her to stay and have her baby, then helped her to get back into her life, maybe find her a job somewhere. Or had your mother received a message of forgiveness from the priest and rejected it? I'll never know. I've asked myself that a thousand times since, if there was anything I could have done.'

'There's nothing you could have done. Nobody would have told you the truth and you could never have traced her.'

My voice broke. She passed me a handkerchief.

'That's right, Father. You go ahead. It's about time you cried. You've held too much inside for far too long. There's only one more thing I need to say to you, and I'm not expecting you to say anything in return. I know you found out something, and then that very night your mother died in dreadful circumstances. If either or both of you had anything to do with it, then I'm the last person to pass judgement. I loved your sister, and I've loved and looked after you and kept an eye on you all these years. All I'm going to say is that I'm on your side, whatever that makes me. Society has its rules, and God knows we need them, but as far as I'm concerned only God understands the human heart and only He has the right to judge. If it was her, and she comes here, I'll help you to keep her safe. You can

343

rely on me to the end, you know that. No, Father, don't say anything. You were going to say it was you, not her. The trouble is that if it was her that's exactly what I would expect you to say. Just forget everything I've said, unless the day comes when you need to remember it.'

She rose from her chair. I stared straight ahead.

'She won't come here, Mrs Raferty. Not now. She's dead.'

She grunted and left the room, briskly. After a few minutes I heard her whistling, dusting the furniture in the hall.

FORTY-FOUR

'I'm beginning to wonder if we're doing the right thing, Michael. I've never liked graveyards and this one's particularly spooky at this time of evening. Nobody else around. What if he jumps out of his grave at us?'

'Good. Then I can tell him face to face. It's not far now, John. Fifty yards along here, Eamonn told me.'

'Michael, I think I'll stay here, if you don't mind. By this tree. This is more about you than me. I feel like an intruder. You go on. Shout if you need me.'

'All right. I won't be long.'

I walked on slowly between the graves, the scent of lilies and honeysuckle sickly in the evening air. A shiny new marble headstone. I read the inscription.

"In Loving Memory of Father Thomas Ambrose, of the Parish of St Jerome's, a blessed spirit who walked humbly in our midst and transformed the lives of all who met him, now face to face with his Maker. Requiescat in Pace."

Freshly placed flowers. Nobody nearby, thank God. I knelt on the bordering grass and addressed the headstone.

'I thought you were a saint and they all still think so. All except those of us who know the truth. So where are you now? Did you confess? Did you make an Act of Contrition? Did you get Absolution? Are you in Heaven? By all the holy saints in that place I hope not. I hope you hardened your heart against God. May you rot in Hell for ever, Father Ambrose, you and your evil collaborators.'

I walked back to the corner where John stood, looking nervously about him. I had expected to feel better. I had expected a sense of release. Nothing. He put his hand on my shoulder as we walked back to the car. Neither of us said a word as we climbed in. I started the engine, slipped into first gear and eased the car into the slow-moving stream of traffic. Rain drove slantwise across the windscreen.

'Put the wipers on, Michael. You can't see a thing.'
'Sorry.'
'Did you find him?'
'Yes.'
'What did you say to him?'
'I said I hoped he would rot in Hell.'
'Do you feel better?'
'No.'

'Angela never came to me for Confession, you know,' he said.

He had interrupted a long silence as we crawled along in heavy traffic. He obviously wanted to turn my mind to her and away from her tormentors. It was a thoughtful gesture, typical of him. I smiled. I liked to hear him talk about her. Our complementary knowledge, mine of her as a child, his as an adult, was now the strongest bond between us.

'She said she would come one day, when she had remembered all her sins. I told her it would be quite a list. She had twenty years to catch up on. I would have to reserve a whole day for her. She said she used to quite like going, when she was younger, before... "Saturday Confession, Sunday Mass with Communion, being wicked all week, starting all over again at the weekend." That's what she said.'

'Her memory was still playing up then. We went to Confession on Wednesdays. All three of us together. Mother insisted on it.'

'Yes, when you were still around. She was talking about later. From when she was fourteen. You had gone away by then. It's funny what she said. I'll always remember it. She had such a way of saying things, it made me laugh out loud. She said, "you don't think I could stay holy from Wednesday night to Sunday morning at that age, do you? Me mam got really annoyed when I changed to Saturday but"...Christ, Michael, what the hell are you doing? You can't just stop here in the middle of the road. The chap behind nearly ran into us.'

'Take the car back to St Jerome's, please, John. I've got to go back.'

I jumped out, slammed the door shut, and ran back towards the cemetery.

FORTY-FIVE

The door to the cottage was open. I searched for a light switch in the hall. I found it and flicked it. Nothing happened.

'I'm in here, Michael.'

I groped my way through the living room, breathing in the chill damp in shallow gasps. The curtains were closed. There was a small halo of pale yellow light from a bedside lamp which had been placed on the floor. Shapes slowly emerged as my eyes adjusted to the gloom. The books and papers were gone. There was a table in the middle of the room and an empty chair in front of it. A shapeless mass stirred on the other side of the table. He was huddled in a black hooded overcoat, his face invisible.

'Sit down, Michael.' The voice seemed to come from the void behind him. 'I've been expecting you. I heard your car. Watched you get out. Are you alone, Michael? Or did you bring Father O'Malley? Is he waiting in the car, until you need him? What about Angela? Did you bring her, so she can exact her revenge in person? If so, she's welcome to come in. I'm tired of waiting here for her, day after day. After I read about your mother, I knew she was back. That was her, wasn't it? There always was a violent streak in your sister. I should know. I knew she'd come for me one day. If she can find your mother's hiding-place, she can find mine. Now you've come, I won't need to wait for her. You have no idea what a relief that is. I couldn't go without telling somebody. You or her.'

'I'm alone, Peter. Nobody knows I'm here. As far as I know I'm the only one who knows it was you. Until recently Angela couldn't remember which of the three of you it was. She may have found out from my

348

mother before she killed her. In which case it is only a matter of time before she finds you. She could be out there watching. Or I could still be the only one.'

'In which case you're being either very brave or very stupid, Michael. I wouldn't have expected either from you. I don't suppose the police are looking for her?'

'No. They've closed the case.'

'I'm glad. She is entitled to be free to hunt us down and then disappear. Only in my case I intend to save her the trouble. But do sit down, Michael. How very rude of me.'

I sat down opposite him. The table was empty apart from two small objects. One was of dull grey metal, the barrel pointing away from him. The other was a slim bracelet of tarnished silver. He stroked the handle of the gun in his slender fingers.

'As you see, I've cleared the decks.'

The voice was the same as before, dry, precise, empty. The emptiness I had thought was only a scholarly mannerism.

'Burned all my books and papers. My researches are over. I have concluded nothing at all from them. I have wasted the last fifteen years in trying to understand. I'm sorry about this.' He tapped his fingers on the handle of the gun. 'No need to worry, Michael. It's just a precaution. A strange thing for a priest to have, you might think. I've had it for years. A parishioner at St Jerome's came to see me one day. Told me he was worried about his brother. Worried he might commit suicide. His brother was a farmer, near Formby. He had had a lot of bad luck. I went to see him. He told me he had thought of killing himself. He gave me his gun. Said he would feel safer that way. It didn't help him. A week later, he hanged himself. I kept the gun. I don't know why. But I did find it useful on one occasion. I didn't have to fire it. I've never done that. I thought I would bring it out of hiding again, for our little chat. Just in case. I suppose you wish it was on your side of the table. I presume you would very much like to kill me.'

'Yes.'

'That won't be necessary, Michael. But I would be grateful if you would stay in the chair. I really don't want to hurt you.'

'I know you don't. It's only women you hurt.'

'Yes. In the past. I've done nothing bad for fifteen years now. I'm old, of course. Grown out of it. I've had fifteen years to think about it, to study all the books I can find on the theology of evil, to try to understand it. I've failed. It must be much easier to study evil from the outside. You can manufacture all sorts of interesting hypotheses and find case studies to support them. Come up with fancy long names for newfangled syndromes. But the fact is that evil is nothing. Just an emptiness. A vacuum. Oh, don't get me wrong. I still believe in God and the Devil, in Heaven and Hell. Only not for me. You see, to know the joys of Heaven or the agonies of Hell, you have to have an immortal soul. I don't.'

'That's blasphemy, Peter.'

'Only if you say that nobody has a soul. That we're all animals. I don't believe that. All I know is that I have no soul. When I die, I will not go to Hell. Nor to Heaven, of course. Not even Purgatory or Limbo. The formation of human beings is a complex process, I'm sure you'll agree. From conception to birth to childhood. Things can go wrong. Some babies are born without limbs, or without a brain. It's like a short circuit in the electricity of creation. It can happen in the spiritual dimension as well, only then you can't see it, of course. You assume you have a healthy normal child, not a monster. You can see a physical monster. In the old days, the midwives would smother it or leave it to die. That should have happened to me. But nobody could see what was missing. So I lived. If you can call it a life. Perhaps I had had a soul once, early in the womb. It died. But the rest of me lived on, like a twitching, severed limb that does not yet know it has lost the reason for its existence. Or like those freakish physical misshapes that still struggle in the womb, desperate for birth, fighting for life and air, unaware of the horror they will induce when they emerge, unaware that they do not belong in the world outside the womb.'

'It wasn't a vacuum that harmed those women. That was a real person with free will. You're deluding yourself, Peter. You will go to Hell. And you're right to say that I would gladly send you there.'

'Hell? What do you think it is, Michael? Goblins with pitchforks, and hissing serpents?'

'No, I never believed that. But I believe what we were taught. That it is the everlasting absence of God.'

He slapped the table with his free hand.

'Right, Michael. I agree with you completely. The absence of God, or to put it another way, the absence of life, the absence of soul. You agree with me, though you don't yet realise it. You see, I know exactly what Hell is like. It is how I have lived all my life. And the worst part of it is that I know that at the end there will be nothing. Just a handful of unconscious dust. I wouldn't care if that were the fate of all of us. But I know it isn't. I envy the souls in Hell. They lived and made their choices. Even as they suffer they sense the reality of their immortal souls. If I had been like them, I would have joyfully embraced my destiny years ago. I would gladly have used this gun on myself, and jumped laughing into the pit.'

'You're trying to make me think you're mad, Peter.

It won't work.'

'Mad? Oh no. I have had moments of terrible madness, but I'm not mad. I wish to God I were. But God would never allow me that mercy. I've prayed for madness as I've prayed for death. I've prayed to escape from the knowledge of what I am. But my prayers don't count. I have no connection with God, you see. There's no telephone wire between us. God doesn't know I exist. He only recognises souls, made in His image. Even when they sin, those souls are still part of His being. I'm not. I can't repent and go to Heaven. And He can't send me to Hell. Father Ambrose understood that. That's why he refused me Absolution.'

'You tried to confess?'

'Yes. Me. I confessed to try to save the immortal soul I never had. It is funny, isn't it? But we'll come to all that in due course. I'll tell you everything, I promise. I'm pleased you're here. So how did you find out?'

'Someone who met Angela before she disappeared made a chance remark. Something she had told him. When she was in her teens, after I had left to go to seminary, she went to Confession on Saturdays.'

'And Father Ambrose only ever heard Confession on Wednesdays. Strange, isn't it, Michael, the trivial little details that catch us out in the end. When you came to see me the last time, I wondered if you had found out. But I was sure you hadn't. The way you spoke to me over the phone. I wouldn't have cared if you had. Not for my sake. I was already tired of waiting. I thought of telling you. But then it occurred to me that you still might not find out. For some reason Angela was obviously reluctant to approach you directly or even identify herself to you.'

'Because I was a priest. So you were trying to spare

my feelings. I find that hard to believe.'

'I was always fond of you, Michael. In my way. I have some accidental residue of human feeling in me. What happened to her...It was never meant to be like that. Things went wrong. I decided it was better you never knew, if possible. You're not a very good detective, Michael. You were on the wrong track. You thought that letter was from the Gallagher girl.'

'So you tried to confuse me even more. By suggesting Father O'Malley might be the culprit, because he knew the name and you said you didn't.'

'I knew that wouldn't fool you for long. You didn't really think the Archbishop would put him in charge of a sensitive inquiry, did you? He got the name from the local paper. I guessed that. I suppose you suspected Father Ambrose next. Who else could have brought the pamphlet to St Jerome's? Not me. I had told you about it. I imagine you were reluctant to believe any evil of him. But he was your mother's confessor, and as far as you knew he was still Angela's at the time of that little episode. And when the trail led to his cousin's house, a house fitting the description in her letter, you had no choice but to believe it.'

'That's right. I went there.'

Keeping his left hand on the barrel of the gun, he raised the other hand and pulled back the hood of his coat. The light threw shadows across his sharp features. For a moment the pleasure of self-congratulation forced his tight lips into a rictus.

'Well done, Michael. You weren't so bad a detective after all. It has amused me, sitting here all these weeks since your visit, imagining you following those false trails. I was sure Father Ambrose would never betray me, if you accused him. He really was a saint, you see. And I knew he was ill. Soon he would be too ill to defend himself, even if he had wanted to.

No, we were safe, unless she remembered. But perhaps she never would. Perhaps you would never find her.'

'And all that stuff you told me about Father Johns?'

'That was all true. You saw the pamphlet.'

'And you really believed it?'

'Of course not. There were times when it gave me a spurious authority for my acts. Times when I was either insane or when my true self emerged. I leave you to decide which. It made me proud to think that I might be following in the footsteps of a holy man devoted to banishing evil spirits. But the rest of the time I knew it was nonsense. Father Johns believed it, of course. He was lucky. He had a lasting spiritual and theological justification for his perversions. So did Father Lamb. I had none. None which lasted beyond the moments in which I was engaged in committing my crimes.'

'I never did accuse Father Ambrose, not while he was still alive. By the time I suspected him it was too late. I was angry with God for taking the opportunity from me. Now I know He was saving me from the terrible sin of making a false accusation to a helpless invalid, someone who had been my friend and mentor. I could never have lived with that. So Father Lamb was your mentor? And later your accomplice?'

'Yes. My mentor and that of Father Ambrose. We knew him at first as Father Callaghan. He was the head of the orphanage where we were both brought up. But he soon confided in us about his past and initiated us into his thinking. He told us his real name and his connection with Father Johns. He had never recanted at all. I suppose they thought that as the principal of a boy's orphanage he was safe, because he would have no opportunity to harm young women. What a short-sighted viewpoint that was. He had the opportunity to do more harm than he had ever done himself, by grooming others to take his place.

'Father Ambrose pretended to go along with him. Then one day he told me he had decided to reject Father Lamb's teachings. He marshalled an astonishing range of intellectual and theological arguments against them. He was still only a boy but he had such powers of mind and spirit. He tried to persuade me to reject them as well. In the end he thought I had. He was convinced that I was like him, a scholarly, humane, if rather old-fashioned, priest. If he hadn't trusted me he would never have let me work with him at St Jerome's. I even began to believe that I was what he thought me to be. I saw myself in his image. What a self-deluding fool I was.'

'So you brought that pamphlet to St Jerome's.'

'Yes. Father Lamb gave it to me. He had realised by then that I and not Father Ambrose was his true disciple. I knew it was banned and that I should burn it. But I told myself that as a scholar it would be wrong for me to destroy any document. Again I was deluding myself. My real reason was that I needed to feel its presence, needed to have access from time to time to Father Johns' obscene words to support my own perversions.'

'But what in God's name persuaded you to be a priest in the first place?'

'Father Lamb was cultivating us to be priests so we could continue what had been his work. Father Ambrose would never have contemplated any other calling. He was a true priest. Spiritual and humble, and far too trusting. I was none of those things. But the calling had its attractions for me. I knew I could never fit into the world. I could never be a man among men or women. And there was something else I didn't consciously understand at the time. Have you ever thought about the power you get when you're a priest?

I suppose not. You're not a very spiritual person, Michael, but you're a man of compassion. Too much compassion to be a good priest. You try to understand, when your job is only to judge. I could tell that when you were still an altar boy.

'I knew your mother was determined you would be a priest. I didn't try to argue against her, but I could see you were never suitable material. You want to help people. There's an innocence about you. In one way, that is. You trust people, believe them, want to help them. That sort of innocence.

'But in another way, you were not so innocent, were you? I always suspected you weren't a virgin. Just something about you. Something in your eyes. The sort of memory that comes only from experience. I'm right, aren't I? So how is that possible? How could you have taken all those steps into the real world, the world of loving women and being loved by them, only to withdraw and become a priest? I know you're not going to tell me. Why should you? Maybe someone broke your heart. You wouldn't be the first. But you should have stayed out there in the world. Tried again. Found someone else. That was where you belonged. You're not interested in power. I'm not talking about power from God. I'm talking about the power all those stupid, gullible people give us. The power of the sacraments. And above all, the power to make them tell us all about their stupid little sins.'

'You became a priest for that?'

'I didn't realise it at first. I thought I was doing good. I thought I had driven out my devils, and so could go on to drive out those of other people. The truth was that I had a chance for revenge. Against the mother who had left me to be looked after by my older sister. And against her. Especially her. I don't blame my mother for leaving, not now. Maybe she saw the deformities in me which were invisible to others. Maybe it was because of my sister that she left, when she discovered she was earning extra pocket money as a whore.

'My sister was fourteen when our mother left. I was eight, very small and undeveloped. My mother had been very strict with her, with both of us. Now my sister was free to do what she liked. What she liked was to beat me and lock me in a cupboard. She left school and earned a living from prostitution. She supported both of us, after a fashion. Later on, she found other amusements. She liked to undress me and make fun of me. She invited her friends round to join in. She took me upstairs and showed me some of her clients, when they were naked and ready for her. Told me she would show me what real men looked like, what I would never look like. Some of them nearly passed out laughing when they saw me. This went on for a year.

'At last a neighbour must have reported to the police what was going on in the house. I was sent to the orphanage. My sister was put in a youth detention centre. I have no idea what happened to her. I expect she's dead now. I thought the orphanage was heaven on earth after life at home with her. I loved to study. I didn't mind the boys making fun of me for being small and weak and not interested in games. I could take that. I could cope easily with a world where it seemed women had been removed from the face of the earth.'

'So when you had the chance you took revenge on women.'

'No, of course not. Not on good women who live by God's law.'

'God's law? You mean your perverted version of it.'

'I never intended it to be like that. But they

reminded me of her. Whenever that happened, something changed inside me. It was as if God had placed a special instrument of justice into my hands. They were like her, so God had decided that I was the one to punish them. Only they were worse than she was because they were hypocrites. They came to Confession. Trying to buy an easy conscience by slipping in some quick reference to impure thoughts or deeds, hoping they'd get a few Hail Mary's to say before going off to do it again. I never let them get away with that. I insisted on knowing all the details. The more humiliating the better. They had to obey, because they knew they would not get Absolution otherwise. Some went away, crying, still unabsolved. Others whispered and stumbled over words they had never pronounced in their lives. I never helped them out. I told them God had to hear them describe their sins in their own words. I told them and myself that it was for the good of their souls. I made them believe it. At the time, I believed it myself.'

He looked at his watch. 'There may not be enough time, Michael. I keep wondering if she's outside and might decide not to wait for us to finish our conversation. Do you want to hear about them? The three of them?'

The chair seemed to rock beneath me. I shivered uncontrollably.

'Three? Did you say, the three of them?'

'That's right, Michael. Three.'

FORTY-SIX

'I thought there were only two. Christine and Angela.'

He shook his head, very slowly.

'No, three.'

'So, who was the third?'

'I'll come to them all in time. Christine was the first. I had been a priest for over twenty-five years. I was well respected. I was conscientious in my duties. I had a growing reputation as a scholar. I had assisted the Archbishop in a number of sensitive inquiries. There was the possibility of promotion to Monsignor. Some spoke of me as a future bishop.

'I knew I was not a holy person, like Father Ambrose, but I did not think of myself as a bad man. After I had conducted one of my inquisitions in the confessional, I did not think about it afterwards. It was as if I were somebody else inside the hushed secrecy of that little box with its scented wood and heavy, velvet curtains. The people on the other side of the curtain were not real. I never saw their faces. I was not real. They never saw mine. After they had gone, I was as before. Dry, detached, scholarly, reliable. The way you knew me.

'It could have gone on like that. I could have ended my time as a priest and taken honourable retirement, burying myself in my researches, believing I had performed my duties well and helped some souls to salvation, forgetting the judgements I had had no right to make, the punishments I had had no authority to carry out.

'Then one Saturday evening Father James asked me to deputise for him at short notice. None of the other priests in his parish was available. So he rang St Jerome's. I answered the phone. I was free. Of course I would be happy to help out.

'Christine came into the box. I could tell from her voice that she was still very young. She confessed to a sin of the flesh, committed in private. I drew the details out of her. I pretended to give her Absolution. But I distorted the Latin words. Only another priest would have known. I did not believe in the words of remorse I had forced out of her, or her promise not to sin again. I knew I had unfinished business with her. I was sure God would find a way to bring her to me again, outside.

'I gave her a penance of fifteen Our Fathers, and insisted she say them there and then in the church, before going home. Nobody else came into the box after her. I left and went into the church. She was there, rattling through the prayers, desperate to get away from the place where she had had to make such humiliating admissions. She didn't see me. I guessed she was about fifteen. Nobody would have given her a second look. I wondered if it really was she who had just been to me for Confession. I could not equate her sin of lonely passion with her nondescript appearance. For a moment, it occurred to me that God had a twisted sense of humour. Why else would He give such feelings to someone while denying them the means to attract somebody who could satisfy them? She did not look up. Apart from the two of us, the building was empty. I waited for her to leave and followed her home, watched her put the key in the door and go inside.

'I visited the house the next day. I did not know what I would find. It was not my parish, so I could not pretend I was on a routine pastoral visit. Her aunt was at home. I told her I was conducting some enquiries for the Archbishop. Drawing up profiles of different parishes for the purposes of comparison, some nonsense like that. I had chosen her name at random from the parish register.

'She was very friendly. We had a long chat. She told me she had been wanting to talk to one of the priests at St Monica's for some time about her niece, who was at an awkward age. I offered to help. I went back regularly, always during the day when Christine was at school. I got to know her well. To say she was scrupulous about religious observance would be an understatement. She was also fanatically puritanical. She denounced everybody and everything, the newspapers, the magazines, the politicians, for their worldliness and obsession with sex. I do not know from where she got her information. She told me no magazines were allowed in the house and there was no television. I told her she was a holy woman, blessed in the eyes of God. She was evidently delighted at last to have found someone who understood her.

'Eventually, she decided to confide in me about her niece. She had obviously concluded I was more likely to be sympathetic to her point of view than her own parish priests. She told me she could protect Christine at home, but could do nothing about the influences to which she was exposed outside the house. She was worried that Christine was spiritually weak and under attack from evil forces. Her manner suggested a deep spiritual unease. She was often wilfully silent for long periods and never confided in her aunt. I imagine her manner was no different from that of any other teenager who has fallen in love with an unattainable object.

'I told her that Christine might be coming under attack from within. She became intensely interested. She begged me to tell her exactly what I meant. I said that Christine had recently come to me for Confession, in my own church. I had to assume that shame about her sin had driven her to go to another parish where nobody would know her. I had been so concerned that I had followed her home. I asked her aunt to forgive the white lie I had told her to make her acquaintance. It had been for Christine's sake. I told her I was pleased she had decided to confide in me. In return I was willing to confide in her. But I could not go on unless she absolved me from my duty of confidentiality. She agreed, apparently unaware or unconcerned that only Christine had that right. So I committed the gravest sin of all for any priest. I betrayed the secrecy of the confessional.'

'You don't need to tell me any more. I found her and talked to her. She told me everything. Only she thought you were Father James, of course.'

'Father Ambrose had told me I could use his cousin's house for study and research, when I needed more peace and quiet than I could get at St Jerome's. He rarely went there himself. It was the perfect place. I know it was madness. If I were found out, I would be thrown out of the priesthood. But I was sure I was in no danger. Christine did not know the real identity of the priest to whom she had confessed. Father James could have given that information, but would only do so if she complained. And I knew she would never do that. Her feelings of guilt and shame were too strong. Her aunt would never betray me. She had authorised everything I had done.

'Then disaster struck, or so I thought. Her stupid brother became involved. He must have realised something was wrong and got the story out of her. He complained on her behalf. There would have to be an inquiry after all. I prepared myself. I would admit everything but claim that her aunt had put so much pressure on me that I had been unable to resist. I would of course resign from the priesthood immediately. Then the Archbishop asked to see me. He told me he wanted me to investigate. I realised I still had a chance. It would be my word against that of Father James.'

'Wait a minute. How could you have accused Father James to his face of something which both of you knew you had done?'

'It was not my job to confront Father James, or even to see him. I was only to talk to the complainant, then send a report to the Archbishop, giving my view on whether or not there was a *prima facie* case. If I thought there was such a case, my involvement was at an end. He would set up a panel. It would be their job to determine whether the accusation was true and if so what disciplinary action to take. Christine refused to see me. Even if she had agreed, I doubt if she would have realised I was the priest to whom she had confessed. Her brother acted on her behalf throughout. I submitted my report, stating that in my view there was a case to answer. I had to say that. If I hadn't, the brother would never have let it rest. He would never be satisfied until somebody was named and expelled.

'Father James was suspended pending the outcome of the panel's deliberations. But he had the chance to go to the panel and defend himself. He could have accused me there. He chose not to do so, so they went ahead and expelled him. The Archbishop sent representatives to talk to him, to try to find out his reasons, so the appropriate lessons could be learned. He refused to speak to them. I think the Archbishop even went to see him himself, but he never broke his silence.'

'How do you know all this?'

'At the time I was given the job, I was not working at St Jerome's. Otherwise I would never have been asked. I would not have been seen as independent enough. But this was some months after the event. I had been seconded to the Archbishop's office to help with some very sensitive inquiries. All sorts of nasty things were crawling out of the woodwork. Allegations of abuse of children by paedophile priests. Our job was to sort them out with the least possible publicity. We sent some of the priests to other dioceses, so they'd be their problem, not ours. We persuaded some persistent offenders to leave the priesthood. We offered some complainants money to shut up and not go to the police. On the whole we did a good job. Managed to put the lid on most of them.

'When Christine's case came along, the Archbishop saw right away that it was even more sensitive than the others. The confessional was involved. The press had already been brought in. He needed somebody he could trust totally. He conveniently forgot that I had been working in a neighbouring parish at the time. Even after I had submitted my report, he often sought my advice on how to handle the follow-up. I was able to keep in touch with the case right through to the end.'

'What about the aunt? Didn't anybody try to get her side of the story?'

'She had moved away, broken off all contact with her niece and nephew. If the press tried to contact her they never got anything out of her. The brother did not know where she was. As far as I know she never knew about the inquiry.'

'Did you really think you had cured Christine of a spiritual evil?'

'At the time I persuaded myself that that was what I was doing. Afterwards, I didn't think about it. It was as if it had been somebody else who had done it.'

'You never wondered about her? About the life she had after you had finished with her and forgotten about her? Let me tell you about it. She tried to kill herself. She was found by chance, just in time. She has suffered repeated bouts of depression. She never married. You saw her as a nondescript teenager. She grew out of that. It amused you to think that God had withheld from her the gifts which would have enabled her to fulfil her passionate nature. But He didn't withhold them. He only made her wait for them, a few years perhaps. But by then they were no use to her. In her own eyes she was always repulsive. You did that to her. But you had suffered no consequences at all. You really must have thought God was on your side. So you did it again. Angela was your next victim, wasn't she? Go on, Peter. I'm waiting.'

FORTY-SEVEN

He leaned back in his chair, his hand still in contact with the gun.

'Your mother had known Father Ambrose for a very long time, but in recent years there had grown a certain distance between them. He was still her confessor. That would never change. Absolution comes from God, but your mother was not alone in believing that Absolution through Father Ambrose somehow conferred a more intense state of Grace than could be obtained through any other priest. But as she grew older he began to find himself out of sympathy with her. He found her harsh and lacking in compassion. When she wanted advice, outside the confessional, she started to come to me. She sensed a kindred spirit. And I visited her at home.

'I met Angela and talked to her, several times. I knew her well enough to recognise her voice when she came to Confession. Your mother was worried about her, concerned that she was out of control. She hardly spoke to your mother any more. She stayed out at night. Your mother had no idea where she was, who her friends were. As with Christine's aunt I found that I had relevant information to give her. Information Angela had so far been too frightened to give to her herself. Again I was released from my vows.'

'You told her Angela was pregnant.'

'Yes. Obviously she would need to be cared for away from home, until the child was born and could be sent away for adoption. I told your mother I could arrange that. But first Angela would need spiritual help.'

'You mean ritual humiliation. For your satisfaction.'

I moved towards the table. He jerked forward and

snatched up the gun.

'Sit down, Michael, please. I really don't want to hurt you. And if you kill me now you'll never find out about the other case.'

I sat down again.

'That's better. You can use any term you like to describe what we did to Angela. I'm not denying anything. Only you must believe me when I tell you that we did not intend what happened. Angela was very different from Christine. Very spirited. She attacked me, hurt me quite badly. I can see that you're pleased about that. Your mother wanted nothing more to do with her. She would never have had her home again, even if she had been discharged and remembered where she had lived. That suited me as well, of course.

'But what would your mother tell you? Then she told me about her niece in Canada, same age as Angela, called to be a Bride of Christ. A good enough cover story, for a while. Until you decided you wanted to go and visit her. Your cousin's death was even more helpful. If Angela died, or never recovered her wits, nobody would ever know. As the years went by, I decided we were safe, your mother and I from exposure, and you from the knowledge of what had happened. Then you came here with that letter from her. I laid my false trails and waited. When I heard about your mother and how she had died, I knew the time had arrived for our punishment.

'But mine had started a long time ago. What happened with Angela was a shock, even to me after all those years of self-delusion. For the first time in my life I tried to look into my soul. I could not see it. I did not yet know it was not there. All I saw was someone who had committed acts he could not now explain to himself. After a year I went in desperation to Father Ambrose and confessed. As I told you, he refused me

367

Absolution. He knew I did not possess a soul capable of true repentance. He knew I had no soul at all. That was when I knew it.

'He was right in his spiritual insights, but he did not do the right thing. He should have told me to go immediately to the church authorities and tell them what I had told him. He couldn't tell them himself, of course. He believed absolutely in the secrecy of the confessional. But I would have authorised him, if he had asked. I would have done whatever he told me to. He must have wrestled with his conscience for days and nights on end. It wasn't just because of our long association. He was desperately concerned for the reputation of the Church. There had been one scandal already involving betrayal of confessional secrecy. It was, in principle, even worse than the sexual abuse scandals. Everybody expects that sort of thing to happen now and then, with the Church's celibacy rules. But this was different. It went right to the heart of the Church's spiritual structure, the sacraments. It threatened to shake it to the very foundations.

'Fortunately it had been contained. Only the local press had taken it up. The nationals never caught the scent. Father James was promptly dealt with and kept his silence. So did Christine. The full details never came out. Eventually the story faded away. But what if it emerged that the same thing had happened again? Connections would be made. It would soon be realised that either the wrong priest had been sacked, or that there had been two of us, in neighbouring parishes, willing to betray confessional secrets. Either way, the result would have been devastating. Rome would surely have got involved.'

'But if you or Father Ambrose had told the Archbishop, could not the lid have been kept on it, as you had managed to do with those others?'

'He couldn't take the risk. The potential destructive power of a scandal like that was far too great. He decided that the fewer people who knew the better. Even Archbishops' offices can leak. There would be no danger so long as Angela did not return and tell her tale. And surely God would intervene to make sure that did not happen, to protect His Holy Church. He told me all this when he had finally made up his mind. He told me he was putting me on probation. I must no longer hear confessions. He kept a close watch on me, or so he thought. Nothing like close enough. A few years later, he told me he had found an opening for me here. He must have assumed I was safe, and he could let me out of his sight. He was right, by then. But in the meantime, because of his folly and neglect, something else had happened. Something even more terrible.'

'What did Father Ambrose do about Father James?'

'He went to see him. Told him he could probably arrange for him to be reinstated, as long as he did not press the case against me. Told him that he had me under his control. Father James declined his offer.'

'So that's what Father James meant, when he said someone had been there before me. And that was how Father Ambrose knew about Angela, when I showed him her letter. Before your attempt at a confession, he only knew the story everybody knew. She had gone to Canada to become a nun and died out there. Now he knew what you and my mother had done. The next time my mother came to him for Confession, he must have told her that he could not give her Absolution any more unless she confessed to the gravest of her sins, the one she had always kept a secret. She would have guessed you had confided in him. We'll never know if she told him everything, but she can't have shown repentance. She showed none when I confronted her.

All those years she kept going back to him for Confession, even after he had moved to the nursing home, hoping desperately for the Absolution he could never give because she could never convince him she was truly sorry. And for her, no other priest would ever do. Only his Absolution was valid in her eyes. After I had shown him the letter, he realised she might be in danger and offered her his cousin's house as a refuge. Probably told her to use her time there to pray and achieve true repentance. Then he asked me to keep him in touch with my enquiries. So he could warn her again if Angela was found. And he set Monsignor Winstanley onto me, to try to stop the search altogether. Must have got someone to send a message to the Monsignor, telling him to come and see him and learn something to his advantage.'

There was a sharp rattle from the back of his throat. After a few seconds I realised he was laughing.

'Monsignor Winstanley? He came to see you to tell you to stop your enquiries? Poor Michael. How you have suffered for your sins. I would never have thought they were so grave.' He looked again at his watch. 'Nearly time, Michael. Just enough time to tell you about the third one.'

I rose again, and again he raised the gun. I wondered if I could reach it and push it aside before he had a chance to pull the trigger. I did not want him to finish his story.

'Don't be a fool, Michael,' he snarled. 'Think of Angela. She may yet contact you, ask for your help. What will become of her if you get yourself hurt or killed?'

'Peter, give me the gun, please. I don't want to kill you any more. God help me, but in some strange way I feel sorry for you. I'll take you back to Seaport tonight. We'll go to the Archbishop tomorrow. We'll only speak to him on the condition that nobody else is present. You'll tell him everything you've told me. I'll be there to corroborate what you say from what I have found out. He will order Father James to be cleared. He won't have to disclose his reasons. There'll be no publicity. You'll just bring forward the date of your retirement. You can go to live in one of the Church's nursing homes in another diocese. Live out your days there. With your conscience for company. You can trust me to keep quiet.'

'And what about the police?'

'We won't involve them. They wouldn't be interested in what happened all that time ago. I'm sure Christine would not want it all raked up again. My mother is dead now, and so is Father Ambrose. It's all best left in the past.'

'I'm not talking about Christine or Angela. I know the Seaport police won't be interested. I'm talking about the Formby police. I'm sure they'd like the chance to close the file.'

FORTY-EIGHT

'What do you mean? File on whom?'

'Frances Pickersgill. Do you remember the case?'

'The name rings a faint bell. Go on.'

I sat down again.

'You can tell them all about this one, Michael. I want you to. The rules of the confessional don't apply here. They had two suspects. They were never charged, but the finger of stupid, gossipy suspicion continued to point at them. You can lift that burden from them. I had nothing against them. Only her. Take this as proof this is not just another crackpot confession. They had a lot of those.'

He pushed the bracelet towards me.

'That was hers. I took it off her wrist, afterwards. Her initials are on it. Her husband will be able to identify it. The case was in the papers. That's why you remember it. She wasn't like the others. She was older for a start, and married. And I didn't get to her through Confession. How could I, when I no longer heard Confession? That was Father Ambrose's mistake. He didn't realise that once the beast was out of the cage it could never be confined again.

'She was a former parishioner. She had moved to Formby. She came back to St Jerome's to see me, for guidance. This was soon after your appointment as parish priest there. She was married to a Formby man. She was a teacher and was having an affair with one of her colleagues. She didn't want to go to Confession because she saw no point in confessing something for which she wasn't sorry. She said she was desperate for a child but her husband was infertile. That was the only reason she was having an affair. Her husband knew about it. He understood her reasons, so she said, despite the pain the affair was causing him. If there was a child she did not know if her husband would accept it as his own, or whether she would have to leave him. She did not know whether in that case her lover would also leave his wife and move in with her. It was all horribly messy, like the lives of so many in the world. But she didn't seem to care about all that. All that concerned her was that she didn't want to be in a state of sin. In her mind she wasn't committing a sin. She wanted me to agree with her, so she could get on with her life with a free conscience. She wanted the best of all worlds.

'She did not hear from me what she wanted to hear. I told her children were a gift from God which God had the right to withhold. She had no right to question such decisions. She went away. Then the next day she told me she wanted to speak to me again. She said she was beginning to understand what I was saying, but needed more guidance. She was ready to leave her lover, and go to Confession, if I could finally convince her it was the right thing to do.

'I told her that I was visiting a friend in Formby that afternoon. I would pick her up from her home when I had left my friend's house. We would go somewhere nearby and talk. If she wanted, I would hear her Confession there and then. We did not need to be in church for that. She could be back home in half an hour. I told her how pleased I was about her change of heart. I didn't believe in it for a moment. I do now. Perhaps she had realised she loved her husband more than her lover. Perhaps she had begun to understand how much pain she had caused, and how likely it was that she would cause much more by wrecking two marriages. It wasn't exactly a spiritual transformation but it was enough of a change of heart to merit Absolution. But I never saw any of that at the time. I was blind by then. My other self had taken over.

'It was late evening by the time I collected her from her house. Her husband was still at his golf club. I drove her to the woods near the beach. She started to talk. She was going on about the things she had done with her lover. Telling me she was sorry she had done them. I had stopped listening. I leaned over to the back of the car and picked up the package I had placed there. She stopped talking and watched me in amazement. I took out the gun and pointed it at her. This very gun. She was too surprised to jump out of the car. She was with her priest. Surely she could not be in danger. But what on earth was I doing with that? That's what she asked me, eventually, with a sort of hysterical laugh.

'I told her I wasn't going to hurt her as long as she did exactly what I said. She could scream if she wanted. Nobody would hear her. Nobody would see us. I was doing God's work, and He would protect us from discovery. I had to purify her, cleanse her properly of her sins. But if she tried to run away I would have to hurt her. I had no fear of any consequences. God had protected me before and He would do so again. I believed the words as I spoke them. I was no longer the soulless abortion of a human being I know myself to be in my sane moments. I was all-powerful again, I was God's instrument, His special agent.

'I ordered her out of the car and into the woods. I told her to undress. She left her clothes there, on the ground. I told her to walk in front of me, out onto the sand. I didn't want her to whisper her Confession in the dark secrecy of the trees. I wanted her open to the sea and the sky and the sweep of the shore, so she could confess her sins to the earth and heavens. She didn't say anything. Just whimpered.

'Out of the woods, there was some faint moonlight.

I could see her body as she walked. I almost started to laugh. It was absurd. There was I, a fifty-five year old man, and I had never seen an adult naked woman before. I was almost sick with disgust. I watched that surfeit of white round flesh, changing shape with every step. What was it for except to serve as an instrument of the Devil? It had been her duty to hide it, to keep it contained within her lawful marriage. But she had not. She had exposed it all to a man who was not her husband, let that man take it in his hands, invited him to explore it. I told her to kneel down and pray. I put the gun down in the sand.'

'You had told her you wouldn't hurt her if she did what you said. You lied to her.'

'I didn't lie. I never meant to hurt her. But she didn't do as I said. I wanted her to know and feel her shame and beg for God's mercy. I wanted her to bare her soul as well as her body before God, there in that vast open space. Surely she could feel God's presence there. That was what I told her, what I shouted to her. But she didn't even try to pray. She never once put her hands together. Even a gesture of shame would have done. If she had just put her hands across her breasts or in front of her private parts, I might have spared her. But they just hung at her sides. She felt no shame. Only fear. I wanted to hear her words of remorse, hear her speak them in a way I could believe. I stepped up to her, ready to put my hand on her head and bid the evil spirits depart from her. Then I understood. There was to be no remorse, no repentance, no Absolution. If I let her go, she would do the same with others.'

'So you killed her.'

'The police were so stupid. I wasn't going to go to them to confess but I would have let them catch me. I waited for them. I made it easy for them. I made no attempt to hide the body or her clothes. I took this bracelet off her wrist and kept it in the drawer in my study, along with the gun which would have had traces of sand on it. I wanted them to come and find them. Her nails left deep marks on my arms. It was weeks before they faded. I never tried to hide them but nobody asked me about them. I didn't even clean the sand off my shoes or off the car tyres. They were looking for a grey car. Mine was light blue. In the dusk it looked grey. They never thought of that. So, so stupid.'

He had let go of the gun and was looking at his hands.

'Look at my hands, Michael. Did you ever notice them? Bigger than those of men of normal size. I've always looked small and weak. But these are my secret. All my strength went into them. I am far stronger than most men. She struggled for a few minutes. Then it was all over. I laid her out, white flesh on white sand, in the moonlight. Her body was beautiful then. Now it could no longer sin, could no longer tempt.'

His eyes were looking into the distance. I prepared myself. But what if he got to it first? What if it went off accidentally? Surely that couldn't happen. It probably didn't work. It had not been fired for decades. He had told me he had never fired it himself. It wasn't even loaded. He was a scholar, not a marksman or a hunter. He would have no idea how to keep a gun in usable condition all those years. He probably had even less idea how to load it or what to load it with. And even if he did, where would he, an elderly priest, get hold of ammunition in that remote spot? No, he was bluffing. He had been bluffing all along. All I had to do was make one quick, determined move and it would be all over. He was small. I was nearly thirty years younger than he was. His reactions were bound to be slower than mine. I could easily overpower him. He would have no choice but to agree to come with me.

I judged my moment and jumped forward. I was too slow. He grabbed the gun and swung it round. The noise threw me backwards, off my chair and onto the floor. I heard voices. To my deafened ears they seemed to be coming from a great distance, though I knew they came from only a few inches away, from the mouths of Father O'Malley and Father Higgins, both of them standing over me and shouting.

FORTY-NINE

All that was a year ago. I now live in a small bungalow opposite the parks where I had received my dressing-down from Monsignor Winstanley. There is no danger of a recurrence of that unpleasant episode. I am no longer a priest. I work in the library where I first met Bernadette. In my spare time I help out at Brendan's hostel, and sometimes at that of Father Higgins. Of Angela there has been neither sight nor sound.

Father O'Malley is still the senior priest at St Jerome's. We meet occasionally for a drink at the YMCA. My successor is a sharp-featured youth who seems to me to have been trained at a management consultants' college rather than a seminary. The church is now run like the branch of a supermarket. The altar-boys are given written lists of objectives and he conducts annual appraisal interviews with each of them. He and Father O'Malley keep a cool distance from each other. For me the new arrival is a blessing. He is allergic to cats, so Fido now lives with me.

When we meet, Father O'Malley continues to pump me for details of my interview with Father Coffey. He is still furious with me for not taking him with me for the confrontation, though I have assured him countless times that Father Coffey would only have spoken to Angela or myself. Though he denies it vehemently I suspect he is writing his own account of the discovery of the murderer of Frances Pickersgill, in which his role as Doctor Watson to my Sherlock Holmes will feature rather more prominently than it did in reality. He understands that any such record can only be for posterity. I will not allow him to disclose anything outside the circle of ourselves and Father Higgins, at least not while I am alive and there is a possibility that Angela might be.

So far, my role has been kept strictly secret and I have no reason to think that will change. I did a deal with the police, once they had accepted that Father Coffey's death was a suicide. My story, corroborated by the others, was that Father Coffey had rung me in what was obviously a greatly distressed state of mind and asked me to visit him and hear his Confession. I had left a note with my fellow parish priest and set out right away. Father Coffey had confessed to the murder of Mrs Pickersgill, and authorised me to pass the details on to the police along with the bracelet. Then he had turned the gun on himself before I could stop him. Father O'Malley, returning home late to find my note, had become anxious for my safety, knowing from longer experience than mine that Father Coffey was a seriously disturbed paranoid personality who might, on grounds apparent only to himself, hold a grudge against me. Enlisting the help of Father Higgins, who was visiting St Jerome's at the time, he had followed me down there, arriving too late to prevent the tragedy.

I pleaded with the Chief Inspector that it would do serious harm to the Church's image, to put it mildly, if it were known that no less than four priests had been present in the cottage when one of them had shot himself. God knows what speculation the press might indulge in. The truth was that I could not have cared less about the Church's image, and neither could the others. But I was desperately anxious that nobody should make a connection between my mother's death and that of Father Coffey, a connection that might lead to Angela. To protect her I needed to be completely outside the frame.

The Chief Inspector did not need much persuasion. The police did not want it widely known that a humble parish priest had solved a murder which had baffled them for fifteen years. According to their official account, Father Coffey had been alone when he killed himself. He had left no note but he had left the bracelet which identified him as the killer of Mrs Pickersgill. As to his motives they could not even begin to speculate.

This is what really happened that night. As soon as I realised I had falsely accused Father Ambrose I had rushed back to his grave and prayed for his forgiveness. I knew what I had to do next and I also knew that I had to go alone. I did not want to go back to the presbytery to get the car. I would have had to convince Father O'Malley and Father Higgins I had to leave immediately and alone on an errand about which I could tell them nothing. After my behaviour earlier in the day the prospect of persuading them was remote. They would never have let me leave on my own.

But I still needed a car. Coming out of the cemetery I walked a few hundred yards up the road until I found a car-hire depot next to the local station. I remembered the route from my previous visit. I drove down in a trance, narrowly avoiding a collision on several occasions.

I had of course underestimated Father Higgins. Back at the presbytery he had told Father O'Malley about his chance remark about Angela's visits to Confession and how I had reacted. Father O'Malley, not exactly known for his mental agility, had worked it out instantly. Until then he had been as convinced as I was that Father Ambrose was the guilty priest, but the lack of conclusive proof had troubled him. Nobody had named Father Ambrose directly. The evidence, though strong, was circumstantial. He had read enough detective stories to know that. Not that it mattered now that Father Ambrose was dead. But I knew he had strong reservations about my plan to visit his grave and accuse him there.

Realising that I might be in danger they had left St Jerome's in the sole charge of an astonished Mrs Raferty and driven down together in the presbytery car. Not having my previous experience of the route, and having a much less powerful car than the one I had hired, they found their journey frustratingly long and made several unintended detours. They had pushed open the door just at the moment when the shot was fired. Seeing that I was in a state of shock they rang the police, and also called for an ambulance to take me to hospital. The nearest hospital was in a market town some twenty miles from Daleford. While we were awaiting the ambulance we agreed on the story we would tell the police. Father O'Malley came with me, leaving Father Higgins to await the police, with only Father Coffey's corpse to keep him company.

I was detained in hospital overnight. The others booked in at a local bed and breakfast. The following morning we visited the police station, made and read over our statements and signed them. I then spent half an hour in private discussion with the Chief Inspector, who spent some of that time on the phone to a senior colleague in Lancashire. As we were leaving we were warned that the press were on their way. It had taken some time for word to get through to them. We got away just in time.

When the dust had settled I wrote my letter of resignation to the Archbishop. I imagined the relief on the face of Monsignor Winstanley when it arrived.

While still awaiting my final discharge, I went to visit Christine Gallagher, anxious that my earlier visit and the story I had coaxed from her might have worsened her state of mind. A young couple who now rented the house gave me a forwarding address, in New

Zealand. They did not expect her to return. I wrote to her, explaining that the priest who had tormented her had been discovered, had confessed and then shot himself. If it was any consolation to her he had lived for many years in a state of terrible mental torment. I never received a reply to my letter.

I sold my mother's house and with the proceeds moved to the bungalow. There I waited. And while I waited, and went about my business, I wondered if she was still watching me, still following me.

FIFTY

Last week I thought my wait was over. My neighbour, a kindly old lady and former parishioner who still calls me Father, caught me on the doorstep one evening as I arrived home from work.

'A lady came to see you, Father. Said she'd come a long way. I said you wouldn't be long. She wanted to wait in the park opposite but I told her I wouldn't hear of it, she had to come in so I've got her inside my front room having a cup of tea. I'll just go and tell her you're here...oh!'

I had already rushed through her open door, the name of Angela on my lips. When I saw the person sitting comfortably on the sofa with a cup in her hand, it was all I could do to clap my hand to my mouth in time.

'Hello, Michael.'

'Hello, Bernadette.'

'Father O'Malley gave me your address. Told me you had left the priesthood. So why did you do that?'

She was sitting in my front room, on the lumpy, moth-eaten old sofa which I had moved in from my mother's house. I had not bothered to get any new furniture. I sat opposite her on a hard chair I had borrowed from the kitchen.

'I realised what you were trying to tell me last time we spoke. That my vocation was a sham.'

'And your mother?'

'She's dead.'

'Thank God. Sorry, I didn't mean that the way it sounded. It's just that I was very nervous about her walking in on us.'

'I sold her house to buy this place. This is her furniture.'

'So, here we are. Your mother and God came between us, in that order. Now they've both gone. Nothing to keep us apart now. Only what we've both become. I'm a lonely widow, dowdy and middle-aged. No, don't say anything, Michael. I know the truth. I can look in the mirror. And you...well, you look as if you've been to Hell and back. If you really have come back. I'm not so sure about that.'

'Are you moving back here?'

'No. No need to look so worried. I've got a flat in Birmingham. Near James. I used most of the money from the sale of my house to pay off his ex-wife. His second ex-wife. He's moving to London next month. Getting married for the third time. If that goes wrong as well he's on his own. I've told him that. I've got a part-time job. Clerical stuff. I thought of going in for teaching. But I haven't the courage or the energy. Not now. And I don't think my brain would work anymore.'

'Bernadette, I don't mean to be rude. After the last time we spoke I was desperate to see you and talk to you again. Clarify some of the things you said. I went round again to your house but you had already left. Now...'

'Now you couldn't care less.'

'No, I didn't mean that. It's just that I think I have some idea of what might have happened.'

'Some idea? No, Michael. I'm sorry. Some idea won't do.'

Her voice shook. I realised for the first time what had finally driven her back to see me. She was trembling with barely-controlled anger.

'For God's sake, Michael, look at you. Look at me. How old are we? Forty-two? And we're finished. Like walking corpses, the blood drained out of us. And we're not the only ones who paid with our futures. No, there are things you need to know. In detail. If only so you know that I wasn't falsely accusing you the last time we spoke.'

I nodded. 'All right. Go ahead. You never wanted to come here today, did you? You resisted, for a whole year. Fought with yourself. In the end you were driven to it. You had to come or you would have gone insane. So go ahead. I don't care what it might cost me. You said I looked as if I had been to Hell and back. What I have been doing is discovering the truth about my past. All of it. What I found out made me realise that my whole life was based on lies. There's nothing you can tell me now that can make it any worse.'

She raised her eyebrows. For a moment, just a brief second, she was the teasing Bernadette of old. She shook her head slowly.

'I doubt that, Michael. I really do doubt that. I'm sure you've found out a great deal. But there are some things you will never discover. And if I were you I would be grateful for that. Tell me what you remember. About that week, after you had proposed.'

'I went home. I told my mother I couldn't be a priest. Her reaction surprised me. I expected her to go crazy, you know, throw things about the place, or even hit me. She was going to hit me at first. She raised her hand. Then she dropped it again. She became calm, very suddenly, almost unnaturally. For the first time in my life, she was kind and understanding. Said it was out of her hands.'

'She said that? That it was out of her hands? Did she ask you whether anything had happened to turn you against the priesthood?'

'No. She just assumed I was getting cold feet.'

'What do you remember about the following day? The Tuesday?'

'I intended to meet you after school as usual. Then

the school secretary came into the classroom with a message for me. A neighbour had rung in. My mother was feeling ill. She had had a fainting fit. Could I go home urgently? This was about three o' clock, I suppose. I was excused and I dashed home. There was a note pinned to the front door. She had recovered a bit and gone round to see Dr Grant. I was not to worry and not to follow her round to the surgery. I was to go in and wait for her to return, so I would be at home when my sister got back. My sister didn't have a key. Mother was away much longer than I expected. When she returned she seemed almost cheerful. She said Dr Grant had prescribed her a tonic. She had gone round to the chemists to get it. The chemist had told her she looked very pale and suggested she sit down, on a chair behind the counter. He had mixed some of the tonic for her with some water and she had taken it. She said she felt a lot better already.'

'I bet she did. I don't suppose you saw the bottle with the tonic in it.'

'I can't remember. I wasn't bothered. Only relieved she was not ill. I was very worried, you see. In case I had caused her to be ill by telling her I couldn't be a priest.'

'She wasn't ill, Michael. She never went to see Dr Grant. She never went to the chemist's.'

'How do you know?'

'I went to meet you in the park. You weren't there. But there was somebody there. A lady. Dressed up as if for Mass. She smiled at me. "You're Bernadette, aren't you? You're very pretty. I'm Michael's mother. I wondered if I could speak to you." She was charming, reassuring.'

'I don't know how she can have known about us, or how she recognised you. I did once tell her I came home through the park. That was when I asked her for

386

some stale bread to feed the ducks. She must have followed me from the school one day and seen us together.'

'At first I thought you had told her about us and sent her to meet me, as her future daughter-in-law. But then I couldn't understand why you had not come with her. Later on, and ever since, I assumed you had sent her, for a different purpose. To do your dirty work for you.'

'No, Bernadette, I swear. I knew nothing about it.'

'As I said, she was friendly. At first. She told me she had reason to understand I had developed certain feelings for you. But it would never do. You had been chosen by God to be a priest. You were in no position to be serious about any girl. I had misunderstood you and your intentions. She showed me a letter, from that seminary you had told me about. I told her you had asked me to marry you. She laughed. It was a sort of pitying laugh. Not spiteful. She said I was too young. I did not understand people, especially men. I was too trusting. You were a kind-hearted boy. You could only be friends with me. But you didn't just want to walk away from me. You had only asked me to marry you to make me feel better. You expected me to refuse, because we were both so young. But I would feel better for having been asked. If by some mischance I had accepted you, you would have waited, for a few days maybe. Then you would have let me down gently. You would have said that things had changed. God had confirmed your calling. Your feelings had carried you away. You were sorry. You hadn't meant to hurt me. Somehow I found the courage to tell her she was wrong. I told her I loved you and had every reason to believe you loved me. I told her I believed you had meant it when you had asked me to marry you.

'That was when she stopped the pretence. The pretence of being concerned with my feelings. I thought she was going to slap my face. She told me I was a slut. Everybody in the parish knew that. She had been watching me. She had seen the way I dressed up to go out. I looked like a whore and behaved like one. I wasn't worthy of you. And she would see you were protected from me, and girls like me. I burst out crying. She left.'

'And you believed her?'

'Yes. She was your mother. Surely she knew what you wanted, better than you knew it yourself. And she was there. You weren't. That was our meeting-place, and she had come instead of you. What else was I to assume except that you knew she was there, to tell me what you were too cowardly to tell me to my face? Yes, I believed her. I believed she was right when she called me a whore. I believed you had deceived me. I had given myself to you, and you had repaid me by proposing marriage when you didn't and couldn't mean it. You hadn't had the courage to come round and tell me to my face that I meant nothing to you. Your mother was your messenger. So I wrote to you to tell you I was going to marry Tom.'

'And then it was too late.'

Again the anger flashed in her eyes.

'Oh no, Michael. It wasn't too late, not by a long chalk. There was still a chance for you to convince me that your mother was wrong. If you didn't reply, if you didn't come for me, if you made no attempt to win me back, to fight for me, then I would know for sure. I would have the proof. You didn't come. One word from you would have done it. One word, Michael. I longed for that word, more than I have ever longed for anything in my life. I dreamed that you would come round, and tell me that I mustn't marry Tom, because you loved me and you didn't believe I loved him, and you would defy your mother, defy the whole world, defy God if necessary, to have me. Well, that would have been quite a few words, wouldn't it? But one would have been enough. But no. Nothing. So I knew. Your mother was right.'

I opened my mouth to speak, but she held up her hand.

'No, let me finish. I never expected to see you again. I used to go to St Monica's for Mass. Then I heard you had come back to St Jerome's as parish priest. I went back there to see you, from a distance. I vowed I would never approach you or speak to you. I watched you every Sunday. That was the limit of my infidelity to Tom. I watched her watching you. I started to understand. It wasn't you who had the vocation at all. It was her. My rival wasn't God. It was your mother. I could have defeated Him. I thought I had. But not her.'

'So at first you believed I had been toying with your affections. Then you believed I had been a helpless weakling, manipulated by my mother and her ambitions for me.'

'No, I never doubted your feelings, from the moment we first met. Not even when your mother spoke to me. But she did make me believe you had never intended to act on them, because you had a higher duty to God. I hated you for betraying me, for making me a false proposal of marriage. But I was prepared to admire you for putting your duty to God first. Something I could never have done. Then I realised it was your mother you had put first. God didn't even come into it. I could never admire you then.'

'You're right. Of course you are. I have been unforgivably weak. I realise now that I should have fought for you, every day of my life, to my dying breath if need be. But I wasn't just weak. I was foolish

389

and arrogant, as well. As far as I was concerned, it was all in your hands. I wondered if I had a vocation. But, at that age, how could I really know? I had often asked Father Taylor that. How would I know in my heart? How does anybody know? He said that God would give me a sign.'

'A sign? Oh God, no. Michael, please.'

'Yes. I thought you were the sign. If you accepted me, I had no vocation. If you turned me down, then I did.'

'How could you have been so...'

'Stupid and arrogant? I don't know. But I was.'

'And how convenient it was that the sign you got meant that you would not need to defy your mother after all.'

'That's unfair. I was prepared to defy her, until I got your letter. I couldn't make sense of it. Why, after what we had done and what we had said to each other, were you telling me you had never loved me and always loved Tom? My first thoughts were that I had been stupid and presumptuous to propose. You had never stopped loving Tom. You had had some silly quarrel, or he had done something to make you jealous. You were using me to get back at him.'

'If you thought that, even for a moment, you never knew me.'

'I found it hard to keep on thinking it. But I had been finding it hard to think you could prefer me to Tom. Then it occurred to me that it had to be God's will. Perhaps what you felt for me was only an aberration of the heart, always destined to be short-lived. God had drawn you back to your proper destiny. He changed your heart back to Tom so He could change mine, so He could call me back to Him.'

'You still sound like a bloody priest.'

'I'm sorry. It gets to be a habit. Certain

390

expressions. A certain way of saying things. I suppose I'll grow out of it. What I meant was, you would be better off with Tom anyway, my vocation was confirmed at last and my mother would be happy. Better for everybody all round. It seemed to make some sort of sense at the time.'

'So you never even thought to come to me and try and find out what was going on. Because you had worked out that it was all for the best.'

'Bernadette, I was eighteen. I had fallen totally and helplessly in love with you. I never expected it to happen because Mother always said it could never happen to me. So I had no defences. You were right just now when you said I had never dared to hope for you. That day when I proposed, I had thought you were going to tell me we were finished, that you were engaged to Tom. Instead...well, it wasn't quite what I expected.'

'I should bloody well hope not.'

'Then I got your letter. Can you imagine my state of mind? I had to try to make some sense of it.'

'That was your biggest mistake, Michael. Trying to make sense of it. That was the coward's way.'

'I know. Tell me something. I never understood why you didn't take up your university place and go on and teach. That was what you had always wanted. If you believed what my mother told you, why didn't you just forget me and get on with your life? You didn't marry Tom just to punish me, did you?'

'No. I didn't think you cared what I did so how could I punish you? So, the question is, why did I marry Tom. You really have no idea? You can't even guess?'

She rose and walked past me to the window. She looked out for a few moments, then returned slowly to her chair. She sat down and faced me.

391

'Okay. Try this. Your mother had called me a whore, and when you didn't come for me I knew you saw me as one too. I decided you were both right. A whore was what I was. Whores don't go to university and have careers. They sleep with men they don't love and they get paid for it. They have clients. Or in my case, one client. I sold myself to Tom, for security and a nice house. When Tom was dead there was nothing left. You see, there isn't any inner me that could have lived on through all that and emerge at the end all radiant and smiling. Maybe for somebody else there could have been. Somebody else could have shrugged their shoulders and become a teacher or gone over to Africa to look after starving babies. But I'm too selfish and incomplete for anything like that.'

'No, Bernadette. I don't believe you. You wanted security. I understand that. You told me that last time. But I don't believe you sold yourself for it like that. Not then, only eighteen, with someone you knew you didn't love. Your parents would have given you security, as they always had done, until you met someone else. Maybe you would never have married for love. But it didn't have to be then, with him, sacrificing so much of your life.'

'Don't press me, Michael. You'll be sorry. I promise.'

'Bernadette, I'm tired of lies. I've had nothing but lies all my life. That's all changed now. Do you really think there's anything you can tell me now that can be worse than what I have already learned?'

'Michael, I've said everything I came here to say today. Yes, it was driving me insane. The thought that you might not know what your mother had done to us. Not just what, but how. All the grisly details. The words she had spoken to me that day. The words I know off by heart and will know to my dying day. The

way she dug her knife into me and twisted it. Then left
me to die of the wound, slowly, agonisingly, over the
years. I had no defences, either. Nobody had ever hurt
me before. Nobody had ever hated me the way she did.
I did not know what hate was. And I had never even
met her. I had known nothing but love and acceptance
and indulgence. I thought it would always be like that
for me. So I had no armour. When she stabbed me I
bled to death.

'The thought that you would know nothing of that
was driving me crazy. Even if some light had dawned
in your brain, if you had guessed she had done
something to drive us apart, I thought you would be
making excuses for her, as her loving, obedient,
understanding son. She only did what she thought was
for the best. And she would have done it in as kind a
way as possible.'

'No, I never thought that. When I realised she
might have been responsible I knew she would have
been ruthless if necessary. That was how she was when
it came to me and my vocation. Only just how
ruthless...I didn't discover that until later. There are
others who have paid a dreadful price as well. I am so
sorry for what she put you through. So, are you going
to tell me the truth? About why you married Tom?'

'Maybe. I don't know. There's something I must
ask you first. Something that might make it easier for
me. Something I suspect. If it's true, if I hear it from
your own mouth, it might just make me angry enough
with you to be able to tell you.'

'What is it?'

'What we did that time. Did you confess it?'

'What do you mean?'

'You know exactly what I mean. We talked about
it. I mean, did you go to a priest and confess what we
did and tell him you were sorry and ask for

Absolution?'

I took a long slow breath.

'Did you?' I muttered.

'Christ, Michael, how can you even ask? For God's sake, don't you understand anything yet? The one thing that meant anything to me, the only time I ever gave myself out of love? A sin? A fucking sin? Michael, if St Peter and the Virgin Mary and a whole host of angels had appeared to me and told me it was a sin I would have told them to get lost. Everything else in my life was a sin, I would have told them. You can send me to Hell for all eternity for everything else about my life, everything else I was and did. But that...that was the only thing that wasn't a sin. I told you then that nobody would ever make me say I was sorry for what we did and I never changed my mind about that.'

She rose and stood above me. I could not look up.

'Look at me, Michael.'

I did not move.

'You can't look at me, can you? Because they made you, didn't they? Oh God, they did, didn't they? They made you say you were sorry. Didn't they?'

Her voice had risen to a scream. I covered my face with my hands. She returned slowly to her chair. After a minute she spoke again, her voice now a dull half-whisper.

'When? When did you confess? Tell me. You owe me the truth. When did you, utterly and finally, betray us?'

I lowered my hands slowly.

'Not for years,' I whispered. 'Not until just before I was ordained.'

She nodded.

'I see. That makes sense. Of course. It had to be then. To wipe the slate clean. To free yourself forever

394

from the past. To wash the sight and the touch and the smell and the memory of me forever from you. Only it's not that simple. Some things don't just wash out with a few well-rehearsed words and an Act of Contrition. All right. I'll tell you the truth. You've earned it. Just promise me you'll stay in that chair and you won't say a word.'

Somehow, I forced my head to move.

FIFTY-ONE

'I knew Tom a long time before I met you. But I didn't think I meant that much to him. We never really talked. He liked to show me off. He was never unkind. But he treated me as if I were one of his trophies, like his prizes for sports. I was the most sought-after girl in our year. Of course he would want to be seen with someone like that. It fitted his image. But anybody would have done, anybody sufficiently attractive. That was what I thought. But I wanted someone who really needed me. When I met you I thought I had found that person.

'God, you needed me all right. You didn't say anything. You didn't need to. The way you looked at me was enough. I was used to being looked at, of course. In a certain way. I was used to the sneers, and the whistles, and the obscene remarks. I heard them all the time. Sometimes they were muttered behind my back when they thought I couldn't hear. Sometimes they were thrown straight into my face, when they wanted me to hear, wanted to see my reaction. Occasionally, when there were a few of them, one would boast that he had had me, would describe how parts of my body looked and felt.

'If only they had known what you knew. There was only one way anybody could have seduced me at that time. You knew. You of all people. Not consciously. But you knew and you were the only one who did. There was no way I could resist someone who needed me like that. You needed me so much you could not begin to tell me. You would never have dared to ask me out, would you, even if I hadn't been going out with Tom? All you could do was look at me and long for me and suffer.

'Don't get me wrong. I didn't respond to you out of

pity. I could never have done that. I don't do pity. If I had, you would have hated and despised me for it. No, I needed you as well. I'm basically selfish, you see. I know it must have seemed as if I had it all. Why would I need anybody, particularly someone as inept with the opposite sex as you? I was attractive. I was confident and outgoing. I could make people like me without even trying. I had been brought up to feel that the world would soon be coming to my door and that there would always be a place for me in it. And I deserved it. I had never doubted that for a moment.

'All this was before your mother got to me, of course. Before you and she between you had squeezed the last drop of life out of my heart and soul.

'So why? You wondered how I could prefer you to Tom. In many ways he and I were quite similar. Or so it seemed. Too similar. He was good-looking and confident. We made such a convincing couple on the outside. I thought he was like me, all shiny on the surface but empty inside. It had all been too easy for me, I suppose. So much love, so much acceptance, just given to me, all my life. A life of sunshine, never a shadow to trouble it, as far back as I could remember. I had never had to work for anything. When I met you I was too young to understand what makes a complete human being. But I knew I wasn't complete. I knew I needed to learn. I didn't think I had anything to learn from Tom. I needed someone who had had to work to make himself whole because life had given him nothing for free.

'Yes, that was you, Michael. I could sense that your life had been difficult. You were not like me. You could never look in the mirror and tell yourself that you were entitled to a place in the world, just because you were Michael Jones. You could have been angry and bitter. Nobody would have blamed you. Nobody who knew your mother, that is. But you weren't. I looked inside you and saw you were sensitive and caring. Even when I was being most cruel to you, when you thought I loved Tom but still insisted on having you in my life, as some sort of add-on as you must have thought, you weren't angry with me. You were concerned for my feelings. You were desperate not to hurt me with a careless word or gesture. When we made love you were worried you might have hurt me. I loved you for your compassion. As other women would have done, after me, if you had just given them the chance. If you hadn't been so utterly blind and stupid as to go to be a priest.

'Through you I might have learned to be that way. To care about others, to care about people not as fortunate as myself. Instead of going through life as a self-centred, heartless bitch. I needed to share my life with someone with your qualities, who would be generous with them, who would love me enough not to hate or despise me because they were not natural to me.

'What about you? What sort of person did you need? What use were your inner qualities if they could never see the light of day? What sort of life would you have if you never found anybody to reflect them back to you? Somebody to say, this, Michael Jones, is what and who you are and it is good, it is of value and you have so much to give the world? What would happen to you if you never found anybody to tell you that you too could look the world in the eye? Your mother would never tell you that, because she never intended you for the world. But when you met me, you realised it could be different. Your physical need for me must have come as a shock to you after the sheltered life you had led. But it was only the beginning. You needed to enter my soul as well as my body, to see the world through my eyes, to see its possibilities, all so much

398

brighter and richer than the dark, cold, narrow life your mother had prepared for you.

'You longed for that new, different life, didn't you? But you did not know how to get it. You were very weak. You had no fight in you. That was something else I thought I had. Enough strength for both of us. I believe we get the chance to become complete people only once in our lives. We had that chance. Yes, we were very young. But that was our chance. The only one we would get. Your compassion for me, my strength for you. Maybe we were too young. Maybe in the end we would have changed too much to stay together. But the point is that we would have changed each other, enriched each other, lifted each other up. Instead of becoming the hollowed-out shells we have both become, God help us.

'As soon as I started to develop feelings for you, I tried to repress them, because of what I had heard about you becoming a priest. In the end I thought you had overcome that. So I went ahead. I fell in love with you. I told Tom I wanted to finish our relationship. He said he was sorry it hadn't worked out. He supposed I had met someone else but he wouldn't press me for details. Then he said something which surprised me. He said he had once hoped we would become engaged. He said he did love me, after his fashion, even if he wasn't very good at talking about that sort of thing. He wished me the best.

'I wondered if I had misunderstood him all that time. Perhaps there was more to him than I had thought. But it made no difference. I had made up my mind. I didn't love him. It was you I wanted. I was sure I was strong enough for you. And you needed someone strong all right.

'I had never met your mother. But I knew from you about her plans for you. I knew they did not include anybody like me. I knew there would be a struggle. But I was confident I would win. I was so sure of myself. How difficult could it be? There I was, young, attractive, confident as only the young can be who believe they will live and be attractive forever, sure of your feelings for me, understanding your needs. There she was, an elderly widow, unwilling to admit the inevitable, that her son had grown up and had his own decisions to make about his life. I had to win.

'But I was wrong, so wrong. Not because she would have been stronger in a fair fight. But because she was a cruel, ruthless liar. I could fight her selfishness, her arrogance, her belief in her right to dispose of you. I could fight those and win. But I was no match for her evil.

'If you had only come to me I would have fought her and won. I had the strength to fight for both of us. All you needed to do was to stand by my side. But when you stayed with her, let her send you away to seminary because for whatever reason lodged in her warped, sick mind it was what she needed, when it was the two of you against me, I knew I was beaten.

'I suppose you remember what I said in my letter. I said I had made a mistake about my feelings and was going to marry Tom. It was all a lie. I hadn't seen or spoken to Tom before I wrote the letter. It was to test you, that was all. You failed the test, miserably. But as you said, I could have moved on. Without you or Tom.

'But instead, a few weeks later, the letter became the truth. I did go to see Tom. I told him I loved him after all. We became engaged. Within a month we were married.

'My mother cried for ages when I told her. Do you remember when you came to see me, after I had been to you in Confession and told you I hated you? I said my mother was heart-broken about Dad's death. But I had already broken her heart, many years before. His death only finished her off.

'She didn't know about my feelings for you but she knew I didn't love him. So she asked me what any mother would ask in those circumstances. I reassured her, of course, as any daughter would. In the circumstances. I mean, they had brought me up to be a good Catholic girl, hadn't they? So I told her. Of course I was still a virgin. Of course I didn't have to get married. We weren't rushing into it. There was no point in waiting for years, that was all. Of course I loved him. I had had plenty of time to get to know him. We had been going together for years, hadn't we?

'She pretended to believe me. But I knew she realised the truth. Not the whole truth, of course. She thought it was only a matter of timing. I had got things in the wrong order. That was all. The cart before the horse. It happens all the time. You know that. You hear it in Confession. Or you used to.'

I gasped. There was a long pause. Then she leaned forward towards me.

'That's right, Michael. Are you getting the message now? As I said, it happens all the time. Eyebrows are raised. Gossips whisper to each other. They try to count the weeks and the months. Work out whether the poor little thing really was a bit premature. But in the end it doesn't matter. There's no disgrace, no bastard. Just one happy family. Only in this case, it wasn't quite like that. It wasn't just a matter of timing.'

She rose, walked over to the window and looked out. She continued to talk, her back to me. There was a matter-of-fact, almost casual tone to her voice.

'It was a very quiet wedding. No reception. Just a few photographs outside the church, after we had signed the register. Then we went back to the house. His parents' house. We were on our own. Both sets of parents and in-laws had gone to the pub for a drink. They were being discreet, leaving us alone. We had decided to live there, until we could get a place of our own. There was more room there than in my parents' house. We couldn't afford a honeymoon.

'Not that we could have had a honeymoon. Not after what I told him, as soon as we were alone together, in our bedroom. There's something you need to know, I said. When we got married today you got a bit more than you bargained for.

'Those were my actual words. There was no expression in my voice. I was standing by the window, looking out, as I am now, my back to him. I found it hard to look at him, just as I'm finding it hard to look at you now. I still had my wedding-dress on. I was still carrying a bouquet of flowers. There was confetti on the floor which I had shaken off the dress.

'When he said nothing, I assumed he had understood. I expected him to hit me. Maybe throw me about the room. Perhaps he would be so violent I would lose the baby. He might even kill me. Nothing like that would have surprised me. But he never said a word. He went downstairs. I thought he was going to leave. I waited for the sound of the front door slamming.

'But none of that happened. He came back upstairs with a cup of tea for me. It was crazy. I wanted to laugh. I felt as if I was dreaming. I assumed he hadn't heard me or hadn't understood. Or perhaps I hadn't said anything, only imagined I had. So I told him again, more clearly this time, to his face, when it was obvious he was listening, so there was no way he could misunderstand me. Again he said nothing. Just nodded. Almost as if he suspected.

'Perhaps he did. Maybe he knew from the moment I had told him I wanted to marry as soon as possible.

Deep down he knew I had been telling him the truth that time when I had told him I didn't love him. So there could only be one reason why I was suddenly in such a hurry. And he had accepted me. Even on those terms he accepted me.

'I told him I wanted to be on my own. I asked him to leave the room while I unpacked and got ready for bed. He went downstairs. It was still early. He came back up a couple of hours later. He wasn't drunk, as I thought he might be. He had been watching television. He came up when he heard his parents come in. For obvious reasons he didn't want to see them. I had turned the light out. He undressed and got into bed. He didn't try to touch me. Of course, he didn't. A woman carrying another man's baby? Why would he? I said nothing. I pretended to be asleep.

'I did not know what to expect. The threatened storm had gone away for the moment. But it would surely return the next day. Maybe he was waiting so he could confront me when his parents were there. What would they say? What would they do?

'But the storm never happened. After a few days he went back to work. I got a clerical job nearby. A few weeks later we moved out into a small flat. I cooked and washed and cleaned. And grew. We did talk. About trivial things. And not so trivial things such as his accountancy exams. But never about my condition, not even when it became noticeable.

'His parents were delighted. They had no fears for the future. Mine were much more apprehensive. They still only thought we had anticipated the wedding. But they were concerned about how suited we were to each other and how secure the marriage would be, with the pressures of so early a pregnancy.

'And still we never talked about it, even when the time drew near and we had to make practical

403

arrangements. He never asked whose it was. He knew I had been out with a lot of his classmates. He must have thought about each of them, one by one. The only one he would never have suspected was you.

'The baby arrived. We moved into a larger flat, then a small house. He looked after me as if the baby was his. He accepted John as his own. He looked after both of us, worked hard for us, provided for us. He never blamed me for deceiving him, never abused me, verbally or otherwise.

'Some months after John was born, we began a married life together. You know what I mean. I could hardly go on refusing him, could I? He had saved my honour and that of our parents. He was providing for me. He was bringing up another man's child, not even knowing who the real father was. He deserved something in return. Only I couldn't give him what he deserved. What I said before, about me feeling like a whore, all that was true. I was paying him for what he had done and was doing for me. Paying with my body. Such as it was.

'It wasn't what it had been, that's for sure. I had started to go downhill pretty quickly after John was born. It's strange. One day you are walking down the streets and you know everybody is looking at you, some of them admiring you, some wanting you, some despising you. But nobody is indifferent. Nobody can ignore you. Maybe vanity is a sin but not a serious one, surely. I was guilty of it sometimes. I enjoyed being noticed so long as I wasn't being abused at the same time. If anybody had told me how soon it would be over, how soon the day would come when I would walk down the street and not attract even a passing glance.

'I don't think Tom minded me losing my attractiveness. What hurt him was the coldness, the mechanical way I lifted my nightdress and opened my

404

legs for him, as if saying, here it is, take it, it's your right.

'And always in the dark. I never undressed in front of him. I locked the door when I took a bath. He never saw me naked. Nobody ever has, not since I became self-conscious as a child and started to hide myself from my parents. Sometimes I wonder what that would have been like. Showing all of myself to a husband I loved, I mean. I never thought I would miss out on that. I never thought I would miss out on anything. But I couldn't bring myself to let Tom see me. I could only give him what he had bought, what I knew he was entitled to. That was all. No more. I wasn't trying to hurt him. It was just that that was all I could give.

'Finally, he broke his silence. He said we needed to talk things over. I thought he was going to tell me he had had enough. He was going to leave. I wouldn't have blamed him. When I heard what he had to say I cried. He said he thought that if we had a child of our own, it might make things different. Bring us closer together. I was crying because I knew I couldn't do what he wanted. The last thing I wanted was a child by a man I didn't love. I had tried to arrange things the way good Catholics are supposed to. The calendar and the thermometer. When he suggested it was time to drop the precautions, that was the time I decided I needed stronger ones. The pill was available by then. Not to good Catholics of course. But that was what I did. I didn't tell him. I pretended to go along with his plan. But he found out eventually. He found them in the bathroom cupboard. Of course he did. I intended him to. I couldn't go on with the deceit.

'He never said anything. But I could tell from his face that he knew. Not just what I had done. He knew it was the end of his dream. I never would love him. That was what killed him. Slowly but inevitably. I

405

knew I was killing him. That's why I stopped receiving Communion. Not because of some stupid Church rule about contraception. Who cares a fuck about that?'

She returned to her chair and looked me in the eye. I stared back at her.

'So now you know. You have been listening, haven't you, Michael? Yes, I can tell you have. Because you have nothing to say. There is nothing you can say. You wanted to know and now you do.

'The funny thing is that I was wrong about both of you. I thought you needed me. I thought you would never survive without me. And off you went to be a priest. And here you are now, no longer a priest but still alive, just about. I thought he didn't need me but he was the one who died. I should have been able to love him. He was the best, the kindest, the strongest man I ever knew. An infinitely better man than you turned out to be, Michael. By the time I realised his qualities, by the time his whole strong, beautiful, patient manhood was revealed to me, it was too late. I could not respond to him as he deserved. I was as empty as I had always known and feared I would be. Most of the time I was married I had no feelings at all. When I did, they were only of hate. For her and for you. I had never known what hate was. Your mother taught me. And I applied it to both of you.

'I had John, of course. A healthy, intelligent, good-looking boy. Any mother's dream. He should have been enough consolation. But I was a crazy mother. Sometimes I smothered him, because he was all that was left of the two of us and I knew the time would come when I would lose him and I couldn't bear the thought. Other times I was cold and angry, as if it was his fault that I deceived him every day of his life. I didn't love him. I did show him my feelings. Anger, panic, desperation, all the feelings which had taken the place of the love you and your mother had cured me of. I showed all those to him all right. Sometimes one at a time, sometimes all together. But however you mix and stir them around you can't make love out of them. That would be alchemy. And we all know there's no such thing.

'But he came through in the end, despite having me as a mother. I know he will make a good life for himself. He is kind and considerate. He has been far better to me than I deserve. It's funny, in a way. He has your compassion and my strength. He has what I wanted for the two of us. So it sort of worked out in the end. He has the best of each of us.

'Now I've lost him. Not the way I lost you. Nobody came between us. We didn't fall out. He grew up and moved on. I'm on the edge of his life, as mothers are supposed to be in the end. Something your mother would never accept.

'When you came to see me that time I was rather surprised by something you said. You seemed confused about John's age. You thought he was still at college. But then I remembered you had never met him. Never seen him. Not been around when he was born. He had left college by then. Moved to Manchester to train as an accountant. Like his father. Like the man he knew as his father. His home is there, not with me. He's twenty-three, Michael. Not eighteen or nineteen as you thought. He has a girl-friend. They're going to get engaged next year. Maybe they'll invite me round to babysit from time to time. That's all the future I have to look forward to. It's something I suppose.

'Just remember these words, Michael. As far as he's concerned Tom was his father. Never forget that. That's the way it will stay. You won't try to find him. You'll never hear any more about him.'

407

She stood up.

'That's all I have to say, Michael. Now you really do know it all. I hope it was worth it. Goodbye.'

She walked slowly out of the room. As if from a great distance I heard the front door click shut.

PART IV

DE PROFUNDIS

FIFTY-TWO

I must have waited for hours, silent, motionless, after she had gone.

Then at last I remembered. It was not yet over. I could not sit there forever. I still had a purpose in life. I rose stiffly out of my chair. It was dark by then. I switched on the light. I made myself some supper and listened to the radio. I went for a short walk to get some fresh air. Then I went to bed. The next day I went to work as usual and performed my duties efficiently, as I always did. In the evening I came home and followed the same routine.

Anybody observing me would have said that my life was aimless. But they would have been wrong. I had a purpose, and that was to wait for Angela. She had found me once, and she could surely find me again. When she did I needed to be ready. I needed to be strong. I would need to comfort her and protect her, talk to her and help her come to terms with what she had done. I would finally be to her what I had promised, after the death of our father. I had failed to keep that promise, as I had failed in every other aspect of my life. But now it would be different. I had learned my lessons. She would at last find in me the brother she needed and deserved.

But inside me I knew this was yet another self-deception. I was the one who needed her, needed to draw some strength from the great destructive, irresistible force of her anger. I had taken many wrong steps in my life. I had lost everybody who had mattered to me. I had lost her, and Bernadette, and the son of whose existence I had been unaware. I had followed a so-called vocation which had not only turned out to be an illusion but had sealed me off from the world and myself. It was too late for me to rebuild my life on my own. But Angela would find me again. Through her I would find a new life and a new way forward.

I prayed each evening on my knees. To her, not to God. Come to me, Angela, for God's sake, come to me. I need you. *De profundis clamavi ad te*. Out of the depths I have cried to thee, hear my prayer.

FIFTY-THREE

Now it really is over. There is nothing more to wait for or to pray for.

My life is over because now I know it all. I committed the ultimate folly of going in search of the truth. And God, or the Devil, or the two of them working together, punished me by giving me the truth. With the arrival of knowledge comes the end of action. Because I do not only know what I have found out. I now have the final piece of the jigsaw, the knowledge that lies buried at the end of the search. This is the realisation that what I know is of no use to me or anybody else. I have knowledge but no wisdom. Life is not for those who know. It is for those who open their hearts and souls to receive the wisdom which tells them how they should live. That was my great mistake. I never asked God, or the Devil, or whoever it is who is in charge, how I should live.

It is too late now. My knowledge bars the way to wisdom. It weighs on my soul with a terrible, crushing weight. It leaves no room for hope or imagination. To start my life again I would somehow have to unburden myself of my knowledge, forget all I have learned. And I know...yes, this is another part of that final piece of knowledge which came to me at the end of my search...that God and the Devil will not allow that. Their punishment for my *hubris*, my insane, Icarus-like wanting to know, is that I always will know, and remember, for as long as my consciousness lasts.

Last night she came, unseen, under the cover of darkness. She left the third letter on the doorstep, like the others. The envelope is addressed with the one word, *Mikey*, large, childish letters scrawled in blue biro. Unlike the others, the letter is in her own hand.

She has not been back to the hostel. She did not use Tim's services. She delivered it in person. For a moment she was within a few feet of me as I slept. Did she pause to look up at the window? Did her hand move towards the doorbell? If so, she thought better of it. She laid the envelope gently on the ground. Then she disappeared into the night, as silently as she came. I know she will never return. God be with you, Angela, wherever you go, whatever you become.

I will read it one more time. Then I will burn it. Like the others. Ashes to ashes.

Dear mikey

I suppose you've worked out by now who these letters are from. Yes, it's me. Your kid sister. I know you didn't know at first. When I went to you in the connfession box that time, you thought I was someone called christine. So who the hell was she?

Sorry I teesed you. I couldn't come cleen with you while you were still a priest. Now you've given it up. Good for you. This is the last you'll hear from me, you'll be pleased to know. Time for connfession, father. Sorry, mustn't forget you don't do connfession any more. And you don't do father any more. I've seen you, going to work without your dog-collar. Followed you home. I'm good at this, aren't I? Following people, I mean. I want to connfess anyway and you'll do as well as anybody.

I killed her. I didn't mean to. He was the one I really wanted to kill. But I couldn't remember his face or his name and the bitch wouldn't tell

414

me. Then I read about them. Both dead. When I read about the one who shot himself I knew it was him. Father coffey. Coffin I used to call him. Did you find out, mikey? I know you were looking for her. That's why I followed you. I was going to carry on following you, to see if you'd leed me to him. But when I realised I had killed her I thought I had better disapeer again. I'm very good at that. When I read about it I did wonder if you found out and shot him. Did my work for me. But somehow I don't think you would do anything like that.

I could have got to her sooner before she ran away. I was going to leave her letters as well. I wanted her to be sitting in night after night shit scared waiting for me to turn up. I was going to draw it out. Follow her without her seeing me seeing the feer in her eyes. Then let her see me just for a moment so she'd wonder if I had really been there. But the bitch ran away. I wondered if you had warned her. Then I knew it must have been him. You showed him my letters didn't you you fucking idiot. You were always so trusting.

I was in the club, by the way. That was what started it all. He got that out of me in connfession. I told him I had been a naughtty girl but had decided to turn over a new leef. That was the truth. I had been screwing around something terrible. I hated meself because she had always hated me. I had nobody to turn to or talk to. I couldn't talk to the nuns and most of me mates were as bad as I was. You might have done I suppose if you had been there but you weren't because you were always away and much too busy lerning to be holey. But the screwing around didn't make me feel any better. Made me feel worse in fact.

So I decided to change. I only went to connfess so I could make a fresh start. Once something had been sorted out about the baby. I went to him because he had been nice to me at home, chatting like he was me mate. Some fucking mate! He said it wasn't enough what I had told him. What did I meen when I said I had been a naughtty girl? I said all right I was screwing around. When was the last time he asked. Six weeks I said. He asked me to give him all the details but the fact was that I couldn't remember so I had to make stuff up about where and when and how and whether it was indoors or outdoors and how much of each other we could see as if all that mattered. It seemed to matter to him because I was sure he was getting off on it. So why hadn't I connfessed before he asked? Why had I waited all that time? Was it because now I knew there were what did he call it consekwenses? I said yes there were consekwenses or there soon would be. I knew he knew what I ment but he made me say it. Yes all right I am in the club I said. So who knows he asked. Nobody I said. And I'm not telling me mam because she'll kill me and that would be a double killing and that would be bad for her soul.

I didn't tell her but he did. I didn't find that out until later. I thought about getting rid of it meself. I knew I needed gin and nitting-needles. I knew what to do with the gin but not the needles. I would never have gone ahed with it. I thought I had been absolved and getting rid of the baby would have been a much worse sin than what I had connfessed already and I didn't want to go back to connfession all over again knowing

416

it would be even worse than before.

I can't even remember who the father was. He kept asking me that and I kept saying I didn't know. I'm afraid to say there were a few who could have been. I didn't exactly turn out anybody's dream, did I? Not yours. Certainly not hers.

I was planning to run away. Even if she didn't kill me I was sure she would send me somewhere awful. A couple of the older girls had had to leave the year before. Nobody knew where they had gone. One of me mates told me they had been sent to work in this laundry somewhere down south. The babies had gone for adopting. But they couldn't come home. They had to stay in the laundry and if they tried to leeve nobody would give them a job or put them up because they would know where they had been and why so they would have to stay there. I was sure that was going to happen to me if I stayed and she found out. So I thought I would steel some money and run away to London and the police would find me on the streets and find someone to look after the baby so I could go and get a job somewhere. I would have been sorry to leeve the baby. But in the end it was much worse than that. Much worse than the laundry. She already knew and I didn't know she knew. I thought I had time to decide what to do. But I didn't.

Mam told me aunt mary was back from canada and had bought this big house out in the country. She wanted to take me to visit her. I said okay. I wasn't thinking about aunt mary. I was thinking about what to do about the baby. We took all day to get there. One bus after the other. I was sure some of them were taking us back to where we had already been. I was wondering aunt mary must have a car to live all that way away from anywhere so why didn't she come round and collect us. Now I know the buses going backwards and forwards were to make sure I wouldn't know where we were going so I would never be able to find the place again.

Anyway, we got to this big house at last. She went up to the door and walked straight in. She never rang the bell. The door was open. It was like she knew the place. It was huge. Dead dark and spooky. I wondered if aunt mary had turned into a vampire and we were waiting for her to come out of her coffin. We sat in this huge front room. Then she got up and went to the door. I thought she had gone to get aunt mary. She turned and spoke to me. Her voice was weerd. As if she'd swalowed some dirt and was trying to spit it out. She told me to stay there and wait. She said she knew all about me. Father coffin had done his duty and told her. I would be taken care of. She would never see me again. I heard the front door slam. I ran out and tried to follow her but it was locked. I was so scared I was shitting myself. There were all sorts of creaks and groans coming from upstairs. I called out but there was no reply. I crawled upstairs. All the doors were locked except one. He was there. You know the rest.

I lost the baby in the socalled hospital. When I was losing it, I heard one of the socalled nurses telling one of the others, did you know this one's been knocked up? Nobody had told them.

Anyway, they're all dead now, the bitch who called herself our mam, the priest who snitched on me, and the doctor who put me away. I remembered where his sergery was and went there. They said he had died. Pity. I would have killed him if I had had the chance.

I'm still not sure if I forgive you. Remember that time you said you would never let her hurt me again? Do you remember, mikey? I do. I know you ment it. But you were no match for her. You were pathetick. Useless in fact. But I know you didn't know where I was. I got that out of her before I hit her. She wasn't going to tell me. I took the poker out of her hand. I kept screeming at her, what did you tell him, what did you tell mikey, tell me, you fucking bitch or I'll kill you. She told me. Said they told you I was dead. Had gone to be a fucking nun and died all young and holey. Only it wasn't me, it was that stuck-up cousin of ours, anne. Just think of it. That toffee-nosed creep in my grave. And you believed them, you stupid prick. You'd believe anything. Me, a nun!

Then I asked her for his name. The name of the priest. She kept shaking her head. I couldn't see her, or anything in the room. Just red in front of me eyes. Then she was lying on the floor. The poker in me hand. Blood on it.

You can tell the cops if you like. Show them this letter. But they won't find me. Neither will you. Or anybody. Not ever.

419

CPSIA information can be obtained at www.ICGtesting.com
Printed in the USA
LVOW041642040912

297319LV00008B/9/P